Horse Punk

LINDA JISUN LEE

Cover image and design by Linda Jisun Lee

ISBN: 979-8-9868333-0-9 (Paperback)
ISBN: 979-8-9868333-1-6 (Ebook)

Library of Congress Control Number: 2022945300

This book is a work of fiction. Any references to historical
events, real people, or real places are used fictitiously. Other
names, characters, and places, and events are products of the
author's imagination, and any resemblance to actual events or
places or persons, living or dead, is entirely coincidental.

First printing edition 2022.

The Animal Instinct, LLC

Dad
you are always
My Dad

1

*A*ll Rose wanted was to stay on.

She squeezed the reins again. The leather disintegrated, leaving a thin line of powdery film across the insides of her curled fingers.

Fender's neck lunged toward her, black mane grazing Rose's nose and lips. He whipped back and up, a thousand rearing pounds of muscle and spook and survival in a moment airborne.

Rose wrapped her burning thighs around him. If she could just get him to slow down...

A frigid wind slapped her cheeks. Horse and human, like a searing cannonball, careened toward the dusk-shadowed trails of Coyote Hills.

Ragged breathing.

Left, right, darting eyes not knowing which direction to trust.

Everything speeding up.

Panicked yelling from back at the stable entrance.

"Easy, Fender, easy!"

Was she pleading aloud or silently screaming?

Pounding—drum-like, from below, then everywhere. Aortas and hooves pumping—too fast, too much.

They cut through that chunk of air right at that moment, dust swirling behind them just as it once did in the setting shadow of a younger star. Burnt-colored leaves, scattering cricket chirps, and cool suburban quiet all whizzed by in an increasingly frenetic blur.

Ahead, something wisped like vapor on a tree branch. Fender convulsed hard. Slipping down against his side, Rose hung on like a torn flag. A part of her just wanted to give up and let go, but her limbs kept searching.

Slower...slower...pause.

Rose didn't dare breathe as Fender came to a tentative halt. A molecule of anything could push it all past the boiling point again.

Ear flick.

Shudder.

It was always like an explosion.

Fender bolted with a new reserve of power, roiling and bloodcurdling into darker forest and strange space.

No need to look up. Overhead, outstretched wings kept gliding in the opposite direction. Beak tucked into chest, he scrutinized the scene below and then pierced the sky with a shrill, cavernous call.

The next thing Rose knew, she was hoping to land on a forgiving patch of earth.

+ + +

Hard and cold pressed against Rose's left cheek. At first, she thought she couldn't move. Where was Fender? The faint sensations in her newly pierced ear throbbed her right back to the present moment. Blinking at the narrow rays of sunlight peeking through the blinds, she shifted her elbows to lift her head: no dirt, no crunchy leaves. Just the familiar hardwood floor.

A warm tongue and cold button nose lapped encouragement over her chin and cheek. Rose gathered herself upright at the side of the bed, petting Milo's black and tan coat. The terrier settled between her crossed legs.

Would she ever stop with this dream? Not only was the dream getting more frequent, but she was also falling off the mattress on a semiregular basis like a toddler still learning how to sleep in a big girl bed.

Rose shook her head in the morning silence. The drumbeat of Fender's galloping hooves faded into an invisible horizon, promising to revisit another night.

Her gaze crept toward the rickety dresser with shiny brass handles, then meandered up to the geese-printed curtains, draped in familiar curves, reminding Rose that she actually didn't just get tossed on the cold trails of Coyote Hills. That was years ago, when she was an awkward preteen obsessed with riding and Fender and everything equine.

But a soft seven-pound creature with adorable puppy breath was demanding her full attention. Rose's shoulders relaxed an inch. She lifted Milo into the air, squealing and cuddling as he wriggled with top-of-the-morning delight.

Satisfied with his face licking duties, Milo plopped back into Rose's lap. The bed was his preference, but he'd take a pair of crossed legs anytime. He gazed up at her as if asking, "You had that crazy dream again, didn't you, Mommy?"

Rose giggled at his inquisitive brown eyes and perfect black triangle nose. Milo was as adorable as he was whip smart. He sighed, curled into a tight ball and tucked his little chin into the bend of her knee.

"Ring of Fire" abruptly alarmed from underneath the pillow. 6:30 a.m., October 31. Rose reached over, her fingers grazing the crystals she slept with until she felt the tip of her phone. Amethyst, rose quartz, and sodalite was last night's combination. Tap, tap. Silence.

"Gotta get ready for school, sweetie pie." Kissing Milo's round forehead, Rose gently placed him back on the bed, pulling the thick blanket over his curled torso as he settled into a position that made sure his tush pressed against the pillow. She gathered a handful of clothes from a flimsy plastic laundry basket, her temporary closet for the past two weeks. Tonight, she could move all her stuff back into her own bedroom. Aunt Esther was leaving for the airport today.

"This room is just too dark pour moi." Aunt Esther always made a point to complain about the guest room whenever she visited from Singapore, Dubai or, this time, Luxembourg. She always seemed to fly into town while breathlessly cutting short one of her habitual glamorous vacations (or equally glitzy business trips). The Moon household clearly wasn't competition for any of her usual ten-star hotels, but Rose knew the lavish frequent flier didn't mince words with any resort staff, either. Her aunt's salary as a top chaebol executive had surpassed her husband's modest earnings decades ago, fading him into the background as a rare yes-man in a generation otherwise mostly full of sexists. Uncle Young-jae didn't make it to Grandma's funeral simply because his wife didn't invite him, and that was that. He had strict orders to stay put in their high-rise capsule home and tend to their son Joon, who was busy training for a top regional fencing competition.

"Rose. You don't mind if I use your room again?" It was more of a brisk order rather than a question. Aunt Esther planted a huge monogrammed duffel bag onto Rose's bed. "I just don't like that guest room, you know."

"Um, sure, that's fine," Rose murmured in the doorway, still aware of the moist spot on her cheek from Aunt Esther's smooch. She shifted her weight. Both arms felt like they were practically stretching out of their sockets from the weight of her aunt's other bags.

Rose watched Aunt Esther silently scan the rock band posters and punk concert fliers taped all over the wall. Social Distortion, Manic Hispanic, Ramones, L7, Dead Kennedys, Agent Orange, X, Siouxsie and the Banshees, and the obligatory Willie Nelson...her aunt had no clue who these people were, but her disdain was obvious. Photos of Milo were also mixed in the hodgepodge, but she didn't seem to notice those.

The door-length poster of five black-clad men especially caught Aunt Esther's eye. Taking a few cautious steps, as if approaching a caged tiger, she simultaneously raised and knitted her brows toward a particularly pallid face with red lips.

Rose suppressed a smile. The Cure poster. Of course, Aunt Esther focused on that one. She had already figured her aunt wouldn't find much humor in having identically shaded lips as the British rock star before her.

"How does a girl sleep with all these scary pictures in her room?" Aunt Esther muttered with a sigh, shaking her head. Then, as if she'd just remembered Rose standing there, she quickly motioned with a whiff of floral perfume and clinking bracelets, beckoning her niece to deliver the rest of her bursting luggage to the closet.

At least it's her last day. Rose scrubbed her head with jasmine scented bubbles in the shower. For a second, she almost felt relief that life would be going back to normal without a house guest, but this time it just wasn't true. Nothing would ever be the same.

Faint purplish suds traveled down her petite frame and swirled into the drain, the latest hair color her parents weren't exactly thrilled about.

"What?" Rose called out, rubbing bubbles from her eye.

For a quick second, she thought she heard someone calling from the hallway. It wasn't out of character for Grandma to suddenly need some random vital thing as if Rose wasn't standing buck naked under a stream of water. Rose kept quiet, but this time she wasn't just ignoring her grandma's inconvenient yet simple request to open a jar or reach something that was stacked too high on a shelf. How many more times would she mistake absolutely nothing for nonexistent echoes? God, she wished she was being nagged right now.

Grandma had lived with them for as long as Rose could remember. Rose held her breath and closed her eyes, letting the warm water pulsate on her forehead. The heat reminded her of how Grandma used to take super steamy, hot baths—and often encouraged a young Rose to do the same, which she'd always hated. But now Rose agreed that nothing felt better than the extra clean feeling after a thorough, Grandma-level scrub.

She closed her eyes and searched inward for sadness, pain, or anything that people were supposed to feel after a loved one left. Once again, she emerged mostly empty-handed. It was all there, swirling and breathing, but she just couldn't settle any of it. And for some reason, she had yet to shed a single tear.

Ignoring the new barbell screaming in her ear, Rose toweled off in the misty bathroom. The reflection of her ear's new holes in the foggy mirror didn't look infected or any more irritated than it should be at this point. Good.

Desiree, an older acquaintance she'd met a few months ago at her favorite boutique in downtown Fullerton, was hoping to apprentice at the nearby piercing spot. While perusing over stacks of artsy magazines together last week, Desiree casually mentioned she was looking to practice industrial piercings. Rose volunteered instantly, and yesterday she finally got the piercing she'd wanted for ages. A little pre-Halloween gift for herself.

Tori is going to love this. Rose swiped the dewy mirror again, this time grinning at the steel bar impaling her cartilage. Tori lived across the street and quickly became Rose's BFF after meeting at the bus stop when they were in elementary school. Tori, unlike a lot of other kids, never got fazed by Rose's random awkward tendencies, like when Rose momentarily froze up when telling Tori her name for the first time. Tori just smiled and extended an open box of jellybeans, and they were pretty much inseparable ever since. Over the years, they developed similar tastes in edgy music and unique, semi-DIY clothes. They lived vicariously through Tori's super-hot (and always backstage) sister Claudia, all the while pushing each other through the pressures of Coyote Hills High School, one of the most competitive public schools in California.

Rose sometimes wished she had an older sister, too. She often wondered if Claudia, as the older kid, ever felt lonely at home. It was an odd thing to puzzle over, and every time she did, she felt like an idiot. There was no way someone who looked like that could ever share the same feelings. But it was hard to accept that no matter what Rose did, how benign she tried to breeze through the day, the gloom always found her. Her younger brother Thomas, on the other hand, somehow seemed to exist in an upbeat, sunny existence under the very same roof. Their conspicuous contrast never failed to make Rose feel like an official freak.

Milo suddenly barked with urgency. He was outside the bathroom door, scratching the door with his paws.

"Hold on, pup," Rose called over her shoulder as she rushed to towel off. His barks were now more agitated.

"Rose?" Aunt Esther's voice impatiently shot through the door. "Rose!"

"Yes?" Rose shoved her black sweater over her head, wincing as the neck hole tugged her tender ear. "I'm almost done." She darted around for the rest of her clothes. Didn't her aunt know she had this thing called "school" today?

"Rose, I need to get in there now." The locked doorknob wiggled urgently, paused for two seconds, then wiggled more. Milo's barks switched to a low growl, disapproving the situation.

"Okay, just a second." Rose scanned the counter for her bra. She must have forgotten to bring it in. She hastily grabbed her jeans from across the counter and accidentally knocked over a row of her aunt's expensive creams and lotions. The other day she'd learned that despite the fancy European and Asian labels, the products were still loaded with gross parabens and other toxic chemicals. She didn't bother to set them back upright.

Water dribbled down Rose's back from her wet hair. She plugged in the hairdryer and switched it to full blast. Her aunt was just going to have to wait.

So much for having a good Halloween hair day, she thought. The dryer drowned out her aunt, but not Milo's protective barks.

When her hair was barely dry enough, Rose quickly wrapped the cord around the hairdryer, hands shaking, and double checked that her long locks covered her ear. Before stepping out, she reminded herself to be extra cautious. No one was over Grandma being gone.

Milo's tail wiggled with furious excitement as he watched Rose spoon a few scoops of his organic breakfast into his very own banchan bowl. He was somewhat of a picky eater, but much less so when his food arrived in the small ceramic plates usually reserved for the humans' side dishes. Milo clearly thought he was human and everyone in the family enjoyed playing into his confident theory. As always, he first sniffed the food with cultured skepticism for three, four, sometimes five seconds or more. Milo had no problem rejecting bowls full of food if he found them non-gourmet in any way. He was picky, but Rose adored that he had such pointed opinions. She grinned once his silver heart shaped tag softly clinked the bowl as he ate. This morning, the tender pieces of chicken, carrots and kibble had passed the terrier's scrutinizing nose.

Rose spread several pages of art history notes on the circular glass dining table, being careful to avoid the crystal vase of this week's fresh cut flowers—white orchids and pink roses—and crunched on cereal in unison with Milo's chomps. He would probably finish long before she reviewed even the first page.

Left, right, left, right.

A slow shuffling came from the foyer, the sound of fabric moving across the tiled floor. Grandma always wore her orchid print house slippers, the ones with the worn rubbery grips on the bottom.

Rose blinked expectantly at the kitchen entrance. Then she realized she didn't have to. That shuffling wasn't there.

I should know better by now.

Milo was already licking his little white bowl clean. The kitchen clock reminded Rose that she had other things to do besides trip out at ghosts—like secretly feed another hungry dog before school.

Milo watched Rose with routine patience as she quickly loaded a second serving of his food and a large bowl of fresh water before he scurried to the backyard. He burst out of the sliding glass door, frolicking past the jellybean shaped pool straight to a patch of grass right between the colorful flower bed and koi pond. From his very first day out of the chaotic city shelter, he'd chosen that as his favorite potty spot.

Almost immediately, Rose's arms and teeth trembled from the biting air. The temperature was probably somewhere in the mid-forties, which felt pretty shivery for Southern California. She walked over to the small waterfall and peered into the oval pond. The koi fish quickly congregated as close as they could to the surface. They always did that. One of her parents would come feed them pretty soon, so Rose continued down the stone lined path toward the side fence. Their next-door neighbors lived in a similar but slightly larger home that sat lower on Camino Drive's gradual slope. Through the black wrought iron fence, Rose scanned their sparse backyard. Poor Koko had spent all night outside in the cold.

Koko had already heard Rose come out and was sprinting up the side yard, bulldozing the vibrant pink geraniums embedded in the dark soil.

"Good morning, Koko." Rose rubbed the dog's heavily matted cream-colored head and slid two bowls under the bottom of the fence. She could see and smell that Koko really needed a bath. For nearly a full minute, Koko lapped the water with an urgency that crushed Rose's heart. Koko then devoured all of the food in just a few lightning-speed gobbles, too desperate to chew. She was like this every morning—thirsty, hungry, and very, very grateful.

Rose grimaced at the thought of her human neighbors, who seemed to think that the two dirty bowls sitting in front of the fancily painted custom doghouse would somehow fill themselves. Once Rose became painfully aware that Koko's bowls were unsupervised for days at a time, she began covertly delivering meals as part of her daily routine. She really didn't have a choice. How could anyone just sit back and watch the poor pup suffer? Rose's vision blurred as she quietly watched Koko. Swallowing hard, she composed herself before a tear could escape. Crying wasn't going to help this ugly situation even though she got triggered every darn time.

Koko let Rose know she was finished by stretching playfully toward her, tail thumping as if she'd just hit the jackpot. Rose gave her a long, satisfying scratch behind her ears and on her tummy, smiling through her worry. She then picked up the bowls as quietly as possible. *What's going to happen to Koko when I leave for college next year?* Her little brother wasn't reliable in that way, and her parents had already warned her to stop the undercover feedings after their indignant neighbor had caught her in the act a few months ago. Again.

"This is the last warning, young lady—leave our dog alone!" yelled Happy Dude. He had a name, of course, but Rose and Thomas had bestowed him with the sarcastic nickname after the first time he'd yelled at them for playing too loudly in the backyard. Their parents had even started calling him Happy Dude, only to Rose and Thomas, of course.

"But she's hungry—"

"Mind your darn business!" Furious that Rose had the balls to argue, he slammed the backyard door behind him. It was the first time she'd ever interacted with Happy Dude directly without her parents. She hadn't seen him much since.

Milo shadowed Rose back into the warm house. Tori would probably honk her car horn any minute now. She had a tendency to honk lightly only a couple of times before her impatience took over, and the whole neighborhood was blasted with some extra-long honkers.

Realizing her warmest jacket was still in her bedroom closet, Rose listened for any signs of her parents or aunt as she climbed the staircase. She paused in the hallway, just for a second, as murmurs floated from Grandma's room. Her dad and aunt were discussing what to do with all of Grandma's old belongings. They sounded tired. Rose winced at the possibility of them throwing away any of Grandma's things. She'd lived a tumultuous life in a region of the world pulverized to dirt by war, poverty, and corruption. To Rose, everything in that room was a precious memory or priceless mystery.

Thomas and her cousin Joon were mentioned a couple of times. Rose carefully trod down the hallway, trying her best not to creak the floor.

Grandma had never been huge on shopping or anything like that. She never bothered with a will, either. Her brother and cousin would probably be favored in some way, Rose guessed. It was fascinating to watch how the living judged things like that.

"These should go to Thomas, I think," Aunt Esther decided as someone rummaged through some crinkly tissue paper. They delved into a deeper discussion about whatever was wrapped in the tissue paper.

Perfect. Rose could pop in to grab her jacket without Aunt Esther breathing down her neck in her own room.

She pushed her bedroom door open and padded to her closet. Her aunt's suitcases were halfway packed for her early evening departure, which meant she'd have to leave for Los Angeles International Airport shortly after Rose returned from school.

The jacket wasn't on the usual wooden hangar. Her aunt's blue wool blazer with chunky gold buttons had taken its place. Rose sifted through the thick mash of garments, all the while avoiding that big brown box. It was there like it always was, that cardboard tombstone. But she wasn't going to get into that right then. After a minute of combing through, she finally glimpsed her jacket sleeve on the floor, smashed between a brown duffel bag and her mom's old Beatles record collection.

The leather bag was heavier than it looked, and it took a few harder tugs before it finally shifted a little. What was in there, bowling balls? A few gallons of milk? Geez. But then, along with her jacket, a corner of something green and flat peeked out from underneath.

A notebook.

Rose bent down for a closer look. Was it one of her old stationery pads? No, the cover was an unfamiliar shade of green. She pulled it completely out from beneath the bag. It was a journal she'd never seen before. The back cover had small Korean words printed in the lower corner.

Milo pawed and sniffed the notebook, enamored with this new object. He lightly grazed his small white teeth against the thin binding.

Rose picked it up. It was a standard journal, small enough to slide into most purses or larger pockets.

"This must be Aunt Esther's," she murmured to Milo.

A quick flash of curiosity coursed through her, but she wasn't sure if she should really take a peek. Could an annoying older relative's journal really be that interesting?

"Rose, are you going to dress like that for the rest of your life?" Aunt Esther had demanded after sharing photos of Joon around the dining table the night before. As usual, on her last night in town, Aunt Esther drilled into Rose during dinner, commenting on her clothes and hair, questioning her academics, and scoffing at her taste in music and art—all with her signature snobbish denunciation. "You look like a ghoul!"

Rose glared down at the journal, her fingers restless. Milo pawed her leg.

"Remember when she was in elementary school, how she used to torture you two by asking for rides to the library *all* the time?" Aunt Esther giggled, jeering over a glass of red wine. "Every single day, wasn't it?" The library was another one of her favorite topics to rant about. Rose had always found it strange that her aunt even thought about the library as some kind of issue.

Oh no, the library! Rose rolled her eyes. Was voracious reading so terrible? Would everyone prefer if she took on another hobby, like inviting dumb guys into her room and locking the door, like some other girls at school?

Rose's jaw clenched as she stared hard at the journal. Even though she still suspected it would just be a waste of thirty seconds of her life, the random opportunity was just too tempting.

She checked over her shoulder and opened the cover.

Her aunt's name and email address. *So far, so boring*, Rose dismissed. The first few pages offered nothing more than random bilingual entries like errand reminders, recipes, directions to some opera house, contact info for a fortune teller, along with some notes comparing all the airports she'd recently flown into, blah, blah...

Rose shifted her weight, concentrating. Aunt Esther's handwriting reminded her of how much she'd hated Korean language school at the local church when she was a kid. Too bad she wasn't all that much better at hangul now.

Listlessly, she flicked through more pages. Sure, the content may be private, but Rose didn't expect to see much more than a stuffy executive's comments on her stuffy, high rolling life. She was just about to yawn and call it quits when the word "Rose"— in plain English—flashed from the blurry shuffle.

Rose blinked with surprise. Was that really her name she just saw? Her fingers rapidly reached back for that particular page. Maybe there was some entertainment in this thing after all! Yup, there it was: "Rose"…then again a few lines down…and *again* on the next page…

With furrowed brows, Rose scanned the pages with growing fixation, as if each word was a bullseye. A rhythmic hammering began to radiate from her chest into her ears. The more the words sank in, the more everything started to make sense. Her aunt's scribble seared into Rose's vision, and she paused to return to certain lines, wondering if the meaning would somehow change. Maybe she had somehow misread or misunderstood…

But all the inked words remained untransformed, refusing to materialize with some sort of overlooked clarification. There simply was none.

2

Mom is going. I just know it.

Talked to my brother in California tonight. Mom is getting weaker very quickly. The doctors advised everyone to prepare.

Flight to LAX is all booked. Young-jae will be staying with Joon. If he really wants to get into the top Ivy Leagues, a tournament win would probably help guarantee a spot.

I'll be staying at my brother's house. I've heard that Rose is doing well in school but that she still dresses strangely. It'll be better that she doesn't influence Joon in any way, cousins or not. Thank goodness Thomas is a normal boy.

Mom has been talking about Rose. We all know why she doesn't want Rose to know. We can't hide it forever, though. Sometimes I feel bad for the girl. Maybe it isn't right for a child to not know her whole identity. But honestly, her life hasn't been nearly as tough as all of ours. And considering what could've been . . .

Joon once wondered how it makes us all look, that we're all hiding it. He thought it was weird, which still kind of bothers me. I explained that it was not our problem. It's just not our place. I think he eventually agreed with me. He always notices how everyone at the family reunions treats Rose so differently. Personally, I don't think anybody treats her too differently, but what else could I expect from such a sensitive and smart boy?

Luxembourg is beautiful. I especially like walking around the streets, just admiring the architecture. Shopping is wonderful, too. One of my favorite eateries nearby has the most amazing pastries. I just hope I don't gain too much weight here.

3

We can't hide it forever...
    Rose couldn't unsee it.

Hidden, somehow out of reach for seventeen years—an explanation, vindication and mystery all rolled into one.

"Oh my god," Rose whispered. She couldn't stop staring at the words that had just scorched her reality.

Magnetized to the page, Rose scrutinized each line, each phrase, each letter, as if doing so would somehow extract new data. Her lungs almost tingled as tight pockets of air barely flowed in and out. She had always felt different in her family, even as a little girl. The connection she knew her brother had with everyone just didn't completely resonate the same way with her. Never had. Relatives were wild cards. Some tried to act normal. The ones who were always outright hostile to her, but not to Thomas, were red flags. People think kids don't know what goes on, but when you're young, you know that's utter nonsense.

And somehow even her cousin Joon had noticed. So, it definitely wasn't all in her head! She and Joon were never close, but Rose felt a new appreciation for him. He was a lot cooler than she had thought.

Rose shook her head, suddenly extremely dazed.

This wasn't only about her and "her whole identity." What about her parents, relatives, grandmother? Who else knew? Aunt Esther's blasé tone was almost as shocking as the words she'd actually written. Who else was in on it?

Everyone.

The only person who Rose was convinced to be out of the loop was her brother. Even the biggest gossips in her family knew that

Thomas couldn't be trusted to keep anything a secret from his sister. They talked about everything—anytime, anyplace—even if they had to do it in pig Latin, which they often did with expert fluency.

Standing at the entrance of the small closet, everything around her instantly appeared alien—the white walls, the assortment of hanging clothes, even her own hands. An unknown had put everything, including her personal space, into question.

Rose scooped up Milo and burrowed her face into his neck, taking in a moment of comfort as he gently cuddled back into her. What was all of this? Was any of this even real?

A car horn honked outside.

There wasn't enough time right now for her to decipher every word in her aunt's casual Korean scribble. What if she forgot something? Somehow Rose knew that was impossible. She'd remember this for the rest of her life. But still, she needed something to look back at, something to confirm later on that she wasn't just freaking out, that this wasn't some sort of random hallucination.

Take the journal? Would Aunt Esther really think she could lose it in the closet? Probably not. Tear out the pages? No, way too obvious. All she needed was some kind of keepsake, something that captured the smoking gun without removing it.

Rose's hands trembled as she pulled her phone from her back pocket.

Snap. Snap. Snap. Refocus, snap.

Her dad's and aunt's voices drifted closer. Sounded like things were settled regarding Grandma's stuff.

"Stupid camera…" Rose grumbled at her phone. She hastily retook a couple of images that turned out too blurry to read.

Down the hallway, a door creaked shut. Footsteps were heading in her direction.

Rose dropped the journal next to the duffel bag and scurried out of her closet, Milo on her heels. She shut the bedroom door behind her as quietly as she could. Milo bounced along with her hurried steps, excited that Rose had suddenly decided to speed walk down the hall. Rose kept her gaze forward, hoping to make it around the corner to the stairs before they caught a glimpse of her.

Right before her dad and aunt reached the straight part of the hall, Rose and Milo turned and bounded down the flight of stairs, avoiding them just in time.

Honk!

"Rose, is that you?" She could tell from Dad's pointed tone that he was concerned about her being late to school.

Darting into the kitchen, Rose bent over to grab her backpack. Her papers were still strewn across the table.

Screw the notes.

Rose kissed Milo's head and ran out the front door.

"Ugh! I just love it!"

Tori's shriek snapped Rose back to attention from the red light. Did all traffic lights have those subtle ridges on the clear plastic covers?

"Desiree did such a good job! I want one..." Tori pined. She leaned up to the rear-view mirror, picturing her own ear with the same piercing.

Rose mustered a shadow of a smile. She reached into her pocket and pulled out a skinny plastic tube. Just as she was about to dab her lips with a trace of clear gloss, she caught her reflection in the wing mirror. Huh. That glare in her eyes was new. She twisted the cap back on and tossed the shimmery goop into her bag.

A few minutes earlier, Rose had managed to race out of the house to Tori's waiting car before having to deal with anybody at home. Taking a shallow breath, Rose shifted in the passenger seat, unable to find a comfortable position, and tried to ignore how her head felt foggy and sharp at the same time. She wanted to be alone, not on her way to a nearly two-thousand student high school. Blueberry crunch cereal somersaulted in her lurching stomach every few moments, but she wasn't quite nauseous, either.

Someone in a beige van honked from behind just as the light turned green. The woman sipped from a paper coffee cup and motioned with her other hand, irritated.

"Yeah, yeah, lady," Tori huffed and tossed her cigarette out the window. A motorcycle cop, who always waited to bust drivers from a discreet spot across the intersection, wasn't paying attention at that moment. Tori steered up Warton Way toward Coyote Hills High School, raising the volume to blast the last song from the Siouxsie and the Banshees album borrowed from Rose.

The morning line of cars crawled into the school parking lot. The two girls slowly neared the array of rides that divulged the school's diverse student body: tricked out imports and vintage cars (some freshly polished and others clearly beloved works in progress), as well as the typical luxury vehicles. A citrus-hued bus hissed to a stop at the front curb, delivering the rest of the students.

Tori parked in a spot along a chain link fence that bordered the baseball field. "Are you sure you can't come out tonight?" She pouted as they marched in their identical knee-high combat boots past the state of the art performing arts center. A big black and orange "Happy Halloween" banner, decorated by the student council, draped the brick wall.

"Your aunt will be gone, so your folks can't say you're being rude by going out, right?" Tori continued, giving looks at random students as she made her case. "Or is it…too soon?" Rose wasn't sure if her friend's smirk was snobbery toward all the costumes walking around or just self-assurance that she was presenting bulletproof logic for Rose's situation.

Rose sighed. Tori continued going off about the evening, not really noticing how quiet Rose was. Not that Rose blamed her for it. Of course, she wanted to go out tonight, too. Orange County hardcore band I Don't Wanna Hear It was playing a last-minute show in downtown Fullerton. Out of all the hardcore shows to go down at the Ice Cave, a Halloween event would be a first. The only reason they even knew about it was through Claudia's new boyfriend. What was his name again? Rose didn't know much about this one, except that he and Claudia had been inseparable ever since he hit on her at the Cloud Nine ride at Knott's Berry Farm, the other local amusement park besides Disneyland. Anyway, Claudia had agreed to cover for her little sister to their trusting Catholic parents, even though she and the boyfriend would be at a house party in nearby Anaheim (he always called it "Anacrime")—and no, Tori and Rose were absolutely not invited to join them.

Tori liked to joke that Rose's folks were hands down the strictest parents at Coyote Hills High—a bold statement considering most of the school was made up of Ivy League bound nerds with ultra-demanding (even delusional) moms and dads. Even though they both knew it was an exaggerated accusation, going out on a weekday was unicorn-rare for Rose, Halloween or not. Plus, there was no "Claudia" in Rose's family to act as a helpful precedent or accomplice.

"Can't you say tonight is something school related, then?" Tori pressed, turning the combination to their locker. "Parents usually chill if they hear the big s-word."

Rose squeezed another worn folder in her already stuffed bag, her back facing her friend. "Already tried, didn't work." She doubted that she was the only one who heard the mean edge in her voice.

Just get it over with.

Rose slammed the locker shut and turned around. "I've got some weird stuff to tell you." Her hand lingered on the rusty metal vents. Did she really want to talk about this right now? Maybe lunch break would be a better time. *But that's hours away—I'll probably explode by then.*

"Oh. I thought you were kinda silent but deadly." Tori opened her black circular compact. "God, these Santa Ana winds—you wouldn't believe these new crow's feet I have. I get 'em every time the air turns dry like this…"

Rose nodded. She clenched one of her fists. Nothing. She clenched the other one, and the skin over her middle knuckle obediently cracked. It was a bad habit, but nothing a little ointment couldn't fix later.

"…but I just chalked that up to one of Rose Moon's random poker face moods." Tori rambled on, smudging her eyeliner with the tip of her pinkie. "Let me guess, your grandma left you her secret book of spells."

"No." Rose shot her a grim look, not joining in on their running joke of Grandma's mysterious "magic."

Tori abruptly looked up from picking at her eyelashes.

Rose paused, fingering her phone in her jacket pocket. Suddenly she felt very protective of her new secret. Maybe it was best to keep it to herself for a while and see how she felt about everything in the morning, or maybe even the next day.

Once the secret was out there, it would no longer ever be one. That kind of permanence freaked out Rose even more than she already was. She had zero control over the situation. That was troubling enough. On the other hand, the gigantic secret was already eating away at her insides. She couldn't fathom when she'd feel "normal" again, if that word meant anything at all anymore. *I couldn't bottle this up for much longer even if I tried.* She had to tell somebody. Besides, this was Tori, her best friend.

"Well?" Tori prodded.

Rose nodded inwardly, psyching herself up. If she didn't share it today, it'd probably happen tomorrow or very soon afterward. Might as well just get it going. With a determined sweep, she handed her friend the phone. "Found my aunt's diary. Look at what she wrote about me." She quickly scrolled to the photos.

Tori's compact snapped shut. As she examined the screen, Rose could tell how quickly her friend was going through the lines, which made sense since Tori and Claudia spoke a mixture of Korean and English to their parents. She was definitely concentrating, but Tori's expressionless face offered no discernible reaction. A couple of times, she scrolled back, rereading. Tori was rarely so silent for so long.

Rose wasn't sure exactly how long she stood there watching her friend, but it felt like days. At one point, she had to bite her lip to stop herself from blurting, "Are you done?"

After what seemed like another eon, Tori finally handed back the phone. Her eyebrows were frozen, raised a tad higher than normal. "What is all that about..." she trailed off.

"I know, right?" Rose burst with relief, leaning in with eagerness. She already felt a little lighter since she wasn't burdened all by herself. "Can you believe I found this before she leaves today? Right there, in my closet! You know how I've always told you that things just never—"

Tori nodded politely. Too politely. And her lips were slightly pursed.

Rose stopped short. "What is it?" Why did Tori suddenly look kind of...wooden?

"It's just..." Tori sort of shrugged and shot a sideways glance at nothing. "I don't know, seems like this could just be a weird misunderstanding. I mean, you've always had that gut feeling, which I get, but..."

Rose swallowed hard. "But...what?" Exactly what was she insinuating?

Tori hesitated, avoiding Rose's penetrating gaze. "Doesn't it seem a little too crazy, whatever this might be? I mean, just because it's in her day planner or whatever...I don't know, maybe it's just the way she writes, like maybe it just came out weird, you know?"

Rose was incredulous. "Just the way she writes? What else could she possibly mean? There's some kind of secret about me, and her words are all right there." She couldn't believe she had to defend something that was so crystal clear...and invisible at the same time. A known unknown.

Rose's vision went dark as a pair of hands covered her eyes.

"Happy Halloween, brats!"

It was Cameron, their other best friend. Underneath his black coat was one of his dozen Bauhaus shirts and shredded jeans, nothing special for Halloween on his tall, angular frame. Last year, though, he'd dressed up as a quintessential "sportsball" prepster, all decked out in a letterman jacket, disgustingly impeccable khakis, and equally nauseating loafers that looked like they belonged on some douche's yacht. Heavily gelled hair and a gallon of cologne rounded out his mocking costume, eliciting an entire school day of double takes and eye rolls. Mission accomplished. But today, Cameron was his normal self. His wavy sandy brown hair was now grown out so that it was considerably longer than Tori's bleached pixie cut. On his pale wrist, a small tattoo of a crescent moon captioned "new moon, new beginnings" peeked out from behind a studded cuff.

Cameron's gray-green eyes sparkled as he exaggeratedly massaged Rose's shoulders like a boxing coach. "You guys ready for tonight?" he grinned mischievously. "I literally can't wait. Hey, let's see that piercing, woman!"

"I can't go," Rose muttered. Both girls avoided eye contact.

He took a quick swig of his bottle, mocha coffee steam whirling in the cold air. "What's going on? You," he pointed at Tori, "look severely constipated. And Rose, you…"

Silence.

"Okay, guys, what's up?"

"So, I found my aunt's journal this morning." Rose finally spoke. She steadily watched Tori, who still wouldn't look at her.

Cameron glanced back and forth between the two. "Yes, and?"

Without saying a word, Rose scrolled to the photos and handed him the phone.

"Um…" Cameron gave her an obvious look. "You know I can't read this, right?"

Rose looked away, despondent. Of course, she knew that Cameron wouldn't be able to read the text in the images, but she just didn't know what to say. It was easier for her to pretend to concentrate on a familiar group of students who always sat in the courtyard under a huge pepper tree. As usual, they were singing along to a guy strumming a Jesus-loving song on his acoustic guitar. Jeff Kim was his name—or was it Jason? She was surprised she couldn't remember even though they both were in Miss Melvin's fifth and sixth grade classes at Willow Drive Elementary.

Tori let out a short sigh. In a sort of business-like voice, she filled Cameron in on the contents of the photos. Cameron's eyes widened, and he stepped in closer as he listened to Tori's translations. Their small triangle tightened as they went through the images together. Tori paused when Cameron gasped and grabbed Rose by the arm.

Cameron swiveled Rose toward him. "Are you okay?" he asked in a very adult tone. "Seriously."

Tori instantly interjected. "It *is* pretty crazy, I guess," she admitted. She seemed to be grappling with the subject as if she just couldn't wrap her head around it. "Rose, I didn't mean to sound like I doubted you or anything. It's just…hard to believe that your family would have some big secret, you know?"

Cameron crinkled his brows at her.

Tori grimaced and continued, a little sheepish. "Rose, so many times you told me that something didn't feel right. Obviously, you sensed that something was up. I just couldn't fathom that something really was." She motioned at Rose's phone. "I'm sorry."

Rose flashed her friend a small but understanding smile. She knew it wasn't easy for Tori to apologize about anything, and she certainly couldn't blame her for being confused. At least she was trying.

"It's okay...I'm not, like, sad or anything." Rose swallowed hard and forced a crooked grin, instinctively backing off from all the seriousness. For some reason, she suddenly felt super awkward. "I just wish she wrote more details about it."

Tori and Cameron glanced at one another. They clearly had no idea how to respond.

"It's weird, I almost feel relieved or something. I mean, lots of things suddenly kind of make sense...but only to an extent because now, I have even more questions." Rose tilted her head back, wincing at the new tension in her neck. "I could never put my finger on what it was, and that was pretty scary when I was a kid. Sometimes I didn't feel like I belonged in my own house. Well, now I know why. Kind of."

"Those jerks!" Cameron stopped, his lips parting ruefully. "I'm sorry, I didn't mean to say that. Your folks have always been so awesome to me, and I totally love them—"

"Don't worry, seriously!" Rose interrupted with sudden force. She lowered her voice a couple of notches. "It's fine, I swear..." She wondered if her casual shrug looked as feigned as it felt.

"Come here," Tori said, pulling her into a hug. "Everything will be all right. I mean, it's gotta be."

Cameron joined the group hug. The bell rang for first period. "She's right, girl. Somehow this will all sort itself out." Like Tori, he was trying to sound upbeat and supportive.

Rose felt their eyes on her as she merged into the noisy river of students in the hall. Her leg muscles tightened. *Don't run.* But she wanted to sprint and break out of this herd: straight, left, through the narrow space between the vampire and nun, down the hall until she reached the line of buses on the curb, along the concrete sidewalk, past the manicured rows of red and yellow rose bushes and down the hill, over the bumpy railroad tracks, on the dirt path until it was just parallel to the main road. But then, where?

Rose knew that she would barely pass Ms. Kleiman's weekly quiz. It was obvious by the time she reached the halfway point. Reading every question was like decoding some obtuse ancient language from another galaxy.

After just a few minutes, Rose gave up and handed it to the bespectacled teacher at the front of the classroom. Ms. Kleiman checked her watch with a quizzical look before placing the paper in the empty plastic tray on the desk.

Rose momentarily stressed about the inevitable fail she'd just submitted as she walked back to her seat. Maybe an A in the course was still possible as long as she aced—like *really* aced—the final essay. Ms. Kleiman weighed these weekly quizzes heavily, though, to make sure her students were engaged all semester instead of just cramming all at once at the middle and end.

Whoa!

Just before Rose reached her desk, her right ankle collided with something protruding and hard. With a clumsy flailing motion, she simultaneously fell down and forward in the aisle between desks, flapping her arms out for balance. Somehow, she managed to jerk out her other leg just in time before totally whiplashing onto the shiny linoleum.

Exaggerated snickers erupted behind her.

Rose knew who it was without even turning around: Chelsea and Eliza, senior editor and copy editor of *The Tribute*, Coyote Hills High's award-winning student newspaper. Chelsea's freckled nose scrunched with delight as Eliza, her loyal sidekick, retracted her outstretched sandaled foot back under her desk. Today the pair was dressed in identical fairy princess gowns, complete with matching tiaras, wings, and long white evening gloves. Barf.

Those two just loved being a total pain in the neck toward Rose. Chelsea was a major reason for Rose declining her arts editor position this year. Once the senior editor role was announced, Rose knew better than to waste any energy pushing her usual pieces on local music and "oddball" art against Chelsea's rigidly mainstream agenda. Their tastes had clashed in the newsroom of *The Tribute* since day one. Rarely a publication went by without both Chelsea and Eliza railing against almost every topic Rose brought to the table.

Besides, Rose had heard the rumors just like everyone else. Ms. Dunbar, the newspaper's supervisor, happened to be a close family friend and golf buddy of Chelsea's mom. It was obvious how Chelsea had snagged the top staff position this year, but nobody could do a thing about it. Even Eliza, who was sometimes even meaner than Chelsea, would've made more sense as senior editor—she was a far better writer than her best friend. Even though Rose was initially reluctant to the change in the newspaper's direction to a more traditional scope, her current position as an occasional contributor was plenty to juggle with the rest of her schoolwork load.

A few faint giggles bounced around the room. Cheeks burning, Rose concentrated on the ticking of the wall clock while the rest of the students slowly turned back to their quizzes. She kept her eyes down and partially obscured by some long strands of hair. As she sank into the plastic chair, she panicked for a second before letting out a silent sigh of relief. At least her phone was still in her jacket pocket. Pride was one thing but sometimes there was nothing more stupidly stressful than worrying about the whereabouts of one's stupid phone.

One last muffled guffaw before Chelsea and Eliza convulsed into one another.

Rose ignored their cackles, kicking herself for not seeing the booby trap of Eliza's mini sausage-shaped toes tipped with chipped green polish. In the back of her mind, Rose felt the faint and familiar swish of fluttering wings and high-pitched chirps swirling around her, over and over. They were so very far away, and she wasn't a kid in her old backyard anymore, but she was okay.

She reached into her backpack and pulled out a wrinkled copy of *Rip It Up*. The local punk zine had instantly become her favorite read after encountering Johnny Oi at the Hub one random afternoon. The last thing Rose thought she'd see when heading to the bathroom that day was the legendary disc jockey casually sitting on a stool at the wooden bar, perusing some papers as he sipped from a glass soda bottle. Stopping in her tracks, Rose yanked Tori's forearm and nudged her chin in the stout man's direction. They gaped open-mouthed for a moment before swiveling their heads toward each other, eyes wide with bewilderment. *What is he doing here?!* Someone they pretty much revered, and one of their crank-calling victims, sat just a few feet away.

Crank-calling was a regular pastime for Rose and Tori, but not all of their targets were people they admired. During the live caller segment of his public television program, local religious fanatic Duncan York periodically accepted calls from a very insistent, heavily accented Korean ajumma, who asked, "You go to hell? Why you go to hell?" Even if that same lady hadn't just crank-called Johnny Oi a few weeks before, Rose and Tori were way too nervous in person to say anything noteworthy besides some dorky comments about how much they lived for his weekly show and the obscure music he introduced. As Johnny Oi politely thanked them, Rose instantly noticed how his grandpa-ish drawl sounded almost the same—though not quite as confused—as when he had patiently explained to the alleged ajumma on the phone that no, he *really* was not expecting a Korean barbecue dinner delivery to the studio that evening.

Rose managed to eke out a few questions—the whole time praying Johnny Oi wouldn't recognize her voice—about the intriguing black and white pamphlet on the counter in front of him. After a couple of accommodating minutes, and most likely to send the idolizing teens on their way, Johnny Oi politely offered his copy to Rose.

The bell rang. A couple of students belted out frustrated sighs as they scrambled to finish. Slowly shuffling with the rest of the class toward the door, Rose tried to finish an article about an Orange County ska-punk band and their growing popularity around the country. And to think, she could've seen them play at the Hub last year when they could barely fill a patio for free.

"Deadline's coming up—hope you have a decent article this time. Nothing inappropriate, mm-kay?" Chelsea made a beeline to Rose on the way out. Eliza waited for her friend at the door, shooting Rose a look even more sour than her usual default jeer.

Rose looked up from her reading. "Inappropriate?" A line of students squeezed past them. What was Chelsea getting at? Besides, she had already submitted her piece on Nebula Records' recent art show days ago.

"You heard me," Chelsea snapped, jumping at the opportunity to make a fuss. "Don't make me do a staff re-org this early in the year. Freelancers like you are the first to get dumped." She scanned Rose with contempt before locking arms with Eliza and sauntering off.

Rose refrained from retorting at their backs.

"The energy you give out to the universe is the energy you get back," Cameron always liked to say, whether he was referencing a good day or a bad one. Rose sure felt like that theory rang true today.

Calculus, her least favorite class, went a thousand times slower than usual. Ms. Sanchez droned on and on about secant line slopes and derivatives as Rose barely looked up from her notes all hour, deep in old, bizarre thoughts. Like Ohio. Why was that place popping up now?

She couldn't remember the last time her family's Midwest stint had entered her mind. As the only non-WASPs in their tiny suburb, the Moon family had been the target of plenty of old-fashioned racism. Ah, the good ole days. If it hadn't been for some of their more open-minded friends and neighbors, who knew how life would've turned out back then? While six-year-old Rose always had plenty of pals in the classroom, recess was a different story—a mini *Lord of the Flies* scenario every time.

Their woodsy neighborhood was often even trickier. One group of aggressive older bullies had a penchant for harassing the lone "Chinese" person from school. Rose's tomboy streak ensured that outrunning or outbiking them was always pretty easy, even when the biggest bully, bowl-cut-haired Victor Appleton, was on his daily hunt for her humiliation. After minutes of expertly zigzagging through the trees and random yards, she'd triumphantly race up the security of her driveway and burst through the front door. By the time she turned back around to look at her predators, they were always further away than expected, slinking off in almost hasty retreat. Getting near a house meant parents were close by. Rose would then run out to the safety of her backyard lawn, singing a made-up tune at the sky until a handful of small sparrows joined her, flying circles around her as she spun and giggled in awe and relief. Every time it happened, she was humbled with the same joyous stun as the first time.

Years later, she tripped out on how those scary bullies were actually just kids. What would they have even done if they had caught up to her? Little Rose was more than ecstatic when her family returned to their Southern California suburb about a year later. But she never forgot those magical little birds.

Instead of meeting Tori and Cameron at morning break, Rose opted for a short walk down the hill. She needed to be alone, just for a little while. Their secret spot was the perfect reprieve from her tumultuous morning.

The morning traffic had long dissipated on Warton Way. A patch of land with a large Quonset hut sat at the bottom of the school property, home to the well-known agriculture program. Sometimes students would secretly smoke at the far end of the Quonset hut, safely out of sight from the school narcs.

Quietly stepping around the patches of vegetation, Rose reached the hidden spot that she and her friends usually claimed. Even the ag students couldn't really see around this corner unless they were purposely looking. Mr. Reed, the sole agriculture teacher, was a super laid-back hippie type who stood out from the rest of the teachers due to his long auburn ponytail and matching mustache. He didn't bother disciplining students unless they were doing something really screwed up, like being disrespectful or violent. He also happened to be a diehard fan of Jackson Browne, a Coyote Hills High alumnus—another reason Mr. Reed was considered pretty cool.

Rose leaned against the side of the Quonset hut and closed her eyes. She could see Aunt Esther's journal floating in front of her, the pages turning rhythmically in her trembling fingers against a backdrop of white noise.

Some uncharacteristic warmth still exuded from her cheeks from the embarrassing incident of getting tripped in first period. Eliza and Chelsea were messing with her even more this year, like they were obsessed or something. Chagrin stung Rose's eyelids open as laughter echoed from the other students, some of whom she had previously thought were okay. She wouldn't be trusting any of them from now on.

Don't, Rose told herself sternly, even though she didn't feel commanding at all. *Don't let yourself go down that dark hole.* Closing her eyes again, she pulled in streams of air in measured inhales and exhales. Longer and deeper, the air flowed through her lungs. A gentle breeze toyed with some strands of her hair, grazing her chin and the tip of her nose.

A faint scent wafted by. Rose knew it instantly—a familiar smell she loved, of horse and hay and precious escape. Rose pushed her hair away from her cheek and gazed down the road. Laguna Lake Riding Club. Every time she smelled horses, a stream of memories from her riding days always flooded back. But today, the sensation of magical rocking canters was marred by new and ugly truths. A stronger breeze swept her nostrils. She inhaled deeply again, searching for just one comfortable, intoxicating moment.

But her aunt's words were all she could see. A shiver yawned up her arms, and Rose slowly slumped onto the cement, utterly exhausted.

Sometimes heartache guides you to the other side.

The voice was calm and ageless and moved like a continental drift.

Just tap in, Rose. You know how.

Rose was almost certain she had never heard this voice before, but the tender tone didn't sound like a total stranger, either.

"Cameron! She's over here…" Tori's voice intruded in the reverberating amber sky.

A presence hung heavy in the desolate silence. Rose squinted at the expanse of dry bronze dirt and random clusters of jagged rocks. Was she sitting or floating? Above, fiery clouds floated with tinged lavender edges, illuminating flashes of other colors she had never seen before.

Her friends' footsteps were getting closer. The sky was quickly deepening into an immense shadow. She was about to wake up.

Near the last tangerine streak in front of the horizon, a tiny silhouette appeared. He faced her head on, light-years away. Despite the distance, Rose knew the instant they made eye contact. A magnifying flash of lightning illuminated his dazzling smile along with his dark, burning, unwavering eyes. She felt him in her veins even though he was from somewhere else. Then he waved an arm, almost hastily, like he knew he was about to be whisked away. An earthy breeze rushed over her face.

Rose blinked awake, momentarily confused at the sight of Tori and Cameron expertly maneuvering around the small plants that lined the Quonset hut's perimeter. A vague hush of disappointment sunk in as she realized the dream was over.

"We were looking for you all break," Cameron said, lighting Tori's cigarette. "Almost reported you as a missing child."

Rose scrambled to her feet. Would she ever actually get any rest while sleeping? "Sorry. Guess I zoned out." She checked the time on her phone as the vivid encounter crumpled into everyday reality. "Oh, no, I totally missed third period!" And her group history presentation, too. Not good, especially since Mr. Lim was gleefully aware of how much she hated public speaking. Like a lot of people, he assumed that Rose's all-black dress code sought attention, but they couldn't be more wrong.

Tori waved her hand in front of Rose's face as if testing her vision. "Earth to Rose, it's already the end of fourth period. Let's just ditch the rest of the day."

Cameron blew a fleeting ring of smoke and coughed. "Jesus, really?" By the time he arched his immaculate eyebrows, the ring had already scattered into nothing.

Ignoring him, Tori appealed to Rose. "Let's go to Hard Times! C'mon, please? You need a break today."

Rose perked up a little at the mention of the pool hall. The trio had randomly gotten into billiards last year, right after Tori had passed her driver's license exam. Tori loved how the classically grungy spot was where older, blue collar guys often spent their evenings. It was usually pretty empty during the day, and Rose found it way less annoying that way.

"Well...okay." Rose ignored Tori's double take of surprise. She was never convinced so quickly. Attendance was strictly monitored, and consequences for unexcused absences were extreme. Ditching was usually never worth it for Rose. "Guess there goes French and physics, too—not like I've been remotely productive today."

They trekked back up the hill and climbed into Tori's sedan. "Christy's or George's?" Tori asked as she reversed out of the parking space.

"George's," Rose answered. "Feeling something savory for once." Although she'd definitely miss her favorite donut shop's incredible apple fritter—not to mention glazed twist, raspberry-filled, and frosted strawberry—her stomach growled for the other mom-and-pop's signature take out.

"You're just full of surprises today, my dear," said Cameron. He pressed a button on the dashboard. "Time for some real Christian Death, not that fake action." Everyone grumbled in agreement, remembering the flyer that someone had left on all the car windshields the other day at the Hub's parking lot.

In a few minutes they joined a handful of other cars in line at the drive-thru. Rose's mouth watered almost every time they waited in front of the big menu display. A neighbor had once told her that George's was originally a Jack in the Box, like a thousand years ago, before the fast food business turned into a big chain. Rose and Cameron each ordered a veggie burrito, and Tori got her usual burger and fries combo. It was too late in the day to order one of their renowned and utterly gigantic breakfast burritos.

"How you stay so thin I'll never know," Rose remarked to Tori, her mouth stuffed with the warm and gooey concoction. Tori's willowy figure never seemed affected by eating whatever she wanted at all hours of the day. "You and Claudia both. Must be the genes."

"Says Miss Donut," replied Cameron, already halfway done with his burrito. "Please, she'd be twice her size if it wasn't for all her barfing sessions—duh!" He displayed an exaggerated gagging finger down his throat.

Rose laughed, nearly choking on her food. They all knew Cameron was just being silly and trying to brighten her mood.

"Liar!" Tori chimed in, looking mildly offended. "You know what a waste that would be, barfing up all that food? I'm too cheap to be bulimic."

"Shut up, you sound like a nutjob," Cameron drawled, dabbing his mouth with a white napkin.

They pulled into a familiar Southern California shopping plaza. This one was composed of mostly older small businesses on a busy street near the border of Fullerton and La Habra. As the trio entered, a random mixture of cigarette smoke, old nachos, and even older carpet welcomed them like a roughhewn friend. The Hard Times smell. A few people were playing, but most of the dozen tables or so looked like they hadn't been touched since the night before.

"Hey, guys." A low but friendly voice yawned from behind the long counter on the left. Harry, one of Hard Times' employees who seemed to never clock out. As usual, he was standing under the big neon beer signs scattered along the wood-paneled wall. Waving a heavyset arm covered in colorful, somewhat faded traditional tattoos, he quickly scribbled on a small notepad. "An hour?"

"Yup. And three beers, too." Cameron quickly pulled out his wallet, waving off his friends' protests. He always had plenty of cash.

"You got it, man." Harry knew Rod, Cameron's brother, from high school back in the day. He seemed to assume Cameron was older than he really was, based on his mature, confident appearance—at least, that's what everyone silently went along with. Personal questions weren't really anyone's thing here if you acted right.

They were careful to keep it cool with their bottles, choosing a table at the dim back end of the room. The last thing they wanted was to jeopardize their beer connection here, or worse, to get Harry in trouble for being so trusting. And they weren't going to get stupidly hammered, which was easy since they all agreed that beer tasted like dung, anyhow. It was more about the cheap thrill of having the drinks handed to them over an official bar counter.

The group quietly meandered around a wiry older man with a graying beard almost as ratty as his Lynyrd Skynyrd shirt. He was a Hard Times regular—Mr. Beard was their name for him. Mr. Beard held his stick upright and let them pass behind him before resuming the strategy for his break. His perennial opponent was Santa Claus, who sat back on a stool with his hands propped on his ho-ho-ho belly as he stared with intense concentration at their eight-ball set up.

A loud crack of resin pierced everyone's ears. From the corner of her eye, Rose watched Mr. Beard subtly thrust his chin at Santa Claus. "Who's the cuck now?"

Not bothering with their usual coin toss at the table, Rose set down her untouched drink and grabbed a cue stick with one hand and chalk with the other. She rotated the cue in the small cube so that the tip was evenly covered in blue.

Cameron went along with Rose's eagerness. He took a quick swig and positioned the rack on the green table surface, making sure the yellow ball was at the top, the other corners each had a striped and solid, and the black eight ball sat snug in the center. Tori chalked up her own cue on the side as Rose carefully lined up her shot, sniper-style. She could feel Tori watching her as she leaned in. Despite their usual joking on the way to the pool hall, she couldn't help but wonder if Tori still secretly doubted her morning discovery.

A real friend wouldn't, Rose thought. She aimed and released her shot. The cue ball splintered the tight triangle into fifteen separate directions. Some balls rolled and others spun throughout the length of the table in different orbits and speeds. Rose stood back and observed the randomness with satisfaction. She looked at Tori as a couple of prime balls plopped into two corner pockets. *Who's the cuck now?* Rose mimicked Mr. Beard silently.

Rose handily beat Tori in the first game. Cameron lost next, even quicker. Despite harboring a hatred for geometry class that bordered on diabolical, angles were easy for Rose in the billiards context, and her spirits momentarily lifted over her morning shock. She drummed her fingers against the wooden paneling of the table as "Welcome to the Jungle" blasted from the jukebox. How great would it be when she finally started college? The thought of such an open road thrilled her every time it entered her mind. Although school could definitely be a drag sometimes, it was also a gateway to a world of new possibilities.

A brief flash of afternoon sunlight burst into the dim interior as the front door suddenly swung open. Two familiar young guys walked in, both in baggy polo shirts, oversized jeans and identical gel-slicked hair. Rose could practically smell their department store cologne before recognizing it was Sung and David from school. The two seniors were both popular, came from moneyed families, and also played at Hard Times pretty often. They were known for their obnoxious sense of humor, sometimes bordering on bullyish behavior. Relentlessly hazing younger students for fun was their specialty. Sung's swagger was at an all-time high because his parents had recently gifted him an expensive black coupe for his birthday. He immediately enhanced it with extra-large rims and a new bass system to blast everything from Snoop Dogg to BTS.

David glanced around the room while his friend took care of

things at the front counter. He noticed Rose, Tori, and Cameron in the back but coolly looked away in that typical *I'm-more-popular-than-you-so-I-won't-say-hello* mode. As the pair sauntered toward the opposite corner of the room, Sung accidentally bumped into Mr. Beard, who was stooped over his table in an awkward position. Sung apologized profusely, which only slightly softened the old man's glare at having his focus interrupted.

"Funny how some people act so differently when they're not at school," Rose smirked. Sung's sudden off-campus humbleness was as bizarre as watching a rodeo clown perform the Dying Swan solo.

Rock music blared over the speakers, and the two groups of schoolmates defiantly ignored each other as they played. But a few minutes later, David approached them.

"Hey…do you think you guys can get us some beer on your next round?" he asked hesitantly, eyeing their bottles with a crisp twenty-dollar bill in his fist. Sung stayed back at his table, pretending not to watch.

"Nope." Tori leaned over the table to aim. She didn't give an explanation even though David lingered for one. Rose and Cameron offered him only blank stares. Sensing defeat, David retreated in silence.

A smatter of high-pitched laughter broke through the intro of an Aerosmith song. Two girls waltzed in and headed straight to Sung and David, their shiny silver bracelets jingling against designer chain-link handbag straps. Grace and Jennie, the main princesses on campus, had entered. They were kind of like a twisted version of Chelsea and Eliza. Jennie tossed her brassy highlighted hair, turning her nose from Rose and Tori as she scuffled by. Close behind, Grace blinked at their bottles, annoyed at being one-upped.

"So that's why they wanted those beers," Rose rolled her eyes, rubbing the cue. "Whatever." Last year the princess duo had talked smack in English lit about how "Rose and Tori must be crazy to dress like total witches."

Sung's head angled to the side. He heard the mild dig. The girls' arrival appeared to mend their confidence, though. David's guttural, look-at-us bellows of laughter reverberated every few minutes. Probably to drown them out, Mr. Beard dropped several coins into the ornate jukebox. Black Sabbath hit the speakers, and he strutted back to his table to resume his game.

4

"Come on, girl. Your stall's waiting."

Ethan grit his teeth. The muscular chestnut had recently moved to Laguna Lake Riding Club, but these mini standoffs were already becoming a frequent thing. Lead rope in hand, Ethan clucked and gently tapped her back hip again, trying to exude an aura of expectant leadership.

Starla didn't budge. She just did the easiest thing, which was to simply stand there, ignoring the silly human. Although the mare was a mere three feet outside of her freshly cleaned stall, Ethan knew that if a horse really didn't want to move, there was no amount of pulling that would change her mind. A clear advantage of weighing about half a ton, among other things.

Quietly chuckling, Ethan released the lead and leaned against the wall. He'd seen every kind of barn in his career, from simple backyard pipe stalls to hedge-lined, polished stables nicer than most houses. Laguna Lake Riding Club was somewhere in between. Of course, letting horses be horses in a monitored pasture all day was ideal in Ethan's mind, but he knew that simply wasn't possible in many places. Laguna Lake Riding Club was a private, full-service boutique facility with spacious in and out stalls, meticulously maintained arenas and round pen, quality hay fed at least three times a day (though many of the owners opted for more), working laundry machines, and access to gorgeous trails. Too bad Starla didn't care about any of that. Yes, the mare was a little obstinate, but her disposition wasn't anything close to the many mishandled horses he'd trained back home. "Range rats," some of his old buddies would probably call a horse like Starla. Ethan never agreed that the term fit the free roaming equines of the West. Some of the most intelligent horses he'd ever known were mustangs. Starla may lack cooperation right now, but odds were it was simply her way of testing her environment...a pretty intelligent move, actually. Ethan could respect that. He'd probably do the same. Having your life uprooted and all of a sudden be forced to live in some new, strange place with new, strange people didn't exactly sound pleasant.

Despite the brisk October air, beads of sweat trickled down the back of Ethan's neck. This morning hadn't exactly gone as planned. Shortly before dawn, he'd discovered that a chunk of the main fence needed immediate repair. Then Javier, one of the barn's most experienced grooms, had to take his elderly mother to the doctor, which added a boatload of extra tasks to disperse to everybody else. And Ethan still had to hack his boss' Warmbloods, per her request. One of them, Spader, was very particular—the old horse absolutely hated turnout (and always returned to the gate within ten minutes, stomping to return to his stall) yet loved any arena work almost as much as he loved competing. Ethan had learned over time that a relaxing trail ride just wasn't up to par for the former jumper champion, so he always arranged a proper ride in the ring for Spader. Taking care of over two dozen horses had its rewards, but an autopilot routine was just not one of them.

Not that Ethan was complaining. As the head of Laguna Lake Riding Club's small staff, his job was to make sure that every unexpected facet of each day was properly managed, no matter what. Health, consistency and comfort—that was the ideal environment in which horses truly thrived, in his opinion. Even with unexpected hiccups, he enjoyed every minute of his job. Through a fortuitous sequence of surprisingly grueling interviews, he'd been able to land the position over several other capable contenders, mostly locals with direct word-of-mouth advantages. And he had received the offer for the position just in time. Ethan wasn't sure how much longer he could afford the grungy, cockroach-infested room he'd spent over two months in, even though it was the cheapest motel in the area.

He didn't come to this part of California with much. That was okay. In his gut, he knew that working with horses would always be the most fulfilling way to some financial flexibility and to finally escape the desert. He loved his hometown, but he just needed to get out of there. He would miss her, of course, but nobody could expect him to tolerate any more. He could not stand watching his naïve mother fall in love with that manipulative loser. Had Mitch waited all those years to swoop in the moment he saw an opening? If she wanted to welcome Mitch into their home—the house he'd ate countless meals in as a trusted friend— that was her choice, but Ethan wasn't going to feign any support or understanding. His father may be gone, but he would always be the sole patriarch of the Soto household.

"You want me to take over, boss?" asked Manuel, a young groom in a straw cowboy hat. He paused with his wheelbarrow.

Ethan shook his head. "I got this, thanks."

Delighted laughter erupted from down the way. "She'll be perfect for the kiddie class at the next schooling show!"

Ethan looked over and saw a couple of young women chattering and cooing as they brushed a sorrel pony barely twelve hands high. Maizie was accustomed to a perennial chorus of "awws" everywhere she went due to her irresistible, diminutive charm. Even Ethan sometimes stopped at her stall during his busy day to give her a good scratch behind the ears or, if she was lucky, a carrot or three.

The eclectic mix at the modest but respected stable was one of the characteristics that had attracted Ethan to the job in the first place. Nestled in a quiet nook of a Southern California suburb, Laguna Lake Riding Club had a solid reputation for catering to a wide assortment of tenants and their needs.

Gina Hartwell, the owner, had three stately bay warmbloods, a small string of saintly lesson horses, as well as a handful of adopted burros. She had taken over the barn just after officially, and very reluctantly, retiring from eventing at the impressive age of fifty-two. Her office displayed some of the fullest trophy shelves and ribbon racks Ethan had ever seen. The stable's trainers worked with both English and Western riders, many of whom competed in hunters, jumpers, dressage, reining, and barrel racing.

A big plus for everyone was the direct access to the chaparral-lined trails of Coyote Hills, a picturesque gem of a nature reserve. Coyotes were still common throughout the area, as well as rare or even endangered species such as the white-tailed kite, the western bluebird, and the coastal western whiptail lizard.

The first time Ethan had ventured into Coyote Hills with Tanner, his trusty blue roan Quarter horse, he knew they'd found the place he wanted to call home, at least for a while. Though it was just a fraction of the open space he was accustomed to, beautiful old trees and lovely hills sprawled in every direction, untouched except by nature and time. The sparkling, duck-filled lake that the place was named after was absolutely breathtaking once you ventured deep into the woods enough to find it. Such pristine wilderness was unique in the area and, judging from the headlines in the local papers, only destined to become more rarefied in the rapidly developing county.

Ethan shook off the emerging pangs that gutted him every time he was reminded of his family home. Would the small ranch still be theirs by the time his mom got tricked this time? They did have a few close calls before. He gently tugged the lead rope again. Starla's ears flattened. Ethan immediately relented, remembering the mustang's swinging head the last time her big ears got all pinny. That was just yesterday.

"You win. This time." Ethan pulled a small carrot from his pocket and waved it in front of Starla until she started toward her stall. Ethan tossed the sweet treat into her bucket when the mare was fully inside and closed the gate behind him. He didn't want to rely on treats, but there were other things to tend to right now besides exclusively catering to a celebrity's unpredictable new horse.

Lula May, a wealthy art student turned artist turned sudden...equestrian. "Huh?" That was what Ethan had muttered to Gina when she informed him of their new client. "Yes, that Lula May," he was told. Her name, presumably not the one she was born with, was all over the junk headlines lately for whatever reason. Ethan knew little about her besides that she didn't know the first thing about horses (a fact she'd admitted, stiffly, during the introductory barn tour). Also made very clear was her preference to always go by her artist name and nothing else. And according to the previous owner, Starla was sound, a pleasant keeper and an easy ride—a sure-footed and reliable lesson horse, even for beginners, despite her former existence as an unowned wild horse.

Somehow that wasn't how it was all panning out. And Lula May wasn't even close to being a "real" beginner, because she hardly seemed interested in the first place. It sounded like their first lesson together would be the first of her entire life—if only she would actually show up. Despite insisting on reserving Ethan as her trainer, she had canceled last minute several times already. Ethan wasn't even one of the regular instructors at Laguna Lake Riding Club. Lula May had convinced Gina to urge him to make special time for her, which Gina had obliged with mild skepticism. But what his boss told him to do, Ethan did. And Lula May was clearly accustomed to getting her way.

Ethan wasn't quite sure what had gone down when Lula May transferred Starla from her first stable in Los Angeles, but the horse's disposition had dramatically changed by arrival. When Starla first unloaded from the trailer, she was in such a frenzy that Ethan almost questioned if the horse had ever been properly gentled at all. She was a prancy, spooky firecracker, the very opposite from the dozen videos that her previous caretakers had sent as additional proof of Starla's once docile demeanor. From patiently packing kids around for their up-and-down lessons to stepping it up for casual cross-country hacks on the field, Starla was a beloved barn favorite.

Ethan paused outside of the stall. Starla didn't pay attention to him in the least, swerving around a couple of times before brazenly kicking the back wall with her left hind leg, like a casual afterthought. She seemed to like that move. Her coat was crusted with dirt, and her mane and tail probably had about a pound of grime to brush out. Too bad Starla wouldn't let anybody groom her so far.

"Just take it day by day with her," Gina had advised. "She'll come around."

5

Rose sat around the living room coffee table with her parents and Aunt Esther. Milo was busy gnawing on his latest favorite toy, a braided rope, as he rested in her lap.

A cluster of luggage waited at the edge of the foyer. How weird that her aunt's journal was somewhere inside one of those bags. Rose watched everyone chatter in the way people typically do when a long term, oceanic separation is looming upon them—almost apologetic, breezy, and magnanimous. They were oblivious to the girl scrutinizing their every move with newfound fixation.

"I have some gifts for you and Thomas." Aunt Esther pushed a crinkly shopping bag forward. "Tell Thomas that Auntie loves him."

Rose nodded at the package in silence, almost afraid that her aunt would somehow discover that her private thoughts had been compromised earlier this morning.

"I just couldn't decide what to get him. He has so many interests!" Aunt Esther continued. Rose's brother was with his best buddy Ricky at an after-school Halloween trick or treat event, so he wouldn't be able to see off Aunt Esther. His absence didn't seem to bother anyone.

Rose sifted through the dense packaging until rough, wiry wool grazed her fingertips. Pulling it out, she held up the itchiest sweater ever created.

"It's going to fit perfectly!" Aunt Esther declared. She snatched the garment out of Rose's frozen hands and pressed its narrow shoulders onto her niece. Stepping back, she nodded with approval.

"Thank...you," Rose forced out. The fibers of the hideous red and brown striped thing pricked right through her own top as if she was hugging a cactus. Milo flinched when one of the sleeves brushed his back. He quickly hopped to the floor, rope in mouth.

"What did you get for Thomas?" Rose's mom asked her sister-in-law. She eyed a long silver-wrapped package that clearly was not a sweater.

Aunt Esther flashed a wide grin. "A skateboard!" she answered excitedly. "I know he already has one, but this one is very popular according to the nice young man who helped me at the shop."

Rose's mouth dropped open. *A skateboard?* And she was stuck with the itchiest, ugliest sweater in the universe?

"Oh, he will love it," Rose's mom gleamed with confidence. "It's good exercise, too. Gets him outside."

"Great." Aunt Esther looked over at her niece. "Rose doesn't seem to like her gift."

"Nonsense! It's a lovely sweater..." Rose's dad said.

Rose tuned in and out as the adults gabbed on. Minutes disappeared on the grandfather clock. Yes, Rose dressed in pretty much all-black almost all the time...no, she didn't care, even during the sweltering SoCal summers...Why? Who knows. But yes, they had tried to convince her otherwise...

*Hurry up...*Rose refrained from rolling her eyes. She'd just about had it, sitting there now for nearly half an hour listening to everything that was so wrong about her, probably for the tenth time this week. This was getting so old!

"I'm sure you're doing the best you can," Aunt Esther said solemnly, shaking her head with a deliberate slowness that implies wisdom. With a pointed finger a few inches from Rose's nose, she remarked, "You have a lot to learn, young lady."

Rose licked her lips and just stared. It was all so mean and jarring. Years of secrets. Pages of secrets. All the wasted time...just how many hours did it all add up to? And then she'd jump on a plane back to wherever, all smug, mission accomplished?

Just who does she think she is? What is wrong with everyone, with everything?

The butterflies from the morning returned in Rose's stomach, this time not whipping against her insides but beating in place, tight, bracing themselves into a knot. Then her pulse bolted and, without thinking, she shot up from her chair and flung the sweater to the floor as hard as she could, wishing she had something more substantial for leverage. The sweater whipped at her aunt's right foot.

Three heads swiveled at her. A mouth dropped open. Rose

wasn't sure whose, and she didn't care. For some reason, she could only focus on Milo. He dropped his rope toy and approached the sweater, sniffing around Aunt Esther's ankles with high suspicion instead of the relaxed familiarity that a two week guest would normally get. He was the only one in the room on Rose's side.

"What…?" Eyes wide, Aunt Esther glanced around at the others, a hand raised questioningly.

Rose scoffed with such force that Milo froze mid-investigation and looked up at her.

Before her aunt could continue, Rose leaned into her face as close as she could without actually touching. "Don't you act all innocent." She almost couldn't believe she was hearing herself say the words—it was thrilling and frightening at the same time.

Even though her logical side was afraid of the consequences she'd face tonight, tomorrow, next week…it just didn't matter. Not anymore. Even though she knew that the family secret, whatever it was, wasn't originally her aunt's fault, the woman nonetheless played a significant role. And this time, Rose wasn't about to stifle herself while everyone took advantage of her presumed ignorance. Their classified information would no longer serve and protect whatever they were serving and protecting.

I know.

The air in the room stirred. Not a single twitch, blink or peep came from the four humans. Even Milo paused with everyone. Something shifted with the clock's ticking. Rose could feel it. Her palms turned heavy and clammy. She could tell everyone else felt some kind of change, too, even if they weren't quite sure what it was.

It had finally happened. Mixed bits of secrets and truth were leaking through neglected cracks in the dam, flowing toward parched soil long adapted to drought.

Had the grandfather clock stopped ticking? Still, nobody moved. Rose's breathing shrunk into shallow flurries. They were all in a team—*their* team—and she wasn't in it. Finally seeing the setup, after searching and wondering for so much of her life, tempered the burn just a little.

Her thoughts and voice and hands began to shake.

I'm done being everyone's scapegoat.

"Rose," Aunt Esther cleared her throat with condescending calm. "I have something to ask you." She paused. "Is it true that you never sent Joon a birthday card or present for his sixteenth birthday?"

Rose, slightly taken aback at the abrupt change of topic, shot her aunt an irritated and distracted glance. "What?"

Aunt Esther slowly reached for her purse and pulled out a blue and white card from the front flap. Rose instantly recognized the old card. It had been returned due to a mistakenly written address, and she never did get around to re-mailing it. But why was it here and not deep inside her desk drawer, underneath a pound of old music magazines?

"You went through my stuff?" asked Rose.

"And I'm glad I did!" Aunt Esther huffed. "I was going to bring this up earlier. Joon sent Rose a card for *her* birthday, but I guess she just doesn't care."

Rose knew it was time. No one else was going to control the pace of her truth.

"Who *cares* about that?" Rose's voice rose to a level she had never used. The manipulation days were over. "You want to know what I found in your big pile?"

As fast as her shaking hands would cooperate, Rose rummaged her phone from her pocket and held up the first journal photo on the screen.

Aunt Esther's face went a little pale.

Rose started reading aloud as she backed up to stand behind the big armchair. If necessary, she could easily run between the sofa and coffee table, avoiding the living room's dead end, directly to the dining room. The dining room led to the foyer and front door.

Suddenly Rose was already sprinting through her planned escape route. She couldn't finish reading it. Her throat was full, tears springing in her eyes. More than anything, she didn't want to cry in front of them.

"Rose, stop!"

She almost dodged them, then someone pulled her shoulder in. It was like they wanted to talk just as much as they wanted to pin her down.

All she wanted was to escape. Desperation and panic blinded her. Rose contorted, accidentally hitting someone or something but unable to see who or what was in her way. Shock muted the feeling of a random fingernail and the clumsy catch of her long hair.

A tear threatened to fall down her cheek, almost more ominous than anything else that had happened. Crying in front of them would never be an option. Eyes burning, Rose ripped herself free and bolted to Tori's blurry house.

6

"Hellooo, konichiwa…" a male voice oozed with slurring perversion.

Rose and Tori ignored the heavyset, obviously drunk guy as his leering friends snickered behind him. Scanning the boisterous crowd outside of the Ice Cave, the two girls quickly spotted Cameron waving from the crowded line. A random arm reached out and grabbed Rose's elbow as they made their way.

"Chill out, dude," Tori warned over her shoulder to the overzealous bloke.

Rose stifled a nervous giggle as her friend pulled her out of reach from the rest of his group, ending the brief tug of war. Even with all the sketchy antics here, she was finally beginning to relax and enjoy herself.

Just a few hours earlier, Tori could tell from Rose's impatient doorbell rings that something was wrong. She ushered Rose upstairs and listened to every detail of the bizarre episode her friend had just bailed while they snacked on pretzels and an array of Halloween candy.

"I can't go back home now." Rose was despondent as she peered through Tori's bedroom window. Her own house looked almost haunted from this angle.

"Don't worry," Tori said, not used to seeing Rose so upset. It didn't take very long to convince her to go to the I Don't Wanna Hear It show together. "I'll have my mom let your parents know that you're out with me and Claudia. It'll be fine!"

Cameron hugged them when they squeezed into his spot in line. The strong scent of Djarums filled the air. "Can your Cleopatra look be any more amazing?" he asked Rose, right before

40

hocking a huge loogie off to the side.

"Dang, maybe lay off the smokes for a while," Tori looked away, revolted.

Rose grinned as they bantered catty comments back and forth. Promptly after Claudia and her boyfriend drove off for the night, Tori had busted out her sister's overflowing makeup case and expertly picked out various glosses and powders. She'd caught the makeup bug pretty hard from many years of observing Claudia primp in their shared bathroom.

"Okay, now open your eyes for just a sec," Tori had instructed as she examined the sharp, exaggerated jet-black points that pricked out from both inner corners. With the concentrated precision of a bioarcheologist studying freshly excavated grave goods, she leaned in again. "Maybe a little more right...here..."

Rose closed her eyes as Tori's tiny brush flicked again. She could feel soft air blowing from Tori's nostrils onto her cheeks. Makeup was never Rose's strong suit, but she had to admit, it always felt pretty nice to get dolled up this way—almost therapeutic, especially after such an unsettling confrontation.

"Hope our queen would be proud!" Tori declared at her finished work a few minutes later. "Or, at least not be too embarrassed with my amateur-hour skills."

Rose gaped at the reflection, both familiar and strange. Her face had taken on the fiercely arched brows and voluptuously rimmed, pharaonic eyes she knew only from *Through the Looking Glass*, not staring in a mirror.

"Hey, remember when you suddenly got ssangapul here that night in junior high? Seriously, I'll never get over that," Tori grinned slyly as she fluffed a brush over her nose and cheekbones.

"Yes, for the hundredth time," Rose rolled her eyes with mock annoyance as she slipped on her favorite pair of earrings. They were another score from downtown Fullerton's classic shop, Safari Vintage. She was obsessed with how the bright beaded red cherries dangled and shined from each ear. Although Rose knew Tori was partially just trying to make her laugh, she brought up the subject of Rose's double eyelids almost every time they were in makeup-mode. After staying up super late watching *Twin Peaks* together during a random Friday night sleepover, Rose's eyelids temporarily (or so she thought) creased just like they always did when she was exhausted. No big deal. Even Tori had seen that plenty of times. But they were both shocked the next morning to see the creases still there.

Tori tripped out hard for the rest of the weekend. So did Rose. The difference that such tiny folds made in the way she looked had her double-taking at herself over and over. At school on Monday, their classmates couldn't believe their own eyes, either.

At lunch break, a smatter of analytical agreement rippled through the large gathering of curious Korean American girls at the aggressive and slightly jealous interrogation. "What did you *do*, Rose?" A lot of them spoke as if Rose wasn't even there. "She'd be *so* puffy if she actually got them done—trust me, my cousin just had the surgery! Look at them—they're not even pink..." Everyone knew about the inevitable and severe post-op swelling, which easily lasted for weeks.

The sleepover's pleasant surprise quickly turned into a mortifying spectacle. Eventually, the scrutinizers concluded that since Rose's entire family already had natural double eyelids, hers were inevitable. She was just a late bloomer.

"And it happened at *my* house—I literally saw it happen!" Tori emphasized with a mixture of envy and exaggerated ownership. Right then, she vowed to get the surgery as soon as possible. Her mom and Claudia already had theirs done years ago, so Tori was resolute on being next.

Slightly shivering, Cameron pulled out a small flask from his pocket. The line was getting louder with anticipation as people inched toward the front. Everyone around them looked older, like mostly in their early twenties at least—lots of wild colored hair, studded leather jackets, tattoos, and piercings. The usual mix of mod skinheads and a couple of Vespas, too. The frosty night air started to teem with the smell of weed, and plenty of people were not-so-discreetly swigging from small glass liquor bottles as they waited. Nobody was worried about security or authority.

From their spot in line, Rose didn't really see other nonwhite people around—and definitely not many with Asian backgrounds, that was for sure. Pretty typical for the Ice Cave, especially at shows of this genre. But that was just how the scene was. Fullerton was diverse, but some of its communities were fully entrenched in their own turfs even though they existed just a mile or two apart.

She loved this world on the other side of the city. It was only a few minutes from her neighborhood in the hills but felt like another galaxy in terms of everything that was actually fun. Here, she and her friends could escape the stress of school or family or whatever else, even for just a few hours.

Wish this could last forever, Rose thought. Frowning, she ran her fingers down the faint scrape that lingered on her arm. Had she left any accidental marks on her mom, dad, or aunt during the awkward scuffle?

"Did you guys hear? They're shutting down this place for sure." Cameron puffed another ring of smoke.

"Yep." Tori shook her head and blew into Cameron's ring, dissipating it. "Scary."

A serious brawl had recently occurred outside the venue after yet another raucous show. The deaths of two of the men involved had sparked an intense debate in the community about why so much violence plagued the Ice Cave, which also hosted events like weddings and parties when not in use for one of Fullerton's infamous punk shows.

Cameron sighed. "I mean, things get crazy here. Everyone knows it."

Tori nodded. "I'm gonna miss it. And think of all the bands that played here before they blew up."

Rose looked down at the asphalt. Sure, they'd had some really memorable nights here. But people losing their lives at something that was supposed to be fun was way beyond screwed up.

She was about to chime in when she noticed Tori staring intently past her shoulder. Rose turned to follow her unwavering gaze. A tall, shaved-headed guy in a leather vest adorned with pins and patches was slowly approaching.

"Hey." He grinned at the group, but his green eyes fixated on Tori. "Think I've seen you here before. Aren't you Claudia's sister?"

Rose smiled inwardly, exchanging glances with Cameron. This guy was just Tori's type—older, tough-looking, and confident. Maybe a little too confident.

"Have you?" Tori looked up at him with a flirtatious smirk. She knew she looked on point tonight in her tight lacy top. "And yes, I am."

The guy nodded, checking her up and down. "Definitely." He extended a heavily inked hand. "Tim."

"Tori." She shook his hand, already loving the attention. "These are my friends, Rose and Cameron."

Tim nodded. "Tori. Cute name for a cute girl."

Before Tori could think of a frisky comeback, Tim jutted his chin in the direction of the clipboard guy standing at the front. "Why don't you guys come up? Skip the line."

"Really?" Tori perked up even more. "Yeah, let's go!"

When the clipboard guy saw Tim, his uncooperative glower relaxed.

"Tim, my man," He gave the rest of the group a quick once over and signaled them in past the beefy security guys. Most of them looked like Sturgis regulars. They all nodded at Tim with slightly formal respect.

The musty stench of sweat and humidity hit Rose's nostrils as soon as they stepped inside. The Ice Cave setup was simple: a large high-ceilinged room with a few thick columns and a small stage at the far end. People were crammed right up to the front, with some guys already jumping off the stage into the swirling, violent pit. Non-Forgotten Hero, the opening band, announced they were on their last song, no doubt chosen to satisfy the crowd's brutal urges. Tori and Tim were already holding hands as they squeezed single file through the throngs of people. Rose and Cameron followed close behind.

"Watch it, fag!" A huge bearded guy got right in Cameron's face as they walked by. "Faggot with a chink, ha." Cameron ignored the insults and shook his head at Rose when she turned around to look back at the bullies. Cameron didn't want any trouble, especially in here. Legit help was at least a few broken bones away.

Tori and Tim finally reached his big group. Most of them were leaning against the side wall, enjoying an unobstructed view of the stage as people thrashed in front of them. It was like a magical protective shell prevented them from getting smashed by the outskirts of the pit.

"What?" Rose yelled. Tori was saying something, but the music was so loud she may as well have been miming in a striped shirt and beret.

Behind her, one of the guys in Tim's posse leaned over to take in the trio, one by one. Rose could see the side of his neck had a gnarly looking scar that resembled a thick earthworm. Short dark hair, pale complexion, no visible tattoos or piercings, and a plain, gray shirt. Something about the way his blunt stare didn't falter when Rose briefly met his gaze made her instantly categorize him as a particular type of Ice Cave guy—inconspicuous at first, but potentially one of the most psycho dudes in there. She wouldn't be surprised if he—not the guy with the face tats, nor the one who already had a black, bloodshot eye—would be the one in the group to kick someone's skull in by the end of the night. Ugh. Rose looked away for a second but somehow ended up making eye contact with him again. *Yep, Scarneck is definitely, very possibly, low-key psycho.* Were her cheeks turning red? She quickly turned away. The dude wasn't even bothering to hide his ogling.

Tori pulled Rose into the group so she and Cameron could straggle closer. A few seconds later, two tall forty-ounce beers came their way, presumably from Tim. Tori clinked bottles with her friends and chugged. She beamed and smacked her lips lightly. She was about to say something but got swung around by Tim, who bent down and kissed her forcefully, groping her waist.

Rose looked the other way. Her cheeks were definitely flushed now, but whether it was from Scarneck or suddenly seeing Tori make out with a total stranger, she wasn't sure. Hesitating, she tilted the beer to her lips. A rust-flavored aftertaste made her instantly crave the bottle of water she'd left in Tori's car.

"Uh oh, the usual crew's getting pissed again," Cameron sing-songed in Rose's ear. With averted eyes, he discreetly nodded toward the far end of the room.

Rose traced the tiny thrust of his chin to the familiar troop of men with arms crossed as tightly as their faces. Everyone could count on those guys to get randomly triggered by the sight of an accidental smirk or a too-close beer.

"Straight edge, dude," Rose commented coolly, keeping her gaze away from them. Sensing their switchblade glares, she casually lowered her drink to the floor and dug into her pocket for one of the individually wrapped candies from Tori's house. Better to play it safe, especially when the drink tasted as bitter as this one.

A few feet from that group, an animated arm in an olive green bomber jacket waved in Rose's direction. Rose instantly recognized the woman's fresh buzz cut, inked neck and cleavage, and most of all, her warm smile. Desiree blew a kiss when Rose waved back.

Cameron took another long swig, still focused on the pent-up guys. "They're not straight edge. They're dorks."

"Oh, come on," Rose said, shaking her head as she bit into the fruity red licorice. It was way too loud to get into a defense of the health benefits of the straight edge lifestyle. When she looked up again, Desiree had disappeared into the crowd.

A minute later, I Don't Wanna Hear It climbed on stage. The crowd blustered with a thunderous drone.

The lead singer grabbed the mic and simultaneously dodged a flying bottle perfectly aimed for his head. He grumbled something inaudible to the crowd. Cameron playfully nudged Rose in the ribs.

The pit was one of the wildest Rose had ever seen at the place. Standing on her tiptoes, she snapped more photos of people getting Armageddon-level bashed in the chaotic churn of (mostly) testosterone, adrenaline, and music-fueled mayhem.

"C'mon, let's get a better angle this way." Cameron led her through the tight crowd, closer to the stage but still on the side. No way were they going right in front to the pit—not tonight. A couple of somewhat "normal" looking guys tried to mess with the band members on stage before launching off the speakers into the crowd. While snapping a photo of one of them midair, Rose realized he was Tim's friend, Scarneck. Cameron then pointed out a dude with a bloody nose who'd fallen onto the grimy floor amid the anarchic disarray. Every time he attempted to stand up, a random body part would fly in his face and ram him down again. Finally, after a few more wild hits, an older skanking guy with a mustache reached out and pulled him up.

"Yay, the pit chaperone!" Cameron yelled with a purposely corny arm swing. Rose cracked up again. Cameron always turned into a comedian at shows. They spent the next several songs analyzing the pit and bantering about the gluttony of dangerous antics and pandemonium.

Tori returned to her friends when she spotted them nearby during the final song. "Hey, you guys," she drawled, clearly a little tipsy. "Gonna head out."

"Where to?" Rose asked. Keeping the party moving forward so late on a weeknight was unexpected. Cameron pinched her arm. He knew what Tori was about to say.

"Um, back to his place," Tori stammered, glancing behind her. Tim was busy joking with his buddies. "Tim's, I mean."

"Oh, you mean, with *only* Tim," Cameron mocked, stroking his chin.

Annoyance tugged at Rose as she realized what Tori was getting at. "So, you're ditching us?" She gathered her thoughts as the ceiling lights flickered on and off, urging everybody out. She hadn't exactly planned on Tori leaving her right then and there. "But I was going to crash at your place tonight!" Rose really wasn't ready to go home. Just the thought petrified her.

Tori's face twisted with alcohol-laden guilt. "I'm sorry, Rose," she whined, shifting her weight as she looked back at Tim again. "He's just so cool! And hot. *And* he's going to take me backstage next time they—"

"Tori!" Rose exclaimed, trying to get her friend to snap out of her gushing. "What am I supposed to do, then?"

Cameron hung his arm over Rose's shoulders. "No worries, I can take you home."

"Actually," Tori interrupted with half-chagrin, half-exasperation. She rapidly rummaged through her purse and dangled a set of keys in front of Rose. "Could you drive my car home for me? My parents will kill me if the car isn't back tonight."

"Are you serious?" This time, Rose knew exactly why her cheeks were burning.

Tori firmly placed the keys in Rose's reluctant hand and closed her fingers over them. "Please? You know I'd do it for you!"

"I'd never ask you to," Rose replied coldly. "You just met this guy. You know he just wants to get laid, right?" She heard the sting in her words, but she really didn't care.

Tori's whole body retracted with offense. "Well, that's a really nice thing for you to say. Funny coming from someone who's never even kissed a guy before."

"Chill," Cameron interjected.

"Tell *her* that!" Tori retorted, blocking Cameron's mediation. "I'm just asking for one simple favor. Rose, we can talk about your family's whatever tomorrow, and the next day, and even all of next week, okay? Can't you just help me out this one night?"

"We'd *really* appreciate it," Tim's deep voice suddenly swaggered into their heated discussion. He draped his arm around Tori's neck and looked directly at Rose and Cameron with reassurance. "We're just gonna get some food. I'll bring her back whenever she wants, no biggie."

Cameron glanced at his phone and instant worry creased his face. "I have to go home. Mom just texted some nonsense. I think she's drunk again." Since the divorce, his mother had gained nearly sixty pounds from stuffing herself with liquor and food the past year. The last time she'd texted gibberish to her son, she'd blacked out and tripped down a long flight of stairs.

Cameron said goodbye, squeezing Rose's hand and promising to text later. He knew Rose wasn't going to say no to Tori.

Rose watched Cameron meander through the thinning crowd and turned back to Tori and Tim. They eyed her expectantly, an exclusive couple wondering what to do with a third wheel.

"Come on, please?" Tori's eyes were wide with urgent desperation as Tim briefly turned to greet someone. She whispered under her breath, "Just leave the keys in the mailbox."

Tim turned back to the girls and shot Rose a smile. "Thanks for being such a good friend, man." Twirling Tori away, he and his friends all sauntered toward the back. Tori twisted around and silently mouthed "thank you" before excitedly squirming into Tim's side.

◆◆◆

Even with the familiar amber-golden glow below Walnut Street's old-fashioned lampposts, the small side street was even darker than Rose had anticipated. She'd always heard that Fullerton was Orange County's most haunted city, though she wasn't concerned about that reputation right then. Walking alone at this time of night wasn't exactly the smartest idea, and that was because of humans, not lingering spirits. But what choice did she have? At least Tori's car was parked just a block off the main drag.

Rose stood tall and tried to exude an aura of confidence, the opposite of how she actually felt. Inside her jacket, her fist was strategically balled around Tori's keys, giving her small hand a set of makeshift claws. Just in case. Ahead, a streetlight flickered, illuminating a young couple strolling in lighthearted conversation. A black witch hat flopped on the guy's head. The tension in Rose's neck loosened a little. Amid all the chaos from the show, Rose had completely forgotten it was Halloween.

At least Tori didn't leave me totally *stranded.* Rose tried to think positively as she approached the white car on the curb. This time she didn't have to call a cab for a ride home, which had happened a few times before. There was no worthwhile reason to stay mad—this was just the way Tori was sometimes, eager to prioritize a dude over everything else. She wasn't going to change anytime soon.

The sweaty heat of the Ice Cave had now completely dissipated in the cold night air. Rose unlocked the car door and shivered in the driver's seat, adjusting the rearview mirror about an inch. The ignition hummed to life, and Rose jumped when "Institutionalized" roared on the speakers right where they'd left off a few hours before. Hastily she lowered the volume before switching it off completely. The unruffled silence, like a buzz of absolutely nothing, was a relief to her ears.

Much of Harbor Boulevard's classic look remained from its humble beginnings at the turn of the century. Mature silk floss trees, gently wrapped with twinkling lights, lined the sidewalks by the Beaux Arts facades atop downtown Fullerton's mostly two-story buildings. Rose drove past the familiar shops: legendary Nebula Records and Safari Vintage, several old school antique stores, Pop's Music School (where she and Thomas learned to play piano), a special occasion dress boutique. The ornate mint green chiffon-ruffled evening gown on the display mannequin wasn't her style, but Rose could appreciate the old school craftsmanship even from the car. Actually, everything surrounding her was old school. And every store, even the smallest ones, took great pride in their window displays all year long. Lately, Rose had noticed how some of the old mom and pop shops were closing, but whether it was due to the economy or retirement, she wasn't sure. This was a part of the city that she hoped would never succumb to out of touch investors.

At the first intersection, Rose considered making a left to drive by the Hub. Nah, it was probably closed. If In Absentia was open, she could slowly browse through the racks full of, as their sign said, *Your Darkest Desires.* But it was way too late for that, too.

Rose headed westbound. To her right, an elegant 1920s Spanish-style mansion hovered from a sprawling hilltop. The Muck was a thriving arts and cultural center owned by the city, with galleries, classes, and amphitheater shows that regularly drew crowds from all over the place. Rose continued for a couple of minutes before randomly turning into an older residential neighborhood off of Malvern Avenue. Without direction or destination, she drove past the 1950s ranch homes that lined the streets near her old elementary school. Most of the house windows were dark. She hadn't seen this neighborhood in years. Despite trying to prolong her drive, the winding streets soon circled her back to the main road.

The pounding in her chest began immediately after she passed the big Korean church and the old apartments by the railroad tracks. After delivering Tori's car, she would have no choice but to cross the street back to her house.

It was late—obscenely late for a school night. 12:49 a.m., the dashboard glowed, fueling her apprehension. All night she'd refrained from looking at her messages in order to avoid the inevitable barrage of texts and missed calls from her parents. She didn't need to see all that to know how upset they were. She couldn't really blame them, either.

Which is exactly why Tori shouldn't have left me! Rose's hands tightened around the steering wheel. Tori had been the one to suggest that if Rose slept over, maybe her parents would cool off by morning. But that was, of course, before this Tim dude had entered the scenario.

Instead of driving past the railroad tracks, Rose quickly turned right. The long way home. Maybe she could enjoy a few extra minutes of peace before stepping back into the mess she'd left. Not the most comforting situation, but it was the best she could come up with.

Coyote Hills High School loomed at the top of the campus hill on her left. The place looked almost unrecognizable from earlier this morning—no lines of cars, no buses, no people. Sitting in a dark classroom until morning sounded a heck of a lot better than the trouble she was about to get into at home. But she couldn't avoid her parents forever. And she knew that Milo was waiting for her in the foyer, probably wondering where she was all night.

A thousand more seeds of fear bloomed inside of her. What

would happen when she opened the front door? Nothing had ever occurred on the scale of what had gone down this afternoon.

Rolling the driver's window open, Rose breathed in deeply and tried to clear her mind. The wind snapped through her hair, and she could feel the icy air whipping on her left cheek. An arctic chill had swept south this past week, delivering unusually cold temperatures for this time of year. She released a long, shaky breath as she slowed to a stop at a yellow light.

A subtle calm soothed the edges of her distraught nerves. That familiar scent again.

The light switched to green. Rose ignored the road home and gassed the pedal in the opposite direction.

7

Sweet hay, dark soil, fresh shavings, pungent manure…

Rose pulled up the dirt driveway. The corners of her lips perked into a covert smile. She couldn't believe how instantly her mood had transformed.

Besides an older Silverado parked on the far side, the parking lot was empty. She clicked the key to make sure Tori's car was safely locked and then scanned her surroundings. The black iron gate with the two rearing horse silhouettes was still there, slightly ajar, almost beckoning her to enter the rest of the property.

Laguna Lake Riding Club had always been her favorite place in the world when she was younger. Just adjacent to Coyote Hills, north Orange County's largest wildlife reserve, it offered a rare cross section of pure nature a mere five minutes from home. The barn owner back in the day, Sandy Kalani, had originally opened it to the public a few decades ago so that other horse lovers could enjoy the special atmosphere in the nearby trails. She'd taken great pride in the property, fixing up every inch that needed repair while maintaining its original classic style. Even with close proximity to the road, Laguna Lake Riding Club had a faraway countryside feel. A random siren from passing traffic was often the only reminder of being in a busy Southern California suburb.

Walking through the gate was like stepping into a time warp. Everything was recognizable to Rose even though nothing was exactly the same: the gigantic oak trees she'd sat under as a kid while waiting for her ride home, the large arena with the jumps and the smaller round pen down the way, spacious sheds for storage, a couple of tidy tack rooms, and locker spaces on the other side. The large main barn still stood out front, with a freshly painted red exterior just like the old European barns. Various rose bushes lined the paths, now substantially thicker and more vibrant since Rose's last ride.

Rose had always been obsessed with horses. She diagnosed it as being born with the horse imprint in her DNA—you either had it or you didn't, and only horse people really understood. Too bad no one else in her family shared her enthusiasm. Horses and riding were overall discouraged, mainly due to danger and expense. Convincing her parents to allow her to muck stalls, clean tack, and help out with other barn chores on weekends to pay for weekly riding lessons had taken years of intense, strategized begging. The day she quit riding was the first time Rose's heart had truly broken.

Rose's curious gaze brightened at the sight of the riding ring equipped with several cavalettis and verticals. She remembered those well. Jumps always reminded her of both the indescribable joy she felt in the air as well as the gloomy evening her parents sat her down at dinner and firmly declared her riding days over. That still stung. It didn't help that Grandma had also harbored a pointed dislike of it all. Sometimes Rose wondered if they were secretly relieved about her fall because it served as the strongest reason for her to drop out of Sandy's program.

"Horse people..." Grandma liked to condemn in her most severe tone. "They care more about horses than people! I just don't understand that—not at all!"

Guilt quickly became the main factor regarding horses and riding. It was like Rose was forbidden to even miss her beloved Fender—the sweetest, most trustworthy and thrilling horse she'd ever had the honor of knowing. Hiding her feelings in order to avoid family difference of opinion was a decision of pure protection. She stashed away all of her breeches, boots, horse books, ribbons, and drawings in a big cardboard appliance box. Just a glimpse of her "horse coffin" in the corner of the closet torched her in the gut for years.

A few grunts and stomps clamored in the air, from the far end of the property where the line of stalls formed a semicircle around the paddock. Maybe the horses had heard her. Some horses were quite active during the night, even tucked in their stalls, according to Sandy's fascinating stories of her old working student days.

Rose couldn't help but grin as she remembered how she and her trainer had instantly bonded after discovering they'd both once lived in the faraway state of Ohio. It was just one of those random coincidences. When Rose was around eight years old, the Moon family had temporarily moved there for work before returning to California a year later. Sandy was the only person around who not only knew of that small Midwest area but also didn't scoff with condescension at the mention of it. At that point, she had already lived in a dozen cities around the world pursuing work that involved horses.

Rose continued walking as quietly as she could, her boots softly pressing the gravel on the walkway. The path was familiar, too, but she'd never been here this late at night. Rose approached the gate to the dim ring and sized up the jumps. Even after all these years, it was hard to look at jumps without feeling totally burned. Once heart fluttering symbols of her utmost desire, they were now just painful reminders of a lost existence.

Don't get caught up in all that. She quickly hoisted herself on the rail and surveyed the scene. This place used to be her heaven, her "dreamland," as she had always told Tori while brushing off her friend's crinkled nose. Even though Tori always wondered how Rose could love such a "smelly place for livestock," she was totally supportive after the incident.

Rose never had her own horse but regularly rode Fender for years, one of Sandy's own picks for Rose's level. He was a handsome bay Dutch Warmblood, a former Grand Prix jumper who also possessed the kindness and patience to become a schoolmaster in his older years.

"Him?" Rose had asked before their introduction, trying not to gape too much at the massive gelding awaiting her in the crossties.

He stood nearly 18 hands tall—quite a change from Jax and Barney, the more average-sized Quarter horse and Morgan she usually rode with. But less than ten minutes into their first ride, her fears about Fender's size had quietly vanished. She quickly got used to his sweeping canter and even felt remarkably safe while flying over jumps with him. Fender was solid, confident, and powerful, yet every move he made was careful and refined. By the end of their first lesson together, she was already in love. He was also extremely intelligent and hilarious. Everyone at the barn knew that a loosely shut door or lid to a jar of cookies would be Fender's for the taking. As Rose progressed from weekly lessons to more frequent trips to the barn, Fender bonded with Rose noticeably more than with the other students (that was what Sandy had told her, anyway). Rose's not-so-secret wish was to eventually, somehow, buy him and have him all to herself.

It was supposed to be just a normal Sunday afternoon trail ride. Nothing intense, just giving the horses a break from schooling in the arena. Coyote Hills offered over fifteen miles of scenic paths, and Rose always liked to imagine she was on a trek in some far away mountain range. Fender loved those trails, too. A certain buoyancy always took over his steps whenever they were deep in those woods.

What did I do wrong that day? Rose asked herself for the millionth time as she sat on top of the railing. She knew to expect spooks with riding—an inevitable part of spending time with prey animals—but to this day, she still felt solely responsible for it. Right on cue, the familiar knuckles of guilt punched right through her.

The trails were gorgeous that crisp November afternoon. Fender had shuddered hard in a very unfamiliar way—not the usual ripple to push a pesky fly off his coat, nor the awkward lurch that meant he was stretching a hind leg at his stomach for a hard-to-reach itch. Rose thought she glimpsed a random piece of litter, but he seemed to react to something else that nobody was able to ever pinpoint. He reared then bolted, hooves pounding into the dirt as if his life depended on gaining as much speed as quickly as possible. Rose still remembered how surreal it was to see his black mane and arched neck jump vertically toward her face.

As they careened through the idyllic autumn scenery, all Rose could hear were Fender's hooves and her own haggard breathing as she used every muscle in her body to try to regain control.

Then she went flying.

Sandy soon found Rose a minute later, crumpled on the ground, one side of her body smeared in dirt. Numb and dazed. The tall old trees loomed as she looked up from the hard ground. Just a few feet away, an assistant trainer retrieved a sweaty but calm Fender and immediately summoned the vet.

Rose ended up with a sore wrist and red gashes in places she didn't expect. By the time she showered that evening, a hand-sized purple bruise had formed on the side of her thigh—not that she really cared. Falling was an inherent part of riding a 1,500-pound partner with a mind of his own, and it was her partner she was solely worried about.

When Sandy phoned the Moons later that night, assuring that Fender didn't even have a scratch on him, Rose deflated from relief.

"You're very lucky to come out of that uninjured," Sandy reminded her. "You handled it like a pro."

But will Fender still trust me? Rose wondered. She couldn't blame Fender if he didn't. If someone had screwed up and let her panic like that in the middle of nowhere...

"You just get some rest now," Sandy continued. "Fender's already over it, and we can all move on from this learning experience. See you soon."

But Rose's parents had other plans. They couldn't fathom allowing their daughter to continue such a risky sport. After a brief conversation with Sandy, they promptly announced that not only were her riding lessons over, she was forbidden to go near horses again. Apart from admiring horses on TV, like the annual Rose Parade broadcasts, her parents wanted equines completely eliminated from their daughter's life and mind.

A tense whinny suddenly cut through the cold night air, dissolving Rose's reverie. She looked over her shoulder toward the stalls. A sharp wind swooped through the property, spiraling loose dirt and whipping her cheeks. At the front end of the row of stalls, a tall gray horse stood calmly. But as soon as Rose turned her attention back to the jumps in the ring, the call sounded again, this time even louder. Some faint grunts followed, then a brief banging ruckus.

Hesitating, Rose scanned the grounds from the paddock to the barn. Most of the stable area was quite dark since the main lights were off for the night, but it wasn't completely pitch-black. Maybe she should check to see if everything was okay in there. What if something was wrong?

Not your horse. Rose swallowed and strained to hear more. *Not your business.* She could practically hear her parents warning her.

Snooping around this late at night—in other words, trespassing—was pretty foolish, but how could she leave without exploring? It was the first time in years she'd allowed herself to return here. And Fender…was he even still around?

Another loud bang interrupted her lingering doubt.

Pumped by the slim chance of a reunion, Rose abruptly swung her legs out and jumped off the rail, landing with an out-of-practice thud. She just had to check the horses. It would only take a minute at the most.

The tall gray in the first stall eyed her with placid curiosity as Rose stepped into the cozy aisle. Though sheltered from the cold gusts, her arms tingled as she took in the long rows of stalls on either side.

"Hi there," Rose murmured softly as a few horses peeked at the unexpected visitor. "Don't mind me, I'm just walking through." Some soft nickers. Two rusty shovels with green handles lay strewn on the ground, most likely knocked over from the sudden burst of wind. Rose took one in each hand and set them next to a nearby wheelbarrow along the wall.

A dish-faced bay Arabian stretched his head over his door as she continued further in. She let him sniff her hand before gently stroking his cheek. He nudged at her sides, lips searching playfully.

"Sorry, buddy." Rose gave him one last pat before walking on. "Guess I forgot to bring carrots."

A tingle traveled down her spine. There was his stall, just about halfway down the aisle. She quickened her steps and her pulse pumped with anticipation. She hadn't seen Fender in years! He might be retired now, but he'd always been perfectly sound, so maybe...

The stall was empty.

Rose's heart sunk faster than an anchor in a shallow pond. No horse and no name sign, either. She walked in with a haze of disbelief from the feeling of bare floor beneath her.

Fender, Rose thought silently. She closed her eyes and inhaled again and again, as if she could conjure his scent into existence. Her upper chest area began to radiate an unfamiliar warmth. With a start, she opened her eyes and looked around. "Fender?" It was almost like she could feel his energy. Or something.

Rose jumped at a loud bang from the other end of the row. That was some kick. The sound was much louder now that she was inside with the horses—no wonder some of them were grunting their acknowledgment. A rapping metallic bang, then a few snorts as they shifted their weights with restlessness. Someone wasn't letting them have a peaceful night.

She followed the noise further down the aisle. In the very last stall, a brownish-rust colored horse paced a few steps and tossed her head. As Rose stepped closer to scrutinize, she immediately noticed how unkempt the horse looked compared to the others. Her coat was dusty all over, and her mane and tail were so tangled that Rose wondered how anyone could refrain from grabbing the nearest brush.

The horse saw Rose and immediately kicked out at the wall again, as if to say, "Yeah, what?" before turning around, rump squarely facing her guest. A couple of small scars dotted her rear quarters.

A chestnut mare. People often joked about that type of horse, as if the coloring and gender meant a certain type of difficult personality. She didn't have any markings—no chrome, as they say—no white socks or a snip on the nose. Still, she was beautiful. Her neck was athletic and arched, and her hindquarters round and stout. Her mane and tail, albeit neglected, cascaded in long, thick strands. She had a slight Roman nose, and the one enormous eye that Rose could see shone like a dark lagoon—large, luminous, and framed with dense lashes.

The horse sure wasn't as dazzled with her new onlooker, though. She maintained a wary side-eye on the human searching for a name sign, which lay haphazardly on the ground near the door: *STARLA - Handle with caution.*

"Starla," Rose murmured, peering over the stall door. "Hello, Sta—"

The mare pawed the ground and let out an indignant screech. Then she just scanned the stranger.

Despite her pounding heart, Rose didn't want to leave just yet. Starla faced her with such acknowledgment, Rose just stood there, breathing.

Starla snorted and pawed the ground with her front hoof again. She kicked the wall behind her, earning a grunt from her nearest neighbor, a brown Appaloosa. Turning her head back toward Rose, she eyed her new guest expectantly. Another restless kick. She wasn't playing around. As if momentarily satisfied with all of the noise she'd just made, Starla then stood motionless.

Rose stared back at her for what felt like nearly a whole minute. It was impossible to not notice the small worried wrinkles over Starla's eyes. She took another tentative step toward the mare. Almost simultaneously, Starla turned her back again, leaving Rose face-to-rump. Her long tail lashed, tossing a clump of shavings in front of Rose, like whirling confetti. She was making it very clear that she had zero desire to engage.

Sighing, Rose stepped back against the empty stall across the aisle. What was she even doing here, bothering this grumpy horse? If this was Rose's own horse, she'd be downright angry that someone was disturbing her like this, even just from outside the stall. The Appaloosa poked his head out of his stall again, trying to see what was going on at this time of night with this weird human.

A buzz went off in her pocket. Rose's throat was parched as she scrolled through the notifications: six texts and two voicemails from her parents. Just wonderful. A quick glimpse of the texts was enough to recognize how concerned and upset they were. She'd never stayed out this late before. Brows furrowed, she moved on to Tori's latest news:

OMG we're having a blast! Just met the bassist from I Don't Wanna Hear It and he says we'll be on the list for their next show!

Wish you were here!

Are u home? Car dropped off?

Rose began typing a reply but quickly deleted it. She restarted but erased it once more. She didn't know what to say to anybody right now, especially to her best friend, who had deserted her at the worst time ever. Besides, on every level imaginable, she wasn't supposed to be at the stables. Her parents were incensed enough, and she could already hear Tori's annoyance at Rose suddenly visiting Laguna Lake Riding Club instead of returning her car safely home.

The cursor on the screen kept blinking.

Nobody would understand why she was there right now. And how could they? She hardly understood, either.

I don't know who I am or what I'm even doing here. Emptiness suddenly overwhelmed her. At school, hanging out with her friends at shows, even at home...she was always an outcast. But finding out that her family had some secret about her all of these years was still a hard, mean shock. But that wasn't what hurt the most. Why all the friction, the unexplained bias? Wasn't keeping a secret from her enough?

Everything that Rose had forced herself to accept as normal flashed in her mind like fireworks, bursting, then fading into darkness. Was any of this even remotely normal? Shivers crawled up her back and scattered down her arms.

Rose suddenly realized what it meant to truly be alone. Being alone was not just feeling lonely. It was more than a temporary emotion. And it wasn't just a physical circumstance, either—plenty of people were physically present in her life.

Starla's rump was still in Rose's face. One of her big ears flicked back in her direction.

If Rose could just feel alone instead of live it...but she *was* alone, and nothing was going to change that. Nothing would ever be the same for her, yet she also worried that everything would somehow remain as is. Or worse. The cards she'd been dealt remained, but the difference now was that she'd finally gotten a glimpse of her hand.

Besides a few nonchalant side glances, Starla hadn't moved much. After a few moments, she turned her head all the way to the side, finally acknowledging the stranger.

"It's okay, I'm leaving now," Rose sighed. It was time to grow up, as well as respect this horse who was sending every "get lost" signal available.

Rose hastily stuffed the phone back into her pocket and started retreating down the aisle. It was only getting later, which didn't exactly help the inevitable punishment awaiting her at home.

Hooves lightly shuffled. Rose stopped in her tracks. Over her shoulder, Rose watched Starla move to the front of her stall, her head lowered and eyes quiet. She was sizing up the human, almost inquisitively.

Rose's heart fluttered. A small but quick draft whiffed through the aisle, knocking over what sounded like a bucket or something. Rose didn't dare budge. She wasn't sure how long she stood there in silence, but the air almost seemed to grow warmer the longer she and Starla watched one another.

Hesitantly, she took a few steps back toward her. Starla's head was now extended over her door, her eyes and ears suddenly riveted.

An abrupt laugh escaped Rose's lips as she took another step. Yes, she'd heard it, too—the sound of crackling candy wrappers shifting in her jeans as she walked.

"So that's why you're all interested now!" Rose giggled, delighted that she hadn't eaten all of the sweets earlier at the Ice Cave. "I should have known…totally forgot I had these."

Starla blinked behind a few rough strands of mane, still very much focused. Rose really wanted to brush her hair aside but knew not to press her luck. Grinning, she walked up to Starla and began to carefully unwrap a round red candy. *Wait—don't just feed a horse you don't know!* Rose bit her lip, feeling like an idiot. Even though every ounce of her wanted to offer Starla this treat that she obviously wanted, it wasn't right. Who knew what her dietary situation was?

But just before Rose lowered her hand, Starla reached over and slipped the sugary sphere into her mouth, wrapper and all. It happened so quickly, Rose just gasped and watched with her own mouth slightly open. Starla turned her head to the side a bit, crunching with quiet satisfaction. Then, as if she'd done it a hundred times before, the mare expertly spat out the clear cellophane right onto the floor. Rose retrieved the wet wrapper, which was still in one piece.

"All you wanted was some candy," mimicked Rose, chuckling at her goofy impromptu twist on the frantic Suicidal Tendencies song. "And they wouldn't give it to you. Just one candy." In the corner of her eye, she could see a few other horses now peering over their stalls, alerted by Starla's loud munches and wondering where their candy was. Starla's soft nose tickled Rose's wrist, asking for more. Pushing aside the echoes of Starla's stomps and kicks, Rose slowly reached out and gently stroked the side of Starla's smooth neck. A spark rushed from Rose's chest to her fingertips as she slid both hands over the mare's coat. A narrow white brand ran along the underside of Starla's rumpled mane.

She's actually letting me touch her! Rose couldn't remember the last time she'd experienced such a simple thrill. She stroked Starla's neck and withers some more until the mare licked her lips.

"Starla," said Rose, allowing herself to indulge in this sweet, secret moment. "Thank you, Starla."

8

Nighttime chirps paused inside the shadows of tall trees. Thundering hooves galloped past, effortlessly bending with the soft curve of the moonlit trail.

The blue roan knew the path well. A young man crouched low and close. Together they sliced through the dark woods along the glimmering lake, a fleeting beam of light.

Dry leaves scattered to the ground as the air settled. The chirps continued under the silent stars.

9

Ethan's calloused hands pushed the rusty lock into place and shut the tack room door. He was still pumped from his ride with Tanner. Late night was the only time he could risk galloping helmetless without a scolding. Every time, Ethan swore it would be his last. He'd seen enough horror accidents to know how dumb it was to not protect the second most important part of his body. He tossed his windbreaker on a nearby post, cooling off in the chilly breeze.

A cold beer sounded like the perfect nightcap. Every horse was checked for the evening. He was just about ready to say goodnight to Tanner and finally retreat to his own storage room-turned living quarters in the main barn. Sure, it was kind of small and even a little musty, but it was all his as long as he maintained his position at Laguna Lake Riding Club. Keeping his employer, clients, and horses happy meant full independence from his mom and that worthless gold digger, Mitch.

As Ethan completed a final scan of the barn, he ignored the chronic worries about his family ranch and turned his attention to his list of things to do tomorrow. In the morning, they were expecting a large shipment of various feed right around the same time he wanted to oversee a couple of veterinarian visits. If he got to the paperwork Gina was waiting for, he'd call it a great start to the month.

Groom Starla. That wasn't a typical task for him, yet it was the one thing he actually hadn't been able to do all week. In fact, nobody had succeeded in grooming her. She was way too upset in the cross ties, and forget about her cooperating in any other capacity. It really bugged Ethan, not being able to clean off the poor gal, but she'd just been too ornery so far and Gina was worried she'd hurt herself or someone else. Starla was just new to the barn, he kept reminding himself. Ethan vowed to try that wily mare again tomorrow. Patience and consistency were key factors at this point.

While leading Tanner to the stalls, one of Ethan's worn-out boots stepped on an unexpected crinkle—just some metallic candy wrappers, leftover goodies from a local Girl Scouts troop's Halloween horsey afternoon. A red foil wrapper printed like a strawberry reminded him of his ex, who used to stash a handful in her purse from the big jar on the hostess table every time they left their favorite gringo Mexican restaurant back home. But those days were long over. Ethan deposited the wrappers and candy in a nearby trash bin. High school sweethearts faded in more ways than one, in his experience.

Suddenly he stopped. Why was another car in the lot? Tanner obediently halted as Ethan turned toward the front gate. An unfamiliar white sedan was parked out front.

Nobody else should be here at this hour, Ethan thought, squinting at the empty vehicle. It was hard to see the details, but he was fairly certain he'd never seen it before. He clucked at Tanner and led him to a hitching post. His boss would be furious if some stranger was creeping around the property, especially if they were anywhere near the horses. Jaw hardening, Ethan gave Tanner a quick pat. He needed to check the horses.

Everything inside the barn appeared the same as an hour ago when he and Tanner left for their ride. Winnie, Buttercup, Dag…they all looked fine in their stalls, but Ethan carefully scrutinized each horse anyway. Always better to be paranoid when it came to their safety, he'd learned long ago. He gave a quick rub on the forehead to Winston, one of the most senior horses in the barn, who automatically nudged Ethan's arm for a treat. Each horse and stall got a close once-over as if the planet depended on it. Horses were incredibly strong, but they could also be unbelievably vulnerable. It was never worth taking any chances.

So far, everyone looked just as they should, some even enjoying the unusual late-night attention. Ethan continued down the aisle. Just as his suspicions were about to subside, he spotted a figure at the far end, right in front of Starla's stall. A girl facing the mustang. She murmured something to Starla and turned to leave. She was petite with long, dark hair—nothing like Starla's absentee owner.

Right when Ethan opened his mouth to say something, the girl abruptly turned back around toward Starla. If she had noticed Ethan standing in the shadows, she didn't let on. Despite the faint lighting, he could tell she had a soft, almost benign, demeanor. She murmured something to Starla, then got closer and looked to be feeding her a treat of some sort. Something about this person made Ethan second-guess his initial instinct to immediately admonish her, even though he probably should. She certainly wasn't Lula May, Lula May's assistant, or even another boarder he recognized. But he didn't want to get too crazy in case she was one of Gina's friends or clients from another time zone, either. Squinting, Ethan took a split second to get a better look. Slim black jeans, tall combat boots, and a little younger, maybe by a few years. Her quiet aura didn't seem to warrant any grounds for him to overreact, but that didn't change the fact that she wasn't permitted there unless he knew exactly who she was.

Ethan started toward her and Starla. It wouldn't have surprised him at all if this stranger had gravitated to little mini Maizie, but instead, she was hanging out with Starla, the most difficult horse in the barn. Not that Starla was living up to that reputation at the moment.

Starla was actually letting the visitor touch and stroke her coat, as if snaking her head at the girl didn't even cross her mind! Her head was lowered and relaxed, ears perky, and eyes the softest Ethan had ever seen so far.

Starla looked like a completely different horse.

What the? Ethan gawked in silence at the unexpected scene. Amused indignation slowly spread across his face. *Does she know her or something?* He almost got pushed to the wall by the mare just the other day in that very spot. It was ridiculous, not to mention nerve-wracking. Even their farrier had given up and sent out for his colleague who had more experience with "those types," so Starla was still barefoot.

But there she was, some complete stranger, petting that unpredictable girl! Ethan quickened his pace. He felt his mouth hanging open. He wasn't sure if it was from mild irritation at having to deal with some random at the barn this late at night, or confusion at watching her interact so effortlessly with Starla, but he was going to get to the bottom of this situation right away.

10

"**H**ey!" A suspicious male voice barked from the darkness. "Who are you and what are you doing here?"

Rose whipped around. In her entranced moment with Starla, she hadn't even heard someone coming. A tall young man, shadows partially veiling his face, walked toward them with swift, authoritative strides. His stony mouth hinted he was in no mood for nonsense. Rose felt Starla slightly shift, but she still allowed Rose's hand on her neck.

"Well?" The guy stopped a few feet from them and crossed his tanned arms.

Rose swallowed. She couldn't blame him for being so obviously perturbed. Who wouldn't be wary of a strange person in the barn at this hour?

"Sorry," Rose started anxiously. "I used to ride here and—"

"We're closed," he interrupted sternly. "What are you feeding her?" His brows creased under slightly shaggy brown hair, and his dark jeans and charcoal shirt showed the usual wear and tear of typical barn life.

"Just some candy. I'm sorry," Rose said morosely, feeling beyond stupid for allowing Starla to grab the candy from her hand. What if Starla had some special kind of diet or condition? "I was just looking for a horse I hadn't seen in a while, and…" She registered the guy's unwavering glare. Maybe she should be careful of him, too. Who knew what kind of nut job this dude was? If he tried to pull anything sketchy on her, it would be tough to escape, considering he was cutting off the way to the car. "But he's not here, so I'll just go." After a quick glance at Starla, Rose started toward the exit.

Starla snorted and stomped hard.

"Hey, easy girl." The guy approached Starla and reached out to pat her neck.

Starla tossed her head away from his hand.

The guy stopped and noticed Rose lingering, halfway facing them. Darting his eyes between her and Starla, he wryly remarked, "I saw she wasn't being her usual murderous self to you." Pause. "What kind of candy?"

Rose wasn't sure what to say. Was this going to get her in trouble? And exactly how long had he been watching? "Cherry drops."

"Okay. Seems you guys were getting along. Well, getting along for Starla," he continued. "She doesn't like to be bothered by anyone here just yet. She's new."

"I noticed," Rose replied, still nervous. "She was making a fuss, so I just wanted to see if everything was okay—"

"So, you used to ride here?" he asked, eyebrows raised. From his pointed tone, he was clearly vetting her, not making small talk.

Rose nodded, motioning down the aisle. "With Fender...I was hoping he'd still be around."

"Fender, huh?" The guy's wary expression seemed to loosen up by a millimeter. "So that was back when Sandy was still here."

"Oh, you know her? How is she?" Rose blurted.

"She moved back to Hawaii a few years ago. Took Fender and some others. Last I heard she was running some kind of sanctuary-slash-horse therapy program for local kids and veterans."

"Wow, so she really did it." Rose exhaled involuntarily, awestruck. Both Rose and Sandy had military veterans in their families, and Rose remembered the endless chats with her trainer about how running a horse sanctuary on one of the Hawaiian islands would be a total living dream. Even Sandy, a native of Hawaii, seemed to think that was all it was—a far off dream, mainly because of the high cost of living in tropical paradise. "I'm so happy to hear that."

"She's the real deal. Met her during her last week here." He paused as if making a decision. With a slight nod, he extended a hand. "Ethan."

Rose took his firm grip and introduced herself. Suddenly she felt shy and awkward.

Starla shifted and reached down to gnaw an itch on her front left leg. Rose pretended to concentrate on her, grateful to have something to look at other than Ethan's auditing stare.

"So, you used to ride here, and you were curious about

Fender," Ethan recapped, shifting his athletic frame into a conversational lean against the stall. "But that doesn't explain why you're here in the middle of Halloween night." He still sounded all-business, but at least the hostility that had laced his voice earlier seemed to be tapering off.

Everything from the day rushed back: the journal discovery, telling Tori and Cameron, confronting her parents and aunt, the Ice Cave show. Rose wondered if Ethan could see the grimace emanating from her insides. Of course, he had every right to question her. She just wasn't sure if she had an answer that wouldn't make her seem like a total freak.

"I was just out with some friends," Rose started. She felt completely juvenile as she heard her own words but forced herself to continue. "Watching some bands downtown. But then they had to go do their own thing, so…" she trailed off, fingering the edge of Starla's stall as if that somehow completed her answer.

Ethan's brow crinkled. "And then you…randomly headed to your old barn?"

Rose nodded, knowing she wasn't giving much of an explanation. "It sounds ridiculous, I know. It's just…this place has always made me feel better. I guess you could say that today was really…weird." She knew how melancholy she sounded, and now she was completely embarrassed for even opening up like that to a stranger. If he were to scoff or dismiss her right then and there, she was ready.

But he didn't. His gaze yielded almost enough to reveal how he might look when fully relaxed. Right then, Rose noticed how handsome he was—not in an overtly conventional, cologne-ad sort of way, nor was he the in-your-face bad boy type like Tim. But Ethan exuded a quiet toughness about him, even without any stylish bells or whistles. He definitely wasn't a high schooler but looked close enough in age to be something of an older peer. His face, while still youthful, was tinged with the sun-kissed look of a life spent mostly outdoors. Rose had never seen someone quite like him: half cowboy, half I-don't-give-a-hoot-what-you-think.

"We all have those kinds of days, don't we," he replied simply.

Starla snorted loudly, still watching them. Taking the opportunity to change the subject, Rose motioned to the mare and asked, "Any reason why she's so dirty? Looks like the last time she was groomed was, like, ages ago."

A trace of irritation instantly appeared on Ethan's face.

"I don't mean to judge or anything," said Rose, now even more curious. "I'd never let my horse get to that point, though."

Ethan shook his head and waved an arm at Starla with fatherly exasperation. "No, no, I hear you. She's just been kind of sensitive lately. Like I said, she's new here."

"Sensitive? She was really banging around just now," Rose continued. "Do you think she misses her old home or something?"

"Could be. She's definitely testing the waters here, just to see what she can get away with. Got some strong opinions, that's for sure. Thing is, she hasn't really bonded with anybody yet, not even her owner. Too busy to try, she claims."

"I like horses with strong opinions," Rose replied. "It's funny, when I first heard the term 'opinionated' about a horse, when I was a kid, I actually thought it was a compliment!" Some horse owners seemed to have zero clue of how lucky they were to even have a horse. Rose was just about to ask why Starla's owner wasn't around when she noticed that Ethan looked like he was going over an equation in his head.

"What?" Rose asked cautiously, seeing the contemplative look on his face.

"I have a question for you, Rose. And don't feel like you have to say yes."

✦✦✦

"She's so pretty!" Rose managed to say before sneezing for the third time in a row. She chuckled at another poof of dust from the trail of the curry comb. Starla wasn't standing completely still, but so far, she was definitely mellow enough for a quick grooming.

Ethan patted Starla's rear with quiet affection. Just a few minutes after Rose had enthusiastically agreed to his suggestion at attempting a quick brush over Starla's coat, the pair was now settling into an impromptu grooming right in her stall. Tanner, now comfortable in his own nearby stall, watched them with calm curiosity.

"Take her to the cross ties?" Rose had initially asked. She'd never known a horse to be groomed without being secured.

"Not for this gal," Ethan answered. He carried over a small bin filled with brushes from a nearby shelf. "Wise advice from her previous owner—groom without tying her to anything. She hates that for some reason."

Rose nodded. "Got it," she replied, rubbing Starla's neck. Every horse was different, so she had no problem with that preference. Starla carefully eyed the blue bin in her domain just a few feet away.

Ethan was about to tell her how to proceed, but Rose didn't wait for directions. She picked up a curry comb from the bucket and brought it over to Starla, allowing her to inspect it for a few seconds. Sensing her accepting it as harmless, Rose started circling the comb as gently as possible over all of the rough spots and unkempt patches, reassuring the mare with low, soothing play-by-plays.

"Don't worry, we'll go nice and slow." Rose talked to Starla as if nobody else was around. "There, better already. Good girl."

Ethan silently watched from the stall door. Why on earth was this moody horse and random girl clicking? He knew that what he was allowing here was definitely not typical protocol. Like his helmetless galloping, he wasn't exactly planning on sharing this with the world. But something about Rose and Starla together seemed to make just a little bit of sense. For the first time since her arrival, Starla was behaving like an adjusted, content horse. Sure, he'd just met her, but at this point a helpful stranger was a godsend compared to all of the staff who'd repeatedly tried and failed to get anywhere with Starla. Plus, Rose seemed like one of those horse girls who just couldn't get enough of horses in general and was more than happy to help clean and groom. This was a win-win for everyone. Especially Starla.

"Starla hasn't been cleaned up in a while, like you noticed, because of her newfound moodiness," Ethan explained, now handing Rose a soft bristle brush. She started on Starla's neck. So far, the mare seemed to enjoy the attention. "Her owner was getting pretty frustrated, so thanks for taking the time. I'll let everyone know that this queen must have her cherry drops, or else."

Rose nodded. Going through the familiar motion of brushing a horse's body was practically hypnotizing her. "So, what's up with this owner?" she finally asked, moving on to Starla's sides.

Ethan noticed how Rose carefully moved the brush along the hair growth pattern on Starla's hip, right above her flank. He tried not to gape at Starla licking her lips. The last thing he'd expected tonight was a sign of Starla actually relaxing. "Starla's owned by someone kind of..." he trailed off, changing his mind. He was about to say "famous" but figured that might be kind of a stretch, recalling some of his grooms' blank faces when he had first mentioned the name. "Ever heard of...Lula May?" Ethan couldn't help but say the name with a tinge of sourness.

Rose momentarily stopped brushing and looked up at him with surprise. Lula May was a high-profile performance artist known for her flashy and sometimes controversial work. "Yeah, I saw her at the county museum last year. I wrote a review of her exhibition for our school paper, but...anyway, it was kind of interesting, I guess." As she went back to brushing Starla, the main takeaway image of the exhibition flashed in her head—the artist stumbling around her own exhibit, undeniably trashed from the open bar mojitos. Rose had actually made a subtle reference to that tidbit in her article but had discovered it was mysteriously edited out by the time it was printed.

"I wasn't familiar with her until everyone started calling her out about some interview. You hear about that?" Ethan asked. "Guess she basically got kicked out of her scene afterward—socially, I mean. That's why she moved to California. But you didn't hear this from me."

"Ha, don't worry," Rose replied, recalling the artist's desperate face plastered on some tabloids at the grocery store checkout. "How's she doing with Starla?"

Ethan grimaced. "Not good. She wanted a more low-key place, without all the judgment and prying eyes, so she moved Starla here from a bigger barn in LA. So she says, anyway."

Rose listened as Ethan went over what he knew about Starla. Her original owner was a retired Nevada rancher who'd discovered his cancer had returned shortly after adopting the horse from the Bureau of Land Management. After months of soaring medical bills, the man felt he had no choice but to give up his now well-trained mustang, among most of his other belongings. At this point, the details became a little fuzzy. A few years and some owners later, Starla ended up in a rural California riding school, where Lula May eventually bought her.

"She's had a lot of bad press, that Lula May. I mean, what do you expect from those crazy comments, right? And no apology whatsoever. So my boss, who owns the barn, wasn't exactly sure if she wanted all that drama moving over here." The hoof pick hanging on the side of the bin reminded him of the farrier's grumbles from the other day. "When they arrived, Lula May's assistant told me that Lula May actually wasn't too fond of horses, but was suddenly inspired to get one."

Rose detected an edge of condescension in Ethan's voice. She softly rubbed Starla's neck. Her hand trailed along the white freeze brand. Although she vaguely recognized the look of the brand, the geometric symbols were a complete mystery to her. Ethan quickly explained how to read the coding of BLM mustangs. One piece of information the brand indicated was that Starla was thirteen years old. Like many things about horses, Sandy had taught Rose about the mustang's intriguing and tumultuous history in America's vast terrains. A slow tingle crawled over Rose's upper arms and shoulders. Standing in a stall with a formerly wild horse gave Rose downright chills.

"Well, since she's fine with the brushing, let me try her hooves." Ethan stood against Starla's shoulder and ran his hand down her front leg to the fetlock. Just as he was about to squeeze to get her to lift her leg, Starla roughly jerked out of Ethan's grip. He tried twice more without any luck.

"Well," Ethan muttered, glancing at his watch. "I think she's had enough primping for her first time here." He declined Rose's offer to try the pick. "Nah, let's not push her."

They both patted Starla goodnight and headed outside.

"You know what, though?" said Ethan as they reached the parking lot gate. "If you have time tomorrow, maybe stop by and we'll try her again."

11

"**I** can't believe you went to the stables last night!"

Tori's bloodshot eyes looked almost not hungover for a moment while she urgently stuffed a handful of fries into her mouth. Tim had dropped her off at home just before dawn. No one in her house was aware, of course.

They had decided to stay on campus for lunch, down at the Quonset hut. "Weren't your parents livid, by the way?" Tori wiped her chin with a damp napkin. The school's classic crinkle cut fries always oozed with an overload of grease.

Cameron shook his head. "That's literally the last place I thought you'd end up."

Rose looked down at her small carton of orange juice, taking her time unfolding the top. She knew it sounded ridiculous to them. Instead of heading straight home with Tori's car, she'd gone to the one place strictly forbidden by her parents. And yes, her folks had been waiting up all night.

After delivering Tori's car keys in the mailbox, Rose crossed Camino Drive, totally unsure of what to expect. Normally she would have been shaking in a cold sweat entering that front door in such an ominous situation. But returning to Laguna Lake Riding Club and meeting Starla offered her something else to dwell upon besides feeling completely wrecked. The apprehension concerning her parents was now countered by a familiar spark that was hopefully back in her life for good. She already felt obsessed again. In a good way. Horses shielded her troubles now, just like when she was a kid. As Rose slid the key in the lock, her brain tightened every muscle in her body, ready for impending chaos, but her heart was elsewhere. Her long-dormant love for horses had been stirred awake, and there was little in the world that would ever penetrate enough to really hurt her. It was like she wasn't available for that anymore.

"They didn't know I went to Laguna Lake Riding Club, obviously." Rose shot Tori a "duh" look and explained what had gone down. Maybe it was because Rose didn't enter the house cowering and quivering as they'd expected, or maybe they were simply still shocked from the confrontation earlier that afternoon. She did know that the haggard looks on her parents' faces weren't typical—even after talking with Tori's parents, they must have been really worried to react with such reserved relief.

"And I'm going back today after school." Rose told her friends about Ethan's unsuccessful attempt at picking Starla's hooves. Her stomach fluttered at the thought of Starla. Would the mare remember her from last night? "I mean, Starla was kind of moody in the beginning, but once she settled down after some candy, she was so sweet. Something about her is so…I don't know. You guys should meet her. She's *beautiful*…" A faint breeze rustled by as Rose chattered on. A tiny whiff of the barn traveled from down the road, so whisper-light she wondered if it was her imagination. It was all she could do to refrain from squealing and jumping up and down like a little girl on her way to pony camp. Tori and Cameron were politely listening, but she knew better than to expect them to fully join her enthusiasm.

"Yuck," Tori grimaced, gulping the last of her meal. "But I know you always loved that stuff for some reason."

Cameron leaned against the wall and dug into a bag of potato chips. "Not that I want to clean hooves with you or whatever, but I think it's cool you're all getting back into that horse stuff. It's, like, so you."

Rose finished the rest of her juice and nudged Cameron's shoulder teasingly. He was right. With a content inhale, she searched the breeze for another trace of the barn.

The lunch bell rang, signaling them back to class.

"Do you think he's still sleeping?" Tori frowned at her phone as they began the walk to the main campus. Tim still hadn't texted her back.

"Um, that's a lot of sleep," Cameron smirked. "I thought you said he passed out as soon as you guys got back to his and his brother's place." After picking up two bags of cheeseburgers and fries at a nearby fast food joint, Tori soon found out that Tim's place was actually his older brother Gavin's apartment. The two lived together just a few minutes from the house they grew up in.

"He did." Glum, Tori stared straight ahead as they trekked to the classrooms. "Well, right after, like, three double burger combos."

"I'm sure he'll get back to you soon." Rose offered Tori some hope. She wasn't going to worry about that guy right now. How could she? She was practically floating all the way up the hill, counting the seconds until the school day was over.

12

ose turned into the parking lot at Laguna Lake Riding Club, her heart thumping. She wasn't sure how people would actually surf in East Berlin, but the quick-fire song matched her buoyant mood. Rose's teachers had loaded her with hours of extra homework for missing classes yesterday, but even that couldn't faze her excitement.

Now that it was officially November, the midafternoon sunlight was already shifting from a crystal canary yellow to a pale honey. Rose closed the car door behind her and skipped to the barn, not caring whether the goosebumps on her arms were from giddiness or the swiftly cooling air. One of the many "No Running" signs reminded her to slow down, in case her sudden movements spooked a nearby horse.

"Good to see you." Ethan waved from just inside the tack room. He set a pile of clean saddle pads on the long wooden table.

Rose got the feeling he was a little surprised that she'd actually showed up. "Same to you. How's Starla today?"

"She's doing well. Her trainer should be here soon," Ethan replied as they headed to the stalls. "It's been iffy with him so far, but maybe today will be better."

Rose's eyes sparkled. She grinned at all the horses chilling on their shavings or eagerly poking their heads over their doors, but she was most focused on the very end of the aisle. Rose had daydreamed of picking Starla's hooves throughout every class at school. Maybe that was a strange thing to fantasize about (that's definitely what Tori and Cameron thought), but she didn't care—cleaning frogs caked with dirt was straight up heaven compared to anything else in her life right now.

Starla calmly poked her head out of her stall like she was

waiting for the visit. Both her ears were perked up and forward, inquisitive and friendly. A soft nicker (of recognition, Rose hoped) trembled from the mare's chest.

"How are you today, Starla?" A huge beam swept over Rose's face. She didn't want to overdo it, but it was hard to hold back. She couldn't remember the last time she'd felt so stoked. Starla sniffed Rose's hand and stood still as Rose slowly stroked her neck. Taking a deep breath, Rose silently tried to give off a sense of calm. She hoped that the more composed she was, the better Starla would feel. "Is it alright to give her some more treats?"

"Be our guest," replied Ethan. He picked up the same blue bin from the night before and suggested grooming Starla with the curry comb and brushes again before attempting her hooves. "Maybe she'll remember that getting groomed isn't exactly the end of the world."

Rose nodded and watched as Starla inhaled the awaiting cherry drop from her hand. She gingerly brushed a strand of forelock away from the horse's soft eyes amid the busy munching. Rose gazed at Starla with curiosity, momentarily lost in the concept that in another life, in her former wild existence, this beautiful girl had used these very eyes to scan the remote plains of her old home. A very long way from cherry drops.

Hoof pick in hand, Ethan jokingly made the sign of the cross on his chest. He gently leaned on Starla's left shoulder and ran his hand down her leg. Starla stood still until the last moment, jerking her leg away in the same manner as the night before.

Rose watched Ethan attempt again. "Can I try?" she asked, trying not to squirm with anticipation. She'd spent all day envisioning this task!

"Okay, just be careful." Ethan handed over the hoof pick and stepped to the side.

Rose patted Starla's rump before standing next to her shoulder, then ran her hand down her leg. Starla did not move.

Rose tried again. Starla lifted her hoof for a fleeting moment before dropping it down, hard. Finally, on the third try, Rose was able to hoist Starla's hoof snugly into her hand. To her slight surprise, Starla was barefoot. And the V-shaped frog underneath was so packed with dirt and shavings, she wondered if she'd be able to pick it all out. Since Starla could easily decide to abort and plunge her leg at any given moment, Rose worked on nudging the debris as quickly as she'd ever done. Just before she got to the last crevice, Starla dropped her leg again, as if saying, "Alright, that's enough."

"Good job." Ethan grinned. "She'll remember now."

Rose was about to point out that she wasn't able to get all the dirt, but a sense of accomplishment rushed through her anyway. It was a small step, but Ethan's approval was noticeable. Rose moved on to the next leg, which was easier. By the time she had circled to the last hoof, Starla actually kept her leg lifted long enough so that Rose could remove every last speck. It was incredibly satisfying to gently set Starla's hoof back onto the ground the same way she'd done with Fender countless times.

"Hello?" A testy voice called out from down the aisle. "Ethan, are you in there?" Impatience rounded out her question.

"Be right there," Ethan replied over his shoulder. He suddenly looked subdued.

"Ethan? Anybody? Where's my horse?" A woman hollered from the breezeway entrance, but she was not walking further in.

"Over here." Stifling a sigh, Ethan ushered Rose to follow him. Rose gave Starla a quick pat and carefully closed the stall latch behind them.

Is that a costume? Rose cringed and had to press her lips together to suppress a laugh. Lula May looked like she was dressed up for a Western themed sorority party, not a trip to the barn. Waxy leather shorts, a matching brown leather vest with fringe that trailed her thighs, a tan blinged-out cowboy hat and equally sparkly cowboy boots. On her left side stood a young blonde woman in striped leggings and a baggy gray crewneck sweatshirt with what looked like faint paint stains. A mustached man in jeans and an ivory wool cowboy hat stood at her other side. Arms crossed and squinting, he gave Ethan and Rose a critical once-over.

Hand on hip, Lula May hovered her phone in the air from right to left. She had that preoccupied stare and slightly ajar mouth typical of someone taking video. Her brown chin-length bob grazed a charm necklace that glistened with every millimeter of movement.

"Ethan, you remember my assistant, Carrie." Lula May didn't look up from the screen. "Has Starla been a good girl? Murray here is going to take her out. Go ahead, Murray." The moment Lula May looked his way, Murray's thick mustache quickly lifted and replaced his blank glare with a toothy smile. He nodded past Ethan and Rose and headed to Starla's stall.

"Lula May, this is Rose," Ethan replied. "She was just helping us with—"

"Shhh!" Lula May raised her finger to shush him, her eyes still on her phone. Everyone waited until she finished. "Carrie, upload that video to my account right now. I want all my other fans to see that I'm at the ranch today." Carrie dutifully nodded and took the phone. For a quick second, Lula May frowned at the caked dirt under her assistant's fingernails, comparing them to her own impeccable French manicure.

Turning her attention to Ethan, she flashed him a broad smile. "And how about you—have you been a good cowboy?" she winked. "You never replied to me about your schedule."

Ugh, Rose cringed even more, laughing silently. *How corny!*

Murray emerged from the stall with Starla in a halter, interrupting Lula May's flirting.

Rose was glad and a little surprised at how calmly Starla followed Murray to the ring. *So she's not that hard to handle,* she realized.

"We'll continue later," Lula May assured Ethan, placing a hand on his forearm. "But now let's watch Murray work his magic."

"She hasn't been lunged yet," Ethan called out to the trainer.

"And?" Murray barked back.

Murray led Starla to the side of the ring. A bridle, cinch, pad, and a Western saddle with rhinestones were on the fence. As Murray began tacking up, Rose couldn't help but notice how roughly he dropped the saddle onto Starla's back. Starla reacted by suddenly raising her head and widening her eyes. Disturbed, Rose glanced at Ethan, wanting to say something. He was carefully watching with his arms crossed.

When Murray yanked the cinch to tighten it all the way in one shot, Starla had had enough. She reached over her left side and snapped her teeth on Murray's upper arm.

"You little chump!" Murray spat and elbowed Starla's cheek.

"Hey!" Rose growled. *What kind of trainer is this?* Her stomach was now rolling. It was one thing to reprimand a combative horse, but Murray had practically begged her to bite him.

"Bad girl!" Lula May yelled. "What's her problem this time?"

Ethan walked over to replace Starla's halter with the bridle. She didn't budge at first, but once Ethan gently prodded his finger in the corners of her mouth a little, she quietly accepted the bit.

"Looking good, Murray!" Lula May hooted from the sideline after Murray mounted the mare. She let out a piercing whistle. As if on cue, Carrie immediately mimicked her.

Rose watched Murray with increasing alarm. The guy was kicking and clucking and then pulling. He almost looked as if he was trying to physically fight Starla, or at least completely dominate her. And was it really necessary to wear spurs, especially such severe ones? Every time Starla listened to his cues and shot forward, Murray jerked the reins back so hard, Rose involuntarily reached up to touch her own mouth. All the conflicting cues were a complete disaster.

"She's got a real soft mouth," Ethan called out to Murray. "No need for all that busy stuff!"

"I know what I'm doing," Murray instantly shot back. Starla spooked in place.

"Let's get out of their way," Ethan directed the group toward some chairs and a well-worn wooden picnic table in the shade several feet away.

"Fabulous!" As if he'd read her mind, Lula May raced to a chair and plopped down. "Oh, my feet," she moaned, slipping off her boots. "Can you rub them, kiddo?"

Rub them? Rose wondered. *What is she talking about?*

To Rose's bewilderment, Carrie dutifully positioned herself face to face with her boss. She cupped Lula May's left foot in her hands, pressing and stroking as if she'd done it her whole life. Both Rose and Ethan awkwardly tried to ignore the strange scenario as Lula May leaned back and began drilling Ethan about Starla's progress. But every time he started to answer a question, Lula May just as soon lost interest and interrupted him about something else entirely.

"I would love to hear all about its diet later," Lula May interjected for the fourth time. "Speaking of which, I'm starving. Does good food exist around here?"

Its diet? Rose blinked. *Its?* That word just didn't sound good in this particular situation.

Ethan stopped his rundown of Starla's feed and switched gears. "Plenty. There's a good Mexican joint on Gilbert Avenue, some good Japanese spot near the corner of—"

Lula May shook her head, grimacing. "Nah, I don't want those. How about something more like—" Scuffling sounds from the ring interrupted her.

The group turned and collectively gasped. Murray was lying on his side on the ground. His cowboy hat was strewn a few feet from his head. Starla trotted away from him, somewhat nonchalant, somewhat sheepish.

Ethan quickly walked over. "Murray, you okay?"

Murray appeared more embarrassed than shaken. "I'm fine," he mumbled, waving off the group. He teetered onto his feet, brushing off the dirt from his clothes and then rubbed the side of his head. "Freaking horse just bucked like a maniac."

"Bad Starla! Bad, bad girl!" Lula May screamed as she ran up with Carrie. Starla stood still and quiet on the other side of the ring.

"I'm…fine…" Murray took a step forward and had to extend an arm to regain his balance. "Just hit my head, that's all. I've had plenty of worse concussions."

Ethan inhaled through his teeth as he watched Murray take another tottering step. "Murray, you should get to a doctor. There's a big hospital just down the road."

"No way," Murray shook his head. He adjusted his hat back on his head. "Said I'm fine, son."

Ethan took a step toward him. "You should just go." His voice climbed a level.

Rose wondered if Murray's refusal had something to do with the pressure of a celebrity client. From the looks of Ethan's annoyed glances at the crew, he seemed to be thinking that as well.

Murray took out a handkerchief and dabbed his damp forehead. His gaze was stony. "No, for the last time. Now thanks for your concern, but I have a horse that needs to learn who's boss." He turned his back and started again to Starla.

The incident was sinking in with Lula May, and now she was beginning to really freak out. "I can't believe Starla did that— what if that happened to *me?* Oh my god…" She turned to Carrie. "I thought they said Starla was *trained!*"

"That's what they said," Carrie replied, looking equally frightened. "Totally broke, or whatever it was they called it— remember how nice she was at first?"

Didn't they see how terrible Murray was to her? Rose stood to the side and quietly watched the two women commiserate among themselves, oblivious to Murray and Starla. Carrie's words made Rose instantly feel terrible for Starla. Sure, it was possible that Starla had been initially upset at being forced to a new home, but at the moment, she was probably much more upset at the abusive handling she had just put up with.

Lula May was spiraling into a raging breakdown. "This is so unfair! Why do *I* have a psychotic horse on my hands? What am I going to do now?" Lula May was fuming so hard her face was flushing. She burst into sobs. Carrie rubbed Lula May's back, murmuring assurances in her ear.

As Lula May bemoaned her "insane" horse, Rose could hear the rapidly escalating conversation between Ethan and Murray. After a few seconds, even Lula May ceased her crying and looked over at them.

"That's not what you do with a horse, man," Ethan said. "Is that how you always ride?"

Murray threw all his weight into Ethan with a hefty shove.

Ethan muttered something that Rose couldn't quite make out, but his disdain was obvious. Whatever he said irked Murray enough to promptly raise his right fist and aim for Ethan's face.

"Murray!" Lula May screamed. "What are you doing?"

The close proximity between Murray's fist and Ethan's left cheek would have most likely guaranteed a square hit in most fights. But right before contact, Ethan turned his head just the slightest. Murray's knuckles barely grazed skin, and he had to catch himself as he stumbled behind the momentum of his own swinging arm.

Ethan was just about to reciprocate but slowly lowered his own fist. Maybe risking his job to screw over this wuss was his main concern. Ethan turned and sauntered by everyone, his eyes steely.

A puffy-faced Lula May and a very flustered Carrie huddled around Murray. He scowled, grumbling to himself.

"We're taking him to the hospital," Carrie told Rose, her voice slightly shaking. "Tell Ethan he'll be hearing from us later." She and Lula May grabbed each of Murray's arms and escorted him to the parking lot.

"What about Starla?" Rose's eyes widened as she watched everyone walk off. Starla was still standing on the other side of the ring, all alone.

Nothing from Lula May, Carrie or Murray. They just kept going.

"What about Starla, you guys?" Rose heard the frustration in her own voice as she called out louder at their backs. Somehow, she knew not to expect them to care.

Carrie finally glanced back over her shoulder. "I don't know, ask Ethan!" she answered dismissively before returning her full attention to Lula May's animated ranting.

Rose looked around helplessly. Where was Ethan, anyway?

Starla was waiting at the same spot in the arena. Her head was low, and, from what Rose could tell, she didn't appear upset at all. *I'm so sorry, Starla,* Rose thought. *Screw that Murray guy.* Maybe she should be getting help from Ethan, but she didn't want to leave Starla by herself now, not even for a minute. She was appalled at everyone's behavior. So immature and selfish.

Starla watched Rose approach her left side. She didn't move a muscle. Rose took a few deep breaths and tried to push the image of Murray's faltering steps out of her head.

"Easy, girl." Rose gathered the hanging reins. She gently rubbed up and down Starla's neck, trying to calm her own trembling hand. No horse should be treated like that, and any reaction to such idiotic abuse was fully warranted. "It's alright, just chill, okay?" Rose wasn't sure if she was telling this to Starla or to herself.

Eyes straight ahead, Rose took a few steps forward. Starla followed her out of the ring without hesitation. Rose again looked around for Ethan. Besides a couple of people by the tack room, the place was pretty quiet. Rose shook her head as she led Starla into her stall. For now, it was just the two of them.

At least Starla looked completely unharmed. Rose searched over her entire body, her mouth, and lifted all four feet. Starla calmly waited as Rose picked out small specks of shavings from her forelock. The mare's eyes were now velvety soft. She took a long sip from her water bucket. Rose ran a soft brush over her coat, humming a random made-up tune. Starla released a deep sigh.

Rose paused and looked at her. "Me too, Starla." She hoped, for Starla's sake, that this afternoon would quickly fade to nothing more than a vague, far off memory.

13

Later that evening, Rose sat cross-legged on her bed, trying to concentrate. A laptop and some folders and books were strewn around her. Milo, tucked between his human's legs, drifted in and out of a light snooze. A text beeped on her phone. Her parents would be staying late at work, so her mom had prepared a simple ready-to-heat dinner in the fridge. That was more than fine with her.

After making sure Starla was comfortable in her stall, a shaken and disgusted Rose had left the barn without even a glance for Ethan. She didn't owe any time to someone who just bailed like that.

This is impossible! Rose stifled a frustrated sigh and tossed her notepad aside. Homework was her last concern right now. The famous artist who didn't care at all about her own horse was bad enough. And Ethan suddenly storming off and disappearing was an additional affront. On Halloween night, Ethan had seemed genuinely concerned about Starla. It was infuriating that some random dude like Murray could suddenly affect anything when it came to Starla's well-being. Starla needed some attention after such a terrible incident. How could anybody not care about that part? It was all just way too much ego.

Rose leaned back on a pillow and retrieved her notepad and pencil. With quick, rough strokes, her hand etched familiar lines and curves on the paper. As a kid, she had spent countless hours filling stacks of notebooks with drawings of equines. Long-legged Thoroughbreds, doll-like Morgans, doe-eyed Arabians, stocky Quarter horses, fluffy burros… None of it was particularly good, but it was amazing how after so many years she still felt acquainted with the process, almost like channeling the offhand sketch through the adolescent muscle memory of her hand. She smiled as she outlined the soft curves of the muzzle, remembering that first candy with Starla on Halloween night.

Out of nowhere, a moving image flashed through Rose's mind: Starla twisting her head away from someone's fist. It was Lula May.

Rose froze. Her pencil hovered, mid-whisker. Was the left side of her nose throbbing? A wave of sheer fright just poured through her bones.

Someone knocked on the door.

"Come in, Thomas." Rose blinked and drew in a slow breath to compose herself.

"Can you help me glue this for my science project?" Thomas asked, lugging in a large, half cut-out cardboard box. He had a diorama to construct and it was due in the morning.

"Sure." Rose sat up and motioned him in. Milo sniffed the materials for a few seconds before losing interest and retreating to Rose's side. Rose and Thomas worked in comfortable silence. Minutes into their cutting and gluing, Milo started snoring almost as loudly as a human, and the siblings giggled every other minute at each snort.

"There!" Rose held up the box, now complete with a small ecosystem of popsicle sticks, pipe cleaners, buttons, and construction paper. "This should get you an A for sure." She listlessly turned back to her own homework.

"Thanks." Thomas paused at the door, balancing the diorama in one arm. "Um..."

"What is it?"

"Do you miss Grandma?"

Surprised, Rose looked up. Her brother was only twelve, and he hadn't mentioned Grandma since the funeral. "Yeah. Of course, I do."

"Oh..." he squirmed, his hand awkwardly twisting the doorknob left and right. "Because, you know, you didn't really cry."

Rose paused. For some reason, Aunt Esther's journal promptly appeared in her head. It made her wonder about her grandmother's connection to the family secret. Another unknown.

"People grieve in different ways," Rose answered carefully. "Not everyone cries when you expect. Some people don't cry at all. Everyone's different."

Thomas nodded. "Yeah." He thought for a moment. "Like Milo...I think he misses Grandma because sometimes he looks for her in her room...but he's a dog, so he's not going to cry. Even though he's sad."

"Exactly." Rose smiled.

Thomas appeared, for the time being, satisfied with his analysis. Right before closing the door behind him, he added, "Nice horse picture."

Rose's smile faded as his footsteps retreated down the hallway. She looked down at the near-complete doodle on the paper.

What was that random, terrifying glimpse of Starla? The fear and the sting on Rose's cheek had subsided, but she could still feel how very real and freaky it was. And so clear. It was almost like she had just shared a feeling—or memory?—with Starla. Or was it the other way around...had Starla somehow let Rose in on something?

"Don't be crazy," she told herself, holding one of Milo's soft, round paws. *Must be delayed side effects from the funeral or something.* He stretched onto his back as she gently massaged the miniature black pads of each paw.

Tears, sobs, puffy eyes...that was all so normal. Sad and normal.

Rose wished, so badly, that things were just sad and normal.

14

The rest of the week passed in a busy blur. Although Rose really wanted to return to Laguna Lake Riding Club and visit Starla, something always came up to hinder her plans—a group project work session for English class one day, helping her parents with a City Hall event another day, and driving Thomas to Amerige Park for soccer practice the next.

The Moon family owned a small but bustling flower shop in the nearby city of La Mirada, and the brief period between summer weddings and the onslaught of the holiday season (when Rose and Thomas spent their entire winter break filling orders and delivering flowers) was the only chance for "easy" ten-hour workdays until the new year. But with everyone still adjusting to Grandma's absence, as well as the lingering tension of that last afternoon with Aunt Esther, things at home were strained more than ever.

One afternoon, Mrs. Happy Dude came by the house to complain about the Moon's gardener and his loud leaf blower, as if he was the only gardener on the block who used those. She had a grown-out perm which basically looked like creepy Ronald McDonald had dyed his hair dark brown instead of getting a badly needed haircut.

Rose didn't bother to hide a visceral scoff. The lady was so good at ignoring her own situation, yet never hesitated to nosy around elsewhere. And she knew about Grandma's passing, too. That entitled nag.

"Why don't you take care of Koko instead of bothering us?" Rose snapped. Disgust clouded her eyes as she watched Mrs.

Happy Dude retreat back to her own house as if she didn't hear. The older woman didn't toss a second glance at Koko, who was panting for her owner's attention at the side gate. Rose made a mental note to bring some extra treats for the pup later that evening.

At the end of the week, Rose suggested she and Thomas order a pizza and watch a movie. They loved spending Friday nights together in the sunken family room.

"Yes, pizza! I want Hawaiian! Extra sauce!" Thomas exclaimed, rubbing his hands together as Rose placed an order on the phone.

"Half Hawaiian and half mushroom, please," Rose told the guy at Frank's Pizza, a tiny immigrant-owned pizza joint a few minutes from their home. She ignored Thomas making a face at her choice and hung up. He was in an anti-mushroom phase, especially on pizza. "Okay, thirty minutes. What movie?"

Milo chewed on his favorite dinosaur toy, tucked in between brother and sister. The classic *Willy Wonka & the Chocolate Factory* was a default favorite. Right when Grandpa Joe—who Rose always made a point to call out as a fraud—jumped out of bed at the news of the golden ticket, Rose's phone buzzed on the coffee table. She expected it to be Tori reminding her of their lunch plans at the Hub tomorrow. To her surprise, it was a pop-up message from one of her social media accounts.

Hi Rose, it's Ethan. Really sorry about the other day. Think you can come by the barn when you have some time? Might be good for Starla to see you. No rush. Thanks.

Rose stared at the message. They had never exchanged numbers or anything, so Ethan must have searched for her online. He'd followed her account, too.

When she clicked on his profile, she was instantly surprised by the large number of followers he had. She hadn't pegged Ethan as someone who cared much for socializing, whether it was online or in person. *Who are all these people?* Rose scanned the dozens of comments and questions on each of his posts. Every photo had a horse or something horse related.

Curling back on the sofa, Rose tried to focus on the group of self-centered humans touring the chocolate factory. They were all jerks if you really thought about it—even the main character Charlie, she concluded for the hundredth time. He did deserve a begrudging pass for admitting his stealing at the end, though.

The most recent afternoon at Laguna Lake Riding Club kept replaying in Rose's head. It still bothered her. Until that day, she'd thought that Ethan was totally caring and fully in control of things at the barn. He clearly knew a lot about horses, and she liked how he wasn't one of those overly tough horse folks, the ones who sometimes made her wonder if they were treating their horses right when no one was looking. He'd actually shown zero indication of being rough or frustrated, even when Starla got testy with him. But his altercation with Murray had revealed a new side to him. Running off and leaving Starla with nobody else around except Rose…what was all that about?

If you care, you protect. Rose remembered how urgently she wanted to check on Starla as well as comfort her. The thought of Lula May revolted Rose even more. That pile obviously didn't care about Starla, either. What was Rose to think about any of these so-called adults?

Rose grimly pushed Laguna Lake Riding Club out of her mind. Never had the place held such an uncertain vibe. This was not the barn she grew up with. Maybe her parents and grandmother were right. Maybe she didn't belong there at all.

15

The Hub was tucked in a discreet row of storefronts across from the train station in a classic part of downtown. Plenty of sudden construction had erupted nearby in recent months. Rose hoped the influx of new money would never threaten the old school café with its original exposed brick walls and beautiful carved wooden bar. The Hub served coffee, tea, and flavored Italian sodas, along with simple light dishes like sandwiches and cold pasta salads. If they were lucky, the small glass display would have freshly baked cookies or other pastries. A few classic arcade games dotted the inside room. Hanging from the ceiling was a huge, quirky upside down chessboard.

Doris, the pretty blonde server, waved her usual friendly hello to Rose and Tori. A long-haired bearded guy lingered around the cash register, trying to get his flirt on. With her genuinely sweet demeanor and cute rockabilly style, Doris was well accustomed to being drooled over by musicians and artists all day at work. But even with the endless creepers who always came by to try to woo her over, she always kept it super professional.

Jazz music played on the speakers just like it always did on Doris' daytime shifts. After ordering the Saturday sandwich special, Rose and Tori headed to the outdoor patio with their favorite raspberry sodas in hand. Rose eagerly made a beeline to the small wire rack by the exit to grab the latest issue of *Rip It Up*. Good thing, only two were left.

A few small groups of twentysomethings with colorful hair smoked and sipped drinks at the wrought iron tables. The clientele during the day was usually pretty similar to the eclectic night crowd.

Tori lit a cigarette before sitting down since Rose didn't allow smoking in her car. She fidgeted with her phone.

"Nothing yet?" Rose asked. She didn't need to specify. Her friend had been waiting for a text from Tim for days now.

Tori frowned. "No. That turd." Before Rose could reply, Tori blurted, "And don't bother with any I-told-you-so nonsense. I don't need to hear that."

"I wasn't going to," Rose protested. "He's probably just busy, anyway." She didn't fully believe her own words, but she felt stuck having to carefully keep Tori's hopes up or get accused of being a hater.

"He did say he had a bunch of rehearsals," Tori reasoned aloud, trying to convince herself. "Nothing4U are getting ready to book a bunch of gigs over the next few months. They might get pretty big this year." Nothing4U was Tim's band, which was already getting props in the local punk scene. Rose listened as Tori rattled off the possible venues they were looking at. "Ice Cave, of course, and that place by the train tracks right over there, the Toy House in Anaheim, and that one spot in Costa Mesa. Maybe Uptown Whittier, too."

Doris arrived at their table with a pair of big oval ceramic plates filled with food and silver utensils tightly wrapped in white paper napkins. "Curry chicken sandwich with pasta salad," she said to Tori. "And veggie sandwich with a side of fruit and your usual hot sauce, Rose." She was about to stop and chat, but someone dinged the bell on the counter inside. "Enjoy, ladies!" The girls thanked her, and Doris skipped off, her sleek bob bouncing over her shoulders.

Tori forked some raisins from the curry chicken and dropped them on Rose's plate. "So, how are things at home?"

Rose popped a pineapple wedge in her mouth. "Could be worse." She eyed the donated raisins. "My parents are still pretty mad. I can't talk about the journal at all with them, much less anything else."

"I'm so sorry, that sucks. You know, your parents are pretty cool. I mean, they're still way cooler than mine...at least yours speak fluent English. They're probably just figuring out what to do. You'll get through this," Tori reached over and squeezed her friend's arm.

Rose couldn't help but wonder if Tori was giving her the same false hope that she'd just offered her about Tim. She nodded anyway, grateful for any support at all. "Thanks. It's been so jacked...I mean, it's not exactly a normal problem to have. I wish I could just look up, 'how to make your family explain their big secret when they don't want to.'"

"I know, it's like a movie or something!" Tori exclaimed. "Does Thomas know?"

Rose shook her head. "No, and I don't want to tell him. He's heard us arguing, but I'm not sure if he gets what we're referring to. Anyway, I don't think he can take much more than that. You know how sensitive he is."

"Don't blame you there. " After a long sip of her drink, Tori changed the subject. "By the way, I still can't believe you met that Lula May chick! She sounds like such a drag." She and Cameron had gotten a kick out of the story about Lula May at Laguna Lake Riding Club.

"She is, from what I've seen. I feel so bad for Starla." Rose picked at her sandwich crust. "You know what's funny? That Ethan guy messaged me last night. He followed me online, too."

"The dude from the barn?" Tori choked on her pasta. "You guys are already online buddies?" she teased.

"Not really," Rose answered calmly, knowing Tori would make a big fuss. "But he asked me to come back and see Starla if I have time." She gave Tori a slow-your-roll look. "It's really not like that."

"Oh, sure it isn't," Tori scoffed, half-joking. "Come on. Why would he reach out if he wasn't interested?"

"Because of Starla, that's why," Rose said a little defensively. She forced her voice to relax a little. "Besides—"

"I can't believe that some hot cowboy who doesn't even have your number has somehow tracked you down, while Tim hasn't even bothered to text me back," Tori pouted.

An obnoxious snort erupted from one of the nearby tables just as Tori was about to launch into another tirade about Tim. A blue-haired girl and her mohawked boyfriend snickered at two men who were scanning the patio for a place to sit. Right away, Rose knew the reason for their laughter. Both men wore Western style shirts with loud prints, stiff blue jeans, big shiny belt buckles, and spotless wool cowboy hats. They were the epitome of the conspicuous cowboy dude that the local punks loved to hate (and vice versa). The area's old school cultural clash lived on with the punks even though it was decades old.

Rose's grin faded as soon as the man in the white cowboy hat turned around enough for her to get a better look.

What is Murray doing here? Rose wondered. It was definitely him. She sharply turned back to Tori.

"Okay, listen," Rose whispered, trying not to freak out. "It's Starla's trainer from the other day." She didn't recognize the other man. Rose motioned for her friend to stay quiet. Tori glanced over discreetly as the pair settled at a nearby table. The two men appeared to be in a serious conversation.

Something about their tone made Rose relieved that her back was facing them. Murray just might have recognized her if she'd been sitting in Tori's spot. The girls ate their lunch and feigned small talk, trying to look like they weren't eavesdropping.

"…man, I'm telling you," said Murray. "She wants to get rid of that horse, like A-S-A-P." He spelled out the letters for emphasis.

Rose's stomach flipped, and her eyes widened as they met Tori's. She didn't want to believe what she was already sensing.

Murray's companion had a rough voice with a hint of an unidentifiable drawl. "Why am I not surprised that another city slicker princess got a horse she can't handle?" He sipped his coffee. "If that thing has an attitude problem, Tanya won't let him step one hoof on our property. Not even for breeding. We got no time for that."

"Understood," Murray nodded and leaned in. "Look, it was trained and doing fine up until recently, as far as I know. We think maybe it was just a random thing or accident that made it change."

"Random thing or accident," the rough voice repeated. "Well, I'm not interested in banging up my skull these days, man. I'm not trying to get in any horse fights anymore. Too old for all that."

Murray stepped up his salesman-mode. "I hear you. Here's the main thing," he lowered his voice. "Lula May needs to get rid of the horse sooner rather than later—and most importantly, discreetly. She can't have *any* bad press. I told her I'd find someone to take it, someone who won't mention her involvement at all."

Rose refrained from turning around. She couldn't believe that Lula May was selling Starla so quickly, after not even bothering to get to know her or even try. If Starla was good-tempered until only recently, she probably just needed a little more attention and care. She was already doing better, so that was a good sign that some extra patience and kind guidance would make her happy and confident again.

Murray continued, "She's willing to just give it up if need be. No questions asked. But it's gotta be done quietly. No gossip or bystanders. She *really* doesn't want any media getting word of this. I cannot stress that enough. Quicker it's gone, the better. Since she'd rather not wait for the next auction, I thought maybe a healthy mustang might be a good pied piper for you, help you to get rid of the bottom of the barrel camp horses festering in that lot of yours."

Rose inhaled a visceral gasp. There was no question what he meant. Her insides churned with horror. Lula May wasn't just selling Starla.

The gruff man paused for a moment. "Now that you mention it, maybe I do have some options before next month, quota-wise. I know some folks who can handle all that. They won't care nor say a word, even if they did know who this Lala-gal is. How much does it weigh, you think?"

Rose's knuckles turned white from gripping her fork. Suddenly the sandwiches on the table looked absolutely inedible. Tori's eyes darted from Rose to the two men, slowly putting together the grisly scenario.

A few more minutes of convincing was all Murray needed. "I'll let her know the good news and get this moving. Thanks again, Don. I knew you'd come through on this."

The two men shook hands and exited the patio. They threw sinister looks at the young group that was still not-so-discreetly laughing and throwing menacing stares right back. It seemed that the punks were picking on some easy targets for fun, and they only found the hostile reaction even more hilarious. Rose heard a jingle-jangle sound coming from the young group and noticed a flash of silver on the heel of one of the guy's leather boots. He was wearing Western spurs, as if the big spiky rowel and long shank were a fashion statement. Pretty kooky.

"Zubie's is down that-a-way!"

The two men looked blank, not understanding the reference. Zubie's was known as an imitation-cowboy restaurant and bar that shared a parking lot with one of main punk clubs in the area. The clashes between the patrons of both businesses were notorious.

Rose watched Murray climb into his truck as Don headed toward the train station. *How could this be happening?* Rose's throat turned dry. A familiar mixture of terror and helplessness overwhelmed her. Flashes of slaughterhouses in Canada and Mexico sizzled in her brain—horrific images that sometimes kept her up at night for hours if she remembered them at the wrong time, images she wished she could permanently delete from her memory. No way would she ever be able to live with herself if Starla was sent down that barbaric path.

"Rose, hello?" Tori interrupted Rose's silent panic attack. Her eyes glistened with newfound excitement. "Did you hear me? Tim just texted! He's going to meet us here in a few minutes." She was already typing back.

"Oh, cool," Rose heard herself mutter. Her guts were still

reeling, and the last thing she wanted was to see Tim right now. She forced a small grin of support despite her terror about Starla. Just wonderful! Instead of figuring out what to do about Starla, she now had to socialize with some guy who could barely be bothered to text her friend back.

Tori sent her message and promptly exploded about how nervous she was to see Tim again and how great it was that he and Rose would finally get to talk more. "You're going to love him, I swear!" She got up to go to the restroom to primp and tripped on the table leg. "I'll be right back. Stay right there, so he knows where we're sitting!"

A few minutes later, loud music came from the front parking lot. Rose looked over at an impeccably shiny black vintage Chevy Impala, windows rolled down. Tim was blasting what sounded like a Fear song.

The people on the patio sat in obedient silence as they watched Tim walk up to the Hub's patio. They seemed to know who he was, so no jokes were in order. Ignoring the hazy skies, Rose pulled out black sunglasses from her purse and crossed her arms stiffly, turning back around so she faced the brick wall.

Tim apparently remembered enough from Halloween night to identify her. "Hey, there," he greeted Rose's back. He waited a moment before pulling up a chair. Glancing around the patio, he asked, "Is Tori around?"

Rose offered a barely perceptible nod in the direction of the restrooms. "She'll be back in a sec."

"Cool." Tim shifted his weight and leaned back, taking in Rose's reticence. "Rose, right?" He pulled out a cigarette.

Rose grabbed the *Rip It Up* copy on the chair next to her and willed Tori to hurry up. She feigned sudden interest in a crass penciled image of the nearby bridge just outside the Hub's parking lot, right on Harbor Boulevard. Rose would recognize it and the "Welcome to Downtown Fullerton" lettering anywhere. But exactly how long would she have to fake-chat with this untrustworthy fool?

Tim removed his sunglasses and nodded at the zine in Rose's hands. "They have a good crew that works on that thing. If it lasts." Rose looked up at him for a second. True, she'd heard all sorts of rumors about the future of *Rip It Up*—it was getting bought, some random cornballs were taking over it, or it was just going to fizzle out on its own. Maybe Tim knew something she didn't, but Rose didn't want to give him the satisfaction of filling her in on something like that.

"Yeah." Rose dove back into the pages.

Tim looked like he was about to say something else but decided not to, instead puffing on his cigarette. He had a rugged, sort of handsome face, the kind that made Tori swoon—piercing eyes, some scruffy stubble, your typical scrappy Orange County tough boy. If he wasn't so shady, maybe Rose wouldn't be as reluctant to agree with her friend on his looks. Today his shaved head was covered with a black beanie, and he had the same vest with patches as on Halloween night. Rose recognized the Cadillac Tramps logo peeking out from underneath it but refrained from mentioning that she had the exact same shirt. That was too much undeserved encouragement for Mr. Can't Text Back.

He appeared to be getting the hint, anyway. "Think I'll check out the arcade real quick." Standing up, he asked, "Interested?" Clearly out of politeness.

"No, I'm good," Rose lied.

"If Tori comes back before I—"

"—don't worry, I'll let her know where you are." Rose finished him off.

"Thanks." He turned and headed into the Cold War Arcade next door.

In a few minutes, Tori returned to the patio alone, a disturbed look on her freshly powdered face. "Tim's inside, talking to *Doris*," she pressed the name in frustration. "He didn't even see me come out of the bathroom. He was that focused on her!"

"Shocking." Rose couldn't help it.

Pouting, Tori ran her fingers through her white-blonde pixie cut and sat down without saying anything. "Should I go in there and get him?" she huffed. "I mean, shouldn't Doris just be doing her job instead of..." She was clearly getting territorial.

Rose shrugged. "It's not her fault." Was Tori seriously twisting the blame onto Doris? "Everyone is into her."

A moment later, Tori stood up as Tim approached. "Tim!" she squealed excitedly. Any wrongdoing was instantly forgotten. Tim dropped a half-eaten cookie on the table before hugging her and spinning her around once. Tori shrieked with delight, her worries regarding Doris now nonexistent.

Pretty lovey-dovey for people who barely know each other, Rose thought as she looked away from the pair's showy affection. Tori hung on Tim's every word about his band's schedule (the reason why he was MIA lately) and their next show. Rose tried to look engaged, but Tori let her know she was failing as soon as Tim took a bathroom break.

"Dude, what's wrong with you?" Tori demanded, annoyance oozing through her elation. "You're not talking enough!"

Rose couldn't believe what she was hearing. Did Tori really expect her to worry about catering to Tim? Now?

"This may be shocking to you, but I'm not really in the mood for Tim," Rose retorted. "Not everything is about *Tim*, you know."

Tori's body turned rigid. "I never said that everything is about Tim!"

A sharp laugh escaped Rose's lips. "You don't have to. It's obvious."

"Are you worried about those old cowboys?" Tori's voice rose. "Or is it your family now? You know, Rose, I just don't know which one it's going to be with you lately!"

Rose felt like she'd just gotten slapped. "We just heard the most disturbing conversation, but suddenly that doesn't matter because—drop everything, everyone—Tim's here! This is exactly how you were on Halloween night!" Hadn't she overlooked enough from Tori lately?

"I didn't do anything wrong on Halloween! And you know what? Those cowboys are dealing with a horse that isn't yours. Just like that dog next door! What is it with you and other people's pets? You can't save them all—you're not their owner! It's not your place! And your parents, well, you're just going to have to suck it up with them!"

"I never said that I'm their owner. I'm their guardian." Rose stood up and pushed her chair back. She was so shocked and angry that she actually felt maniacally calm. "Ownership means nothing if you don't care. Have fun with your precious boyfriend."

16

I can't believe I wasted all that time babysitting Romeo and Juliet! Rose mentally kicked herself as Laguna Lake Riding Club appeared in the distance. The scent of the stables fueled her racing adrenaline.

Ethan's truck was parked out front. Although she really didn't know him well, she was slightly comforted by the sight of the old panels and rusted bumper. *He'll know what to do.* Or would he? Rose's head was spinning, and she wasn't sure of anything except that she needed to tell Ethan what she'd just overhead at the Hub *right now*. She eagle-eyed the grounds for any sign of him. A few people with their horses chatted near the mounting block, but he wasn't one of them.

Rose headed to the ring and released a small sigh of relief. There he was, riding a brawny blue roan. They were a handsome match, with Ethan's obviously expert skills astride the horse's commanding movements. The most amazing part was that the horse was completely tackless—Ethan loosely held a little mane just above the withers, and that was it. Captivated, Rose watched them canter an accurate figure eight, lead changes and all. They slowed to a walk when Ethan noticed Rose standing at the gate.

"Hey, Rose." He hopped off and walked to a nearby hitching post. "Really glad you're back."

"Me too," Rose murmured, eyes widening at how the horse just followed Ethan. "Who's he?"

"This is Tanner," Ethan grinned. He slipped a halter over Tanner's head. "My baby since his first day on earth."

"Wow, he's stunning. And obviously amazing." Rose was floored at their connection. And she hadn't even considered that Ethan would have raised a horse of his own. "I've never seen anyone ride here without tack! And he just follows you without a lead rope, too. Quarter horse, right?" A big Quarter horse butt like that was hard to miss.

"You got it. Yeah, he's good about no tack. We don't ride like that too often though. It's more about reminding him of the concept, and for me to get a different perspective." Ethan quickly checked each of Tanner's hooves. "Starla will sure like seeing you." He paused and faced Rose directly. "I apologize about the other day. I should've handled it better."

Rose shook her head. "Don't worry about it. As long as Starla's okay, it's fine. Look, I have to tell you something that—"

"I found out you brought her back," Ethan continued. "A couple of boarders saw and told me. Thanks for doing that."

"Don't mention it." Rose was sincere but eager to move on. "Now, I need to tell you something important. About Starla."

The seriousness in her voice got Ethan's attention. As they walked along the dirt path that wound around the property, Rose breathlessly explained the conversation she'd overheard at the Hub. The two men never said the word "slaughter," but it was too easy to read between the lines. "Then I rushed right over here to tell you," Rose finished, her voice shaking a little. Verbalizing the details of the two men's plan was downright painful.

Ethan was silent for a while. Tanner turned to some grass on the side of the path and began nibbling. "Did you recognize the guy with Murray? What did he look like?"

"Never saw him before. Guessing he was around Murray's age, maybe a little older? I didn't have the best view. I think his name was Don or something. Kind of a bigger guy, all decked out in a fancy shirt and cowboy hat, a little sunburned in the face. He might not be local, because I saw him go to the train station when they left." Rose tried to think of other details.

Ethan glared ahead. Tanner momentarily looked up at him from the grass before resuming his snack. "You go see Starla now. I'll meet you after I put Tanner back home."

Starla's earnest snorts were already familiar to Rose. The mare knew that if people walked past a certain point down the aisle, they were most likely headed for her.

Rose laughed when she saw Starla's head stretching far out over the stall door, intently watching her. Now that she was all cleaned up, her chestnut coat exuded a new sheen that really showed off her strong, noble frame. A petrifying vision of Starla being forced into a filthy trailer bound for somewhere over the border invaded Rose's head, and she struggled to kick it out. She hated when her imagination ran wild with the most disturbing images. She stepped inside Starla's stall and immediately wrapped her arms around the mare's neck.

When Ethan appeared, Rose could tell from his face that he was even more troubled than before.

"So…" She was desperate for a solution. "What do you think we should do?"

Ethan shook his head. "Hard to say. Not much we *can* do considering she's not—"

"Our horse," Rose finished his sentence with a tinge of impatience. "Yeah, I'm aware of that. But we can't just let her…you know…" she looked away, barely stopping herself from having a panic attack.

"Hey," Ethan sighed and briefly patted her shoulder. "Look, no horse should be put in this situation. But it happens all the time by people who don't care, one by one, down the line. A combination of greed, nonchalance, and plain evil."

Rose ran her fingers over Starla's nose. Just beneath her cute whiskers, the skin felt softer than velvet, almost like Rose was touching whip cream vapor or something. Starla lowered her head, eyelids closing halfway.

Ethan stared at Starla's placid interaction and recalled his last conversation with the horse's previous owner. "No one can figure out why she suddenly changed—not even multiple vets. She used to be really friendly and quiet, always up for anything, any rider. But now…" he shrugged with a slight shake of his head, "She's most like her old self when you're around. When I give her treats, she's cool but still, like, 'whatever dude.' I mean, I'm not into those pony fairy tales or anything, but there's at least something going on with you two, candy or no candy."

A small smile broke through all of Rose's worries and stress. Being reminded of her vibing with Starla totally outshone everything else going on.

Stroking Starla's cheek, Rose closed her eyes. She leaned into Starla's neck and took in her scent. Starla exhaled and lightly licked her lips. As much as their friendship had blossomed in such a short amount of time, Rose knew she had to be realistic. Enjoying one another's company was cool, but a massive obstacle still stood between any future they potentially shared.

She wasn't sure how long they stood there together like that, just breathing.

I will make sure you're safe, Starla. That's a promise.

A potent warmth charged through Rose's rib cage and then steeped through her whole body.

Starla understood.

17

Lula May let out a prolonged, moaning yawn. She poured coffee into a red SAX mug, one of many gifts the posh gallery had sent when her *Insider* exhibition had first opened. That was more than two years ago.

Now that the gallery owners weren't even returning her calls, the mug was yet another reminder of just how badly she needed to revamp her career…and reputation. The silver spoon clinked against the sides of the mug as she swirled in a generous splash of hazelnut creamer. She could almost hear her personal trainer's daily admonition to avoid sugary frills. Maybe if she actually listened to his advice, she'd have a taut physique more like his other famous clients. But all that fitness and eating healthy just wasn't her thing.

"And who needs looks with this brain, right Royal?" Lula May asked her German Shepherd, who followed her into the dining room of their spacious Spanish-style home. Royal was probably hoping to jump into the car for a jaunt at the Silver Lake Reservoir, but Lula May really didn't have the time nor desire for exercising around the urban lake with hipsters today. The outdoors was not exactly her favorite concept.

Lula May hunkered down in front of her laptop at the marble table and took a long sip of liquid caffeine. Closing her eyes, she let out a long "ohm" and tried to ignore the relentless chirps from outside. *Hello?* Like, how was she supposed to relax with all those birds? This was a daily ritual that her therapist had suggested, but even with her pricey Beverly Hills-rates, the lady had never advised on how to deal with pesky interruptions from nature. So far, therapy wasn't helping Lula May forget the unfortunate mistake from last year. Some might call it a disaster.

The memory of her verbal gaffe during that important interview intruded her "ohm" again. Not a day had passed without Lula May remembering the appalled look on the *Times* reporter's face right after she'd uttered those ill-fated words. She had begged them not to publish the interview—and when that didn't work, *demanded* they hold back or else face legal consequences. Of course, none of that had worked, either. The daily onslaught of critical online conversations, nasty emails, unwanted calls, and random dirty looks even at the local grocery store was now a normal part of her life. Her parents spun it as "Just the price of being famous, dear."

Lula May really missed the East Coast, but this part of Hollywood was actually much more peaceful. And, interestingly, a lot of regular people didn't really seem to care about her all that much in Los Angeles. It was unclear if that was because they didn't recognize her or if they were simply avoiding her.

Sheila, her manager, insisted she not worry. Either way, a big floppy hat was pretty much a requirement when going out for errands these days. Heckling scared her. On the bright side, though, Lula May now owned a large house complete with a nice yard and two-car garage, things she'd only experienced back home when visiting relatives in the suburbs.

Of course, her parents' privileged lifestyle—her father was a banking mogul and her mother a successful abstract painter—was still totally accessible to her. She visited them as often as she could. While they were supportive of her move to Los Angeles, they would never, ever leave their luxurious penthouse. "Everywhere else is for hicks," they often joked.

In a lot of ways, Lula May agreed with them. Her old home was the center of the universe that no other place could ever compete with. And for a while, it was her urban domain in which she reigned queen—her perfect safe space—especially after all the glowing praise that *Insider* received in the art scene. She was grateful for her family's extensive media contacts, but there was no way she could credit social connections for her own success. She had earned it.

Lula May was on top of the world. For a while.

Then, like a wild nightmare suddenly invading heaven, she gave an interview. *The* interview. It was one of many, but there may as well have only been one because it was all people seemed to remember about her exhibition, her work...her whole being. Who knew that some careless statements about class and race in America would have such outrageous repercussions?

The bearded guy standing behind her favorite bread booth at

the weekend Farmer's Market. The receptionist at her spa who always smelled like cigarettes. Even one of the neighborhood dog walkers and her pack of wagging tails and twisted leashes. Was it her imagination, or did anything with a heartbeat all of a sudden couldn't stand the sight of her? Maybe if her assistant (at the time) hadn't forgotten to pick up that extra coffee she'd requested that morning, Lula May wouldn't have been so hungover. That stupid oversight had clearly affected her alertness and overall communication during that dumb interview!

"Stupid political correctness." Lula May slightly jumped and looked around before remembering that she was alone. Whew. Her posture relaxed back into a gentle slump as she scanned her emails. Of course, she would never repeat those words in public. She was keenly aware of how people assumed her life was all about entitlement. Even if it was true, was it really her fault? Regardless, since the interview fiasco, Sheila had instructed her a thousand times to never touch political subjects again.

"It's just not your area, babe," Sheila explained during one of their many emergency phone calls. "Don't worry. Now that you've locked down your social media accounts, we'll put out a huge PR blitz that'll cover all of this up—make people forget. For the most part."

Starla was indirectly a small part of Sheila's work-in-progress scheme. Her manager had originally suggested Lula May look into getting involved at a big animal charity or something similar. "Everyone loves animals. It'll be a great look for you," she instructed. Lula May considered herself an animal lover, too, even though she usually couldn't stand smaller dogs or any cats at all. Or birds. Fish and hamsters were questionable.

Lula May skipped over the many emails from strangers, most of them with scathing subjects like "You're a Disgrace" or simply "I Hate You." Some of them, like the one that began with "Your Amazing Art," seemed safe until she actually opened and read it. At this point, she was pretty accustomed to reading about how disgusting and shameful of a person she was and how she gave all women a terrible look.

Things got so difficult at one point that Sheila had advised her to consider a humble public apology.

"Never," Lula May had answered breezily. "I don't do apologies."

A few more scrolls on her computer and Lula May knew she just had to let out some steam.

Reaching over for her trusty beige hand towel, Lula May held it up tightly to her heated, reddening face. Sprawled on the oval maroon dog bed, Royal barely cocked his ears, unfazed by the routine scream into the muffling fabric.

"Those nobodies!" Lula May gasped a few seconds later, sulking to the kitchen to hunt down the new package of brownies she'd been eyeing all morning. Her trainer would kill her if he knew this was her first meal of the day—but he wasn't the one getting harassed all the time, so who was he to judge?

As gooey chocolate melted all over the insides of her mouth, Lula May returned to the table and focused her attention on today's goal. On the side of her computer screen, a yellow sticky note stared back at her with the scribble: *Strategize!!!* It was a reminder to figure out what was hot, what she should do as a creative figure—whatever it took to get back on track. She had more talent in her big toe than anybody's entire portfolio. In fact, at a family dinner when she was only eight years old, her esteemed architecture critic uncle had literally told her that she was artistically gifted.

Research time. Lula May quickly clicked people's names into her expectant browser. She had a hate-love relationship with the Internet. Hate, since (besides how it was screwing up her traditional and reliable media support system) most people online seemed to severely dislike her and made it very known every single day. In fact, she had abandoned her online activity for what felt like ages, strictly allowing herself a peek at her accounts once or twice a week. With all the abuse, that was the maximum her therapist allowed. Once she got Starla, she cautiously began posting updates again. How else would she get credit for saving some animal? The newspapers that used to hound her for pieces didn't even reply to her emails anymore. A lot of the vitriol had simmered down, but plenty was leftover and would probably always be around to some extent. And though she still had a lot more followers than most users on a given platform—two of her recent posts actually went pretty viral—ultimately, Lula May couldn't deny that she had been effectively "canceled."

The Internet did serve a critical purpose, however, no matter what people thought of her. A plethora of new and amazing ideas were all over it, just waiting to be absorbed…concepts she would have *never* conjured up on her own. The online world was an absolute goldmine in that way.

"Just saw this interview with that no-wave gal—what's her name again? Kind of got me thinking," Sheila quipped one evening after returning from a business trip to London. "You know, Lydia Lunch?"

"Huh?" Lula May asked, deadpan. Sheila's references were

often nothing but total mysteries to her.

"Never mind," Sheila dismissed, jet lagged. "Anyway, she's calling out celebrities who rip off ideas from the underground and use them for their own mainstream platforms. Pretty interesting stuff."

All it took were a few initial online searches. Once Lula May got beyond the most obvious search terms and their generic results, she started getting the hang of what Sheila was suggesting. As her searches got deeper and more specific, Lula May unearthed tons of people with tastes and lifestyles and talents that frankly surprised her and made her a little envious, even. They were all strangers, many of them younger and none of them remotely famous like her, but so much of what they shared with the world was perfect fodder for the taking. Like, inspiration. Lula May never used the word *copy*. It was simply a part of being an open artist and a busy celebrity. How did the saying go…"bad artists copy, great artists steal"? She always forgot to look up who originally came up with that. Anyway, none of her peers admitted to spying and stealing from people, so why should she?

During her expansive online exploration of Southern California locals, it took less than an hour before her random clicks led her to Laguna Lake Riding Club. While searching profiles into the night, she'd stumbled upon Ethan's fascinating account, which brimmed with his impressive and intriguing life filled with horses. He was pretty cute, too. Definitely potential boyfriend material.

"Awesome idea!" Sheila yelled on speakerphone the very next day after Lula May explained her spontaneous plan to acquire a horse. "Lula May saves a horse from becoming a bowl of dog chow—*genius!*"

Lula May never actually liked horses. Growing up, she'd always hated the piles of stinky poops that tourist carriages plopped in their wake along the streets, but she agreed that it was a great look for her critically wounded career.

Too bad getting a horse had ended up being much more of a hassle than she had ever anticipated.

She surveyed the latest photos on Ethan's account. His newest update was an image of a dark blackish-gray horse. He posted that same horse often, so Lula May didn't bother reading the caption. Ethan actually had a decent number of followers, considering he was a complete unknown. Impressive. She clicked on his friend list. The most recent addition was a girl named Rose Moon.

Lula May spent the next few minutes on Rose's page. She remembered her from the barn—some quiet Asian American chick who didn't even look like she could order a martini. Until just recently, Lula May had no clue that Orange County wasn't all lily-white. The few times she'd even heard about the place, that was exactly how it was described.

Most of Rose's photos showed the local music scene. Lula May didn't know a thing about that world, though some of her younger acquaintances had recently mentioned it was part of a cool, under-the-radar area. She had initially dismissed them. How could some suburb of Los Angeles be remotely cool? Weird photos of rough-edged bands filled the screen as she scrolled. The latest from Rose's account was from a few days ago, a serene photo of the entrance to Laguna Lake Riding Club.

Lula May immediately memorized the girl's screen name and bookmarked the profile in both her laptop and phone. Surely this kid would post some interesting ideas that could be utilized.

Technically, she should be flattered that someone famous actually finds her interesting, Lula May beamed smugly.

A Celine Dion tune from her phone abruptly broke the silence. "Hello, Lula May? Ethan from Laguna Lake Riding Club."

Lula May stiffened for a moment. What an eerie coincidence to get a call from Ethan just now. As if he might see her computer screen through the phone, she closed her laptop and stood up.

"Hi, there," Lula May swallowed a mouthful of coffee and settled in a dining room chair at the other end of the table. "What's going on? Did Starla attack someone else today?" She rolled her eyes at the thought of the problem horse she was stuck with. After paying Murray's hospital bill, she'd told him to get rid of Starla as quickly and quietly as possible. She could easily find another hobby that wasn't so much trouble.

Ethan was all business. "No, Starla's been great, actually. I'm calling to let you know about my schedule the next few weeks—"

Lula May sighed, her nails drumming the tabletop along with her shaking leg underneath. Starla sure had seemed fun in the beginning, but the horse was much more of an expensive inconvenience now. It didn't want to be ridden or even groomed, and misbehaving with Murray was pretty much the last straw. Besides, Lula May had already received public kudos for "saving" a horse. It was time to move on.

"I guess Murray hasn't called you about it yet." Lula May figured she might as well explain. "I'm getting rid of Starla."

"What? Already?" Ethan's voice filled with concern.

Lula May bristled with a smudge of irritation. She'd only told a few inner circle friends about her plans for Starla, and a couple of them had responded with the same worried tone.

"Yes, *already*." Lula May said in her firmest voice, the one she usually reserved for insubordinate staff. "It's useless. I can't ride it. What's the point of keeping it, then?" She took another quick sip of coffee before Ethan could interject. "And then it practically kills my trainer. I don't want something like that. In fact, I should complain to the sellers. They sold me a lemon!" She slammed her coffee mug on the table, warm splashes of brown splattering over the hard surface.

"Starla's owners—previous owners—they're good horse people," said Ethan.

Lula May scoffed. "Yeah, right. Then why did I have to punch her when she—" She pressed her lips tight. That was close. She had never told anyone, not even her therapist, about her first time alone with Starla. That horse had deserved the hard whack on the face, but Lula May doubted that Ethan would understand.

"What?"

"You're cutting out," Lula May said the first thing that came to mind, hoping he didn't catch her accidental disclosure. "You were saying?"

Ethan went on explaining why a horse wouldn't behave perfectly under all circumstances. Lula May couldn't help but let out a few dramatic huffs of frustration. She was in no mood for excuses. Was he really trying to cover up for some dumb horse?

"Okay, then," Ethan paused. "How about leasing her to someone? I'm sure we can help you find a good match."

As Ethan explained the concept of leasing out a horse, Lula May scowled at the floor-to-ceiling palm tree sculpture by the dining room wall, a pricey "never mind the critics" present from her father. "Ethan, I really don't have time to deal with something ongoing like that. Starla just isn't the right horse for me. I know I haven't really tried it out for myself yet, but honestly, I'm not interested anymore. Besides, Murray can handle everything else just fine. He's got plenty of connections at auctions and stuff." She chomped off another chunk of brownie. This was really none of Ethan's business, but she was used to prying people. Maybe he had nothing better to do than to get involved in the affairs of the one celebrity boarder he had ever known.

"Here me out," Ethan replied cautiously. "When a horse goes to auction, you never know where they might end up. It actually gets pretty dangerous for them very quickly. Look, we can help you find a real buyer."

Chewing the chocolate morsels, Lula May pondered his words. Clearly, he was insinuating that Starla could end up in the wrong hands, and she assumed that meant being killed in some way. But wasn't that the typical path most livestock went down, anyhow? Maybe it was unfortunate, but she'd much rather Starla completely disappear than have the media discover her failed plan. The last thing Lula May wanted was to look like a deadbeat or an insensitive opportunist who'd simply used the horse. She just couldn't afford another ding on her social record.

On the other hand, if word did somehow get out that she'd sold Starla to an abusive or fatal situation, she'd be permanently labeled something even worse. No amount of Sheila's slick public relations would ever mend that damage. From every angle Lula May viewed the situation, it was pretty much a lose-lose for her.

"I shouldn't have bought it," Lula May thought aloud. She massaged her eyes with her index finger and thumb. "I just didn't see all this coming." A few crumbs tumbled off her chin onto the floor.

"Don't think that way, Lula May," Ethan replied. "Look, I think Starla has a lot of potential. Really. She just needs a little work. Like a refresher course."

"Really?" Lula May's eyebrows shot up with doubt. "Do you even know that Starla totally gave Murray a concussion? The hospital bill wasn't exactly cheap. The way I see it, Starla owes me some money." She returned to her laptop and opened the screen to her inbox. If Ethan was trying to drag her into a longer drawn-out scenario with Starla, she would have to end this conversation quickly.

"I know that was scary for Murray—and you, of course," Ethan added. "But Murray was pushing her way too much, and Starla hasn't exhibited anything like that since." Pause. "How about we make another plan?"

"Like what?" Lula May stared at a new email that accused her of being a "hipster racist."

"If we can retrain Starla, you keep her here at Laguna Lake Riding Club. What do you say?"

Lula May narrowed her eyes. "Who's 'we'?"

"Me and Rose. You met her the other day, remember? Starla really likes her. She's actually super cool with Rose," Ethan answered, sounding upbeat.

Rose Moon. Lula May bristled, but let Ethan's offer sink in. Maybe it would actually be convenient for her work schedule to let those two deal with Starla for now. That way, she could prepare for her next project without getting dragged down with horse problems in the meantime.

"Couldn't hurt to try," Ethan pressed. "If you change your mind, we'll call the whole thing off. You're the boss."

Lula May nodded to herself. Yes, she was the boss. And the more she thought about it, the more his suggestion sounded like a fair option for her. At least for a little while.

"Fine," Lula May slowly agreed. "But only if you guys get Starla back to perfect before my next exhibition. After that, she's in Murray's hands."

18

"Tanner's riding English today?"

Ethan looked up at the half-teasing voice. It was Gertrude, a longtime boarder, on her way to the cross ties. She raised an eyebrow at the English lesson saddle with accompanying pad and girth in his arm.

"Unfortunately, no," Ethan joked. He had gladly ignored the untouched saddle in the tack room that Lula May had proudly brought on her first day there. It was adorned with distracting and gaudy decorations and he was secretly relieved it remained out of sight, collecting dust.

Rose and Starla were already at the ring. Starla kept her head close to Rose's shoulder as they entered the gate.

They both look nice and relaxed, Ethan observed. *So, do I disturb the peace now or later?* He hadn't forgotten Lula May's slip up during their last conversation. She probably thought that he hadn't heard, but he did. Lula May had hit Starla—at least once. It all actually made sense now. No wonder the mare didn't like the woman. He would tell Rose soon enough, but one thing at a time. He first had to reacquaint Starla with the basics to get her confidence back. She was definitely an educated horse, so Ethan was counting on her cooperation to kick in sooner rather than later.

"Don't worry," said Ethan. Rose was already warily eyeing a black lunge line and whip on a nearby table. He knew he didn't have to explain how the whip was just a visual cue, but the ugly incident with Murray was probably making a guest appearance in her head, too. "I'd never treat Starla the way he did." Force and disrespect were the opposite of expertise. Murray had proven himself a pseudo-horseman.

"You read my mind." Rose's gaze settled with relief. "So how much time do you have before..." she trailed off.

"*We* have about a month," Ethan emphasized. Though Rose was nothing close to a professional trainer, Ethan was experienced enough to know how helpful it could be to have a calming companion nearby for such an edgy personality.

"That'll go by quick," Rose replied. "Well, let me know what you want me to do."

"Just observe," Ethan said. "That's good enough for now."

After securing the lunge line onto Starla's halter ring, Ethan carefully went through his usual steps with the mare. Starla started with a working walk, first tracking right. She was engaged and responsive.

"Good job, girl," Ethan called out as Starla agreeably broke into a collected trot. "Keep it going." He saw how Rose focused on every detail of the process, so Ethan made sure to go over what he was doing even if she already knew some of the explanations. "We have to practice everything going both ways. Horses compute things differently than we do. It's like they've got a brain for each direction."

"She's doing great!" Rose beamed, leaning over the rail excitedly.

"I'll give her that," Ethan replied, pleased that the mare had chosen to face him before turning. Starla continued in an engaged trot. Despite his usual default skepticism, he had to admit that this session was already going better than he'd anticipated.

When he wasn't starting horses back at home, Ethan had spent several years applying his personalized training methods to Tanner and many others. Almost all of them had ended up in great homes as trusted riding partners. But some of them just didn't seem to want that lifestyle, and Ethan had no problem letting them live out their lives as pasture buddies for those who needed a companion. To him, every horse had a role on this planet. His father had taught him that a respectful horse-human partnership—whether or not it involved riding—was the foundation for a mutually beneficial connection that was impossible to break if done right.

What made you change? Ethan wondered as Starla promptly responded to his signal for a canter. *Is this all because of Lula May, or is there more?*

Starla's old owners had fondly reminisced about their favorite trail rides around their property. According to them, Starla was always the first horse to meet them at the gate, as well as the horse who was the most excited about getting tacked up, even for lessons. "Kind of like a dog seeing her leash," was their exact quote. They had even shared some notes about Starla when she used to give rides to kids on her days off—Starla did it all with a bright, happy-go-lucky spirit.

"Too bad we'll never know what really happened to her," Rose reflected, her eyes locked on Starla's every move.

"We actually might." Ethan watched Starla complete her circle and then slightly closed his fingers. Starla immediately slowed and took a few steps toward him in the center of the round pen.

Rose blinked at him. "What do you mean?"

Ethan quickly relayed his recent phone conversation with Lula May. Even though he kept his delivery as neutral as possible, the shock on Rose's face was undeniable even before he finished.

"Punch?" Rose repeated. "She *punched* Starla?"

"Her words, unfortunately," Ethan replied. "I'm not saying that's the only culprit of Starla's complete one-eighty, but it sure didn't do any good. Either way, at least we know a little more background...you okay?" Rose suddenly looked distracted, like she was remembering something.

"I'm fine." Rose snapped back to attention. "Let's just continue."

The afternoon air rapidly swirled into dusk. Harsh, dry gusts picked up as Starla worked in tandem with the sun lowering in the sky. She didn't seem bothered by the random bucket that teetered off a nearby plastic chair, nor was she fazed when the wind skidded the same chair over on its side in plain sight. Everything Ethan asked her to do, Starla completed with an air of pleasant certainty.

"I have to say, she looks amazing. Good job, teacher—Starla and I both learned a lot today." Rose glanced at her phone and hopped off the rail as Ethan unclipped the lunge line. "I should be heading home."

"One last thing," Ethan handed Rose the lead rope.

"You're going to ride her?" Rose asked. Her eyes sparkled as she watched him get the nearby saddle.

"We'll see how it goes. First, I'll saddle her up, see how she reacts." Ethan gently laid the quilted saddle pad on Starla's back. Starla didn't flinch. Ethan patted her rump, reassuring her the way mares nudge their little foals from behind.

So far, so good, Ethan thought. He lowered the saddle squarely over the pad and buckled the girth, purposely going extra slowly. Even unflappable Tanner didn't appreciate a rushed girth buckling.

Starla looked behind at him for a split second, paused, then turned back around.

"Good girl," Rose reassured her, scratching under her mane. "She seems more than okay so far."

"We'll see." Ethan stepped back and appraised Starla's stance. "Think I'll get the bridle now. You have some extra time? Won't take long."

Rose nodded eagerly, still holding the lead rope. Go home now or stay a little longer with Starla? That was an easy one.

Ethan made a beeline to the tack room and quickly returned with a bridle. He unbuckled and removed the halter before gingerly holding the bit just below Starla's mouth. Starla instantly cooperated by lowering her head. She deliberated for only a moment before separating her lips. Ethan barely had to nudge his thumb in the corner of Starla's mouth to position the bit right in.

"What a polite girl," Ethan praised as he tucked Starla's ears and slid the headpiece over. "You know, Murray had trouble putting this on the very first time, too. You should've seen that."

"I'm glad I didn't," Rose muttered. "Isn't that Murray guy some hotshot trainer? Somehow I doubt that Lula May would hire him if he wasn't."

Ethan tried not to stir. "I've never heard of him."

Starla chewed the bit, her head and neck loose, and stood quiet.

A certain spark lit in Ethan's gut. It was the sensation he always got just before mounting a green horse for the first time. Starla wasn't green by any means, but Ethan empathized with her recent ordeal. She deserved fair communication and kindness. Every horse did.

Ethan took in her disposition. Soft and engaged.

"Let's go for it," Ethan decided firmly. It might as well be today since everything else had gone so well.

Rose's eyebrows shot up. "Great!"

Ethan lifted his knee and set foot in the stirrup. Starla took a few steps forward, reacting to the human on her side. Ethan hopped once, then swung his other leg over and gently lowered himself into the saddle. Starla turned her head to get a look at her new rider, then lurched forward a few steps.

Ethan shifted back. Not a surprise. She calmed to a slow walk and he slackened the reins to the buckle. After she continued a walk at that pace for a bit, Ethan quietly pressed his legs for a trot.

Rose admired the two as they passed. They already looked synced. Riding obviously came second nature to Ethan, even when things took an unexpected turn.

Ethan urged Starla into a canter. Immediately he was impressed by how smoothly the mare moved with him. They went around once, twice. The first canter with a horse always reminded him of the first time he and Tanner cantered together, the day he knew he'd fully earned Tanner's trust and respect.

An unexpected bang fractured the air. Starla hopped and swerved to the side. Ethan quickly got her attention back and turned toward the parking lot.

Murray stood outside of his truck. A second slam quickly followed as a portly man climbed out of the passenger seat. They briskly approached as if about to conduct some high-level business.

"Hey!" Murray boomed, cupping his hands.

Without warning, Starla skittered to the side.

The two men chuckled as they stopped at the gate. They stood right next to Rose, ignoring her through their laughs.

"Better be careful. It doesn't seem to like you!" They erupted into obnoxious cackles.

Right when Starla looked like she was over it, she surprised Ethan with another lurch, then a tiny buck. Ethan easily leaned back into the motion, muscle memory flowing from the many times he'd sat on horses specifically bred to fling off anything from their backs. This was no big deal.

The two men mocked applause, howling with glee.

"What do you want?" Ethan growled at them after Starla came to a halt.

"Sorry, dude," Murray grinned. "Just wanted to bring my friend to check out the selection."

"Are you guys alright?" Rose approached Ethan and Starla as calmly as she could.

"We're fine," Ethan replied, still facing the two men. "What 'selection' are you talking about? And who are you?" he demanded to Murray's companion.

"I'm the guy who's gonna take that horse off your hands. But you can call me Don."

"Like hell you are," Ethan countered.

Rose chimed in. "Starla isn't for sale."

Murray threw Rose a fleeting, withering glance. Paying her any mind was obviously a waste of his time. "Is that right, missy?" He turned back to Ethan and firmly tapped Starla's hindquarters. She shuddered under his touch. "Lula May called and told me all about your little idea. Didn't think much of it then, and now—well, seeing how this nag ain't worth a dime—"

"It'll be better when we take the dumb stinker off your hands," Don interrupted. "Plenty of broomtails in this world with manners."

"Get out of here," Ethan retorted. It was always bad news

when people spoke of horses this way. "Now."

They didn't acknowledge him as they surveyed Starla. She stood there quietly, but when Don ran his hand over her croup, Ethan saw her body tense.

"That's enough!" Ethan snapped, guiding Starla away. "Like we said, she isn't for sale."

The men snickered.

"Yet!" Murray bellowed at their backs, elbowing Don. "It isn't for sale *yet.*"

19

"Where have you been?"

Rose jumped. She didn't notice that her mom and dad were near the side of the foyer when she walked through the front door.

"Just with Tori." She slipped off her boots, grateful that her parents seemed more preoccupied with rearranging furniture. Milo stood on his hind legs, sniffing wildly around her pants.

Rose's dad looked up from behind a loveseat. "What's that on your pants?"

"Not sure." Rose glanced down. She should've done a way better job at shaking off. Riding horses wasn't necessary to get dusty from the barn. Sometimes all it took was some walking around the place. "I'll change right now."

Without risking a closer inspection, Rose dashed up the staircase, Milo bounding after her. Her brain was still reeling from what Ethan had revealed about Lula May.

Late afternoon sunlight spilled from her parents' bedroom windows onto the hallway floor. When she got to her room, she blindly changed into a fresh pair of leggings and her favorite "Mommy's Little Monster" sweatshirt. The notebook with the horse drawing was still on her desk, reminding her of that vivid, mid-doodle flash of Starla getting hit. It was like a shocking movie clip. She felt crazy for even having that visual. She hadn't told anybody yet about it yet. How could she explain seeing something like that? And Ethan basically confirming it took the freakiness to a completely new level. What was happening?

She carefully coiled her clothes into a tight ball and stuffed them in the bottom of her laundry hamper. Yup, they smelled like the barn. If her parents even got a whiff, who knew how they'd react? She really couldn't risk her visits with Starla now.

The intro track of *First and Last and Always* played in the background as Rose stretched out on her bed. Milo immediately took advantage of her position by standing on her chest and covering her laughing face in wet kisses.

A bubbly, familiar voice drifted from outside. Peeking through the window blinds, Rose spied on Claudia tiptoeing to kiss a tall, lanky guy with long brown hair. They both wore denim jackets with a big symbol on the back, but Rose couldn't decipher what it was. The guy definitely wasn't that loser Marvin, and he looked nothing like Chris, Claudia's ex from just a couple of years back. Chris was from the South Bay, and he'd always been pretty cool with everything having to do with Claudia. Waiting hours for her to get ready to go out, letting Rose and Tori tag along with them to see Morrissey at the Hollywood Bowl—no problem. He'd even made sure the two young girls didn't get roughed up while paying for t-shirts when overzealous fans raided one of the merch tables during that sold-out show. Too bad Claudia eventually got bored of him and moved on.

Yawning, Rose retreated to bed. Her parents couldn't stand it if they ever found her napping. They considered it lazy, especially if she'd just supposedly spent the day having fun. Naps were only tolerated after all-nighters for school, and even then, just begrudgingly. But a heavy wave of fatigue was hitting her hard.

Just ten minutes, she promised herself. She covered her face with a pillow, but it wasn't any use. Every time she closed her eyes, she saw—and felt—that secret glimpse of Starla.

Someone briskly knocked on the door before entering. Her mother was holding something.

"Look what I found." A familiar piece of brown leather dangled in the air.

"Whoa, the bracelet from Moose!" Rose scrambled upright.

"It's still in good condition. Found it while we were cleaning out the downstairs closet." Her mom smiled. Before Rose could say anything else, the door closed behind her.

Rose's fingers grazed over the slightly frayed edges and each hand-engraved dip in the leather. Moose, a burly former biker gang member, was a neighbor during their short stint in Ohio. He had striking blue eyes that appeared even brighter against his sun beaten skin. Long hair, mustache and beard, always in worn denim and leather boots—he was hard to forget. Despite their obvious differences, Moose and Rose's father somehow became friends. On random humid summer nights, Moose would pull up to the house on his big motorcycle, which was always exciting for Rose. As he and her dad shared some cold beers on the front porch, she would quietly hang out on the other end of the stoop, eavesdropping while weaving dandelion necklaces and marveling at the swarms of flickering fireflies. When the neighborhood kids congregated with their glass jars to catch the glowing bugs, Rose would always decline their invite if Moose was around—that's how interesting and fun he was.

Even back then, Rose always questioned her mom about why the two men were friends. Why would someone like Moose want to hang out with her dad—or even on their front porch, for that matter? Most folks in the area seemed to want nothing to do with them.

"Because they're both different from everyone else," her mom had replied simply. "This area is very traditional for Moose, even though he's from here. He said most people don't feel comfortable around him. That's why he likes talking with Dad."

On their last day in Ohio, Moose stopped by in the early morning to see them off. The rumbling of his motorcycle sent Rose racing out to the driveway as usual. Outside the big moving van, Moose hugged her parents and gave Rose a silent smile, showing her the leather bracelet he'd made special for her. He loved carving leather almost as much as motorcycles. Although Rose was relieved to move back to California, it was near impossible to hold back tears while watching him shrink from the backseat window as they drove down Simpson Lane for the very last time.

Rose wrapped the bracelet on her narrow wrist. Her name, carved in old English style lettering and surrounded by flowers and elegant curlicues, looked even more striking now. It fit perfectly after she adjusted the ties. She reached for her books and laptop. Might as well try and get some homework done. For an extra boost, she pulled open her top dresser drawer. Half of it was filled with socks and underwear, and the other half held her small collection of crystals. Selenite, citrine, lapis lazuli, malachite, smoky quartz. The carved mala bracelet her parents got for her from a mountaintop Korean Buddhist temple was also in there. It was one of her most treasured items, so she rarely wore it. Rose picked the reddish orange swirled carnelian, sliding the smooth egg shape in the palm of her hand.

As soon as she finished the draft, Rose took a breather to check her emails. The title of her essay would come to her soon enough. Starla was back on her mind. Rose wasn't sure if that would ever *not* be the case.

Humming, she scrolled down the screen. A message from

Chelsea caught her eye.

> *Subject: Your article*
> *Rose,*
> *Thank you for submitting your article to The Tribute on the art show at Nebula Records. It has been accepted and will be published in the next issue in the "Local Arts" section.*
> *-Chelsea*

Rose had practically forgotten about her submission. Grimacing, she stared at the generic message from her bully of a classmate. What a fake.

20

"Guess I missed a bunch of weekend drama," Cameron chided Rose and Tori as they headed to their classrooms on Monday morning.

The girls grinned at each other, slightly sheepish. As soon as Rose climbed into Tori's car that morning, Tori apologized to Rose about their Saturday lunch at the Hub. The girls squabbled once in a while, but so far always made amends quickly afterward.

"Ha, ha. How was the wedding?" Rose asked. Cameron's journalist cousin had just married her arborist fiancé in Santa Barbara over the weekend.

Cameron finished off a long swig of coffee. Today it smelled a lot like dark chocolate. "It was alright. Long ceremony, open bar, all that stuff. First problem started at the rehearsal dinner the night before—our cousin Cara, remember, from up north? She got hammered! Everyone could hear her shrieking and slurring from her corner table, even during the old folks' speeches."

Rose rolled her eyes. "Ugh, I hate weddings."

"And get this—the next day, before the actual ceremony, Cara actually stands in front of the bride and groom during the group photos. The photographer had to physically move her to the side!" Cameron continued incredulously as Rose and Tori cracked up. "I tried to say something, but what's the point, you know?" He made a wry face. "Then, at the reception, she spilled wine all over herself—at least that was funny. Of course, she blamed the wine glasses for being a certain shape or something."

"Classy," Tori drawled, shaking her head. "What is it about weddings that bring out the worst in people?"

Or funerals, Rose thought silently.

"Like, can't you just enjoy your free meal with some

composure?" Tori continued. "Anyway, see you guys later." She waved and headed across the quad toward her classroom.

"I seriously can't believe you're training a celebrity's horse!" Cameron exclaimed as they continued down the crowded hallway. He was already filled in on the details about Starla. Lowering his voice a notch, he added, "Poor horse, though—do you think she'll be alright?"

"I think so," Rose replied. "She's doing so much better. But really, I'm just helping out. Ethan's doing all of the real work. There's no way I could do what he does."

"What's up with this mystery man, by the way?" Cameron inquired teasingly. "Anything going on there, hmm?"

Before Rose could reply, a smattering of hoots and hollers erupted behind them, accompanied by a familiar loud rolling noise that echoed off the corridor walls.

"What's up, Brody?" Cameron muttered as a group of guys whizzed by on skateboards. One of them tapped him on the shoulder. They didn't care that skateboarding was banned at school. When the narcs weren't looking, speeding down the big slope in the middle of campus was just too tempting.

"So, he's back." Rose watched as the group reached the end of the hallway, scooped up their skateboards, and triumphantly strutted off amid whistles and claps from amused onlookers. Brody's white cast and sling didn't seem to faze him in the least as he half-raised both arms like a warrior returning from battle.

Cameron shrugged. He didn't say anything. He just stared straight ahead.

It wasn't even two months ago since it happened. Brody and Marcus drove down to Huntington Beach one Saturday afternoon. On their way home, they crossed paths with some day-drinking driver who ran a red light near Pacific Coast Highway. Brody was fortunate enough to walk away from the totaled vehicle with a broken arm. But Marcus spent a few days in the hospital before succumbing to his injuries. Something about internal bleeding and blunt trauma to the head, they said. The sudden death shook up the entire school, which wasn't accustomed to heavy media attention outside of perfect SAT scores and record Ivy League admissions.

Cameron and Marcus were once best friends. Marcus used to come over to Cameron's house to skateboard all the time, since his own parents hated skateboarding with a passion. He couldn't even begin to count how many hours they must've spent on his driveway, just messing around on their boards until sunset. Eventually, Marcus got just about as skilled as Cameron already was. Sometimes Cameron still wondered why they drifted apart. Maybe it was because Marcus had gotten so sucked into Brody's rowdy social circle when they all started high school. Cameron had nothing against those guys, but he just didn't find them all that interesting. With Marcus now gone, Cameron would never know the reason why they went their separate ways. Not that it really mattered anymore.

Rose nudged Cameron gently. They were now standing right in front of his classroom door.

He blinked and quickly returned to attention. "Sorry," he stammered. "Kind of spaced out for a sec. See you at break." He shoved his conflicted thoughts about Marcus to the back of his head and made his way to his desk.

The truth was, Brody had never dared to bomb that long downward corridor slope until Marcus had shown him and everyone else at school. Over the years, that slope had somehow morphed into Brody's domain. Funny, considering the guy had originally entered Coyote Hills High as a hardcore Rollerblader. But with Marcus as a blueprint, Brody quickly learned to cast aside his "tootboots" (Marcus' reference) in favor of a skateboard.

Cameron couldn't help but smirk to himself as he always did whenever he pictured that first day of freshman year.

It was early morning before the bell had rung. Marcus was inches behind him, weaving through the crowded hall of blurry students with surprised or approving grins, balancing on his own board at top speed with utter glee. A walkie-talkie narc in a school golf cart whizzed after both of them, desperately trying to catch up to send the boys to the principal's office.

Nobody else seemed to remember that.

21

"Where's Starla?"

Rose didn't expect to see Ethan at the cross ties on her way to Starla's stall. Tanner stood quietly while Ethan cinched the girth by a notch. A tall black bay stood next to them, already groomed and tacked up.

"Hello to you, too," Ethan joked. He slid his fingers under the girth to check its hold before moving on to Tanner's bridle. "You okay with joining us on a trail ride before we get to Starla? Nice day for a little outing."

A trail ride? So that was why Ethan had the two horses tacked up. Rose had contemplated her bizarre vision of Starla all day at school and had assumed the rest of her afternoon would entail watching Starla and Ethan work in the ring while she sat safely on the sidelines. She fidgeted with the brown paper bag clutched in her hand. The night before, Rose had baked a tray of horse cookies from the same recipe that Fender used to love so much. She couldn't wait to see if Starla liked them, too.

"I...I haven't ridden in a really long time." Almost as if apologizing, Rose stammered the first thought that came to mind, then motioned down at her clothes. Even though she sensed that getting back in the saddle was inevitable, an actual ride was the last thing she had anticipated for today. "I mean, I'm not even dressed properly." She couldn't remember taking a single lesson without breeches, paddock boots, and her favorite half chaps.

Ethan half-scoffed. "Horses don't care what you're wearing. Just grab a helmet from the tack room. I have to take Anya out before dark. You can ride Tanner. He'll take care of you for sure..." He finally noticed her silence. "But no worries if you're not comfortable."

Rose pursed her lips and contemplated Tanner's sweet, placid expression. How could she think she could spend all this time with Starla and Ethan at her old barn and somehow not get back on a horse? Fender, Sandy. Mom and Dad. That one ride. Years of dreams that wouldn't let her forget. Whirling in a mental hurricane, conflicting thoughts pushed and pulled.

For nearly all of junior high and high school, Rose had tried to forget about Fender and riding. She always made sure to look the other way when driving by on Bastanchury Road, as if the sight of Laguna Lake Riding Club and any horse there would permanently blind her. Messages and chatter of lessons and shows from her old barn buddies were also meticulously avoided. It was just too depressing. Those girls eventually faded into casual acquaintances and then just blue, distant memories. She had tried so hard to forget. But some flames just keep flickering no matter how much wind blows.

"I'm up for it," said Rose. She disregarded her suddenly clammy palms with a small grin. Walking to the tack room, she offered a warning over her shoulder. "I'm pretty rusty, though."

About a dozen well-worn helmets, in different sizes and in no particular order, lined the tall wooden shelf in the back of the small room. They were mainly for beginner lesson students who hadn't yet committed to buying their own gear. Rose's old helmet was stashed in that box in her closet somewhere with all of her old riding clothes, horse books and stacks of horse sketches, but she couldn't remember the last time she'd seen it. Not that it mattered. Once you fall with a helmet on, you get a new one. That was the rule. She eyed the cleanest helmet that looked like her size and slid it on, but it was too large. Helmets had to fit just snug enough to actually protect the head but not squeeze so much to cause a headache. After trying on a couple more, she settled on a dusty navy blue one that felt pretty good.

Rose tried to steady her nervous hands as she twisted the adjustable dial in the back and clipped the strap under her chin. A small circular mirror was still nailed on the wall, right next to the saddle racks. Seeing herself in a helmet again was a trip. Even though she looked and felt older, the eyes in the reflection stared back as if she'd never left the place. Her whole face sparkled with anticipation. Taking deep breaths like she used to before each ride, Rose counted imaginary strides and pictured her and Fender cantering toward the first jump.

You're just helping Ethan! Rose snapped out of her daydream. *Which means you're helping Starla.* Determination instantly swelled inside her at the thought of Starla.

"He likes 'em long and loose." Ethan handed her Tanner's reins when Rose met him back outside.

Rose attempted her best "it's all good" nod as they led the horses to the wooden mounting block near the round pen. Stepping to the top, she was relieved to look down and see Ethan standing close to Tanner's side. *Don't hesitate—just get on.* She swung her right leg over the saddle and slowly lowered herself. Sinking into her heels as much as her boots allowed, she took in her immediate environment—Tanner's head, neck, the reins— then turned her gaze to Ethan.

"Looking good," Ethan smirked and petted Tanner's withers. "Even in a Western saddle."

Couch potatoes! As Rose watched Ethan mount Anya, the relic of a phrase appeared in her head. It was one of many snooty labels used by some of her old barn mates who liked to sneer at Western riding. Rose was never quite sure why they did. It always just made her feel bad for the horses involved. Sometimes on barn chore days, they even made fun of Rose's black and turquoise cowgirl boots, a Christmas gift from her parents that she'd spent weeks dropping hints for. The teasing was usually all in good fun, so Rose brushed it off every time. Now as a nervous re-rider, the Western saddle's deep structured seat and protruding horn offered a certain amount of initial comfort. Still, contact through the darn thing felt muffled compared to an English saddle—or was that just her paranoia? At any rate, it only fueled her rattling nerves.

"The stirrups feel long," Rose commented nervously.

"They're just right," Ethan replied. "Shall we?" He steered a chomping Anya around them and took the lead to the trails.

Rose swallowed hard. This autumn afternoon was a galaxy away from her "legs of steel" days. Maybe suddenly riding was a huge mistake, even if it was just a trail ride. What if Tanner spooked? Maybe switching horses would be better. Staring longingly at Anya's more familiar saddle, Rose wondered if she'd feel more secure in that. *Just chill out—you'd probably be sweating for the Western saddle if the situation was reversed.* It wasn't about the saddle at all. Ethan knew Tanner inside and out, and he also knew Rose's last ride was years ago. He wouldn't have her ride Tanner if he thought it'd be risky. Probably a good idea to let him handle Anya's high-strung strides, anyhow.

"Ready." Rose's mouth was so dry she barely heard herself answer. She switched reins to one hand and squeezed her legs. Once the insides of her calves pressed Tanner's barrel, Sandy's golden rule bubbled in her mind: *When riding, you have no right to think about anything except your horse's well-being.* Rose believed every word of the golden rule from the moment Sandy had uttered it during their first lesson. It made perfect sense. How could someone think about other things when such a majestic, powerful being—one who could kill you if they wanted—was allowing you to climb atop their back and then dictate where to go and how to move? Riding was such a privilege. Thinking of it in any other way was a disgrace.

Tanner responded to Rose's legs with a springy walk that any rider would be crazy not to appreciate. Was he always this perky, or was Anya's blue ribbon-strut just rubbing off on him? Rose loosened her hips to adjust to the gelding's eager steps. Stretching into the two-point position, she searched for a familiar leg stance. Ethan had guessed pretty well. The stirrups still felt long, but only because she was so used to them on the shorter side for jumping.

As they clip-clopped down the white fence-lined path, a warmth radiated in Rose's veins, tingling then fluttering with more intensity as they neared the trails. Thick green bushes of red, pink, and white roses softly swayed in the afternoon breeze. Autumnal sunlight cast a pale golden glow on everything in sight: the buckles of leather halters hanging outside the stalls, an assortment of poles and jumps in the main ring, a couple of bays led by their grooms, and Rusty, a petite brown barn cat lapping water from a silver bowl by the picnic bench.

Rose couldn't believe the sensation swelling in her chest. The ultimate. This was where she wanted to be. This was what she wanted to do. Nothing else even came close.

"Oh, no you don't," Ethan chuckled at Anya as she tried to munch on a bright pink bloom on the last rose bush right before the exit. She missed and tried again, triumphantly yanking off the odd snack and swallowing just as quickly.

"Anya always wants to eat roses, thorns and all," he said, shaking his head over his shoulder. "But she doesn't like peppermints. Go figure."

The path widened, and the white slats of the wooden fence came to an end on either side, replaced by wiry trees and dry brush. A bird's call echoed from somewhere high up.

It's even more beautiful than I remember. Shivers prickled up Rose's neck. The canopy of old forest enveloped them as they walked in silence for a while, interrupted only by the occasional horse snort.

By the time Rose glanced behind them, the path to the stables had stretched further back than she had expected before curving into obscurity behind the low-hanging branches over the last turn.

Laguna Lake Riding Club felt so far away, its comfortably groomed grounds replaced by gorgeous, untouched nature. It was another world, full of unknown, and absolutely perfect.

"Whoa!" Tanner suddenly broke into an eager trot. Without a second thought, Rose squeezed the reins a little to bring him back, only to instantly regret the hasty signal. Despite her thumping heart and years from the saddle, those first few steps of his trot felt unbelievable—buoyant yet smooth and collected.

"He's used to getting ready to gallop around this area, that's why he sped up," Ethan commented when he heard the change in gait. "Just hold him back for a few steps, and he'll know to take it easy the rest of the way."

Gallop? Rose's fingers gripped the reins again, fearing an unannounced surge and almost anticipating the familiar nick of leather trimming into her skin from her dreams. Even though Tanner stayed mellow, she could tell by his pricking ears and hoppy forwardness that he felt every inch of her body tense up. Cursing herself for reacting so viscerally, Rose tried to forget what Ethan had just told her. She couldn't allow that last ride with Fender to affect her ride with Tanner today. That was literally the opposite of the golden rule.

"Talked to Sandy the other day," Ethan quipped, turning left in the path's fork going uphill. "She says hello."

Rose's eyebrows shot up. "Oh! Tell her I said hi, too. How is she?"

"Loving life in the heart of the Pacific, basically," Ethan replied. "She married and divorced, and I don't know much else. But she seems otherwise happy as long as she has the horses. One of my buddies might take a ranch hand gig on the same island." Pausing, his usual rough-edged gaze flickered with curiosity. "She mentioned you were some big deal rider...called you the barn psychiatrist or something..."

A surprised giggle escaped Rose's lips. She couldn't help it. The phrase "big deal rider" surely didn't fit with Rose now, and Ethan was probably getting the wrong idea. Sure, Sandy had encouraged Rose to compete more after that first reserve champion win with Fender, but Rose had a hunch that their winning streak wasn't quite what Sandy was referencing by the "barn psychiatrist" part. Of course, Rose didn't expect Ethan to know about her brief stint as the gal who rode the horses nobody else was willing to. Either way, she had never heard such complimentary words come out of her trainer like that, ever. Were they even discussing the same Sandy?

"...but she's not surprised in the least how you're helping out with someone else's horse," continued Ethan. "I told her about Starla and the whole situation. Her advice is to not let it get personal."

Not let it get personal? Something about that line didn't quite sound right. As they rode deeper into the woods, she realized why it bugged her. What was more personal than deciding to actually run a horse sanctuary? The Sandy she remembered took abused or neglected horses extremely personally—a trait that Rose both admired and related to. What was up with this new, hands-off tip?

"You okay?" asked Ethan.

"Of course," Rose answered. Maybe she was just misconstruing it. She didn't hear Sandy talk firsthand, after all. "Can we trot?" It wasn't until she'd already blurted the question that she wondered if Ethan would agree. She couldn't blame him if he secretly thought she was too nervous or out of practice, but suddenly all she could think about was just a little more speed.

Ethan didn't give a verbal answer, but Rose knew what the subtle press of his legs meant, and so did Anya. Rose squeezed her legs, too. Tanner's buttery jog melded with her seat and spine as she sat the trot, her lower back loosening and conforming with each step. The sensation of a nice sitting trot wasn't something she ever took for granted because Fender's trot was by far the most challenging she'd ever ridden—big, funky, and a guarantee that every rider earned solid legs and seat.

Ethan and Anya were just ahead, looking like they'd ridden together for years. Rose really admired the way Ethan rode. He had that innate calm and confidence that rubbed off on everyone around him, an especially fortunate trait around skittish creatures like horses. It was still a surprise to her that she would be of any help to someone as skilled as him when it came to Starla. She also knew to never underestimate the random quirks of their four-legged equine friends. If anything, it only proved just how traumatized Starla was. And the important thing was to support her now.

Trying to sink deeper into her heels to absorb the motion, Rose began posting. *Gotta get real riding boots as soon as possible!* Her regular boots just weren't cutting it, even though they had a small heel and were narrow enough to slip in and out of the stirrups. Still, while moving up and down, a rush of electricity coursed through her body as muscle memory kicked in, her legs stretching into position on Tanner's sides. She could feel the familiar line of hips, knees, ankles, awkward boots and all…

"Tanner is amazing!" Rose gushed as they trotted side by side.

Sheer exuberance bubbled out of her. "He's, like, the perfect ride." She really meant it.

"Thank you." Ethan's pride in his horse was obvious. "You should feel his canter. Cream of the crop." He scanned ahead then looked back over at her. "We've got a flat straightaway coming up...do you think you want to—"

"Yes."

Rose held her left leg steady and pressured with her right. Tanner's trot gracefully morphed into a powerful, balletic canter.

They picked up speed, hooves hitting the ground with the powerful unison of competing teammates. The trail dimmed and cooled the further they ran, and Anya's longer strides quickly caught up and pushed ahead, her competitive personality now unrestrained.

Rose heard the wind careening in and out of her lungs, but this wasn't a dream. Leaves, branches, rocks, purple and orange wildflowers...everything around them turned soft, in slow motion, still rocking with the three beats of Tanner's flowy canter.

This is it. She was back. Time never existed here, in this temporary place where one skims air and earth energy. She wanted to go faster, forever, but the more they ran, the sooner they'd reach the shift. *Keep going.* Rose then remembered that she and Tanner weren't alone. She stole a tiny glance to her left, just barely, still breathing and rocking, and their eyes locked for a stride. With a sharp inhale, everything blurred back, *one-two-three, one-two-three, one-two-three...*

Wrenching away all of her conceivable body language toward complete aloofness, Rose directed everything back to Tanner. The horses accelerated in tandem as if responding to the increasing whirring winds brushing the very top layers of trees around them. Dry leaves spun and scattered in a cold sweep, dead and wild. When the next curve came into view, everything slowed back down.

Rose was almost certain Tanner could hear her heart hammering against her insides. No mirror was necessary to check if her cheeks were flaming red—she could tell by the way they scorched, just like when Eliza had tripped her in art history class. This time, though, it was from climbing a mountain of adrenaline, only to get momentarily stunned before reaching the top. Did she just imagine the way Ethan had been staring at her? Why did she even look over at him? What was up with that disorienting, milky moment?

Human-wise, the ride back to Laguna Lake Riding Club was silent. Each step the horses took only fed the new bewildering awkwardness that Rose was almost convinced now hovered between herself and Ethan.

It wasn't exactly a romantic awkwardness, which made her core reel with confusion. The exhilaration of running through Coyote Hills was a lost dream returned, and it overshadowed almost everything Rose had ever known. But another abstract realization was settling in. Ethan was unlike anybody she knew, and being able to spend time with a horse like Starla was the ultimate surprise gift. Ethan had never displayed any amorous interest in Rose. In fact, he'd been very clear of that from the start. Starla and Lula May's cryptic deadline was their sole focus—and Starla needed them to keep on that focus, not suddenly get all soft and googly-eyed. Even though Tori and Cameron loved to tease her about Ethan, wasn't that just the typical, immature illusion that everyone would push about two people spending time together? Rose was used to brushing off her friends about him by now, but the unexpected energy she and Ethan had just shared during their ride made her nervous in a whole new way.

When the barn's white fence came up in the distance, Ethan finally broke the dead air between them.

"Ever notice how most things you worry about never end up really happening?"

Not even close. That statement couldn't sound more opposite from Rose's reality—not to mention timely, considering her still-blazing cheeks. "Gonna have to think about that one." She kept her eyes pointed twelve o'clock sharp.

"You were so nervous about riding Tanner, but look at how it turned out," he explained. "You guys looked awesome."

Rose's shoulders relaxed. Ethan was talking about her riding, that was all—so he did notice she was petrified at first. Grinning, she patted Tanner's withers. "*He* is awesome. Thanks for letting me ride him. I can't tell you how much I appreciate it." In the wholesome safety of talking about Tanner, she forced herself to finally look over at Ethan again and plastered on the most all-business look she could manage. She considered herself an expert at making sure the friend zone boundary was razor sharp.

Rose caught a flash of understanding in Ethan's eyes right before he gave a brisk nod and then promptly extended Anya's walk. Any lingering question of whether she had conjured up that intense, mid-stride connection dissipated.

Rose soaked up all of the nature surrounding them on the ride back to the barn, as if gliding on an invisible cloud, doting on every different tree, plant, bird, shadow, and breeze. It was the only way to return to the bigger picture. And after a ride like that, she couldn't help but feel even more positive and convinced about helping Starla. It was all falling into place—she could do this. *They could do this.*

A large squirrel stopped in the path in front of them, nibbled on something in his or her hands, then zipped across the way and disappeared into a thick grove. Ethan and Anya still maintained a slight distance ahead. Even though there was plenty of room to walk side by side, she didn't nudge Tanner to catch up. She was mostly relieved to just enjoy the last few minutes with Tanner.

The trail cleared up and widened around them as they got closer to the barn. A distant whinny emerged from the stalls. The commanding tone was instantly recognizable.

"Was Starla waiting for us that whole time?" asked Rose, half-joking.

"Probably. Hoped she wouldn't notice you were here before we left, but I guess you can't get anything past her these days." Ethan turned around and grinned. "Who says horses are dumb, huh?"

"Only idiots," Rose answered earnestly.

They untacked Tanner and Anya and took them back to their stalls after a quick grooming, working as efficiently as they could amid Starla's eager snorts and the occasional "hurry up" stomps from down the aisle.

"Starla, we didn't forget about you," Rose cooed, glowing with anticipation. She slid open the door, halter and bag of cookies in hand. The mare's big ears perked up even more when she sniffed the round treat in Rose's flattened palm. The cookie was made of oats, bran, applesauce, carrots, and molasses, and topped with a single red and white peppermint in the center. Humans could eat them, too. Starla carefully lipped the cookie once before it vanished into her mouth. Rose laughed and offered another as she began grooming the mare. Although Starla was pretty much acting like a docile puppy, Rose still made sure to use an extra gentle hand while brushing her and cleaning out her hooves.

When Rose finished, she stepped back to admire her. Starla gently nosed Rose's arm and sighed. She seemed more and more comfortable with everything at Laguna Lake Riding Club. *And if she keeps progressing this way,* Rose beamed, *I just know we'll nail Lula May's deadline!*

Never in Ethan's twenty-one years would he have guessed that some random student would be so valuable when working with a horse. But then again, he never anticipated such an awful predicament with a neurotic horse owner, either. With a demanding sunrise to late night schedule managing the barn, he barely had time for a "normal" life, whatever that was supposed to be. But he couldn't turn away from Starla's case, and Ethan was glad to have Rose's support in whatever way she was willing. After experiencing the difference in Starla before and after meeting Rose, Ethan's professional opinion was that Starla's improvement only accelerated when Rose was around. All of the mare's physical necessities—food, water, comfortable and clean living quarters, vet checks—were fully met at the barn, but it was clear that Rose somehow satisfied Starla's emotional needs that had been screaming for attention.

What he wasn't so certain about was why he accidentally let Rose catch him looking at her during their trail ride just now. Sure, he quickly glanced at plenty of people during rides to check how they were doing. But who would've guessed she would actually look over at him too, especially at such a pace? He couldn't recall a single time that had ever happened.

Ethan swallowed a tight grimace and tried to clear his head as they brought Starla to the ring. Considering how much time he and Rose had spent together so far, the number of words uttered between them was relatively few. Still, he felt a comfortable, almost familiar, connection with Rose. What it was, he almost didn't want to know, and he certainly didn't want to force or even pursue anything. He had a job to do.

When he opened the gate and entered the ring, it was all about Starla. Going one-on-one with a horse, getting into their thinking, questions, and instinct—that was in his blood. Not even a girl sitting pretty on the rail, no matter how intriguing, could distract him once the gate closed.

Ethan used a nearby stepladder to mount and asked Starla for a walk. Her ears were forward and attentive, occasionally pricking back and forth at the sounds of nearby people, horses, and random cars on the road. Once they started trotting around the ring, Ethan realized he had to really steer Starla away from Rose almost every time they passed her.

It's like Starla's magnetized to her, Ethan thought as the mare again tried to veer toward Rose—the exact opposite direction he wanted. With a firm leg, Ethan urged the mare to maintain the imaginary oval. Rose giggled as she mock-shooed them away.

Confident with the trot, Ethan pressured with his legs again. Starla responded with a slow, steady canter.

"That was a great transition," Rose enthused. "She even got the correct lead!"

Good. He could feel how Starla picked up at just the right moment. They circled once without any problem. On the second round, though, Starla suddenly jerked and tossed her head.

"Steady, girl," Ethan said as they tried the canter again. After a few more rounds, they slowed to a walk on the other side of the ring, opposite the gate. He glanced at Rose, who was staring at Starla with a concentrated, almost checked out gaze. "What are you thinking?"

Rose blinked, as if she'd just remembered he was there. "Oh," she shrugged a shoulder with a hesitant grin. "Just that when Starla was born, I was, like, in kindergarten." She let out a modest giggle.

Ethan only nodded. He couldn't recall the last time anyone had expressed something like that about a horse. It was kind of refreshing.

Rose hopped off the rail and walked over to them. "Such a good girl," she patted Starla's neck. Starla snorted and blinked her dark eyes.

"Let's give her a rest now." Ethan led Starla out and secured her to a post. Lately, she'd been okay with being secured like that as long as he stayed nearby. He grabbed two bottles of water from a nearby cooler and offered one to Rose.

"Thanks." Rose followed Ethan to a group of chairs near the big oak tree.

"What made you stop riding here? Was it because Sandy left?" Ethan asked casually. Truth was, he'd been curious about it this whole time.

"No, it was way before that. I didn't even know Sandy had left until you mentioned it," Rose replied.

"I see. And you rode Fender, right? He's a really good horse, from what I remember." Ethan crinkled his brows. "So, if you didn't stop riding because of Sandy leaving..."

"I kind of had a scary fall. Well..." Rose hesitated, lowering her eyes. "...not kind of. Fender spooked pretty bad on the trails, which was totally out of character for him. Thankfully, he didn't get hurt." She sighed. "My parents pulled me out of training the very next day. They already thought it was dangerous enough in the first place."

Ethan shook his head. "If it's any consolation, you ride like you haven't missed a day."

Rose blushed. "Highly doubt that," she mumbled, grateful for a sudden breeze that brushed a bunch of her hair across her face.

"No, seriously." Ethan's eyebrows shot up with sincerity.

"You're catching up really quick for someone who's just starting again. Must be taking secret lessons at another barn or have some kind of weird equestrian tricks up your sleeve." He chuckled and downed the rest of his water. A minute later, he pulled out his phone.

"By the way, think you'll ever follow me back? You know, online," Ethan broke the quiet between them as he teasingly waved his phone in the air.

Rose shrugged, smirking a little. "Didn't think it really mattered. You have so many followers on that thing."

"You'd be surprised what people assume on social media," Ethan scoffed. "All that stuff is pretty corny, but it can help for work, so I'm told. Anyway, you haven't answered my question."

Rose reached for her phone and clicked a few times. "There. We're officially friends. Happy?" she chided.

"Cool." Ethan winked and stood up. At least they'd returned to casual banter. "So, ready for a little more trabajo?"

22

"I completely agree, Murray. Thanks for keeping an eye on things. Gotta go now, my agent's on the other line." Lula May hung up and tossed the phone onto the passenger seat.

Maybe it was a little odd that Murray had taken it upon himself to nose around Laguna Lake Riding Club on her behalf, but she had other things to worry about at the moment—like driving around completely lost for the last fifteen minutes in this strange city. The semi-busy street continued uphill, bordering a large public park. Lula May vaguely recalled driving by its green grassy hills and huge fields last time. After turning the red leather steering wheel onto Euclid Avenue, she breathed a sigh of annoyed relief. Things were looking familiar again.

Get me out of here, Lula May thought, stepping harder on the gas pedal. From what she could tell, Fullerton was typical Southern California suburbia. Lula May wasn't sure if she actually hated it or if she was just miserable at being there today.

Regardless, she didn't drive all the way down there for fun. Adjusting the rearview mirror, she cranked the air conditioner and frowned at her rapidly frizzing hair. A sudden, dry-as-hell heatwave was announced throughout southern California this week, expecting to push temperatures toward record numbers. As if June gloom wasn't bad enough, now this? She was starting to think that California weather wasn't perfect at all.

Once she sped through a red light in front of the local high school, Laguna Lake Riding Club soon came up on the left. Lula May skidded into the lot and released some of her frustration by slamming the car door with the most force her arm could muster. It was easy to ignore the disapproving look from the older couple loading a dark horse into a trailer. Had they, along with the rest of the world, read her infamous interview too? She couldn't tell.

Pricks, Lula May sneered. She shaded her eyes with her latest pair of designer aviator frames. *You don't know me.*

Her mood brightened when she saw Ethan riding Starla in the ring. He looked as cute as ever in his cowboy boots and old jeans. Lula May's eyes descended onto the horse. Starla's generic, orangey-brown coat certainly wasn't her favorite thing in the world to look at, but the only light-colored horse up for sale at the same place was too feisty, way out of her league—an Arabian or something.

"Oh, he's for experienced riders only," the owner assured Lula May. So, Starla it was. If Lula May hadn't been in such a rush while horse shopping that weekend, maybe she would've been okay with leaving empty-handed. Too bad that just wasn't realistic for her busy agenda.

"Hey, Lula May. Ethan's just about done with Starla today."

Lula May hadn't noticed that Rose Moon chick standing by the rail. She greeted Lula May with a pleasant smile.

Ugh, she's here! Lula May reminded herself to not—under any circumstances—slip up that she'd been lurking on this girl. This was the first time Lula May had physically encountered an online nobody she regularly spied on.

"Hello. And you are…?" Lula May raised her eyebrows, feigning ignorance. From behind the safety of her sunglasses, she scrutinized every detail of the young woman—her t-shirt had something with "Rozz" on the front, a pair of shredded black jeans, tall laced-up black boots. The girl's long hair had a dark purplish sheen and almost reminded Lula May of her Beverly Hills stylist's locks, but she highly doubted that what she was looking at were pricey extensions.

"I'm Rose. We met the other day when you and Murray came over."

"Ah, yes, that's right." Lula May nodded abruptly as if just now remembering. At least Rose didn't seem to know that that particular day wasn't the last time Murray had been around the barn. "Well, I'll be out of town for the next couple of weeks, so I wanted to see what's up with my horse."

"Starla's doing great." Rose seemed eager to deliver some positive feedback. "Today she's been practicing some—"

Lula May stuck her fingers in her mouth to blow a piercing catcall whistle at Ethan. "*Hello!*" she waved wildly and motioned him over. No sense in wasting any more time talking to this insignificant kid.

Ethan and Starla walked over to them. "Hey, Lula May—can

you not whistle like that around here?" he reminded her. "Just to keep things on the safe side."

Lula May rolled her eyes teasingly. "Come on, it's fine," she drawled, reaching her arm through the rails to lightly spank Starla's hip. "Hi, my precious little thing!"

Ethan stifled a sigh. "She got a little skittish a few minutes ago and seems fine now, but let's just make sure she stays that way." He jumped off and rubbed Starla's rump with affection.

"I'm in a hurry, so this will have to be quick," Lula May quipped as she typed on her phone. "You have *no* idea how annoying the traffic was getting down here—I don't know how you people do these freeways!" She looked up to shake her head at them with genuine disapproval. "Anyway, I have a flight tomorrow afternoon and won't be back until the end of the month. Can I ride Starla today?"

To Lula May's irritation, the pair exchanged looks of surprise.

"Not a good idea." Ethan's tone was careful but firm. "I mean, Starla's doing great. Now, if we had actually started your lessons—"

Lula May's gaze flicked at the sky. "C'mon, you know how busy I've been! Besides, if *she*," she pointed her index finger at Rose with a short, high-pitched laugh, "can ride that big darkish blackish horse, I know I can ride little Starla! I was born with really good balance."

"You saw me and Tanner?" Rose asked, taken aback.

Lula May mentally kicked herself for leaking Murray's covert detail. "I was—I mean, someone mentioned they saw you guys riding or something." She tried not to react to the quizzical look that Ethan shot at Rose.

"Whatever." Ethan shook his head. "Anyway, don't judge a horse by size. Look, once you get the basics down—"

"Fine!" Lula May cut him off, aware of Rose's cautious stare. She needed to change the subject before that girl opened her mouth again. "I was hoping to have some good news for Murray. He's a little impatient."

"He's got nothing to be concerned with over here," Ethan's voice sharpened. "Doesn't he know that we already have an agreement?"

"We still have plenty of time to work with Starla," Rose added, sounding worried. She still appeared wary about Lula May's previous comment.

Frankly, Lula May didn't appreciate either of their tones. It was like they were making her the bad guy. "Of course he knows. But this is *my* horse. You guys may think it's all innocent, and everything's going so great, but let's not forget the reality here. Starla is violent!" she barked, forgetting that she'd just argued about wanting to ride the very same horse. "Do I have to remind you of what happened? I'm lucky Murray's not suing me, so spare me your jealousy about the guy who could barely see straight for two days, okay?"

"No one's jealous," Ethan said. "Look, we're just trying to help. And remember, Murray wasn't exactly doing the right thing by getting after Starla the way he did. He should've known that would—"

"He's a *star trainer*." Lula May's phone rang, interrupting the strained exchange. "Shh, this is important. Hold on." She held up her finger to silence Ethan as she turned to the side. "Hi, Sheila!"

"Have I got some wonderful news for you, babe!" Sheila explained that one of the contemporary art world's hippest galleries had just agreed to host Lula May's work in its new space. "They moved to their new location a little early and have a few extra weeks before their next exhibit! Perfect time for a pop-up show. The only thing is, you have to meet me out here first thing in the morning. So switch tomorrow's afternoon flight to a quick red-eye tonight. Sound good?"

"Sheila, that's amazing! I love you! Yes, see you tomorrow morning." Lula May hung up and immediately texted Carrie the instructions about her new schedule. Her assistant needed to book a new business class flight right away.

"Change of plans, guys. I'm leaving tonight and still have to pack—like *now!*" Lula May squealed, jumping in place as Sheila's news really started to sink in. This could be a whole new beginning for her broken career! "I swear, you have no clue how crazy things just got! Ethan, real quick, can you at least show me some of Starla's progress since I'm here?"

Ethan gruffly nodded and mounted Starla. He held the reins loose and gently squeezed Starla's sides with his calves.

"Incredible," Lula May murmured as she watched Starla calmly follow the rail. "That horse is actually listening!"

They continued the next loop in a trot. "Why does Starla keep going toward *her*, though?" She pointed at Rose, standing at the rail a few feet away.

Ethan chuckled. "*She*," his own finger pointed down at Starla, mocking Lula May, "...just really likes her." He exchanged a quiet grin with Rose. "Don't worry, Starla's starting to realize that she doesn't need to stand so close to Rose all the time."

"That's weird." Lula May threw Rose a sidelong glance, not registering Ethan's sarcastic smirk. "Have you ridden Starla?"

Ethan steered Starla toward Lula May. Starla took a few steps but refused to move further.

"Whoa, it's okay," Ethan reassured Starla when she tossed her head and jigged sideways. Ethan directed her a little further away until Starla finally calmed to a halt.

"Uh, what was all that about?" Lula May demanded. Any desire to ride Starla had disappeared. "You said Starla's doing great—that did *not* look great!"

"Sometimes things just happen," Ethan explained patiently as Lula May glared up at him. "They're horses."

"They're horses?" Lula May repeated. "This horse just needs some discipline—*tough* discipline. You know, my dog used to act like that, all wild and jumpy, but after proper doggy education, he's fine! Why can't you do the same for this thing?"

"We can't really compare the two," Rose interjected.

"I just remembered something that Murray suggested." Lula May's red lips pursed at Ethan. "He mentioned that if Rose can ride Starla, then that's when we'll know she's all better."

"What?" Ethan quickly shook his head. "Why Rose?"

Lula May shrugged. "He was joking at first, but Murray thinks it'd be a good test of your training skills, Ethan."

Ethan squared his shoulders. "First off, Rose isn't a beginner like you. *Far* from it. And when it comes to training—"

"You know what? I'm over it with this horse. Murray's right." Lula May paused, enjoying the bewildered looks on their faces for a few seconds. "Look, guys, I know you probably mean well, but I have some really big power moves coming up in my career. I just can't have that kind of baggage." She tossed a disgusted hand wave at Starla.

Ethan's face darkened. "I don't know where you got the impression that he's such a good trainer, but he clearly doesn't care about Starla. Or horsemanship in general."

Sighing as if dealing with a petulant child, Lula May dug inside her gold crocodile leather purse. She handed Ethan a prewritten check for the month and turned to Rose. "Now, for the second time—have you ridden my horse?"

"No," Rose answered quietly. She darted a confused glance at Ethan, whose narrowed eyes glared at the artist.

"Well, I guess you'd better practice then." Lula May jutted her chin out in a defiant challenge. "I'll be back in two weeks to judge. Then I'll decide what to do with it."

"What's 'it'?" Rose asked, looking slightly confused.

"Don't you know English?" Lula May exploded. The nerve of this girl. "That pain in the ass horse!"

23

Rose and Cameron settled in a shaded corner table, glad to be at the Hub after a busy day at school. Tori was supposed to join them but was running late. The pesky winds had sent the other few customers indoors.

"Let me get this straight. Lula May wants to see how *you* ride Starla?" Cameron shook his head ruefully as he smoothed a napkin across his lap.

Rose heard him, but she was still distracted by yet another deep dive into the situation with wild horses and the Bureau of Land Management. The federal government's ongoing plan to capture wild equines via helicopter roundups, and then offer money to people who adopt them, was not what they were supposed to be studying. From what she'd read so far, the subject was clearly very contentious. Some supported the plan due to claims of overpopulation, that the horses and burros were decimating the landscape and even starving in the wild, so it was better for them to be rounded up and sterilized.

Those opposed to the government plan pointed at "welfare ranchers" who used the same public lands for grazing of their privately owned livestock soon after the wild horses and burros were removed, effectively contradicting the landscape decimation claim. There were also highly disturbing denunciations about destructive drilling and fracking.

Was this land management? Rose always thought that ranchers had this innate philosophy of leaving the land better than its original condition. That sure didn't fit into this equation. And she was obviously no biologist or veterinarian, but neither were the most vocal supporters of forced, permanent sterilization. All of it just seemed really dangerous for the animals.

Despite the romantic notions of the wilderness, Rose knew that nature was also dangerous and rough. Whether wild or feral, animals want food, to not get killed, and, ultimately, breed. Rose had glimpsed enough of the circle of life to recognize it wasn't all about living free and beautiful. Even in her own backyard, trails of gray rabbit fur leading to nowhere on the morning-dewed lawn was a common sight.

The other night she'd watched startling footage of a herd of wild horses galloping for their lives as a huge black bear bounded after them. The bear looked like she would easily overtake them with her mind-blowing speed. And Rose couldn't forget the video of another group of wild horses getting released (was it after receiving some sort of fertility control?). While most of the horses galloped off as soon as they unloaded, one mare kept gently nudging the human standing by the trailer, perhaps not wanting to leave the newfound life of readily available food, water and shelter. Though hard to watch, the reality was even more heartbreaking. Out of the thousands of horses and burros rounded up, only a tiny fraction actually got adopted to safe homes.

But the most revealing part of Rose's research was actually an article from twenty years ago. A mystery group of environmental and animal rights activists had burned down a notoriously putrid and scream-filled slaughterhouse in Oregon, known for swamping the local sewers with blood. What animals were being killed in that plant? Horses—many of them BLM mustangs, discreetly rounded up, bought and slaughtered for human consumption in Europe.

Horse slaughter was no longer legal in the United States, that Rose knew for sure. But too many horses of all breeds and backgrounds were still in kill pens and auction houses and shipped out to be slaughtered over the border. Whether from the racetrack, rodeo, show arena, lesson barn, someone's backyard, or anywhere else in between, all those equines had at least one thing in common: a money exchange that valued profit (however meager) over their safety and well-being. Just the actual transport was excruciating…long journeys without water, food, or medical care, even with injuries.

The more Rose looked into the subject, the worse the entire government—and humans in general—looked. The violence of the BLM roundups was undeniable. Witnesses had shared plenty of graphic videos with the public. It seemed that there were hardly any roundups that *didn't* end up killing or severely injuring equines in the process. Those who made it then got crammed into overcrowded and understaffed holding facilities. The BLM had already admitted on record that mysterious diseases had already killed hundreds of horses on their watch.

Adopters got a thousand bucks for each equine. It wasn't a surprise that so many individuals were adopting the maximum number of horses allowed, which added up to a hefty sum of money after the waiting period. Then the animals could go anywhere, even be sent to slaughter. And it looked like many of them were.

Was the current plan some sort of an updated façade to continue getting rid of the horses legally? And why were these particular horses and burros such a focus in the first place?

Money. Wasn't that always the answer to almost every disturbing question when it came to humans? Government was no exception. This violence was all taxpayer-funded. And adoption was not a solution for sloppy, large-scale government violence. Who were the horses affecting so much, and exactly whose interests were being funneled to the BLM through elected officials?

"I mean, such a dumbass, that Lula May and her crap idea," Cameron continued, rolling his eyes. "Is this like celebrity idiocy or something? Who *does* that?"

Rose picked at the bright miniature lemon tart on her plate. She set her fork aside. She was troubled enough, and now the mere mention of Lula May just made her stomach twist into tighter knots. "I know. I'm so nervous, I can hardly eat or study or do anything. Apparently, it was Murray's idea, that prick. He must think I don't know how to ride." Even Doris' rare and delicious dessert tarts were no distraction from the snowballing pressures weighing her down.

Cameron continued about how sexist, and probably racist, Murray must be to come up with such an outlandish and presumptuous idea. Rose sat motionless in her chair, half-listening. Pages of notes flapped in the breeze. Major exams were coming up in both of their schedules. She briefly glanced up just in time to catch a familiar sight walk by—a guy with a waist-length ponytail in his trademark flowing black trench coat and industrial boots. He always looked like he was on his way to something pretty important. She didn't know his name or age but had witnessed him stroll around the area for as long as she could remember, even when she was a little kid in the backseat of the family car.

Ever since Lula May's proposition, Rose made sure to see Starla every day after school. Despite Ethan lunging the mare beforehand, Starla seemed to have acquired a jittery disposition again. She was still affectionate and engaged during groundwork, but each time Ethan thought that maybe, just maybe, Rose could try riding her, something unexpected would call the whole thing off: a series of small spooks one day, staunchly refusing to pass the gate the next, and a jumpy, keyed up trot another time. Each day, Rose drove home from the barn more and more worried.

"Don't worry, I've seen this before," Ethan said to try to cheer her up when he sensed Rose's mushrooming panic. She wanted to believe him, but it was getting difficult to see anything in Starla's future besides Lula May, Murray, Don...and much worse.

Sitting at the table, a surge of warmth beamed through Rose just as she remembered her silent conversation with Starla the other day.

Starla, did you send me that message of Lula May hitting you?

The mare, facing the side of her stall as she drank from her water bucket, promptly lifted her head and stared at Rose. For a few long seconds, neither animal moved.

Rose looked at Cameron across from her. He had been so understanding about the whole diary thing, right from the very first moment. Maybe he'd have some insight into her unexpected flash about Starla, too.

His phone beeped and he let out a bemused scoff.

"So, I guess Tori and Tim are actually a thing," Cameron chuckled as he read a message on his phone. He reached over to fork a bite of Rose's lemon tart. "She just said they're still at his place and just ordered some Chinese. We're invited to come by before getting back to the books."

24

Tori peered through the plastic blinds as she watched Rose and Cameron walk up Whiting Avenue. They had just parked on the street between an old white van with stickers all over the back and a black lowered hatchback with peeling tinted windows.

"They're here," Tori called out over her shoulder. Tim, her new boyfriend (or so she hoped) sat leaning forward on his black couch, controller in hand. He was mesmerized by the booms of the video game in front of him.

"Already? Good, I'm so hungry." Without taking his eyes off the screen, he reached for an open can of soda on the rectangular glass coffee table.

"Not the food. My friends," Tori clarified, keeping her eye on them to make sure they didn't walk past his place like she did the first time. She carefully lit a sandalwood incense stick by the window and propped it in a ceramic elephant-shaped holder atop a portable toolbox. The elephant was a souvenir Tim had brought back from a trip to Thailand three years ago. The toolbox was one of several scattered throughout his apartment. All kinds of weird screwdrivers, pliers…too many to keep track of. There was always something that needed fixing in there, though, so Tori didn't mind. It was cute how Tim, a part-time assistant to his full-time handyman brother, never had to call their landlord for any maintenance.

The modest apartment was part of an older building just about a block from downtown Fullerton's main area. It was a peaceful, quiet street for many generations, before all the new bars and restaurants began claiming spaces along Harbor Boulevard. Lots had changed in the last few years. At least the mature blue Jacaranda trees still shaded long stretches of the sidewalks with their immense canopies, sprinkling vibrant lavender blooms around the classy old-fashioned lampposts that were now practically extinct.

Tori just loved Tim's place and the neighborhood. The apartment could definitely use new carpet, not to mention another room, and, ideally, a kitchen area that didn't make her feel like she was in a shoebox. Still, Tori felt like she was on another level here. Tim played his guitar, stayed out late, and slept in as much as he wanted when he wasn't working with his brother Gavin. Tim also happened to write incredible music. Tori found it all very cool and intriguing, even if he wasn't the most dependable person all the time.

"Hey, guys!" Tori buzzed Rose and Cameron inside and hugged them in the doorway a few seconds later. Her friends entered tentatively, looking around the cozy bachelor pad.

"Nice place," Rose said and gave Tim a small wave. Tori immediately could see the stiffness in her demeanor.

She's probably just stressed about that horse, Tori reassured herself as she reintroduced Tim and Cameron. Even though they had all met at the Ice Cave on Halloween, she somehow doubted Tim would remember everyone's names.

"So, this is where you've been hiding out," Cameron joked as they all settled around the coffee table. Tim put on a T.S.O.L. album and Tori passed around some ginger ales.

"Oh, I wouldn't say hiding out," Tori smirked as she wedged herself next to Tim on the couch. "But we've been having fun. Right?" She poked Tim's ribs.

"Yup," Tim grinned broadly and stretched his arm around her shoulders. He was done with his game for now. "Now, where's that food? They usually deliver pretty quick."

Tori jumped up and whipped out her phone. "I'll call them and ask right now!"

"No, that's okay, I was just wondering. Don't worry, the Yangs have brought me kung pao like a million freaking times. They're never late." Tim motioned for her to relax.

Tori ignored Rose's critical gaze on her as she sat back on the couch. She could practically hear her friend thinking, *Calm down, eager-beaver!*

"Whoa, you actually got one of these!"

Predictably, Cameron had meandered to the sizable record collection at the end of the living room. The two guys began nerding out on some new vinyl Tim had just picked up from nearby Nebula Records. As they chattered on about his latest UK imports, Tori plopped on the closest chair to Rose, trying to melt the ice between them. She knew she'd been super unavailable lately.

"How's the whole thing going with Lula May's horse?" Tori asked. She crossed her fingers that Rose would say the horse's name first since she wouldn't remember on her own.

"Not so good," Rose answered abruptly as if coming out of a deep thought. "I mean, Starla's improving, but Lula May's the problem." She gave her friend a quick rundown of Lula May's plan.

"What a loser," Tori replied. Her eyes gleamed with mischief. "You know what? You should leak this story to the tabloids! Imagine the headlines—*Lula May Sends Her Horse to Slaughter!*"

"Lula May?" Tim's shaved head popped up from behind one of the shelves of records. "You mean that silver-spoon artist? She's so gross."

Everyone burst out laughing just as the front door buzzed. With triumphant relief, Tori noticed that even Rose let out a genuine giggle.

Tim waved away the cash the group offered to pitch in. "Hey, Mrs. Yang, how's it going?" A few seconds later, he returned with two large bags of steaming food. "Someone give me a rundown."

Tori skipped to the kitchen to grab some plates and utensils. "Rose is helping take care of Lula May's horse and—"

Tim's hand froze while reaching inside one of the big paper bags. "That beast has a horse? This is sounding bad already."

"I know, right?" Tori returned and spread plates and forks around the coffee table, explaining the current situation. "And it was all for show, too—she's not horsey at all, as if that needed to be said. It's, like, if *I* were to suddenly get a horse, but even worse, can you imagine? Not that I would ever use a poor animal just to look good. She's hiding behind that horse because she knows the jig is up!"

"Do you think you and this trainer dude will be able to get the horse ready before Lula May sends her off?" Tim asked Rose after Tori relayed the rest of Starla's circumstances. "And what are they killed for? Don't tell me it's for food."

"I think we will," Rose nodded. "And yeah, sometimes they're slaughtered for food, whether for other animals or people. Some countries still consider horse meat a delicacy, I guess. Or some of them will be bought for next-to-nothing for other horrendous reasons like illegal rodeos or other abusive stuff." Rose bit her lip to stop the involuntary outpouring. Just verbalizing such barbaric facts was instantly upsetting.

"I didn't even know people eat horses. Sounds disgusting."

Tim shook his head at the fork Tori hovered in front of him and opted for a pair of metal chopsticks already on the table. "Nah, tastes better with these," he joked, snapping the utensils between his fingers. Tori rolled her eyes but laughed.

Before Rose could reply, the door buzzed again. Since they weren't expecting anybody else, Tori questioningly turned her head to Tim. He shrugged and got up.

"Just in time for free food, don't know how you freaks always sense that," said Tim. Two guys followed him inside. One was Scarneck from Halloween night.

"Everyone," Tim said, pointing at Scarneck, "this is Mike and that even uglier thing is Darrell, my band's drummer. Fill your plates before they inhale everything."

Tori stood up, taking it upon herself to introduce Mike and Darrell to her friends. She watched Mike make a not-so-subtle beeline to sit near Rose. She'd hung out a couple of brief times with these guys already and liked the idea of bridging everyone together. With both sets of friends now in the mix, Tori kind of felt like it made her relationship with Tim just that much more committed. More real.

If this was a group of typical high schoolers, the impromptu lunch might have gotten off to an awkward start. But these older guys weren't exactly timid. Darrell let out a huge belch and then talked nonstop about bombing a job interview at Disneyland. While he explained how it went awry because of his visible neck tattoos, Mike began putting the moves on Rose. Actually, he was just trying to strike up casual conversation, but Tori knew a casual come-on in disguise when she saw it.

"Dude, that was so crazy when you jumped into the crowd like that," Cameron remarked to Mike. He dunked a crispy egg roll in some hot mustard and nodded at Rose. "You should see some of her photos."

Rose took a long sip of ginger ale. Sometimes Cameron just didn't know when to keep things mellow. The last thing she felt like was to share her photos with new people, especially one of Tim's friends.

Mike pounced on the topic. "You got pics from that night?"

Rose tried to downplay it. "Just a few," she answered, shrugging.

"More like a few dozen," Cameron scoffed. If he noticed Rose's reticence, he didn't let on. "At least show the ones with him."

Rose was on the hook now. "Sure." She slowly reached for her purse.

"Yeah, let's see 'em," Mike said, clearly amused. "I've never actually seen myself doing all that."

Rose scrolled until she found the photos from the I Don't Wanna Hear It show. The curious group peered over her as she quickly went through the images. Tim and Darrell howled when Mike's airborne moments came into view.

"Clown!" Darrell exclaimed through a mouthful of noodles.

"You look like you're taking a dump!" Tim cackled.

"Shut up," Mike smirked, lingering on the image of himself. After a few seconds, he turned to Rose. "What do you think about putting some of these in our zine? Not the ones with me, but..."

Rose blinked. "Zine?" she repeatedly bluntly. "Uh...no."

Tori's eyes brightened. "Mike, that's such a good idea! Isn't it?" she asked Tim. Rose was always reading *Rip It Up*. Tori waited for a response, trying not to squirm at the ideal set up. It was practically a done deal to her. Rose had so many fun photos, why hadn't she thought of it before? More importantly, it would also be a good distraction for Rose to get away from all that drama with Lula May and her horse. That couldn't possibly be healthy. And double dates would be way more fun with Mike instead of that guy from the barn!

"I...don't know about that."

Tori couldn't believe how unenthusiastic Rose looked.

"I'm super busy right now at the barn, and if anything, I need to focus more on my grades this semester," Rose replied.

"Your grades are fine! You could squeeze this in," Tori protested. *What was up with all these excuses?*

"No worries, just wondering." Mike quickly acknowledged Rose's reluctance and backed off. "So, what do you do at the barn?"

Tori twisted some noodles around her fork and listened as Rose and Cameron shared the details about Starla, Ethan, and Lula May. She had to hand it to him—either Mike was a really good actor, or he was genuinely interested in hearing about all that horsey stuff. He even mentioned how he'd done a couple of trail rides somewhere in south Orange County, which, of course, loosened up Rose right away.

Maybe this isn't a total lost cause. Tori watched as their small talk flowed into a comfortable conversation. She reminded herself to pass along Rose's number to Mike before they left.

25

Ethan wiped his forehead with a handkerchief and surveyed the row of freshly mucked stalls. Earlier, he had given a longer-than-expected tour of the place to a prospective boarder. She was relocating along with her Morgan from somewhere near San Diego. Ignoring his empty stomach, Ethan headed to the tack room for Starla's saddle and bridle.

Sure, he was pretty disappointed when Rose had texted about her tight exam schedule, but he knew it wasn't right to depend on her too much. She had a life outside of this place, and Ethan had already heard plenty from locals about uber-ambitious Coyote Hills High. That kind of academic stress and competition for top university spots sounded like a complete nightmare to him. He honestly couldn't imagine what it felt like to deal with Starla's situation on top of all of that. So he figured it best to not pester Rose about coming by. She had enough on her plate. But time was running short.

I'll be back in two weeks to judge...

Lula May's words haunted Ethan as he led Starla out of her stall. Left, right, left right...he thought of their situation as he walked along to the sound of Starla clopping into the dirt next to him.

Ethan paused and patted Starla's rump, a wave of compassion hitting him hard as he hoisted the saddle gently over her. Starla had already been through so much, and she still had no idea what else her owner potentially had in store for her. He tightened the girth a little more since it usually got extra loose after a few of her strategic exhales, typical of horses countering a firm buckle around their bellies. Ethan closed the gate, mounted, and took a deep breath.

Starla's ears flicked back and tuned in to Ethan as they started with a forward walk. She was listening. Good. Ethan shifted back to slow her down a notch, then extended her stride, still at a walk. He had to make it clear to Starla that two-way communication was of the utmost importance right now.

They circled a couple of times without any issue, so Ethan decided it was time to trot—or jog, just depended on who he was talking to. Ethan barely had to close his calves to get Starla going. She was no lackadaisical lesson horse, that unfazed, bombproof type accustomed to patiently ignoring amateurish signals. Starla definitely still had a good trace of the wild mustang blood running through her veins—not a big deal, but Ethan could pick up on things like that. Faint, but still pure electricity. What Ethan needed was to corral some of that spark through a mutual understanding…especially if Rose were to ride her anytime soon.

The thought of Rose riding Starla still made him a little nervous. Rose definitely had the skills that were quickly returning after such a long hiatus from riding. She looked confident enough on Tanner lately, and she was clearly a better rider and horsewoman than the lesson students at the barn, that was for sure. But he worried about Starla's feisty moods, even when it came to a lifelong rider like himself. And now, he was responsible for the safety of both Rose and Starla. If something were to happen…

On top of it all, Rose was always on his mind these days—and not only for Starla's sake.

Stop psyching yourself out! Ethan sternly warned himself. But he couldn't help it. The more time he spent with Rose, the more he thought about her when she wasn't around. Every time his phone rang or a car pulled up at the barn, he hoped it was her. He was on her barely-updated social media pages so much lately, it was getting kind of embarrassing. He'd never known what it was like to be so preoccupied with someone so categorically *ungettable*.

Later that night, Ethan scrolled through his phone in front of the TV. He guzzled a long swig of amber beer and went through his new messages. Two of them were from a relentless young woman he'd never met.

He stared at her latest bikini-clad photos. *Hey, when should we talk?* The same phone number she'd sent at least three times was typed again next to a row of hearts and winking faces.

Ethan finished off the bottle and twisted open a new one with his teeth. Leaning back in his chair, he looked out the window into the night sky. Full moon.

26

ose kept her eyes shut. She wasn't sure if the feeling of being watched was in her imagination or from her dream. The longer she tried to resurrect some details, the faster it all dissolved in the morning blaze. Another restless night.

She crept out of the bathroom, her hair still damp from the shower. The house was silent. Everybody must still be asleep since it was so early.

Grandma's bedroom door was still closed. Odd. What was she up to?

Rose's body froze right when her fingers grazed the knob. When was she going to finally realize that nobody was in there? Lifelong routines were hard to break. It was a weird feeling, standing there in a deep, hollow realization.

Milo and Koko both gobbled up their breakfasts, but Rose wasn't hungry. She texted Tori that she'd meet her at school instead of carpooling. Sometimes on high-pressure exam days, Rose just preferred to be solo so she was fully in the zone.

After morning classes, Rose darted into the school library as soon as the lunch bell rang. She needed to sit down, alone, and take a few minutes to just chill. The place still smelled of old books despite the rapidly shrinking stacks. Over the past school year, many of the publications had been transferred electronically into the school's computer system. Ms. Nadeau, the head librarian, nodded a silent greeting over her wire frame glasses. Rose wound past a table of scruffy geek guys in windbreakers and khakis. They were muttering, huddled over a laptop. Rose snuck a glance between their shoulders and glimpsed a video of a rocket launch playing on mute.

The small partitioned desks in the very back were always her choice seats. Rose swung her bag over a wooden chair and settled in, pulling out a s'mores granola bar that would have to hold her over until dinner. The most important exams were done for the day, but she still had an economics paper to submit, as well as a couple of lectures to take notes from, before it was officially the weekend.

Rose pulled out her report to scrutinize key points she was bound to be asked by her teacher if her luck had anything to do with it. But by the time she swallowed the last marshmallowy mouthful, she was already in deep search-mode on her phone. *Random visions. Information in daydream comes true. Premonition about animal.* Every phrase that Rose searched online came up with results that only partially related to her flash about Starla. Nothing fit similarly enough for her to feel like she was getting a real explanation. *Animal beaming thoughts to human.* Rose stared at the words she'd just typed. What the hell?

As the big wall clock ticked, the occasional shifting of chairs was the only other sound in the otherwise silent library. Outside was a different story, full of laughter and chatter as students enjoyed the midday reprieve. Most people didn't venture into the library during lunch. The place was strictly for ultra-nerds, loners, or weirdos. Rose always figured she probably fit into all three of those stereotypes in some ways, but now she was sure that was the understatement of the century.

The bell signaled the return to the grind. Rose slowly gathered her things and was just about to hoist her backpack over her shoulder when she noticed a folded newspaper on one of the nearby desks. *The Tribune* always came out midmorning on Fridays. Her impatient fingers flipped through the pages to the Local Arts section. There it was! Her piece on the art exhibit at Nebula Records, the second article in the small section.

Biting her lip, Rose slowly walked to the library exit, carefully examining the piece. She already knew her article word for word, but it was still pretty cool to read her piece in actual print: *Fullerton's seminal vinyl shop, Nebula Records, hosted their first art exhibit this past weekend featuring some of the area's talented, and mostly underground, artists of all mediums...*

So, Chelsea must have decided that Rose's topics weren't all that "inappropriate"! And even if they were a little different from the rest of the articles in the Local Arts section, it certainly didn't mean that *The Tribune* couldn't use a little variety in its scope, right? Rose couldn't help but grin a little as she continued reading.

...and while some of the photographs and sketches were indeed interesting, it goes without saying that this type of art isn't much more

than a temporary fluke in the real art scene...

Rose stopped in her tracks. Those were definitely not her words.

"Uh, excuse me," a polite voice creaked behind her.

Rose popped her head up. It was one of the guys watching that rocket video. For a couple of incredulous seconds, she just stared at the dark mole right above his thick left eyebrow, racking her brain. Why was that line even in her article? How did it get there?

"Sorry," Rose finally mumbled, realizing she was holding up the exit. She stepped aside and checked the article again.

Someone had tampered with her piece. Was this some sort of prank?

Her pocket vibrated. Fidgeting, she pulled out her phone.

Hey Rose, just checking if you have some time to swing by the barn soon. Hope you're okay. —E

27

Lula May paced around the sparse gallery. Hands gripping her hips, she muttered expletives under her breath. Carrie and the gallery staff watched in uncomfortable silence.

The walls were crisp white, ready for hanging frames. The floors were polished smooth and matched the precise, soft lighting she'd repeatedly requested from the curator and her help. Even though a dozen people had been assisting her all week, progress was still far off.

Too far off.

In only a matter of days, some of the most influential art critics in the world would descend on this very room to judge Lula May's work. This was her very first exhibition not centered on performance art. Sheila had recommended that Lula May expand her body of work in order to create distance from anything associated with *that* interview. Lula May had her peripheral performance pretty much nailed and ready for opening night, but her photographs and assemblages were nowhere near where they should be at this point.

Lula May picked up a hammer and approached the centerpiece of the exhibit, a mass of thick glass and wood. It was supposed to resemble a crisp diamond from one angle and a flawed one from the opposite viewpoint. But right now, it was just a meaningless pile of disconnected materials lying on the floor.

She, along with a handful of staff assigned to this particular piece, had already assembled and disassembled the dumb thing three times without success. Nobody was sure what to do next, especially after her screams about everyone's incompetence last night. Sure, it wasn't Lula May's most elegant moment, but she was stressed and extremely tired. Could anybody really blame her?

To top it all off, two interns had failed to show up this morning, which further incensed her. They just didn't seem to understand that this show, *her* show, was going to be under the tightest scrutiny imaginable and could very well define the rest of her career.

"But no one cares about that part, do they?" Lula May lamented bitterly as she flung the hammer to the ground. It landed with a series of heavy clunks, the sharp end chipping the otherwise pristine floor.

With a brave face, Carrie stepped forward and picked up the tool. "Okay, Lula May, let's just calm down and figure out—"

"Calm down?" Lula May repeated menacingly at her assistant. "Screw calming down! You said you knew how to make this piece work. What kind of assistant are you?"

Carrie's lips quivered. "I really thought I could get this set up by now. I'm sure I can do it with just a little more time."

"We're all here to help, Lula May," a young man's voice chimed in. He crinkled his brows at a sheet of paper in his hands. "Carrie's blueprint for this piece makes enough sense. We'll figure it out soon enough."

"Give me a break, Peter!" Lula May burst. "You haven't been able to figure out anything!"

The tall skinny guy swallowed and looked directly into her eyes. "It's Ronald, actually. For the third time."

Lula May sighed with frustration as she watched Ronald grumble something to the rest of the group and swiftly exit the gallery. Why did she keep calling him Peter? And more importantly, where did he think he was going? She actually didn't want this helper (or gallery manager or whatever he was) to leave—his sawing skills were a lifesaver so far. Who knew how long he'd be gone now?

"Well, one more down. Anybody else?" Lula May demanded at the sullen, demoralized troop.

Nobody said a word.

After a long silence, Pat spoke up. Her voice was reassuring and patient. "Lula May, you need to cool off a little. Please."

Pat, the gallery curator, had plenty of experience handling a packed roster of artists for her job. "Let's just focus on getting the measurements of the larger pieces for the north-facing wall." She pulled her curly mahogany hair back into a tighter ponytail and smiled pleasantly, trying to salvage some semblance of positivity.

"No, no, no." Lula May shook her head back and forth with each emphatic syllable. "I want to build the centerpiece. It's a mess. It's going nowhere, and it looks *nothing* like the outline that

Carrie—er, *I*—drew!"

Pat shifted her weight and pushed her glasses higher up her freckled nose. "Lula May, we can tackle that after Ronald comes back. We can't do much on that piece without him, you know. Besides," she motioned at the remaining team, "everyone else here needs to help lift the big frames to the walls. Meilin, Shanae, and Ernesto have to leave earlier today, so let's just work on the stuff that needs hanging first. Sound good?" She was clearly trying. The three assistants she'd just named stood awkwardly behind her.

Lula May tilted her head with exaggerated concession. "Fine!" she relented. "I guess I can focus on that. But I swear…"

The front door slowly opened. The staff looked mildly surprised that it wasn't Ronald.

A tall, muscular Ken doll type in a navy blue tracksuit clutched a large black suitcase and scanned the room. His brows crinkled on his chiseled, sun-kissed face.

"Um, is…" He quickly checked his phone. "…Lula May here?"

Lula May stepped forward, extending her hand. "That's me. You must be Kevin," she cooed, offering a broad smile. "You're just in time. Follow." She led him toward the desk at the far end of the gallery.

Pat cleared her throat. "Um, Lula May, what are you doing? The frames are over on this side."

Kevin rummaged through his bag and pulled out what looked like some type of elaborate folding chair.

"You guys get started. I know time's tight, but my shoulders have been killing me, like, no joke." Lula May leaned forward into Kevin's portable massage chair, squeezing her face into the cushioned ring at the top.

Pat walked over briskly, her eyes darting between her gaping staff and the artist. "Lula May—are you serious? This really isn't the time for a massage."

Carrie discreetly tapped Pat on the arm and silently shook her head as a subtle warning.

"It'll only be an hour, Pat." Lula May waved a "shoo" hand without looking up.

Pat frowned. "No. This is unacceptable."

Lula May raised her head, genuinely surprised. "I said it'll only be an hour. Just get started on the hanging. Geez!"

Pat shook her head. "This is totally inappropriate. In all our years, we have never experienced such ineptitude and disrespect while setting up a show." She turned to Kevin. "I'm sorry, but you have to leave. We don't allow…massages here."

"Um, okay." Kevin glanced at Lula May, unsure of what to do.

"Kevin, you're not going anywhere!" Lula May scrambled to her feet, knocking over the massage chair. Kevin bent down to retrieve it as Lula May got up in Pat's face. "Pat, I can't believe you!"

"Me?" Pat retorted. "You're getting a freaking massage while all these people are busting their butts setting up *your* show—which, by the way, doesn't look like it'll even be ready by opening night!"

"Look, this is *my* show—not yours, and not your little interns' show either!" Lula May trembled. Her entire face flushed with indignation. "If we're not ready by opening, it'll be all *your* fault because you guys don't know how to work as real artists! None of you!" Her shrill condescension bounced off the white gallery walls.

Ronald suddenly burst through the front entrance, holding up his phone in a tight grip. He bore his eyes into Lula May and went straight at her, oblivious to the rest of the room.

"Guess who just called me?" Ronald's delivery was so confrontational that Pat instinctively raised an arm to slow him down.

"Who just called you?" Lula May knew her defiant, mocking yell was unprofessional, but really, who the hell did he think he was speaking to?

"The manager of Nothing4U," Ronald snarled. "I've never heard of that band, but you have. Right, Lula May?"

Lula May's inflamed face slowly drained of color. Her hot gaze flamed out and searched for Carrie, who just shrugged and shook her head, confused.

"You seriously didn't think someone would find out?" Ronald demanded, taking another step toward Lula May.

"Find out what, Ronald? What's going on?" Pat sounded almost afraid to hear his reply. She shot Lula May a bracing, apprehensive look.

"Well?" Ronald just stared at Lula May, giving her a chance to speak. Everyone in the gallery held their breath, including a wide-eyed Kevin, who had stopped packing up his massage chair to just stand in place and watch.

After a long enough silence, Ronald released a frustrated sighed and turned to Pat. "You know the centerpiece of the show? The two-way diamond? The image on *every* ad we put out?"

Lula May scowled down at her shiny ostrich leather shoes. Usually, she loved it when an entire room stared at her, but this felt just terrible.

"Lula May ripped it off. Like, *exactly*. From some Southern California punk band called Nothing4U. See for yourself." Ronald handed Pat his phone. "Look at their album cover...it's not even arguable. What am I supposed to tell that guy? He was pissed!" Exasperated, he threw his arms in the air before turning back to Lula May. "What the hell? You didn't even tweak it—not even a little! We all look like fraudsters, thanks to you!" Now it was Ronald's anger belting off the walls. Pat adjusted her glasses and carefully compared the album cover on Ronald's phone to the posters for Lula May's show that hung by the front desk. After a long minute, she handed back the phone, nodding introspectively. Considering the situation, she appeared totally neutral.

"It's not that bad, right, Pat?" Lula May asked in a small, hopeful voice.

Pat looked Lula May over from head to toe to head. Frustration briefly appeared on her face before she regained complete composure. "Just get out. Now."

Lula May's mouth flew open. "You can't do that!" she shrieked, stepping closer to Pat. "This is *my* show!" She resisted her assistant, who was silently attempting to hold her back by the arms.

Ronald smirked. "Sure have a lot of people working on *your* show."

"Excuse me?" Lula May blinked. "You pathetic, sexist—" She stopped mid-sentence, catching Carrie in the corner of her eye. What was that? Had her assistant cracked a grin at Ronald's comment?

Carrie quickly straightened her face and stared hard at Ronald, trying to redirect Lula May's attention back onto him, but it was too late.

A sarcastic grin stretched across Lula May's lips. "You know what's really funny, Carrie? You're *fired*. Get your belongings out of my hotel suite before I hurl all of it off the balcony." She ignored her assistant's open mouth and turned to the staff. "In fact, all of you are fired! I'm out of here."

28

Rose silenced the speakers blasting 45 Grave once she saw the familiar wooden fence ahead. The tension in her neck that had bothered her all day was gone. A pleasant smile danced on her lips. The school day couldn't wind down fast enough. But, finally, she was back. And classes hadn't ended too shabbily either—an A for her history essay. Whew. Life at home was still up and down lately, but neglecting schoolwork would only add to her troubles. She was relieved that, at least for the time being, things were looking up, GPA-wise.

She was even more grateful for the chance to return to the barn. The place was like entering a portal to another world, a magical bubble of horses where Rose's heart fluttered with contentment and comfort. *I have to find a way to come here more often*, she promised. Despite all of the Lula May drama, the barn was still the only place in her life where she actually felt the most connected to herself, even for just a few hours.

Where was Ethan? Rose hadn't seen him in a while, not since the last time they had worked with Starla…and ridden on the trail together. But Ethan was nowhere to be found. Rose headed over to check the stalls. She paused to say hello to some of the horses along the way. Tanner peered at her inquisitively and stretched out his head, suggesting she give him some love. She scratched under his chin for a few seconds and continued.

Starla belted out a loud nicker as soon as she saw Rose's figure. She was by herself.

"How are you doing, girl?" Rose cooed as she stroked Starla's soft nose. The mare stood still, enjoying the attention. She loved that spot.

Hey Ethan, I'm here with Starla, Rose typed on her phone. There was no way he had somehow forgotten about Starla and her urgent schedule. He would turn up soon enough.

"Until then, it's just you and me." Rose grinned at Starla's coat. Her entire left side was covered in a fresh layer of shavings. "Geez, roll much?" Rose grabbed her grooming kit and began brushing, relishing every second of doting on her beautiful friend.

Thirty minutes soon passed. A couple of other boarders walked by, some saying hello and others ignoring her as they quietly tended to their own horses. Still no Ethan.

Rose texted again. She loved to just hang out with Starla, but they had work to do, too. Should she continue waiting for Ethan or just start without him?

"Hi, do you know where Ethan is?" Rose asked a pretty, bronze-skinned woman in a nearby stall. Rose had seen her with the dappled palomino a few times, but never got her name.

The slim woman shook her head, her wavy caramel locks grazing her maroon sun shirt. "He was here earlier, but I saw him take off in a rush." She hesitated. "I did hear him kind of arguing with someone just before he left."

"Do you know who he was with?" Rose asked.

"I don't, hun. Sorry."

Rose thanked the woman and walked out to check the grounds again. Sure enough, Ethan's truck was not in the front lot. She'd been in such a hurry earlier that she hadn't even noticed his empty parking spot.

An older man with sunburned cheeks and brown field boots led a tall black horse from the jumping arena, praising him. "At this rate, you'll be ready for the Thoroughbred Classic in no time, big boy," he said as he rubbed the horse's neck.

From under the sprawling oak tree, Rose watched them return to the stalls. Her hand lingered on the trunk, fingers grazing one of the many cragged crevices that ran the length of the thick bark. She remembered this tree from her childhood. To think, she thought it was huge back then. It was always the perfect spot to watch Sandy train a horse or teach a lesson. The cool mushroom-shaped cover always provided welcome shade as young Rose enjoyed a snack and soaked up as much knowledge as she could from afar.

This was the first time she'd bothered to stop next to the tree despite passing it frequently lately. It felt a little strange to be in its omniscient cover again. The tree's obvious growth since last time was a breathtaking example of thriving nature, as well as a harsh and inescapable reminder of how brief human life really was. A dry breeze weaved through the looming branches. The arena was now empty.

A short, grinding screech drew Rose's attention to the parking lot. When she turned to look, the car had already peeled out of sight.

Ethan or no Ethan, Rose decided, *we have no time to waste.* Immediately, she marched to the tack room. She was no horse trainer, but she had watched Ethan enough times to know each step of Starla's routine so far. At the very least, some walk-trot-canter, while they waited, was doable. She could definitely handle that, as long as Starla was okay with it.

Any worries of Starla being nervous or suspicious of Ethan's absence faded as Rose tacked her up. The mare almost seemed more eager than usual, even before nuzzling the bulging side pocket of Rose's jeans. After adjusting the pad and saddle and gently securing the girth, Rose unwrapped a peppermint. The crinkling of the clear wrapper prompted Starla to nod her head up and down with excitement. "I'll bring you even more treats tomorrow, baby," Rose assured while Starla crunched on the candy. She held the bridle over her nose, and Starla quietly accepted the bit. Rose ran up both stirrups, took a deep breath, and led her to the arena.

Here we go. She stepped onto the mounting block and exhaled while slowly sitting in the saddle. Then she stood in the stirrups, stretching her calves and sinking her heels under her hips before lowering herself again. A little too long. She lifted each leg to shorten the stirrup leathers by a hole. Starla let out a long breath. Rose reached out and stroked her neck.

"Glad we're on the same page," Rose grinned. "Let's have a nice ride, just the two of us." Starla's left ear flicked back at her.

They started with a relaxed walk in the same way she'd watched Ethan practice. First counterclockwise, then the opposite way. Aware she lacked Ethan's expertise, Rose tried her best to tune in with every one of Starla's movements and reward her by removing pressure as soon as she responded.

Rose swallowed and squeezed her calves, asking for some more speed. *Whoa!* Unprepared, her torso swayed forward with the first steps of Starla's trot. Frowning, Rose scolded herself and sat back. Being unprepared for her own request was the exact opposite of what she should be doing as a rider. The communication had to be clear and honest—anything else was confusing and unfair for the horse. Rose squeezed her legs again. Starla bounced into another trot, and Rose was ready this time. She smiled when the mare noticeably collected underneath her after a subtle half halt. Maybe Starla had a little less suppleness in her strides than Fender or even Tanner, but overall she felt very solid.

Heels down! Engage your core…no pinching with your knees! A sharp and familiar voice burst out of nowhere.

Rose couldn't help but nod in acknowledgment at Sandy's empty spot by the fence. Core muscles turned on, thighs adjusted, Rose's seat shifted from a decent grip to a firm, wrapped balance. That small modification immediately improved the immersion between them. Rose then lightly pressed her leg on Starla's right side while maintaining a steady left leg. The mustang accelerated her trot instead of transitioning to the canter. Rose sat back, and they returned to a walk before Rose asked for the canter again. Starla immediately bounced into a staccato trot again, but her ears were now flicking back toward Rose. She was listening. Just as Rose was about to bring them to a walk, she felt the initial sway she was waiting for, that very first step into the canter.

Telling herself to breathe, Rose kept her legs on and allowed her seat and hands to move along with the three-beat motion. They cantered down the long side without even a slight hesitation at the gate and continued all the way around the ring. Rose wasn't sure if Starla's canter felt a little quick. She could probably use some fine-tuning from a more experienced rider in order to round her out and better engage her hind end, but Rose used her legs and seat as much as she could to achieve that "connected and collected" feeling she was looking for.

Things got even better when they switched directions. For whatever reason, Starla clearly preferred tracking left. She moved with power and complete collection, all the while maintaining a big, almost slow-motion rhythm. Rose was about to glance down her shoulders to check if they were on the correct lead, but it simply wasn't necessary. She could feel every step. A familiar featheriness rippled through Rose's chest as they went around the ring once more.

"Who are you, an undercover Warmblood?" Rose joked as they slowed to a walk. She rubbed Starla all the way up and down both sides of her neck, which the mare seemed to appreciate by letting out a long sigh. "You're incredible. Don't let anybody tell you otherwise, especially you-know-who!"

Rose heard distant rumbling overhead but didn't give it a second thought. Then she noticed Starla's distracted ears. The noise got closer and louder, and the mare bobbed her head a few times.

"Easy," Rose murmured, carefully watching Starla's body language as they came to a halt.

The rumbling continued over Laguna Lake Riding Club. Starla lifted her head and looked up, eyes locking onto the helicopter traveling across the sky. For a few motionless seconds, Starla didn't even look like she was there.

She remembers. Rose sat as still as she could. She had never seen a horse staring at a helicopter before. In fact, she couldn't recall any horse ever noticing objects in the sky. A few strands of Starla's mane wisped up in the breeze. Rose glimpsed the freeze brand on Starla's neck, but she was no longer a human staring at horse. She was a soul in a human body staring at a soul inside a horse's body.

The helicopter whirred on, shrinking in the distance.

Starla blinked and lowered her head, snapping out of the mysterious moment. She let out a conclusive blow through her nostrils.

"No way," Rose whispered shakily. She couldn't fathom what had just gone through Starla's mind. "You're safe. I hope your family is, too." Stretching all the way forward, she wrapped her arms around Starla's warm neck.

The remaining coral sunlight dimmed above Laguna Lake Riding Club. A long, slow shadow stretched overhead, as if pushed by the arid gusts streaming through the darkening sky.

29

Milo tackled Rose's legs as soon as she stepped into the house. The panting terrier bounced over and over, begging to be scooped up. Rose held the wriggly pup and kissed his face as they ascended the stairs. Cheeks flushed, she was still on a high from Starla, and coming home to Milo was the perfect end to the day.

"Anybody here?"

Heavy silence greeted her back. Everything at home felt so disconnected lately. She didn't have a clue where her parents or brother were now. For a moment, she thought she heard Grandma's shuffling slippers again. Energy doesn't die, and certainly not when charged through a vessel like her.

"Miss you so much, Grandma," Rose whispered, nuzzling into Milo's soft coat. Sometimes she tripped out on the fact that he had experienced Grandma in his existence, too—what a precious, living connection he was. "We all miss her, don't we, sweet boy?" Milo's dark brown eyes turned down the hallway toward the last room. Rose followed his gaze. *He's looking for her again.* She'd lived for over ninety years, so although her passing wasn't exactly a surprise, the frenzied and grief-stricken funeral plans still took a painful toll on everyone. Rose couldn't imagine how Milo perceived such a huge and abrupt absence. He still hung around Grandma's room sometimes, all by himself.

Instead of leading Rose to her bedroom, Milo headed straight to Grandma's. He pawed the door and stood upright, his front paws scratching to push it open. With a hesitant smile, Rose followed him inside. Maybe it'd be nice to sit in there, just the two of them.

She hadn't entered the immaculate room very much lately.

Everything looked the same—the crackly crisp white sheets, cherry wood dresser set with large mirror, and wall of framed pastel watercolors Grandma had painted in her youth. A bookshelf covered one wall, rows packed tight with mostly old hardcovers on religion, history, and art. In one section were the old workbooks that Grandma used to teach Korean (or hangul) to Rose and Thomas. Rose immediately felt homesick at the sight of them, remembering how often she'd squirm and complain during the lessons in this very room while hearing the neighborhood kids play outside.

The room quickly blurred. Keeled over the dresser, her entire body convulsed with deep, silent sobs.

Milo's small sneeze finally coaxed Rose to lift her head and steady herself. He was curled into a tight ball on Grandma's bed, right next to her pillow.

"Come on, Milo," Rose murmured, dabbing her puffy face with a tissue. Grandma's tidiness continued even from the grave. A box of the wispy papery pullouts was always available in her room. "Let's go."

Usually, he'd leap off the bed and scramble down the hall at her signal, but other than his eyes, which followed her every move, Milo remained in his curled position. When Rose walked over to pick him up, she noticed the bottom drawer of the small bedside dresser was slightly open. Through the narrow opening, a cream-colored object was just visible. It was strangely familiar. And plush.

"My Pound Puppies!" Rose exclaimed even before pulling the brass drawer handle. A pair of her beloved childhood toys, one cream and the other slate gray, looked up at her with their sad, sweet, plastic eyes.

She kept them in here this whole time? Grandma was never the mushy, sentimental type. Rose remembered designating random nooks of the house with toys. This room was her favorite to play in, especially while Grandma read books through her black-handled magnifying glass.

The doll puppies were as adorable as the day Rose had received them on her fourth birthday. Seeing them again, side by side, made her wonder when she last put them in there. It was almost like peering into a time capsule, evidence from the final day she played with the toy pups before growing out of them and eventually forgetting their whereabouts. Scooping them up, she nuzzled her face into their velvety softness again.

The front door opened downstairs. A cluster of footsteps and rustling sound of grocery bags filled the foyer. Milo sprung in the air and disappeared down the hallway. A few seconds later, he bolted back to Grandma's room to pant at Rose, tail swishing and pink tongue beckoning her to join him.

"Go on, cutie pie," Rose chuckled. "I'll be right there." Milo whipped back around and tore down the hallway again. Checking out all of the new groceries was always such an exciting activity.

Someone would probably call her to help put things away any second now. As if handling a pair of delicate fossils, Rose placed both toy puppies back inside the drawer. Her hand paused midair when she heard the distinct sound of metal rolling on the wood bottom. She pulled the drawer all the way open.

What was this little metal thing connected to a feather? Rose eyed the small, bronzish, dome-shaped trinket. Some kind of a bell, with a short brown leather strip attached at the top. It tinkled as she picked it up. Connected to the bell was a small tag with handwriting, which was carefully wrapped with a thin rope to the light gray feather. Rose held it up against the light of the window. The feather had some brown specks faintly lining one side. She couldn't recall Grandma talking about any birds. Rose pushed the drawer shut. She'd have to dig into all of this later. Keeping everything right where they were when Grandma was still alive was somehow comforting. *Our little secret, Grandma.*

She could hear that something sounded off downstairs. Instead of the usual post-grocery shopping buzz—the fridge door opening and closing, sliding drawers, filling the snack cabinet—all activity had ceased. Rose quickened her pace. Her mom was murmuring in a tone so concerned that it viscerally startled her. When she reached the empty kitchen, paper bags lay on the ground, still full. Then a high-pitched yelp pierced through the walls. It was coming from outside.

"Milo!" Rose shrieked. Two paws bounced on her leg, and she almost collapsed with relief when she saw her pup next to her. "What's going on? Where is everyone?" She heard the backyard door slide open. Her parents entered the kitchen a moment later. Their expressions looked clouded and sharp, like they were really disturbed.

"What happened?" Rose demanded, gaping back and forth at them.

"Thomas, don't go over there!" Mom called out behind them. She sounded so worried. When she saw Rose, she blocked her with an outstretched arm. "Rose, don't go out there, either."

Her brother, eyes wide, scurried in without a word.

"Why not?" Rose eyed Thomas, who was already stretching over the kitchen sink to peer out the window. "What's going on?

Somebody, say something!" Her temper was about to boil over.

Another pained cry walloped through the air.

"It's Koko!" Rose had never heard her beloved neighbor sound like that. "Is there a coyote or something?"

"It's not a coyote." Her dad's solemn reply stopped Rose in her tracks. "He's hitting Koko."

Dad's words sunk in for a second. Then Rose shoved through her parents, blindly rushing to the backyard door. She had just stepped outside when Koko cried out again, this time so loud and scared that Rose could barely see straight as she made her way to the border fence.

Happy Dude, barefoot in green plaid pajama pants and a loose white undershirt, leered over the wooden doghouse. Koko cowered behind it, trying to dodge her owner's attacks. Happy Dude's right hand gripped a long black leather belt.

"*Stop!*" Rose screamed so hard her voice split with rage. He was shifting his weight and raising his arm again. "Stop right now, you son of a bitch!" Specks of saliva spat out over the top of the fence as her words shot all the way down Camino Drive.

Happy Dude's graying head turned toward her. Even in the midst of the clash, Rose noticed how different he looked—more haggard and unkempt than she'd ever remembered.

"Get off my fence, you little brat!" As if to spite her, he cracked the belt at the desperate dog, grazing her side.

Rose's lungs heaved with pain. Shaking, Rose gripped the fence and searched for a place to step over. She could wrestle that belt out of the old man's hand.

"Step one foot on my property..." he snarled.

As much as Rose wanted to fight him, something about the way he sounded was just too ominous. Stopping him just for right now wasn't enough—she needed more help.

Rose turned and sprinted back into the house to get her dad. Everyone was still in the kitchen.

"Yes. Thank you very much." Her father was on the phone. Pacing in a tight back and forth line between the counter and the table, he added, "Please hurry."

"Dad!" Rose cried, reaching for his arm. He didn't have to say who he was talking to. She knew he had read her mind. "Dad, Dad..." She exploded into sobs, unable to say anything else.

It was the first time in years that her father hugged her like this. Maybe the first time ever. His arms wrapped tightly around her shoulders, and he patted the back of her head, reassuring her just like he used to back in the old Victor Appleton bullying days, but for longer this time, and without the encouraging pep talk. He just held. Rose held, too, her heart beating right next to his. More tears rolled down Rose's cheeks and disappeared into his blue denim shirt. It was quiet. When she finally composed herself and looked up, Dad's eyes were as watery as hers.

A few minutes later, a uniformed woman and man arrived outside. Rose stayed with Thomas while their parents briefed the officers.

"He doesn't remember hitting Koko," Dad explained when they came back.

"What a lie!" Rose interrupted. "He knows exactly what he did!"

"That could very well be," Dad continued in a let's-stay-calm voice. "They asked Mom and I if he always talks about all the aliens." He paused. "We told them how you give Koko food and water. Then his wife came outside by herself. She was very upset and said she needs to keep a closer eye on him because he is not doing so well. Mentally."

"*Right*. Obviously." At that moment, no matter how sad the predicament was, all Rose could muster was icy sarcasm for what sounded like an old man's brain going downhill. "If he does anything else to Koko, I swear I'm going to take her—and you guys will *not* stop me." She was more than ready to launch into a full-on debate about minding her business, but nobody argued.

Koko didn't let out another peep the rest of the evening, and they didn't hear any more commotion in the backyard. After all the lights went dark next door, Rose walked out back with fresh water and a bowl of food, sprinkled with extra chopped leftovers from dinner. She petted Koko through the fence until bedtime. Thankfully, Koko felt okay—no welts, bumps, or cuts. At least for now, Koko and her wagging tail seemed to be back in cheerful spirits.

With Milo cradled in her arms, Rose headed upstairs to turn in. She was still very disturbed. It just really bothered her to be right next to Koko but not be of more help. She knew, without an iota of doubt, that if something violent should happen again, she simply would not be capable of refraining from physically extracting Koko from her dangerous environment. Was that breaking the rules, the law? Yes, fine. But much more than mere rules and laws had been broken before this egregious point. Only the most corrupt point of view would cherry-pick a breach and then designate it as the starting point of a crime, even though way more transgressions had already occurred. How could all that be glossed over? Rose wasn't about to allow the big picture—Koko's safety—to be ignored, no matter how tragic the human circumstances may be.

As she neared her bedroom, she noticed a dim crack of light peeking out from Grandma's room. The door was open, just enough to peek in.

Mom and Dad stood on the rug in the middle of the room. They spoke so softly and seriously that Rose could barely make out their conversation even though she was only a few feet away. Something about time. She had never seen them so solemn. And sad. No tears, just heavy, quiet sorrow sprinkled with words.

Rose stepped away from the light of Grandma's lamp, backing into the darkness of the hallway. The floor creaked beneath her. They didn't notice.

Before dawn, Rose promptly woke from a soft noise. Someone had just called her name.

Someone, or something, was in the room with her.

Rose shut her eyes again, telling herself she was just dreaming. But she and Milo were not alone, and she was definitely not asleep. Milo sat up, ears perked. Rose scrutinized the darkness, trying to pinpoint what it was. It didn't scare her, but now she really knew it wasn't just her imagination or a dream. She could literally *feel* the space right next to her bed.

"Grandma," Rose involuntarily whispered. There was no question, there was no doubt.

The space was listening. It registered her faint whisper with a connection so powerful and definite, a surge of reassuring acknowledgment melted through Rose's whole body at once. Rose said it again, in clear, sharp awe. Although she could see right through the space, the mountainous density was undeniable, as if anchored by a living, invisible planet.

Go back to sleep. You need more rest.

The message sighed into Rose's aura, in the form of something between an image and a soft breeze. It radiated love beyond human comprehension. A heavy blanket of fatigue cradled Rose's body even though she was desperate to continue.

When the alarm went off later that morning, Rose buried her face into her pillow, determined to keep sleeping. A final glimpse of gold barren desert, framed by enormous plateaus, dissolved with each passing second. The drum of hoofbeats raced further away until they vanished into what she could not remember.

She lifted her head and eyed the space by her bed. Slender beams of sunlight illuminated through the window. She didn't have to check the calendar. Rose knew this day was the forty-ninth day since Grandma had left her physical body, an important memorial in Buddhism.

Milo kept snoring, happily oblivious to the man singing of falling into the fire.

30

$\mathcal{S}$queak. "I'm not sure what you're referring to." *Squeeeak.*
Hand cupping the side of her face, Chelsea rotated on her noisy swivel chair and shot Rose a bored stare. "What exactly are you complaining about, again?"

Rose kept her expression as unfazed as she could.

After ten minutes of going over her original Nebula Records art show article versus what was actually printed in *The Tribute*, Chelsea was now pretending to have no clue about the obvious discrepancies. Her stubborn denial was predictable, all smug in her swiveling throne. It was possible that the editor had nothing to do with the tampering of the article, but her instant and hostile power trip about the matter was highly suspicious.

The rest of the newspaper staff had already gone home for the day. If only Rose had an opportunity to bring it up earlier, maybe someone more reasonable could have helped. But in Ms. Dunbar's otherwise empty classroom, Chelsea seemed keenly aware that without any witnesses around, she could give Rose the second-class citizen treatment and still maintain her goody-goody reputation.

"Since you're having a hard time, I'll try to keep it simple," Rose replied. Screw being nice, that wasn't getting her anywhere. She pointed at the newspaper spread out on the desk. "Those aren't my words. How did it get published like this?" She really wasn't sure how much more direct she could be at this point.

Shifting, Chelsea sighed loudly. "When you write an article, you email it for submission. It gets reviewed, then goes to print. That's how it gets published." Her voice oozed with patronizing patience. "It's the same for everyone. Honestly, I'm concerned as to why you suddenly don't understand the submission process, my dear. Do you need another copy of the official guidelines?"

Rose took in the amateur fascist, noting Chelsea's visible pride at her rude comeback. So cheesy, like something out of an 80s sitcom. "Never mind. If you ever figure it out, let me know." Being gaslit was one thing, but Rose couldn't justify wasting another minute engaging in such small-fry drivel. It was all precious time that could be spent with Starla.

Rose gathered her belongings and left the newspaper and original article on the desk. She felt Chelsea's eyes clawing into her back as she headed to the door. Rose momentarily considered lifting her hands over her shoulders and flashing two middle fingers on her way out but decided against it. Chelsea would spin it as an unprovoked attack for sure.

Tori's bursting cackle erupted from down the hallway, even through the closed door of the classroom. It was too far away to have anything connected with what had transpired in the newspaper room just now, but the timing was one of those convenient little boosts of hilarity that take the sting away from an otherwise annoying situation. And it was an earnest cackle. Someone must've said something genuinely funny in order to get that particular laugh from her. Tori was waiting to drop Rose off at the barn before hanging out with Tim for a few hours, so that was probably another factor for her more-hyper-than-usual tone.

The door to Ms. Dunbar's classroom closed behind Rose without another word from Chelsea. At that moment, a group of junior and senior varsity football players crowded the hall as they made their way to an awaiting bus at the front of campus. Rose squeezed to the side and decided to let them pass since the shortest path to her friends was congested by the migrating herd. The players all looked pumped. None of them really knew or noticed her, and the honest blankness was mutual. Were they all going somewhere for training or an official game? Rose couldn't really tell. She never did pay much attention to the school football team. Nobody really did. It wasn't just that she lacked interest, but it hardly even seemed real to anybody except to the players. This was unranked Coyote Hills football, not the renowned private school team just twenty minutes south.

The last of the student athletes were about to pass, so Rose began making her way across, eager to get to her friends. She wanted to repeat every stupid syllable of belligerence they all knew to expect from Chelsea. She also wanted to get their honest opinion on what to do about Chelsea's suspicious evasiveness. Take it to Ms. Dunbar? But since she was Chelsea's family friend, would that even help? It was frustrating that there were so few legitimate recourses because of certain social connections.

"Oh good, you're done!" Tori called out.

Rose was surprised to see the shaved head next to Tori and Cameron. What was Tim doing here?

Cameron looked up from his phone. "How'd it go in there?"

"As expected," Rose mumbled. She offered Tim an awkward wave. It was odd seeing someone so obviously not a student in the hall. "Hey."

Tim gave a friendly nod. "Hey, how's it going?"

Cameron jumped right in. "What did she say?" As avid Nebula Records supporters, they all felt they had to get to the bottom of the article fiasco.

"She twisted it into me not understanding how to submit an article properly," Rose answered. "My gut says she was in on it." She wanted to get into the details, but not with Tim right there, even if he was listening with amused curiosity. The last time they'd hung out at his place was pretty fun and all, but she was still warming up to the guy.

"We'll discuss later," Cameron said, eyeing Tori and Tim now wrapped in a goofy bear hug. "Well, I'm heading over to Nebula now to pick up a special order. Hope Will doesn't kick me out. Text you guys later."

"Let me know if they all hate us now," Rose half-joked as he waved back. She wouldn't blame anyone at the legendary record shop if they did, but she doubted a high school newspaper was on the owner's reading list.

"They'll understand once we tell them how our resident dictator tampered with it," Tori declared. Then she glanced over Rose's shoulder. Was that a mischievous glint in her eyes?

Before Rose could turn around, someone else spoke up right behind her.

"Resident dictator? Sounds serious."

It was Mike. Tim and Tori smirked at each other, then erupted laughing.

"You should see your face, Rose!" Tori exclaimed. Her giddiness was echoing throughout the corridor again.

Rose felt her face flush with surprise as they exchanged hellos. What was this, a set up?

"Well..." Tori exchanged a look with Tim. "I'm getting hungry. Let's get some food."

As if on cue, Tim's stomach expelled a noticeable twisting groan.

"Was that a fart?" Mike asked loudly. Tori playfully swatted him on the arm.

Rose relaxed a little and turned to Tori as the two guys began bantering. "Ready to go? I'm dying to see Starla."

Tori darted her gaze at Tim and Mike. "I wanted to ask you," she hesitated. "Since they came in Mike's car, can Mike just drop you off?"

"Seriously?" Rose asked in a low voice. Mike, some dude she didn't really know, dropping her off at Laguna Lake Riding Club. Was that really necessary?

Tori, sensing a roadblock, pulled Rose out of earshot from the guys. "He's *really* cool, trust me. I wouldn't suggest it if I didn't know for sure. Plus, Tim thinks he's into you." When that didn't get a reaction, she continued with more urgency. "I've already asked Mike to drop you off, and he knows where the barn is. After Tim and I get dinner, I'll pick you up just like we planned. That's okay, right?"

Rose racked her brain. She really didn't feel like sharing a short car ride with Mike, even if he did seem nice. On the other hand, Rose could tell her friend was pretty determined about this idea. Arguing would probably only steal time she'd otherwise have with Starla.

"I know what you're thinking. This is the last time I'll pull this, okay?" Tori whined. "And if it's not, you have my permission to kick my butt every day for a week!"

Rose shook her head. "Fine, whatever," she grimaced, sneaking a glance at Mike. The guys were now coming over, and she'd just committed to it, so all she could hope for was that this dude wouldn't try anything stupid. "But I swear, you owe me big time."

"Yay!" Tori hopped in place. "Text you when I'm on my way."

"Yeah, yeah," Rose muttered with a small grin. Tori's dream come true was to have her best friend dating her guy's homie. And Tori was clearly in sheer bliss as the two "couples" walked across campus. Every passing student stared at them, some of them turning to their friends to speculate who Tim and Mike were. As ridiculous as it was, Rose couldn't help but smirk a little at the looky-loos. As they approached the parking lot, Tori and Tim drifted off to a different row of cars.

Rose wasn't expecting Mike's car to be so nondescript: a beige family sedan, nothing like Tim's old-school classic. She was also surprised when they sat inside, and all she smelled was a soft whiff of lemon instead of smoke or general griminess. The bright citrus scent came from a small and shiny disk-like object stuck to the light taupe dashboard. And unless Mike just had the car detailed and deep cleaned yesterday, he seemed to keep it as spotless as an operating room. It hardly even looked used.

When two people settle into a capsule-like car, a narrow window of opportunity to say something opens. Any benign and casual chitchat, or at least some kind of effort at communication, helps to set the situation off to a comfortable start before things slink toward the awkward direction. Mike was silent for the entire walk to his car. After both doors closed behind them, Rose tried coming up with an easy conversation starter that would last the few short minutes to Laguna Lake Riding Club. *So, are you from around here? What do you do, besides hang out at shows and Tim's place? Is your car always so clean and empty?*

Mike turned the ignition and twisted back to reverse out of the spot. As his left hand reached to clutch the steering wheel, it slightly trembled.

"Laguna Lake Riding Club," Mike recited the words as if reading a billboard. "How's the horse training going?"

Rose realized she was crossing her arms and let her hands relax on her lap. At least since it was later than usual, the line of cars cramming to leave campus had trickled to just a few stragglers.

"It's going fine," Rose replied in a pleasant tone. She'd probably see Starla in just about five minutes at the rate they were moving. "I'm not really the one training her, though. I'm just helping out and learning."

"I see." Mike stepped hard on the brakes as the light ahead turned yellow. "Sounds really cool." Silence grew between them.

Has this red light always been this long? Rose caught herself right before she was about to cluck at the light. She was glad to not have to explain to this guy about quirky equestrian reflexes.

Mike then pulled out his phone and pressed a number. It went on speaker. He noticed her looking and explained over the first ring, "Have to call in my order for an early dinner. Ever had Mama Lu's Sandwiches?"

"Who hasn't?" Rose answered. She couldn't count how many times she had devoured their food. The chewy French baguettes were especially delicious.

"Want to grab something real quick?" he blurted abruptly. He flinched right when his voice cracked. Rose stifled a sigh. She really didn't appreciate this setup now. Did Tori give him the idea that she'd actually want to get a sandwich instead of seeing Starla? "No, thanks. I just need to get to the barn."

"Hello, Mama Lu's!" a young voice answered. Probably one of the owner's kids on after-school duty.

Mike seemed unprepared for both Rose's answer and his call being picked up at the same time. "Oh, okay—um, can I order a pickup? Great, I'll take the large Friday special. Wait—never mind, make that a large, uh…" The traffic light turned green.

"Are you there? Hello?" the young woman asked, her voice cutting out.

"Bad reception," Mike muttered. "Yes, can you hear me? Hello?"

"Did you say a large torpedo combo?"

As Mike repeated his order a few more times, Rose looked down at her phone and went through her emails. By the time he clarified his order, Laguna Lake Riding Club was just up ahead.

"Thanks for the ride," Rose said hastily. They hadn't yet reached the parking lot, but all she wanted to do was jump out.

"You bet." For the first time, Mike smiled. His teeth were straight and almost as white as his knuckles gripping the steering wheel.

They turned into the small parking lot. Gravel crunched underneath the tires. It was a welcome sound. Horse-time was about to begin.

"Since you're busy today, how about grabbing lunch some other time?" It was a quiet and hopeful invitation.

Such a timid conversation was definitely not the scenario Rose expected. Why was this guy, an apparent expert at aggravating scary mosh pits—someone she silently referred to as Scarneck—so hesitant? Some girls loved seeing a tough guy all nervous, and Rose could definitely appreciate that. Sincerity was always cool. Tim could benefit from displaying some of that sometimes. But right now, when her life overflowed with more pressure and questions than she'd ever thought possible, the last thing she wanted was to be around someone who would add more uncertainty. Her hand hovered on the door handle.

Suddenly Rose knew she just needed to leave. Getting tangled up in some forced double-date romance would not be a part of her reality.

The car slowed to a crawl. Even before they reached a full stop, Rose pushed the door open and let her boot land on the passing gravel. She just couldn't hide her eagerness to flee, even if it meant coming off as a little rude. Mike's invitation lingered.

"I'm pretty swamped with school and horse stuff," Rose scrambled, her mind already a mile away. She hoped her answer was a clear brush off that was also nice enough that his ego didn't sting too much. She'd still see him around as long as Tori and Tim kept dating.

A big truck delivering hay was reversing in the lot. Its piercing warning beeps momentarily drowned out the whirring ambulance that careened by on the main road.

"Cool, have a good time," Mike said over the ruckus. The sudden noise was a convenient wedge between their clumsy exchange. It was unclear if he got her message until he added, "Already got your number from Tori—maybe I'll text you later when you're done with the training."

Rose walked away from the car, shaking off the cringe of the last few minutes. So Tori *did* give him Rose's number without asking. Big surprise. Rose drank in the cool air as the sound of his car faded behind her. Tori had been dropping hints all week about what an awesome guy he was. Maybe that was true. But now was not the time.

Once the hay truck finally teetered into place, a blanket of serenity settled over the stables. The stable looked so lovely in the partly cloudy afternoon light. Rose breathed it all in: the trees overhead, the dirt under her boots, and the beautiful energy of the horses. A petite sorrel and a dun raced in the round pen, taking turns to playfully buck in front of the lady with an Angels baseball cap who was supervising their turnout. Some riding students carefully groomed Georgia, an older bay lesson horse. The mare was well known around the barn for having the thickest, longest tail anyone had ever seen. It wasn't unusual for people to ask if it was fake. A random snort from the stalls, and another, reminded Rose to hurry up.

Rose shut her eyes for a moment, pushing aside all the worries and confusion that had recently crept into her life. Horses were so energetically in tune with humans, it was only fair to clear oneself before entering the barn. Breathing in, then slowly out, she quietly indulged in the horses' presence. Soon she felt herself grounded with calm and stillness.

A deep nicker interrupted. A small brown streak torpedoed across the cloud-streaked sky, a world above the barn. White speckled underbelly flashed against a frame of copper to cocoa feathers. A Cooper's hawk. Rather petite, so maybe a male.

Determined to witness where he was headed, Rose watched without blinking until her eyes stung. The hawk cut a sharp line away, extending in the open space and soon disappeared into an invisible end.

"Over here, Rose." A small cloud of dust poofed over the stall next to Tanner. "Recognized your footsteps."

Tanner's head stretched over to watch Ethan. Rose patted the gentle gelding and peered inside the open stall. With forest green flannel sleeves rolled up past his elbows and his face uncharacteristically flushed, Ethan forked around the remainder of the fresh shavings. The rubber flooring was covered with a thick, mattress-like layer of softness. "I'll be done in just a minute," he said, still focused on his work.

"No problem," Rose replied cheerfully. *Probably busy covering for someone*, she reasoned, shrugged off his mildly subdued tone. Ethan usually wasn't mucking stalls, especially at this hour, so maybe it was just one of those days. "I'll get Starla ready." Rose was about to ask how Starla was doing when a deliberate nicker interrupted from the far end, sending butterflies of excitement straight to Rose's stomach.

Humming softly, Rose entered the nearby tack room for Starla's supplies. Ethan could fill her in on yesterday while she groomed. Small talk was always better with a horse listening. Starla's grooming box sat on the sturdy wooden shelf near the tack room entrance. Just in case, Rose also grabbed a bottle of fly spray.

Eyes soft and beckoning, Starla watched Rose approach. A glow spread over Rose's face. Besides Starla's adorable gorgeousness, Rose was now perpetually in awe of the unconventional (and thrilling) secret they shared. She paused a few feet away to snap a few quick photos.

"I'll gush over these later." Rose blew softly into Starla's nostrils and stroked her neck. Starla's eyelids began to close halfway. Rose giggled, gently rubbing her palms on the mare's cheeks, then reached into her pocket for a cookie. For a moment, Starla looked like she'd pulled her lips slightly back and up into a funny "smile," investigating the scents around her. Rose smiled along with her.

Rose loved riding horses with all her heart, but she loved caring for them just as much. Was that so weird? Some of her old barn friends viewed grooming as a drag and often pawned off their responsibilities to either Rose or nearby staff. Sandy called them the "ride-and-runs." Even though Sandy discouraged Rose from picking up their slack, Rose was always happy to step in as long as Fender was already taken care of. She was really down with anything that got her more involved with the horses, and there was no better way to get to know a horse—and animals in general—than to just hang out and tend to their well-being. Being turned off by big poops and grime was just weak, in her opinion.

"Let's back up a little," Rose clucked and placed a soft hand on Starla's shoulder. One ear flicked to Rose and then Starla took a few steps back, straightening out and giving Rose more space to comfortably maneuver.

Rose adjusted the brown halter over Starla's head and let the lead rope hang to the floor. Starla still didn't like cross ties. Nobody knew why, except for her. Meeting animals when they were a little older came with inherent mysteries and quirks that had to be respected and accommodated, no matter the species. So grooming in the stall, or really any appropriately free space, was fine with Rose. Starla stood as still as if she were clipped to invisible cross ties for the most part, anyway. Rose wasn't going to force her to do everything the "proper" way right now, and she was grateful that Ethan was cool enough to be flexible about Starla's preferences, too.

Such an underrated activity! Rose suppressed an inward grin while brushing Starla's back. She remembered Tori's face, all scrunched and grossed out and utterly incredulous at how being in such close proximity to large pieces of poop could ever be fun. The last time they'd talked about it, on the side of the school Quonset hut, her friend's dramatic and disgusted expression had said it all. Clearly nothing had changed since they were little kids. Yes, the poop was smelly, and there was always plenty of it. "Just be thankful horses don't eat meat," Sandy often liked to point out. "The smell would be a whole different story, my dear." Rose mischievously reminded herself to borrow that line next time to really gross out Tori. Ha!

Rose's smiling cheeks suddenly dropped, remembering the Quonset hut conversation…it was on *that* day. The journal day.

Focus on Starla, she told herself, pushing aside the images of her aunt's handwriting. With soft sweeps, she brushed Starla's dusty croup and down her hind leg. While going over every inch of the mare, the rest of the world faded into the background. The two of them alone in the stall was just as wonderful an escape as riding together out in the arena or trails. Rose felt her heart tingle and warm up, almost like it was shining, right there in their secret universe. She watched Starla's breathing slow down, and then Rose closed her own eyes along with her. It was so relaxing and peaceful, just sinking in the moment together.

Rose had completely let go, in a state of just existing, when a horse unexpectedly pulsed in the stillness of her mind. Frail, tall, and dark bay, maybe black. Hunger exuded from this horse.

Her eyes shot open. *What?*

"Sorry about that," Ethan ambled in. "One of my main grooms is off for the rest of the day."

"No worries," Rose swallowed the sharp, abrupt image of the

horse. Starla snorted with a swish of her tail. *Maybe it's from an old article or something*, Rose reasoned. But that just didn't seem right. She'd remember a horse in that condition.

Ethan picked up a brush for Starla's other side. They worked in silence for a few moments. "That prick Murray was here yesterday. He was creeping around all over the property. I actually first saw him digging through the shelves near the main office," Ethan revealed, frowning. "When I confronted him he got all ornery, as if he had a right to be doing that."

"Was he here because of Starla?" Rose asked. "Maybe Lula May sent him over."

Ethan bent over to pick up Starla's front right hoof. "Looked like Murray had zero interest in her. That's really what got me suspicious—he was interested in everything here *except* Starla."

"That is suspect," Rose frowned. She couldn't think of any reason why Murray had to snoop around the barn.

Ethan moved on to Starla's next hoof. "Next time he steps on this property, I'm going to kick his—"

Starla let out a big, rough snort and shifted, her head stretching to her front leg.

Rose zeroed in on the spot that Starla was trying to reach. "Looks like she agrees with you about Murray," she joked, scratching the itch for her.

They stepped back, admiring the new shimmer on Starla's coat.

"Let's continue where we left off," Ethan instructed as they all went to the ring. A bold gust swirled around them then swooped down the path, forcing Ethan to push his hat further down his forehead. He squinted as bits of dust blew around like microscopic confetti. "We'll walk and trot as usual, and if all goes well—which it should—you'll canter her. Again."

Rose nodded with both anticipation and acknowledgment. She knew Ethan was not-so-subtly referencing her first ride with Starla without his supervision. They both knew it wasn't exactly the safest decision she'd ever made. Stray hairs flew around her face from an abrupt, dry gust.

"Her canter is still a little quick, as you probably already know," Ethan continued. "But we have a few more days to practice. Go ahead and grab her usual saddle and girth. She's been particular about wearing that one lately, and it fits the best. Plenty of pads to choose from on the left. I've got the bridle over here." He reached for a leather bridle hanging on a nearby hook and slung it over his shoulder.

Rose headed to the tack room. She pushed the door open and clicked on the light switch. A fluorescent bulb flickered overhead.

To her surprise, Starla's wooden saddle rack was bare. Rose scanned the rest of the wall to make sure someone hadn't accidentally misplaced it or switched spots. All of the other tack seemed to be in place. Rose triple-checked the small room, even in ridiculous places like behind the shelves and under the small desk.

"Would her saddle be somewhere else, by any chance?" Rose asked Ethan when she returned. "It's not in there."

"Maybe it's on another rack." Ethan went to check but returned empty-handed. "You used it just yesterday, right?"

"Yes, and I put it back where it always goes." Rose was one hundred percent sure. "Do you think someone borrowed it?"

Rose stopped. Ethan's face had suddenly clouded over. Rose turned, following his gaze.

Lula May and Murray were marching toward them from the parking lot. Don followed closely behind, gabbing on his phone.

"Wasn't expecting you here today," said Ethan.

Lula May's stony face didn't reciprocate any pleasantry. "You know why I'm here. Let's see the progress on my horse." She pointed to Rose, explaining to Murray and Don, "She's going to ride now, and we'll see if it's all back to normal."

Ethan held up his hand. "Now, wait a minute, you said we had two weeks."

Lula May angrily pulled off her oversized sunglasses. Dark bags hung underneath her eyes. "I don't care, Ethan. I'm here *now*." She finally looked at Starla and motioned at her with exasperation. "See that color, Murray? I don't like how it looks like an old penny. I want a horse that looks like the ones in fairy tales."

Murray nodded thoughtfully as if that description actually meant something. "No problem. I'll check the local market, see what's out there."

"You've got to be kidding." Ethan looked disgusted.

"What do you expect?" Lula May crossed her arms and looked down at her watch. "Come on, let's start this dumb thing. I don't have a lot of time."

Panic rose in Rose's chest, and her palms began sweating. Ride for Lula May today? Racking her brain, she stammered, "Lula May, can't you give us more time? You're really early and—"

"I know I'm early!" Lula May snapped as if highly offended. "My exhibit was...postponed. So, yeah, I'm here early. How observant of you. Now hurry up, let's see if this crazy horse actually knows anything at all."

Rose shot Ethan a wide-eyed look. She had barely ridden

Starla, and Starla's future was potentially on the line.

Ethan spent the next few minutes trying to change Lula May's mind without success. Murray tapped his fingers impatiently against a post, smugly exchanging silent glances with Don.

"We can't find her saddle right now, anyway!" Ethan declared, a last attempt at stalling.

Lula May looked up from texting on her phone. "So? Just use another one."

"There isn't another one that fits," Ethan replied, doubling down.

Rose mentally crossed her fingers as Lula May hesitated. Of course, Lula May had no clue that there were plenty of saddles that would fit just fine. Maybe the misplaced saddle was fortuitous after all.

Lula May turned to Don, muttering something. Suddenly her shoulders tensed, and her hand shot up to her face. "Ow! What was that?" She rubbed her now-watering left eye. Before something else could fly into it, she quickly shoved her sunglasses back on. "Why is there a dust storm all of a sudden? This disgusting place, I swear!"

"Santa Ana winds." Rose couldn't hide the slightly defensive irritation that automatically came with explaining particulars to insolent transplants. "Not exactly ideal conditions for riding."

Don's mouth curled into a sour frown. "Bareback then. No saddle needed. Come on now, we don't have all day." He flashed Ethan a fake, cheerful smile. "Before the winds get worse," he mocked.

"Bareback?" Lula May repeated, dumbfounded and hopeful.

"That's not what we agreed to. Besides, Starla's never even done that," Ethan answered.

"Horses are here to *serve* us!" Lula May huffed. "I'm sure Starla can handle it! Now, hurry up—I'm not going to change my mind, so don't even waste your time arguing."

Ethan shook his head and took Rose aside. "We're not doing this. Let's just forget it."

Rose's heart dropped as his words sunk in. The awaiting trio dove into their own discussion. Starla stood off to the side, quietly waiting at a nearby hitching post. "But what about Starla? We can't just let her..." she trailed off, remembering her promise.

"We'll figure out something else," Ethan insisted, more firmly this time.

"Nothing else to figure out, kid." Murray sucked on his front teeth. "Deal's over. We're headin' out."

"Wait!" Rose stepped in front of them. "Lula May," she

pleaded, hoping to tune in with the artist's sensitive side, the genuine part that must have existed somewhere within her to ever have wanted Starla in the first place. But even through the dark and blingy sunglasses, she could feel Lula May stare back with nothing but hostility. Rose knew what she had to do. "Let's do it."

"Rose!" Ethan threw his arms up. "You're not—"

"I am!" Rose retorted sharply, eyes flashing at him to settle down. Just what did he think he was doing? Certainly nothing along the lines of what they'd been working toward this whole time. *He's crazy if he wants to give up now.* She ignored the gleeful looks in her peripheral vision and took deep breaths while walking back to Starla.

"I know you don't want to hear this," Ethan spoke under his breath so nobody else could listen in. He lifted the reins over Starla's head and put on the bridle. "But neither of you should be doing this right now."

Rose kept her expression neutral while adjusting Starla's forelock from under the headpiece. She took Ethan's opinions and thoughts on horses very seriously. But at this moment, he couldn't be more wrong. Of course, this wasn't the ideal situation. *But do we really have a choice?* They could either take a chance on this one ride today or just sit back and pray that Starla wouldn't end up in danger—a much more frightening and dangerous risk than any kind of riding. Maybe Rose was being foolish, but she was no liar. Promises still meant something to her, no matter what circumstances may have changed along the way.

"I thought orientals were supposed to be smart," Don chuckled behind them. "Why she cares so much about some old broomtail is beyond me."

"Eh, the girl's probably better at math," Murray piled on, earning a bubbly giggle from Lula May.

Creeps. Rose tried to tune them out.

Starla's bridle was all set. Rose looked up and grimly realized that without stirrups, the mare suddenly appeared twenty hands high. She needed help mounting.

"Give me a boost." The words came out more curtly than she intended, but there wasn't any time to pad dialogue with manners.

Ethan reluctantly stepped closer. "Lower your knee, then swing your right leg over." At this point, he knew there was no turning back.

"Thanks." As soon as Rose felt Ethan's cupped hands lift her, she hoisted the rest of herself up and over. Even though Starla didn't stir, Rose's limbs trembled like thick jelly. She'd ridden

Fender bareback a couple of times before, but only on very brief walks around the barn—nothing along the lines of what Lula May and her cohorts were expecting.

Engaging every single muscle in her legs, Rose lowered herself as delicately as possible until she was sitting all the way down.

Starla immediately turned her head to look back at Rose, taking in the newfound sensation.

"Good, Starla. We're going to ride like this for just a little while, okay?" Inhaling deeply, Rose took the reins and touched Starla's neck. Starla then looked ahead, contemplating. *At least she's calmer than I am*, Rose thought. Her heart was thumping like a possessed drum. Wrapping her legs around Starla's barrel, she pressed her heels down and adjusted her seat with competition level focus. *Just pretend it's a no-stirrup lesson day.* She could feel Starla's spine shift toward her, not to mention every warm micro-movement that a saddle would typically cover, or at least somewhat muffle. Starla's back was rounder than Fender's, a characteristic that presently worked in their favor. But even while completely still, and with Ethan standing at Starla's shoulder, Rose couldn't help but feel highly insecure without a saddle and stirrups.

"Are you two ready yet?" Lula May whined. "I have to leave in about…" Just then, her eyes closed into slits, and her mouth hovered open. She stood silently for a few seconds before a violent sneeze expelled into the palm of her hand. The Santa Anas were picking up, and so were her allergies. One, two, three, four…Lula May covered her mouth, but the sneezes kept shooting out, exacerbated by a warm, prolonged current. After several more bellowing discharges, Lula May was finally able to regain composure and wipe her pink nose and eyes with the back of her sleeve.

Ethan gave Starla a firm, confident pat on the neck. "You sure about this?" he asked, putting on as upbeat and positive expression as he could manage. Once Rose nodded, he looked over his shoulder at the group. "All set."

Breathe, Rose reminded both herself and Starla. *It's the same groundwork we've been working on, just without a saddle this time.* She'd never realized how important the air in her lungs was until mounted bareback on an unsure horse in front of a hostile audience.

"Back, back, back," Ethan instructed everyone to move away from Starla's hind end. To Rose's surprise, all three shifted away a few steps but quickly crowded up toward Starla's tail again. Ethan shook his head and nudged them further away with his arms.

"Okay, Rose. Let's start at a walk, tracking left. Remember, I'm right here, so just relax." He sounded like his confident self again.

Squeezing her legs a little, Rose signaled Starla forward. Her walk felt brisker than before, but Rose wasn't sure if it was just her own paranoia. One of the men let out an obnoxious hoot.

Starla flicked an ear but wasn't fazed. Rose tried to push them out of her mind, focusing on completing the first circle. Starla felt extraordinarily huge and powerful this way, and Rose's seat bones had never connected to any horse like this before.

If we could just keep this up a few more times around the ring, maybe we'll be alright, Rose thought hopefully.

Ethan looked satisfied with the way things were going as horse and rider approached the starting point. But Lula May was uninterested and restless.

"This is boring. I'm sure I can *walk* on it, too," Lula May complained as Rose and Starla passed by. "Make it go faster!"

"Hold on, Lula May," Ethan snapped. Rose pretended not to hear them and maintained Starla's walk, trying to practice bareback walking for as long as possible.

"Rose, do you think you're ready for a nice, slow trot?" Ethan asked carefully as they finished their loop.

"Slow?" Lula May asked, irritated.

Rose nodded quickly, afraid Lula May might demand more speed if she didn't agree right away. She pressed her legs. *Yikes!* Starla sprung into motion. Riding Starla's already perky trot, saddle-less, was a completely new experience. Legs on, heels absorbing the motion, core lit. Rose knew she had to get back to the basics to feel comfortable. She barely thought about a half halt and Starla collected into a smooth, relaxed trot.

"Yes! Good!" Caution edged Ethan's encouragement. "Nice and easy, you don't even need to post that one! Let's try a canter now."

Rose jaw relaxed. Ethan wouldn't suggest a canter unless he thought they were riding really well together. And she was actually beginning to enjoy herself. Wisps of Starla's mane swished from a passing gust as they cantered around the ring. Rose guided Starla with her legs, keeping her hands super soft on the reins. At this moment, Starla was fully in sync with her. All of their recent hard work had paid off, even if it was cut short by Lula May's unexpected arrival.

I hope we can do this again, Starla, Rose thought as they cantered around the ring one more time. Starla was moving pretty much perfectly—Lula May couldn't possibly dump her now! Rose would be shocked if the artist failed to see what a wonderful horse she was lucky enough to have. Maybe it would be possible to continue training Starla at Laguna Lake Riding Club, now that Lula May witnessed how much progress had been made here. Rose was almost afraid to hope.

In the corner of her eye, she caught Murray and Don and their matching crossed arms. They weren't happy. Lula May kept observing with a blank stare. At least that was a step up from her bored, mean whining.

"Excellent, Rose." Ethan's relief was evident as Rose slowed Starla to a halt in front of the group. "Good girl, Starla!" He patted Starla's neck with playful affection. Starla sighed, sensing she had done her job.

Lula May looked unusually satisfied with Starla and Rose. "That...wasn't bad," she said slowly. She turned to the two sulking men behind her. "Right, fellas?"

Murray nodded and shrugged at the same time. "It was alright—it seemed a little tight though."

"You could tell it was her first time bareback." Don directed an aloof scan across the rest of the property. "You know, this is a sweet little piece of land right here in this part of town. A developer friend of mine, a real good dude, would be all over this place..."

Lula May held out her phone. "I want a souvenir of the day my horse decided to stop being a psycho. Hold on while I get this shot." She clicked a few times from the side then walked behind Starla's rear end. She steadied the frame. "Ugh, it's blurry, dumb phone. Wait a sec," she ordered, reaching out to yank some shavings from Starla's tail.

Everything happened in slow motion. Lula May's fingers clumsily tugging at the tangled shavings, Starla's head jerking up, ears flattened back. Sensing trouble, Ethan lunged at Lula May to push her out of the way. The next millisecond, Rose felt herself jolt forward. Starla's rump sprung in the air as she kicked out behind.

Instinctively, Rose pulled her body back, balancing as best as she could. Just as she was convinced she was about to eat dirt, it was over. Heart pounding, she steadied herself. Afraid of what she was about to see, Rose turned around.

To her horror, Lula May sat a few feet away, on the ground, right on her butt. She was looking around in a dazed but increasingly furious stupor. A pair of sparkling sunglasses lay next to her.

"Are you okay?" Ethan asked.

Starla still seemed a little perturbed, shaking her head a couple of times. Rose's heart was pounding so hard, she almost felt like she was the one who'd almost been swiped with a hind leg. A wave of dread crashed over her. The ride had gone so well. Why did this have to happen?

Lula May stood up and dusted herself off, mumbling that she was fine. Ethan had pushed her just in time.

Murray approached Rose. "Now, that was a tantrum!" he whistled. "Stupid horse doesn't know right from wrong, now do ya, dummy?" He laughed heartily, then leaned in with a lowered voice. "By the way, might wanna check the storage room. I heard some mysterious tack's in there."

So that's where it went! Rose's jaw dropped. "You hid Starla's saddle?"

Murray grinned and raised his arm high before slamming it as hard as he could on Starla's rump.

31

Starla shot forward like a bullet from a rifle. Her side grazed the edge of the creaky gate and she careened past the group, legs battering with burgeoning force across the property.

Everything quickly turned into a blur. Rose barely had time to think as two young girls jumped out of the way, one shrieking with surprise.

"Watch out!" Ethan yelled from behind. It almost sounded like he was coming after them, but Rose knew that no one would be catching up anytime soon. His voice quickly faded.

Trying not to completely panic, Rose held the reins and steadied her legs and core. It was the only option she had to not hurl off at any moment. Riding at this speed on a bareback horse was definitely not something she had anticipated doing today. And Starla wasn't listening at all—not even to Rose's steering. The mare was in sheer stampede mode, oblivious to everything.

Starla's hooves soon hit the softer dirt of the trails just outside Laguna Lake Riding Club. Rose heard herself shakily pleading with Starla to calm down. Branches scratched across her limbs— was Starla also getting scraped? The air whipped around them as if they were cutting through a gathering storm, a combative mixture of the dreaded Santa Ana winds and their own velocity.

Starla kept veering off the well-worn path, precariously bending into the rustling borders of the brush and vegetation, most of which were too thick to comfortably ride through. Rose aimed them back to the path as much as she could, hoping to at least keep her on a safe surface. Their speed was way too high for off-roading.

The stretch of thick trees was coming to a brief end up ahead. Rose remembered this part of the path well—a straight shot for nearly an eighth of a mile before narrowly curving back into the shady trails. It was one of the most popular spots for riders to snap selfies, and an especially scenic area for a walk or trot.

Autumnal leaves blazed by in a fiery blur. Starla, sensing an open track in front of her, accelerated even more.

"No! Easy, Starla!" Rose cried out. But her words were futile, especially since she was really beginning to wonder if she'd be able to stay mounted for much longer. She managed to wrap her shaking fingers around some strands of mane, but the extra grip did little to calm her.

This is crazy! Rose thought as a squirrel high-tailed it up a tree and watched them with interest over his furry shoulder. *I'm never going to get her to stop!*

Starla's breaths now heaved with a ragged tinge, but her body did not let up. She burst through the remainder of the stretch, Rose perilously clinging on with all her strength. She prayed no other riders were turning on the trail approaching them. What a disaster that would be—a horrific, blindsided crash!

The path curved to the right into the woodsy microcosm of Coyote Hills. Rose wasn't sure if she should feel relieved or even more frightened. If Starla continued on the dirt path, they'd eventually wind back to Laguna Lake Riding Club. But plenty of potential obstacles stood between them and the barn—a small stream near the trail border might very well freak out Starla even more if she veered off the path. There was also a clearing with several overturned logs that some riders used as jumps, another conceivable hazard area.

Starla's taut muscles expanded and contracted as she blasted onward. Her sheer power was almost overwhelming. For a moment, Rose contemplated just giving in, letting herself tumble down, and end this ordeal. Maybe that would be easier...

Years ago, Starla had galloped in a panic like this before, sprinting and sweating across the boundless plains as deafening enemies in the air attacked her herd. It wasn't a play-by-play memory, but more of a feeling—frosty morning sunshine, charging toward an undecipherable black hole ending, bleeding, disoriented, fragmented...breathing only to protect.

Unlike her delicate bay colt with a tiny off-center star on his forehead, Starla had survived.

A high-pitched call from the clouds reverberated through the entire forest. Rose squeezed her right leg as hard as she could, steering Starla haphazardly back onto the dirt and away from a clump of bushes they almost blindly crashed into. Struggling to balance her seat was almost overwhelming in the frenzy, but

Rose's own stubborn instincts were kicking in as well.

Starla's pummeling hooves began to conform with the wind in a turbulent yet discernible rhythm. The flow pounded in Rose's head like a mesmerizing drumbeat as a sharp pulse coursed through her entire body. Up ahead was the cluster of trees. Somewhere in there was the spot that Sandy had eventually found her lying on the ground, not far from Fender.

What was that? A tranquil sound from some corner of the chaos.

Hoping someone from the barn had somehow caught up to help, Rose darted her gaze around but saw no one. Just when she thought she'd safely turned Starla back toward Laguna Lake Riding Club, the mare swerved into an unassuming gap in the brush. They burned into the sheltered cove of trees to the open patch of jumps. Even though the back end of Laguna Lake Riding Club was just on the other side of the thicket, it felt like they were a hundred miles away.

"Rose!" Again, the unfamiliar called out, this time from somewhere ahead.

Disoriented, Rose scanned the blur of woods.

Starla shifted direction with another delirious sprint. Rose's head buzzed with adrenaline. Something was on the ground up ahead.

A pair of huge logs, side by side, greeted them.

No! Rose's lips quivered. She mentally braced herself.

A nearby jagged branch swayed from the wind's increasing violence, bouncing a flash of sunlight off the shade of another tree.

Starla cocked her head to the side for an instant. A glint shimmered, ephemeral, in her large brown eye.

An atom of images and voices exploded.

"Horse people…"

Aunt Esther's green journal…

A childhood of averted gazes…

A chill shot through all of Rose's flesh. Some part of her had done this before, elsewhere, in another time. The whir of the Santa Anas went silent for a fleeting second, and Rose willed her terror far beyond the gigantic logs. She really didn't have any other choice as Starla pounded onward. Pressure scorched through every vein and muscle until even her fingertips and toes felt like steel.

Starla was on a warpath of her own, the kind without a target or specific plan—the gallop of prey. *Run…*a deeply ingrained sensation inherent since birth and reborn at the end of her independence. She didn't have to hear any aerial whirring or chopping. The logs ahead weren't going anywhere, and neither was she.

A sea of fear crashed against the insides of Rose's chest, each wave hurling into a froth with every haggard breath. But she *had* done this before—it was as built-in to her as the mindset of prey was to Starla. Rose pivoted forward into a two-point position as much as she could, her intuition bounding up and down like a seesaw. One moment, Starla felt almost fluid underneath her, but as soon as Rose gave into the cycling rhythm, she lost it, only to jerkily halfway meld into the movements again.

Just as Starla launched off the ground, Rose leaned into her, giving the reins. They sailed through the air as effortlessly as the very last time Starla commanded her desert homeland.

Nothing else mattered in that flash. Space stilled. Front hooves hit the dirt, landing, straightening out. Starla collected herself and continued galloping without missing a beat.

Starla's proud snort was the most glorious sound Rose could ever imagine at that moment. The fogged tunnel of trees sharpened into focus as her strides gradually shortened with each deep exhale. Their lungs heaved together, winding down in tandem.

Suddenly Starla tossed her head. But before Rose's seat could prepare for the powerful buck, she was in the air again, this time alone. A nearby craggy tree branch didn't soften her fall but cut along the underside of her left arm as gravity hurled her to the ground.

Rose could've sworn her bones cracked a little when she landed, butt-first. Both hands clutched the ground at her sides, fingers pressing into the dirt with both relief and shock. Was it her imagination, or did the ground feel a million times harder now than it did when she was a kid?

Starla's curious muzzle was the first thing Rose saw when she looked up. The mare's dark eyes gazed down at what she'd just tossed off her back. Bemused acknowledgment tinged her look with a trace of "Oops!"

"Oh, Starla," Rose heaved, managing a faint grin. Starla snorted again, quietly. The reins hung down the sides of her neck.

Rose exhaled and slowly stood up. She'd be a little sore but she was alright, especially since Starla looked more than fine. Patting Starla's neck, Rose gathered the reins. She would hand walk Starla back to the barn. That would give her a few minutes to decompress…as well as figure out how to deal with Lula May's inevitable wrath.

32

"Ethan, wait up!" Lula May huffed. She stumbled on a scraggly overgrown tree root again, barely catching herself.

Ethan offered a grunt of acknowledgment but didn't slow down. Despite having no idea where Rose and Starla were, he wasn't going to waste any time following the designated paths to find them. And if Lula May wanted to tag along, that was her choice.

"Argh!" Lula May yelped, tripping on a jagged rock. Her mouth curled into a stupefied sneer as she watched Ethan's back trudge on without so much a glance behind. "I thought you cowboys were supposed to be gentlemen."

Was she baiting him? Ethan turned around.

Lula May smirked and raised an eyebrow. Her face said it all: *Boys—so predictable.*

Dried leaves pulverized under his boots as Ethan backtracked a few steps toward her.

Lula May flashed a flirtatious grin, trying to get him to crack one back. "You're going a little fast. You wouldn't want to lose me, would you?"

Ethan looked down at her with pure condescension. "You know, you've been nothing but an entitled pain in the neck."

"*Excuse* me?" Any leftover trace of Lula May's coyness instantly vanished.

"Entitled is putting it nicely." Ethan knew that addressing one of the stable's income sources this way could get him into trouble, but Lula May was no proper boarder.

Lula May clenched her fists. "How dare you. You don't know a thing about me!"

Ethan shrugged. "I do know that you punched Starla, and who knows what else. And now you just want to get rid of her without anybody finding out. She's nothing more to you than some kind of shield for your pathetic career." He turned back around and resumed his brisk pace. "You don't deserve her."

"I'm not pathetic!" Lula May yelled. "And that dumb horse is a hot mess—a total drain of my money, and it tries to kill almost everyone it sees! If you had any real clue…"

Her tantrum shrunk into the background as Ethan zeroed in on the approaching figures. Rose was leading Starla. Both were walking calmly. Neither looked in distress. Although he couldn't see much more detail from this distance, a shock of relief hit his gut and it was all he could do from breaking into a sprint.

33

"Well, what happened?" Don inquired, stubbing out a cigarette with the toe of his leather boot. He and Murray were still waiting by the ring. Don looked impatiently behind Lula May as she approached. "Where are the three stooges?"

Murray laughed and spit out a marble-sized grayish glob from the crook of his mouth.

Lula May stopped, slightly panting. Since firing Carrie, she'd spent the last several days doing absolutely everything all by herself. And now this! It was utterly exhausting. "I don't know. I'm sure they're fine." Her hand gestured back toward the trails with a "who cares" flourish.

Murray and Don exchanged glances before talking at once.

"So, what do you wanna do with that animal?"

"Now *that's* a suicide mission!"

Chuckling, Don revealed a row of dull, crooked teeth. "Seems futile to me."

Lula May scowled. "Guess so." The incredible hassle called "Starla" dawned on her for the millionth time. What a waste. Uncooperative, ungrateful, even making Lula May look bad...

A stern voice interrupted from behind. "Excuse me. Is that a cigarette?" A petite woman in a gray jacket and matching breeches approached the group. Her gaze focused on the ground near Don's feet.

Don's spine practically melted with caginess. "Yeah, so?" he answered, shifting his weight. He didn't welcome authority, especially from some woman.

Lula May simmered with annoyance. Didn't Gina remember her? If Gina knew what was good for her, she wouldn't be addressing her top boarder's guests with such inconsideration.

"Gina, it's Lula May. Starla's owner, remember?" She made sure to edge her voice with a little domination.

Gina coolly registered her. "Lula May, yes. How are you?"

Satisfied that Gina now understood her rightful place, Lula May relaxed. "These are my friends, so you really don't have to worry about the smoking—"

"—burning down the entire stable, and all the animals in it?" Gina interrupted, her eyes heating with intense, turquoise anger.

Lula May frowned. "One cigarette isn't going to do that," she muttered.

"Please spare me your advice on fire safety," Gina replied, carefully maintaining an even tone. She pointed to a large sign on a nearby shed. "Does it look like smoking is allowed here?"

Silence.

With an irritated sigh, Gina continued. "Obviously, anyone with eyes that work can see that smoking is absolutely not permitted."

The two men ignored the berating and began shrugging their way back to the parking lot, nodding their departure to Lula May. They certainly weren't going to stick around for any more verbal abuse from this lady.

"Let me know," Murray said to Lula May. "You got my number."

Don defiantly lit another cigarette as the pair sauntered away. The sharp flick of the lighter almost triggered Gina to go after the pair, but she decided to just let them leave.

Lula May turned toward the sound of clopping hooves. Ethan, Rose, and Starla were returning from the trails. She looked the group up and down. Ethan was walking a few steps ahead of Rose and Starla, aiming directly at his clearly perturbed boss, probably ready to offer an explanation of the odd scenario. Rose led Starla, much of her clothes covered in a layer of dirt. She looked a little…windblown. But it was Starla who took Lula May by surprise the most. Her eyes, usually distant and uninterested, scanned the grounds with a cheery spark. Instead of pulling or head tossing, Starla followed just behind Rose, happily, as if she'd never had an uncooperative moment in her life. Was that how she always was with that girl? How was this the same horse? A glower crept across Lula May's face. Even on Starla's best days, the nicest thing she'd ever done to Lula May was completely ignore her.

"Hi, Gina," Ethan called out. "You're back early. How was the trip?"

"Never mind that. What is going on here?" Gina demanded.

Lula May stepped forward. All of this nonsense was ultimately because of her horse. She probably owed Gina some sort of explanation. "You have no clue how hard the past few weeks have been, Gina. It's been total nonsense with Starla." She pointed at the placid mare. "Don't be fooled now—it's usually totally mean and dumb no matter how much you try. I'm so done. We'll be leaving Laguna Lake Riding Club as soon as possible." She turned on her heels and quickly got her phone. "Murray, it's me. Are you still nearby?"

"Hey, hold on a minute!" Ethan hollered. He handed the reins to Gina's unsuspecting hands, muttering something about explaining everything later.

"It's okay, Starla," Rose heard the barn owner say. When she looked over at them, Gina was petting the mare's withers.

Ethan and Rose caught up to Lula May just as she was about to get in her car.

"Didn't you see what Murray did?" Rose's voice shook with anger. "He's been screwing with Starla this whole time!"

"She's right, Lula May," Ethan leaned against the car door. "Murray's done nothing but harm."

"Murray, let me call you back." Lula May shot Ethan a threatening glare to move out of her way. These two animal justice warriors were really getting on her nerves. "I'm sure you guys mean well, but it's none of your business now. Just stay in your lane." She plopped into the driver's seat. "I mean it. Don't make me call the cops."

"Funny coming from someone who's using Starla for PR and then just throwing her away," Rose shot back. "Do you even know that Murray came here earlier and hid Starla's saddle? Or did you put him up to that?"

"What did you just say?" Lula May's keys missed the ignition and dropped to the floor mat. "Are you accusing me of something?"

"It's nothing, Lula May." Ethan reached out and pulled Rose's shoulders gently back.

"That's what I thought." Lula May fumbled for her keys and revved the engine as loud as she could without scaring herself. She screeched out of the parking lot with an obnoxious cloud of dust. In her rearview mirror, she eyed Ethan and Rose. They looked like they were in a serious conversation.

Nosey losers! Lula May fumed. Clearly, they'd all been gossiping about her. The more she thought about it, the more Rose's comment about Starla and PR bothered her. How did she know about any of that—was it possible the girl had just made a lucky guess?

Lula May steered right and slammed her foot on the gas, accelerating down the curving road so fast she almost missed the big intersection at Beach Boulevard. At the last second, she managed to swerve into the left turn lane toward the freeway.

"Shut the hell up!" she hollered, sticking her middle finger out the window at the car behind her. The nerve of that couple honking at her like that. Searching around the insides of her purse, she clutched the small white box and pulled out a cigarette. She hadn't regularly smoked since her early post-interview days.

The left turn arrow turned green just as her phone lit up. Murray was calling her back.

Lula May clung to the steering wheel, her foot still on the brake. Could everyone just leave her alone for a minute? Where was her scream towel when she needed it?

The phone screen flashed again. Murray was probably wondering why she wasn't picking up all of a sudden.

Funny coming from someone who's using Starla for PR and then just throwing her away...

Rose's words drilled in Lula May's head, over and over. And what did she mean about Murray hiding Starla's saddle?

"I'll show them," Lula May grumbled. Her temples were pounding from all this drama with these morons. She hurled the phone at the passenger seat with all of her might. Slamming her foot on the gas pedal, she roared, "You don't mess with Lula May!"

34

ose watched her father in the corner of her eye.

He pushed the button that closed the car window and shifted in his seat. He had that far off look, a gaze that surfaced only while ocean fishing or driving on a long, deserted highway. This time it was the latter. But unlike their usual family road trips, it was just the two of them. Although Rose was pretty convinced that she knew why, she still had no idea what to expect.

The morning was a blur of her parents' plans. Shortly after waking up with a sore lower back and butt, her parents knocked on her door to announce the impromptu day trip.

"Dirty Boot Town?" The last thing Rose thought she'd hear from them was the silly childhood nickname that she and Thomas had given the desert ghost town. Thanks to Dad's keen interest in remote landscapes and buried bits of local history, the family had taken the three-hour drive enough times to claim a certain jokey familiarity with the place. Thomas pouted a little after hearing he wasn't invited this time, but immediately perked up at the mention of an outing to the local skate park. After packing leftover sandwiches from Ruda's Deli, some of Mom's homemade rice and veggie rolls, and several bottles of water and apple juice, Rose climbed into the waiting sedan.

Should've brought my headphones. They had been on the 5 North freeway for nearly an hour without so much of a single word between them, other than benign comments on the scenery. The longer her father went without talking—*really* talking—the more trapped and claustrophobic Rose felt in the passenger seat. And the last thing she would ever do was start the conversation herself. She was way too full of dread. Had she scrapped her plans to check on Starla at the barn for this? Rose sent Ethan a brief text asking for an update. What if Lula May decided to take Starla away today? Even the view of the shiny high rises of downtown Los Angeles, usually so striking and dramatic from the road, couldn't attract her attention when they switched lanes to the 101 North.

Now well beyond the cityscape and its far-reaching flats crammed with concrete humanity, Rose drummed her fingers on the armrest, fixated on the horizon. A vibrant blue sky, streaked with wispy cirrus clouds.

Her dad turned on the radio. A song with his favorite musician promptly started. Any real conversation would have to wait until after the highway robber crossed the universe in his spacecraft.

✦✦✦

"We're here."

Rose jerked awake, her entire left side prickling from dozing off in such an awkward position. Lunchtime sunlight and an expanse of golden dirt in a shallow basin greeted her. The makeshift parking lot was distinguishable from the rest of the barren surroundings only from repeated flattening by tires. Drivers had to leave their vehicles somewhere adjacent to the cluster of dilapidated structures. Even through post-nap grog, Rose was stunned by a totally new characteristic of the abandoned town: tourists. Lots of them.

"What are all these people doing here?" she blurted, eyes widening at the sight of another car turning in. She pointed out the windshield. "This place was always empty!"

"Guess everyone has discovered Dirty Boot Town."

A silver Range Rover pulled up on their right. Rose studied the middle-aged couple through the semi-tinted windows as if they'd just arrived on a UFO. The man's wiry beard covered most of his face, and his wavy locks were twisted into a loose bun at the nape of his tattooed neck. His companion leaned her lavender-hued head into him and snapped a quick photo as they made funny faces at the phone.

Rose shook her head. Never in a million years would she have guessed that one of her dad's quirky road trip destinations would end up becoming a backdrop for hipster selfies.

"Let's take a short walk before lunch," Dad suggested. He motioned to his daughter's backpack. "Hold on, let me get something."

The crisp, dry air nipped at Rose's cheeks as soon as they stepped out of the car. The sunlight was piercing. She slipped on a black Toy House cap with "Anaheim, CA" embroidered on the back. Nothing4U was hoping to play at the small venue soon, which Tori was ecstatic about.

Dad went to the trunk. Rose could hear him sliding aside his heavy box of tools.

"Nice hat," Dad spoke with a playful tone that matched the mischievous twinkle in his eye. On his head was a familiar brown hat of his own.

A delighted grin spread on Rose's face. The wool cowboy hat was custom made by a local hat maker during a family trip to Montana. She was too surprised at the sight of it to come up with a joke, even though she knew Dad probably expected at least a few. *Asian cowboy—yee, hao!* She and Thomas had relentlessly made fun of him all the way from Big Sky back to Orange County, choking with laughter at their father's new look. Dad always had a zippy funny bone. He didn't mind all of their wisecracks for that entire drive through the West, even pushing rather non-politically correct jokes right along with them, albeit at his own expense.

"Thought I should wear it out here today," Dad chuckled. He adjusted the hat again. "Still fits."

Rose got the feeling that he had brought it out after all these years to help ease the tension between them. Despite her teasing, she had to admit that her father actually looked pretty good in the skillfully creased hat. Maybe it was because he was a little older now. Cowboy hats tend to complement age—at least that's what mustached Carl, the philosophical hat maker, had mused in his wood paneled workshop while taking Dad's measurements.

A certain smell was floating around. Animated yet muffled laughter escaped from behind the almost rolled up windows of the Range Rover. Rose glanced inside. The man and woman were puffing on what looked like a small joint, apparently getting primed up to trip out. Dad didn't seem to notice them, or if he did, he didn't pay them any attention.

Despite the numerous visitors milling about, the main street still looked just as lost in time as when the Moon family had stopped by years before. No cement lined this street—dirt, rocks, or scrubby weeds met every footstep, and the dozen or so structures on either side of the drag were mostly comprised of ramshackle wood and haggard stone. Old cobwebs weaved around cragged points of glass in broken windows, so dusty they appeared to have been abandoned even by the spiders. Some kids chased after a tumbleweed scuttling across the street until it passed the other side of the buildings and disappeared somewhere in the open range.

Rose's stomach growled. It was definitely past lunchtime. Unlike some of the other ghost towns they had visited, Dirty Boot Town didn't offer brochures, souvenirs, or a functioning restaurant. When someone came to Dirty Boot Town, at least for now, they were still pretty much on their own.

As a group of tourists posed for photos in front of the general store, Rose and her father continued toward the center of the street. The peeling "Saloon" sign above the narrow entrance hung crookedly from years of dry rot and overall desert roughness. Three shallow porch steps creaked under Rose's weight. At the entrance, a lone remaining swinging door precariously hung onto a rusted hinge, its matching counterpart nowhere to be seen.

The saloon looked and felt a lot smaller than before. Splintery wooden walls framed the room and the rickety bar that ran about half the length of the back wall appeared almost fuzzy with grime. Some brown chairs with missing legs were strewn along the sides. A thick layer of tanned dust blanketed just about everything. The only signs of life were the faint footprints on the chalky flooring and the random gnats that hovered in the still, musty air.

"See it?" Dad had beat her to it. He walked briskly to the far side of the bar, turned around, and pointed at an object on the floor. "Still here."

"Ugh!" Rose came over and bent down at it, wrinkling her nose. There it was—the dirty boot.

Whether or not it was the same rotted leather boot that she and Thomas had seen in the saloon every time they'd visited was unclear. On the bar counter, under a back table, or next to the entrance…it always turned up in a different part of the saloon, but it was always somewhere in there. She and Thomas had stopped wondering whose it was or how it got there, instead just nicknaming the whole darn town after it.

She took a photo to send to her brother, but the message wouldn't go through. "No reception," she grumbled, reminding herself to try again as soon as they got closer to civilization. That was probably why she hadn't heard back from Ethan, too.

Footsteps creaked up the front porch, quickly followed by giggly chatter. It was the couple from the Range Rover. They nodded with puffy grins and instantly became fascinated with the dusty details of the old bar.

Rose and her dad left the saloon to the giddy couple. While exploring the old post office, bare-bones schoolhouse, and tiny restroom, Rose remembered reading about the initial economic boom of the area and how adventurous settlers from all over trekked to California hoping to uncover sudden wealth from the region's pristine natural resources. From the looks of the unlikely town, their plans had indeed worked for at least a little while. But she couldn't remember much about how it all ended. Why did it vanish completely, and where did everyone go? How long did it take for this tiny town to dissolve into nothing more than a community skeleton, an obscure day trip for tourists in the know? The place was a trip all by itself, no joint necessary.

"Ready for lunch?" Dad heard Rose's stomach grumbling again. "Let's go to that spot we ate at last time. If it's still there." Those last four words were always mentioned on their repeat road trips. Anything could always disappear.

The empty wooden shed still stood all by itself in a vast and lonely stretch of scrub, an easy uphill walk from the main street but still far enough away to experience a slice of desert solitude. An uneven, sun-bleached cloth awning extended off one side of the shed, offering minimal but welcome shade from the harsh sunlight. They reached the padded bank of dirt and oval rocks and unloaded their lunch packs.

Mom's scrumptious veggie rolls quickly disappeared. "The ones from the grocery store are a joke after you eat these," Dad commented as he reached for another. "Ah, nothing better than eating good food outside." He took a long sip of water and looked out at the expanse of land and sky.

Nodding in silent agreement, Rose savored the last roll of chopped tofu, carrots, spinach, and rice. Although swatting flies between bites was always annoying, her dad was right on both counts. She leaned back, wincing from the tender bruises on her side, and faced the opposite direction of Dirty Boot Town. This was why they really came out here all these years: an unobstructed view of hard, beautiful, impossible life. Rose used to eventually get bored with the arid panorama as a little girl. But now, as she looked closer at the intricate fabric of the unforgivingly patient land, a sense of incredulity engulfed her.

Clumps of thriving shrub covered the land for miles in every direction until reaching the distant, imposing rolling hills. The insistent finger-like branches of Joshua trees also sprinkled the terrain like unexpected starfish on stilts. The pale blue sky enveloped the horizon so wide and low that a couple of wispy clouds appeared almost touchable. A squiggly movement next to Rose's leg caught her eye. The small brown spider scuttled to safety behind a vibrant orange poppy. Somehow she had not noticed the delicate flower. Rose suddenly felt smaller than a molecule, humbled by such a quiet, far-fetched existence just a few hours from home.

"Well, we know you've been going to the stables." Dad was matter-of-fact, as if they were already ten minutes deep in conversation. It was the first time he had mentioned the barn in years. "What are you doing there?"

Rose blinked and refrained a bug-eyed double take. She drew in a rapid gulp of air but kept looking straight ahead at the desert openness.

"Did Aunt Esther write that in her diary, too?" Her reply came out harsher than she intended, but she just let it hang.

Dad made a sound that was halfway between a chuckle and a scoff.

They both sat in rigid silence for what felt like minutes. Rose concentrated on the far-off rounded hilltops, not really focusing on anything. Nothing was there, nothing that she could see, anyway.

"You shouldn't have found out that way."

Rose's heart convulsed before he even finished that sentence. Even though she'd read those shocking words with her own eyes on that Halloween morning, none of it was ever truly confirmed. Until now.

Suddenly Rose was no longer sitting on the outskirts of Dirty Boot Town, leaning on the side of a fossilized shed with her reticent father. She was back in her bedroom closet, clutching her aunt's journal. She was a kid, overhearing strange murmurs about her. She learned to keep quiet and observe. The concept of empathy was something she grew up giving more than receiving, and she quickly learned to pinpoint ill will at an age far younger than anybody should. A random sequence of events and timing had aligned in such a way for a hidden truth to finally emerge from those handwritten pages, sucking her entire existence into a crystallized enigma. Now, in the middle of a desert basin with her father and facing the edge of what may both separate and connect them, Rose just wanted to throw up.

"It wasn't my fault that I found out that way." The begrudging retort flew out of her mouth, bitter and eager to seize any opening. It was cathartic and a little scary at the same time.

"That's not what I'm saying." Dad spoke evenly, but Rose could tell his mind had a storm of thoughts hurling around. "I don't know why she was writing about that."

"I know I shouldn't have snooped," Rose interrupted earnestly. "I wasn't trying to. I was just getting my jacket, and it was there, right in my closet—her journal, I mean." She paused and tried to steer back to the more pressing issue at hand. "Dad, you know it's been really…obvious."

"What has been obvious?"

Rose's head swiveled at him, her eyes scorching from the searing heat that was now simmering the blood in her veins. "What?" She couldn't believe he was acting like there was even a question to ask. And did he truly think that somehow Rose had never noticed? "Your stupid secret, whatever it is!"

Reee! A bird's simultaneous and vehement screeching stole the effect of her yell, but Rose knew her father had heard it all. His perennial I-can-handle-anything expression shifted as the bird's insistent calling echoed off distant surfaces before flying off. The creases from Dad's brows and mouth slackened and he turned to her. Light coffee, almost hazel. Sometimes in certain lighting, he almost looked as if he wore colored contact lenses. Who knew where that gene came from because no other relative she'd ever met had an eye color in that shade.

"I heard that horses know right away if you don't know how to ride. And some of them will totally reject you, just throw you off."

Rose blinked, switching gears from her frustrated outburst. "Um, depends on the horse, depends on the person." Before she could ask where he had gotten this factoid, he continued.

"But Rose was always...brave." For a second, her dad seemed to have forgotten she was sitting there with him. Then he smirked. "Your hair doesn't hide it, you know."

"Hide what?" Just as the words left Rose's mouth, her hand involuntarily floated to her ear. "Oh."

Her dad chuckled. It was reassuring.

A muffled musical note pinged the easing awkwardness between them. Dirty Boot Town's patchy reception had finally let a text come through.

Are you ok? Keep getting your voicemail. Lula May is freaking out, said she's coming to the barn. Not sure what she's planning. Call me when you can.

Rose's stomach dropped to the dirt. "Dad?"

The change in her voice instantly got his attention. "What is it?"

Rose tried to quell the noose of panic tightening around her throat. "Can we go home now? Something's wrong at the barn." She hated to interrupt this long-awaited conversation, but she was already starting to freak out. They were so far away. Was there a faster route to take back? "I'll explain everything in the car."

"Of course." Even though Dad didn't have a clue about the circumstances surrounding Starla and Lula May, he instantly began gathering their food, wrappers, napkins, and bottles with meticulous speed. He'd always had a sharp instinct for unforeseen distress.

Rose tried replying to Ethan all the way back to the car but kept getting the dreaded error message. "So much for technology," she grumbled in the passenger seat, huddled over her phone.

"The service will get better near the highway," Dad assured. He glanced at the mirrors and turned the jangly set of keys in the ignition. The radio crackled to life with a fuzzy churn for a few seconds before Rose leaned forward and switched it off.

As they bumped along the grit road, Rose watched Dirty Boot Town's reflection shrink in the side mirror. Something about the forgotten buildings and dirt street that held the shoddy place together had always compelled her father. Whatever it was, she was glad he shared that with her.

Dad glanced at the phone in his daughter's hand. "So, what's been going on?" He sounded genuinely curious.

Rose glared at the useless device as another error appeared. Sighing, she plopped the phone down. No sense in trying to return Ethan's text until those precious reception bars reappeared.

Let Starla be safe.

About a week before Grandma left for good, Rose had perused a flimsy booklet that someone had left behind on one of the Hub's patio tables. The title had something to do with the power of thoughts. She couldn't remember the author's name, but their simple explanation on executing those thoughts into real-life outcomes was more than intriguing. Manifesting, that's what it was called. Apparently, people did it all the time. Was it real or just wishful thinking? Squeezing her eyes shut, Rose thought about Starla again, and then the other horses at the barn, and Laguna Lake Riding Club itself.

Dad's question still dangled in the air between them.

Trying to get him to understand her tunnel-vision love for horses was always difficult enough. How was she going to now justify everything else that had gone down, especially with a horse who wasn't even hers? Rose squinted out the window at a small white cap that jaggedly topped a mountain on the horizon. The sunlight was now so bright that lowering her gaze onto the shadier hillsides actually lessened the pressure on her eyes.

A steady ripple cut across Rose's peripheral vision. Pacing an unbroken horizontal line across a plateau of dry brush, a dark silhouette crossed the land with commanding speed. Though far from earshot, Rose knew the drumbeats were not imaginary. The shadowy form then curved toward the hills and blended with the native turf, protected behind the camouflaged cloak of wilderness and inertia.

"Did you see that?"

Rose didn't reply even though she knew they'd glimpsed the same thing. Scanning the general area where the flat range met the base of the mountain line, she tried to locate the fleeting motion again.

"Almost looked like..." Dad shrugged. "Eh, maybe it was a big deer or something."

Rose kept her eyes focused. She knew what he was thinking. Deer didn't live in this area. Coyotes and big horned sheep, maybe, but not deer. The way the shadow moved had nothing in common with those animals.

Willow, bittersweet, and ash in the distance hushed into uncaptured motionlessness, expertly eluding the intrusive stares from the two aliens inside the humming metal object on wheels. On this faraway plane, the energy of a crooked tawny weed was no different from that of a long-stemmed Andes mountain rose. A warm wind stroked that isolated piece of the planet's surface. Every desert hue trembled. Unseen, the running shadow breathed in the strand of foreign texture in the air. Confirmation was futile.

Dad gently stepped on the brakes. Rough dips dotted the uneven road ahead. A steady and pulverizing crunch filled the inside of the car as they carefully pressed on, a granulated cacophony that instantly churned an underground image of Grandma's pale, strong arms.

There she was, hovering over her old gray mortar stooped over the kitchen tile, grinding the club-like pestle until the tiny globes of seeds cracked and released. Rose's lips lifted into an inward, private smile. She smelled (or could've sworn she smelled) the nutty aroma of freshly ground sesame seeds inside the Moon's sedan. Then it was gone.

What were those sesame seeds even for? Rose wondered. She'd always jumped at the chance to take over the pestle when Grandma had other tasks, but she couldn't recall what dish or recipe those seeds were for.

Avoiding the overwhelming emptiness wasn't what Rose had ever intended. The funeral had played out like a surreal exercise in desensitization. Was it normal for people to reveal their usually hidden selves at funerals? Almost everyone with a pulse seemed rude, judgmental, and self-centered. It wasn't surprising, just very disgusting. One would think that at such a somber gathering, guests wouldn't pose for photos in front of a casket or casually remark how the luncheon afterward didn't meet their sophisticated palette's standards.

In some ways, those folks were the most disturbing part about the funeral because they could walk out and live. After the black-clad guests went back home to their everyday existences, the void latched on to Rose, darkening and swallowing. It was sharper than a cracked glass shard, and when it cut into her eyes, she realized she had more than the two to see with. Then every haughty cackle, every sour look, and every single screw, exclusion, and lie just blasted in her midst. *Boom.* Days ahead or behind her back, it didn't matter. Rose watched them all come and go. Nobody was remotely subtle, no matter how slick they thought they were. *So that's who you are, you smiling, miserable, mini-sandwich vilifier.* Rose's heart clenched whenever she remembered those vapid grins and picky gripes in a sea of compassionless stares. Instead of looking away, she wished that she'd wrenched that stupid Leica and hurled it into the nearby pond. Rather than brushing off the criticism of the food, she should have stuffed thirty sandwiches right into that ugly yapper. Whether or not anyone else cared, believed, or cared enough to believe was on them. Loyalty was truth, the rarest form of love.

What an anchor she had been. If only Rose had realized it during that bend of time when Grandma's heart was still pumping. Foolishly, she thought—no, *assumed*—the woman would last forever. Headstrong and fiery beyond hell…how had Rose never learned that such an immense existence could one day simply vanish?

It went both ways.

She and her father bobbled in the car toward the main highway, the road gradually smoothing out again. Her throat was suddenly parched. The sun's rays versus air conditioning, final round. Ignoring the emerging throbs behind her right temple, Rose searched the outlying terrain as far out without having to squint too hard.

The sunbaked expanse remained simultaneously rooted and airborne, offering only the eonian silence that had always been. Rose felt tiny. She squirmed against the now uncomfortable angle of the car seat and kept searching out the window. They had driven far enough from Dirty Boot Town that not a single car or road sign was around.

Dad was silent. Rose could feel him still wondering what was going on.

Her connection with Starla was not in her imagination, and she certainly wasn't trying to meddle in some ridiculous, romanticized delusion of mustang drama. She respected horses too much to seek self-serving tales from them.

Screw hiding.

The freeway onramp was coming up. Rose drew in a measured breath of air. The tingling in her hands she knew well. It always crept up her shoulders the longer she hesitated at the cusp of being heard. Grandma's arms kept grinding. Most of Dirty Boot Town's shabby road had already shrunken out of sight in the mirror, replaced by tenuous lines of shallow tire tracks in the desolate desert moonscape.

Tick, splat.

Tiny brownish dots specked the front windshield, splattered corpses of dozens of unknowing insects that had met their big bang fate, courtesy of the Moon family car.

Rose was glad to be leaving. The land was healthier and safer without humans and egos. A final sense of reprieve blanketed her. The past could wait.

Maal. *Maal.*

The monosyllabic word meant both "talk" and "horse" in the Korean language. Funny, she'd never recognized that before.

Rose sank back into the seat like she'd just finished a paralyzing solo presentation in front of her entire school. But unlike almost every other consequential instance in her life, Rose knew exactly what to say. Starla had opened up to her, and now it was time to open up about Starla.

35

Ethan ransacked his vest pockets before the caller hung up. "Hello?" He drooped when he heard the voice on the other end. "Hi, Gina."

"Everything okay?" she asked.

"Yep." Ethan yanked off both torn gloves. "All fixed now." He quickly went over the details of the morning as he headed back to the main barn. Some driver had crashed into the fence on the eastern side of the property during the night. Temporarily fixing the sagging gate had eaten a significant chunk of his workday.

He listened to Gina's plans to hire an additional trainer for their hunter jumper students, but his mind kept drifting. Of course, he was grateful at how quickly their little barn was growing since he'd started the job. The equestrian scene wasn't nearly as robust as it was years ago. That was the trajectory both here and back home. Blame it on technology, a changing culture, land development and greed...in any case, everyone had to be even more on point these days to make a decent living with horses. He stifled another deep yawn. The reason he'd hardly slept last night kept bugging. Squinting in the afternoon sunlight, Ethan stuffed what was left of his gloves in his vest. Pair number four this year was already done, and it wasn't even Christmas.

The news from back home wasn't a surprise. Not at all. Should he let his mother go about her business and get screwed in the process—again—or go and try to fix her mistakes, just like he did with the stupid fence, and disrupt his own life in the process?

A burst of wind rustled through the property. He quickened his pace. Thanks to the weather, he and the horses had woken up to several minutes of howling gusts throughout the night. A nap would be nice. But even with Gina not around (she was visiting a horse up north for a client), Ethan knew that catching up on any rest was nothing more than a fairy tale. The gritty coffee in his old thermos would have to take him straight through the day as usual. Fine by him. Compared to going back home to survey the damage caused by his mom's inelegant romantic fling, a little fatigue at Laguna Lake Riding Club was straight-up heaven.

"Mitch loves me," she implored during their brief and testy call last night. "You really don't know how good he treats me. And sweetheart, I am going to add him to the documents. Please understand, okay?"

Mitch, you washed up gold-digger.

Ethan studied the old eucalyptus trees that protectively lined the property and sage-covered hills in the distance. This year, he had originally planned on staying put for the holidays in order to save money. But the more he thought of Mitch's shifty intentions with the family ranch, that scenario was looking way too risky.

A trace scent of hot, crackling wood drifted in the air before dissipating as quickly as it had appeared. It reminded him of the craggy river rock fireplace in the living room of their old house. One of those rocks had his first initial and a tiny smiley face etched on the side, right under the one with his parents' initials. He missed those evenings after dinner, the three of them relaxing with music and banter as the late afternoon heat dissipated to prickly night chill. Even from the grave, his dad probably wanted to pummel Mitch in the face.

The idea of "Uncle" Mitch secretly lusting after his mother all those years incensed Ethan so much that sometimes he almost couldn't see. Looking back now, Mitch's desires were nauseatingly obvious: the lingering stare whenever his mom walked by, the incessant jokes of how a two-jump chump wrangled such a gorgeous specimen, always finding a reason to quietly amble into the kitchen or barn when his dad wasn't paying attention. How could he—*they*—have been so blind?

Mitch was no godfather. Too bad Ethan didn't realize this until two months after the burial. What he really should've done that unforgettable evening, when he unknowingly walked in on their sundown Cabernet escapade, was smash the bottle into the ground and run him off their land for good. Instead, he packed up and left the next morning—right after an explosive argument with his still-grieving mother. He didn't win.

Ethan stopped in his tracks. It still hit him in the gut sometimes. Nothing on the planet could knock the wind out of him like that cozy, revolting scene on the creaky front porch. He heard himself going over the farrier's new schedule with Gina, but all he could think about were those smitten gazes of pure betrayal. How could they be so proud to indulge in their newfound connection while prancing around on the very porch his father had built?

Not only was Dad's mysterious death a tragedy of a lifetime, but it had also opened a gateway to what looked like a losing battle. Mitch had a very specific reputation. He could make bulls prance for him like cute little ponies, just for fun. Those same traits always went far with the ladies, even with the one who was supposed to be off-limits.

Mitch probably thought he was going to get away with it. All of it. And so far, he'd done a pretty bang-up job. But no way in hell was Ethan going to sit back and watch that fake outlaw bear down into their family hearth without a real fight.

"Last thing is Starla," Gina's voice skipped as the connection crackled. "Lula…at the barn until…"

"What was that?" Ethan asked. "Gina, your connection is breaking up."

His boss kept talking, unaware of his reply. "…now under Murray's care…all paid for the month…"

The line snapped and went silent.

Ethan kept walking until he reached his room and flicked on the light switch. He roughly yanked out his old black canvas suitcase from beneath the bed. It didn't roll smoothly anymore but was functional enough. With a couple of hasty scoops, he emptied the contents of the two compact dresser drawers and smashed the pile of clothes into the open suitcase with his fists. Good. Still enough room for a few more things.

As he walked across the small space to grab the old alarm clock by the bed, he caught a glimpse of his blistering eyes, reflecting in the window back at him.

Ethan had heard enough to piece the ugly news together from Gina. Starla was a goner. And since he'd failed her, he now had no choice but to confront another battle. He had waited long enough.

36

Muffled steps vibrated through the steady churn of the bubbling waterfall.

A legged one was approaching.

Her white caudal fin swished into position so she could claim the space right up in front, using her advantage as the largest koi in the pond. The others anticipated, just behind, scaled patterns flashing orange, gold, black, and red.

The legged one peered down, its gigantic figure wavering through the blurry surface.

They glided and weaved with increasingly shorter strokes. The pellets sprinkled over them, floating on top of the liquid border. The warm air dabbed the tips of their mouths as they relished their meal, curling and rippling until every piece was gone.

37

Lula May spun in front of the wall of mirrors, the bright pink silk dancing through her fingers.

In the center of the enormous walk-in closet, cozying in a plush purple velvet armchair, sat Sheila. She looked up from a thick stack of glossy fashion magazines and let out a low whistle.

"Wow," Sheila nodded with approval. "I like you in the loudest pink possible—it's feminine *and* rebellious. It goes nice with my new streak, too." She toyed with a slender section of freshly dyed hair just above her right ear.

Lula May examined her reflection up and down and then turned, flashing herself a smoldering look over her shoulder. Sheila was right. The dress was absolutely perfect. Knee-length, a smidge of cleavage, and flowy enough that she could eat whatever she wanted at the upcoming event.

The Wags and Women fundraiser was one of the coolest events of the year, in Lula May's opinion. Every fall, the committee honored an artistic individual for her work that helped animals of any kind. Up-and-comers of all creative genres had been picked in previous years—the organization had a penchant for spotlighting hard-working and emerging artists often overshadowed in their competitive fields. Sheila had long insisted that Lula May getting recognized by something like Wags and Women would catapult her reputation far away from the days of that unfortunate interview. She'd spent the last couple of months campaigning hard on her client's behalf. After numerous rejections from the board, based on the fact that Lula May was already an established artist, Sheila found a clever loophole in the system to use in their favor.

"I'm gonna rock this thing so hard!" Lula May set a hand on

her hip and scanned the floor for her new shoes. "Imagine me walking out on stage to accept the award in *this!*"

Sheila laughed as she quenched her thirst with a prolonged sip of chardonnay. The zesty citrus notes vaporized through her nostrils.

Lula May blew an exaggerated kiss to her reflection. Without the nuisance of Starla, she was already smiling more (and screaming into her towel less). At first, Lula May still got that tiny ping of guilt whenever she thought of the horse, but now all she felt was mostly contentment. And she was certain that Starla was in proper hands. Murray had assured her that Don would find Starla a new zip code to call home—fast. He just needed to pack in his trailer with as many horses as possible so the haul made financial sense, whatever that meant. Lula May didn't quite understand all of the details but their confidence in Starla being untraceable was the main selling point for her. The dark cloud from her old interview was finally clearing, too, so this was all perfect timing. The relentless horde of hateful emails and messages had cycled to a manageable trickle. And despite the abruptly canceled gallery show, other opportunities were being discussed. Just like Sheila had promised.

True, the exhibit would've been huge. But no matter. Several major media organizations, thanks to Sheila, had gotten word of Lula May officially caring for and owning a horse that nobody wanted—an extremely good look. Of course, Sheila had embellished in her usual way. Nobody actually knew that Starla would soon be heading to some kind of auction, but that wasn't the point. This time tomorrow, Lula May would be enjoying her celebration at Wags and Women! Getting picked didn't come easily at first, even with Sheila's harping influence. Luckily, Lula May's father had agreed to arrange a prestigious summer banking internship to help out a board member's college kid.

A timid knock rapped outside the closet.

"Come in, Vivian," Lula May called out, stooping over as she peered behind a small pile of off-the-runway handbags. Where the heck were those shoes?

Lula May's new assistant immediately entered, clutching a stack of mail against her red and white striped blouse. She exuded the typical high effort zeal most people have when still excited about their new job. "That dress is amazing!"

"Isn't it?" Lula May and Sheila replied in unison.

Vivian's long strawberry blonde ponytail bounced with her nods. "Absolutely!" She sorted through the envelopes. "Lots of mail today. I already separated the bills, so I'll send out all the

payments first thing tomorrow. Junk mail's in the trash, and…
this was at the front door." She shrugged and held out a
handwritten note.

Lula May pushed aside a small chevron-patterned ottoman,
half-listening. "Vivian, have you seen my new heels? With the
super pointy toe?" She frowned, scanning the space again. "I
swear I put them here right when I got back from Beverly Hills
last night."

Vivian shook her head. "Nope, sorry."

The doorbell rang downstairs.

Sheila pointed to the small glass table next to her. "You can put
all that right here, Vivian. Thanks." She sifted through the small
stack as Vivian left to answer the front door.

"What's so funny?" Lula May asked.

"This letter from your neighbors." Sheila's eyes scanned the
note, her eyes bright with amused disbelief. "You painted their
curb?" She erupted when Lula May nodded. *Why?*"

Lula May sighed, increasingly irritated. Her new shoes seemed
to have completely vanished. "Honestly, I need more room when I
back out of the driveway. So I painted part of their front curb red,
to block anyone from parking there. It's scary driving around
here."

Sheila tilted her head. "Darling, you can't just go around
painting your neighbors' curbs, you know."

"Tell me about it." Lula May huffed and grabbed the sheet of
paper. How annoying. The last thing she had time for was to
arrange a sandblasting!

Vivian suddenly bounded back into the closet. "Found your
shoes!" She lifted the lid to the torn box. "Looks like Royal beat
me to it, though. They were next to his bed."

Lula May snatched the box. "Oh no!" Deep teeth marks dotted
all over the thrashed leather. *"Royal!"* she roared, making both
Sheila and Vivian jump. "Where is that dumb dog? What am I
going to do now?"

With the calming air of a mother dealing with another tantrum,
Sheila expertly took the box from Lula May and exchanged it with
a very full glass of wine. "Dear, we have a whole day before the
event." A gurgling sound emanated from her stomach. "Was that
the food?" she inquired to Vivian, hoping the front doorbell was a
delivery. She'd ordered them all a late lunch from her favorite
steakhouse nearly an hour ago.

"I'll check!" nodded Vivian.

Lula May took Sheila's seat in the purple chair and flipped
through the mail. *"Rip It Up?"* Her brows knotted. "What is this

thing?" Examining the strange array of black and white sketches, photos and scribble on the front page only perplexed her more.

"Looks like a zine." Sheila leaned over to get a better look. "Didn't know you were into that sort of stuff. But I definitely approve, my friend—very au courant." She carefully poured more wine into her glass, beaming with a satisfied smile.

"That's short for magazine, right?" Lula May squinted at the angular font. *A magazine for freaks, that is.*

What she saw next made her nearly spit out all the wine in her mouth.

The Lula May Scam! Page 4

What was her name doing on this wretched thing?

Her index and middle fingers began to twitch. It was a reflex she could never quite get rid of, one that sometimes started the instant she got nervous. Lula May hastily turned the cover, already afraid but simultaneously desperate to see. Familiar dread swarmed over her when she saw that page four was neatly folded at the corner, beckoning to be found. She gulped another swig of wine.

A familiar image of a diamond, Nothing4U, and the gallery's advertisements. She skimmed the page as quickly as she could as if that would somehow lessen the blow of the incriminating words.

SCAM ARTIST.

"What is it? What's wrong?"

Lula May hardly heard Sheila. In the margin of page four was her name handwritten in blue ink and all caps, followed by a few sentences. The penmanship was surprisingly proper. The message of the ominous lines was clear: hundreds of copies of this zine would be distributed at the Wags and Women event tomorrow night unless Lula May got Starla back.

And that's just the beginning, Scam Artist.

A warm itch prickled up the back of Lula May's neck. The sensation was all too familiar—another itchy rash, just like the one that had suddenly appeared when that nightmare of an interview was first published.

Not again! Lula May's fingers quivered, and she lost her grip. Pale yellow liquid splashed down her dress. The glass landed on the peach carpet with a barely audible thump.

38

" Stretch out your suspenders with pride, kids," Johnny Oi graveled through the airwaves. "Next up is an exclusive world premiere from those Pogo Dog regulars, yadda, yadda…"

Rose skipped across her bedroom to dial up the volume. The Santa Monica Boulevard fast food joint was notorious for its raucous LA nighttime crowds back in the day (not that she'd ever been). She lingered in front of the speakers for a few seconds to hear every sound of the new song's intro. A thick, finger-tapping bassline made way for a funky blast of martial snare. Nice. The first few moments of a song were usually enough to determine if it would be one of those repeat-for-days scenarios, which drove Tori nuts.

Rose walked back to her closet, taking in a few measured inhales. She and Milo had spent the last hour reorganizing her clothes into two basic categories: stuff that could double as riding apparel and everything else. She glanced back at the clock for the hundredth time, not quite sure if she wanted the minutes to move faster or stop entirely.

"No turning back either way." In the reflection of the dresser mirror, Milo lifted his head to look at her before resuming his very important paw-licking.

The clothes sorting was a decent distraction. Even with all of the riding and barn time lately, Rose still hadn't stopped by the OC Saddlery. She didn't exactly have tons of money to spend at her favorite old tack shop. Nothing about horses was cheap, even basic riding gear, so for now she had to be malleable and creative with what she already had. Anything with spikes, pins, and hanging chains were out, but her two pairs of worn boots were okay for now. Some patch-covered vests and jackets were works in progress, but she was now happy to move them as-is to the "in" section. Nice and flat, they wouldn't catch on anything. Most of her leggings and jeans would suffice, maybe except for any denim that was more shredded than necessary. She scooped up a stack of mostly-black band shirts—dark cotton was perfect for riding—but moved the white tees off to the side. White laundry was already a hassle without the unavoidable barn dirt or slobber from horse kisses.

Rose stepped back, satisfied at the assortment of her "new" barn wardrobe. The crucial missing piece, however, was a helmet. Borrowing the lesson spares was getting inconvenient since she never knew which one would be available, not to mention pretty gross. Swapping old sweat with other human heads, blech. She needed one that fit her own head anyhow. For sure, her very first purchase once she got some cash would be a crisp, brand new helmet.

Come over, let's head out soon! I'm pumped!!

Tori's text pinged just as Rose pulled a crisp black Nothing4U tee over her head. She'd purposely singled it out for tonight. They all had.

The familiar clatter of kitchen utensils and the rich aroma of spicy tofu stew filled the air as she marched downstairs. Home.

"You sure you don't want to eat before you go?" Her mom stirred a pot at the stove while her dad filled a few glasses with water.

"No, thanks. Smells delicious, though." Rose sat on the bottom step of the staircase and pulled her boot laces tightly over the bottoms of her jeans. Now that she was actually about to leave for the event, she almost felt like she'd never be hungry again.

Her dad walked over and put his hand on her shoulder. "Be careful." He offered a small grin, but his voice was very serious. "Keep a full-circle view. Don't lock your knees."

Rose nodded, looking directly at him. "Got it, Dad." He knew what he was talking about. In his college days in Korea, Mr. Moon had participated in plenty of demonstrations with much more dicey circumstances. "But don't worry, I don't think there's going to be tear gas or anything like that."

Dad's face froze for a second but quickly relaxed when Rose chided him with a nudge. "Okay." He paused. "As we used to say, in a rough translation—love, rage, and teamwork." He raised a fist above his head and chuckled.

"I put your bottle in your backpack," Thomas chimed in, his head peeping out from the kitchen doorway. "Just in case you need some water." His eyes sparkled with eagerness.

"Thanks, everyone." Rose kissed Milo's head and hoisted her backpack over her shoulders as she opened the front door. She looked back at the room, savoring the comforting atmosphere of support and transparency. "Save some soon tofu for me."

◆◆◆

"Oh my god, you're pink!" Rose gasped with a delighted laugh.

Tori's megawatt smile radiated from her porch. "Thought I might as well do it up for such an important event." Her fingers grazed her choppy, electric rose spikes of hair. "I was already so blonde. It was easy to just use a bottle at home."

"It looks amazing," Rose gushed. Tori's new hair color was definitely a nice distraction from her fluttering stomach. "Have your parents seen it yet?" She followed Tori inside. With the indoor lighting, the pink almost looked neon.

Tori made a wry face. "Oh yeah, about an hour ago. No bueno," she lamented with a giggle. "But they calmed down when I assured them it'll wash out just like those fruity juice powder packets we used to slather on our hair. C'mon, let's get my things."

Claudia was sitting on the family room couch in an animated phone conversation. She briefly looked up and smirked as the two girls walked by. "So funny you guys are doing this, I swear," she commented.

"Wish us luck," Tori replied. She picked up a canvas messenger bag at the bottom of the staircase. Several colorful pieces of poster board were folded neatly inside. "Oh!" she reacted to her phone. "Cameron's here."

"Wowzers!" Cameron hollered once he saw Tori's pink head. He looked extra tall in a slim black coat and burly boots. As they went to Tori's car, he quickly rummaged through his backpack and thrust a small plastic case at Rose before hopping in the back seat. "Pop this in ASAP—these guys are rad. Nebula special order."

Over the music, they excitedly discussed their plans during the half-hour drive to Los Angeles. The heavyweight guitars and clobbering drums of Burnt Machine, a locally revered hardcore group, pumped through Rose's veins as she went over the possible sequence of events once they arrived at the venue.

No one in the car knew what to expect. Sure, they'd spent the bulk of their high school years devouring rebellious music and literature, but actually taking part in a protest was on another level. And the sheer act of starting one—even a tiny one—as opposed to joining a protest already taking place, was incredibly intimidating to Rose. She got full-blown stage fright before simple class presentations, so what the heck did she expect now? This might be the most audacious thing she had ever attempted. If it weren't for her friends' instant and eager feedback when she'd first brought it up, Rose would never have had the guts to pursue Lula May in this way.

A sense of warmth and appreciation anchored deep in her chest. Rose pressed her lips together and relished how smoothly the details had snowballed into a concrete plan of action. It only took a few minutes for them to weave a strategic web around the fiasco of Lula May. Essentially, every detail was ready for the taking because the artist had done it all to herself. They merely had to direct a spotlight on her actions. A few fired up phone calls later, they had formed a decent road map. It was simple: show up with the visuals, spread the information, and hopefully exert enough pressure to make Lula May reverse course with Starla.

"Remember we have to be flexible," Rose thought aloud as they exited the freeway and turned onto 2nd Street. "Keep a full-circle view, and don't lock your knees." Downtown Los Angeles used to be known for being totally dead on the weekends, but a recent influx of pricey high-rise lofts and craft beer-infused gastropubs had transformed significant sections from a utilitarian landscape of strictly nine-to-fivers to a bustling 24/7 community.

"Those are some fighting words," Tori remarked. She steered into a line of cars creeping toward the valet in front of a shiny and clearly brand-new hotel.

The car fell silent for a moment as they all took in the impending environment. The hotel's minimal façade at ground level was all white horizontal-beamed fencing, neatly separating the imposing glass tower from the street ruckus in a tight sandwich between an ancient looking laundromat and a dimly lit check cashing service. A handful of black and white uniformed valet drivers jogged back and forth between the ticket station and the awaiting luxury vehicles. A montage of attendees donned in colorful print dresses, funky glasses, fedoras, three-piece suits, and designer handbags lingered along the red carpet out front as they quipped for reporters. Cameras clicked, veneers flashed. A taut white banner hung over the entrance, greeting all of the guests before they breezed through the revolving glass doors: WAGS AND WOMEN PROUDLY PRESENTS AN EVENING WITH LULA MAY: ARTIST & ANIMAL ACTIVIST.

"No, we're not *getting* into trouble," Rose answered. "We *are* the trouble." A short laugh escaped her. Cornier yet truer words had never been said. This event's level of hypocrisy and lies deserved all the hassle it could get.

"That's right, mama!" Cameron leaned forward between the two front seats and stared through the windshield. "Hey, is that Tim?"

In a black suit jacket and matching pants, Tim stood on the sidewalk just a few feet from the gate entrance. He kept his head low, in that aloof way that very tall people tend to do when trying to go unnoticed, while other gala guests milled around. Every few seconds, he glanced up. If it weren't for his signature beanie and ink-covered neck, Rose might not have even recognized the guy.

"Yeah, it's him," Tori took in the unusual spectacle with a dopey grin. A bomber jacket fresh from the dryer was the fanciest she'd ever seen him. "And the rest of the posse."

Rose then realized that the other people lingering closest to him actually weren't other random guests. Mike, guys from Nothing4U, and a couple of others nonchalantly waited, all donned in similar gala-appropriate outfits.

"I thought they were all going to wear their shirts, too," Cameron commented. "I mean, *they're* the actual band she ripped!"

"Maybe they're wearing the shirts under their jackets," Rose suggested, noticing that none of the guys had shirts with collars. "Helps them blend in better in this obviously uptight crowd."

As the line of cars moved forward, Tim finally saw them. He jutted his chin further down the block.

Tori nodded back her confirmation. "Okay, we're parking on the next street over, just like we planned," she told her friends.

As they passed the hotel, Rose gawked at the growing melee. Mike stood off to the side on his own, in a navy jacket and pants, already staring into their car. His expression was mostly indifferent, but Rose could've sworn she glimpsed a mischievous flicker in his eyes.

At least someone's having fun. Rose quickly turned straight ahead. The more people she saw, the more her stomach threatened to unload all over the glove compartment. Suddenly she was very glad to have not polished off that second slice of boysenberry toast from lunch.

Once they made a right turn at the next intersection, the scenery instantly transformed. Gone were the spotless new businesses cropping up at every other storefront or so. This row of neglected buildings was untouched by both sunlight and money. The largest of the structures was a dilapidated twelve-story hotel with rows of cracked windows and crooked or missing shutters. Below its barely legible "Xander's" sign, much of the damp sidewalk was lined with shoddy tents and clusters of people. Some of them walked by and vacantly peered into the car as Tori parallel parked in an empty metered spot, but most didn't even seem to notice nor care.

Rose had never seen so many people living on the street. As Tori secured the brake, a rollicking laugh caught their attention. The smartly dressed group was hard to miss: all shiny hair, chunky watches, bright lips and healthy struts—it was like watching lasers cut through a bank of soil.

One of them, a young man immersed on his phone as he blindly paced forward, bumped into an oncoming pedestrian with a severe limp and a loud yet undecipherable yell. He detached from his phone long enough to look up with entitled irritation at the elderly man and then muttered something to his friends. They all laughed again as the gray-haired man hobbled on, once again deep in his own world.

"We're right on time," Tori said as she typed on her phone. "Tim just overheard some of Lula May's people say she's in a white limo."

"If anything happens to me, tell my parents that I love them and to bury me with all of my records." Cameron stepped one foot out of the car. "Shall we?"

Rose nodded, forcing herself to look away from the limping figure shrinking into the crowd. She opened the passenger door and stepped out. All of her senses shot up and out, all the way up the distant skyscrapers and simultaneously scrutinizing every ground level face, bus exhaust, piece of litter, traffic light, and car whizzing by. The smell of nearby donuts and pungent urine mixed in the cold swirling air dictated by traffic currents and thick bursts of fumes.

"Oh my, I love this place!" Cameron practically bounced as he tried to contain himself from skipping too far ahead. Rose grinned. A part of her couldn't help but feel a tad guilty at getting everyone involved in this plan, so his enthusiasm was comforting.

Tori and Rose quickened their pace as Cameron easily weaved through the busy sidewalk. When he reached the crosswalk, he abruptly stopped to stare down the street toward the hotel.

"There's the limo," Rose observed when she and Tori caught up. A long ivory limousine was waiting in the valet line behind several other cars. Despite its opaque windows, the valet drivers and lingering gala guests seemed to know exactly who was inside, as they visibly swished about with animated jabber.

"And there's Tim!" Tori added with an amused giggle. "Look at him, he's so ready to go for it."

Tim was standing next to a group of pretentious air-kissers. "Oh my *god*, I haven't seen you in forever!" one of them shrieked to a friend right beneath his goatee. It was hilarious to see the guy in the midst of a frenzy that she knew he found totally gross. Tim kept his eyes between the approaching trio and the white limo. Once a valet driver started waving the limo into an awaiting space along the side of the circular covered driveway, Tim rubbed his right temple and coughed into the arm of his sleeve.

That was the signal.

One by one, Mike and three others turned, each cutting different paths into the crowd.

Already?! Rose squeezed both of her friends' wrists, unable to slow the rapid thumping in her chest. Maybe it was better to just dive in. Waiting around would only feed her anxiety.

They had several people participating in their little surprise. Tim and Mike were the designated lookouts for Lula May's arrival, as well as if or when the security guys had their heads turned or guards down. Tim's brother Gavin and friend Zack would help Mike and Darrell scale the front awning. The rest of Nothing4U, Elliot and Billy, were going to put their vocals to good use while Rose, Tori, and Cameron did their parts.

Tori's lips switched between tightly pursed and softly mouthing something as if going through all the steps in her head. Cameron's previous playfulness on the way to the hotel had completely disappeared. He now scanned the crowd, the cars, and the red carpet with a focused and unsympathetic glare.

"Wooooo...!" Appreciative cheers and a smatter of applause erupted. A white-gloved valet driver opened the limousine door and beckoned with his arm to the red carpet. Tori and Cameron briskly joined the small crowd edging closer to the guest of honor while Rose veered to the back of the group.

A sturdy and panty-hosed leg, capped with a pointy emerald green dress shoe, stretched out of the vehicle and dangled for an extended hold-your-breath moment. After a flurry of camera flashes, the rest of Lula May graciously emerged in a floor length caramel fur coat. With a hand on her hip and a wise and magnanimous smile, she reveled in the hoots and clicks for a full minute before teetering her first step.

Nobody noticed the deadpan, open-mouthed stare from the back. Seeing the con artist in some manufactured celebration was beyond gross, but the fur coat was a shockingly tone-deaf topping to an already unbelievable pile of trash. Sure, this wasn't an antifur function, but really—a fur coat at an animal charity event? Even though she'd rather spit in Lula May's eyes, Rose forced a bubbly smile and clasped her hands together as if seeing Lula May in person was a dream finally realized.

A woman in a canary yellow Chanel jacket, microphone in hand, rushed up to the artist. "Good evening, Lula May, welcome to the most exciting Wags and Women gala in years! Before I dive into how *amazing* it must feel to be here with so many supporters, I just have to ask—is this real fur?" She was practically yelling despite standing a mere inch or two from the artist.

"An heirloom from my mother," purred Lula May, nodding approvingly along with the reporter's every word. "All of this is incredible, Emma. Anyone who's ever known me knows how much I adore and cherish animals, and I'm so honored to be recognized at this wonderful event. First, I'd like to thank a few people who made all of this possible."

Emma? So she must know this reporter already. Unless she somehow missed it, Rose definitely didn't hear the reporter saying her own name. Rose slowly edged closer as the interview hammered on, settling into an empty space just behind one of the gold stanchions.

Behind the velvet rope across the red carpet, a tall woman in a long black dress scrutinized the interview like a coach watching her team players. A bright fuchsia streak stood out in her otherwise dyed black hair, and a white name badge lanyard hung from her neck. Her unsmiling face was a sharp contrast to the overall giddiness of the scene. Next to her, a man with slick brown hair and green glasses eagerly leaned forward with his microphone hovering upward, the fronts of his red pants pushing the velvet rope. The woman then quietly tapped the man's back and muttered, "Okay, go!" Just as he hastily lifted a leg to climb over the red rope, she grabbed his arm and added, "Remember, she *saved* the horse," to which he firmly nodded.

The horse. Rose's heart ricocheted in her chest. While standing in this ridiculous gaggle of phoniness, Rose wondered where Starla was and what she was doing. Taking a deep breath, she tried to ground herself back to the task at hand. The only shot she had at ever seeing Starla again was standing just a few feet away. Rose squeezed between several onlookers and found a decent space a little closer to the two reporters flanking Lula May.

"Lula May, you're here as an artist of the people," the young man pleasantly reeled off, thrusting the microphone to Lula May's face. "Word on the street is that you've also taken it upon yourself to actually *save* the lives of horses. Can you elaborate for us mere mortals?"

Lula May joined his benevolent chuckle briefly before quieting into seriousness. She slowly shook her head as if deep in thought and went silent while the two interviewers waited with starstruck patience.

"Where do I even begin?" she said falteringly, directing her eyes to the sky. "It's been a hard, painful journey, Ben. As an animal lover, nothing hurts me more than seeing something suffer. I came across this wonderful horse, a wild mustang that needed a home. It wasn't in good shape and—"

"How so?" Ben asked curiously, adjusting his glasses with interest.

"Um, let's see," Lula May paused. "Well, it was neglected. Hungry and sad—and very skinny."

Ben nodded solemnly. "Go on."

Lula May cleared her throat. "Anyhow, this horse really hated everyone. It had trust issues and lashed out at every person. Well," she ticked her head to the side, "every person but me, that is."

"So, despite all odds, this abused horse took a liking to you," Ben offered. "That is simply incredible!"

Nodding with the glow of good fortune, Lula May waved her hand around her head. "Incredible, indeed. We met, and there it was, following me everywhere I turned! So, of course, I had to take it with me. And the rest is history!"

Ben's eyes widened with astonishment. "Amazing. I seriously think I'm about to cry. One more thing before I let you go. What's your horse's name? And where is it now?"

"Now?" The beam on Lula May's face flickered. "Well, um, her name is Starla. She's probably just at home, I think." She looked questioningly over her shoulder at the woman in the black dress, who was now gesturing a silent neck-cut to an oblivious Ben.

Wanting more, Ben nodded for the artist to elaborate. "Oh, I'm sure Starla misses Mommy! So, it lives with you?"

"Uh…" Lula May kept glancing between him and the woman on the sidelines. "No, at a barn down in—"

"Okay, thank you very much, but we're running out of time!" The woman in the long black dress expertly swooped into the conversation. She draped an arm around Lula May's fur-covered shoulders and nudged her past Emma and Ben.

She's leaving! Rose searched the crowd for any signs of her friends. Just as she started to wonder if they'd gotten cold feet, Tori and Cameron stumbled over the velvet ropes to block the artist's path.

"Lula May, it's an honor!" Cameron greeted with his most sincere gush. "We're with *Rip It Up*. Did you like the special issue we dedicated to you?" He then cheerfully motioned for the two reporters to rejoin them.

The woman pushed Lula May onward, more forcefully this time, but Tori stepped in their way with an aggressive smile. "We have plenty of copies for the press here, plus anyone else interested in your exclusive backstory!" She motioned to the nearby curious crowd.

"Exclusive?" Emma asked quizzically. She squarely faced the artist and her handler. "Sheila, I thought *we* had the exclusive."

"Yeah," Ben chimed in, blinking with uncertainty.

Sheila shook her head with a nervous laugh. "Of course you do. I don't even know who these people are!" She reached over and pushed Cameron's shoulder to move out of their way.

"Don't touch me, lady," Cameron immediately warned. "Tori, please remind them of what we put together for Lula May."

Tori pulled a copy of the zine from her bag. "You mean this?" she asked politely, holding it up.

Sheila snatched the zine out of Tori's hand. "I'm calling security," she seethed in a low voice. "You'd better leave *right now*."

"Scam artist?" Ben had already glimpsed the cover. "What's that supposed to mean?"

"Do you know Nothing4U?" Cameron motioned at his and Tori's shirts. "They're a local band, and this is the cover of their latest album."

The group finally seemed to notice the shirts for the first time. Ben and Emma exchanged dumbfounded looks.

"What the hell do you think you're doing?" Sheila's face flushed into a deep shade of crimson.

"Okay, everyone, shut up!" Lula May snapped. She side glanced at the nearest onlookers, who were cautiously exchanging whispers. Leaning in for what little privacy she could retain, she lowered her voice. "This is harassment. What do you want?"

"Rose," Tori called out, looking around behind her. "We're ready for you."

Rose calmly passed a rubbernecking couple and stepped over the rope to join the terse conversation. Everything suddenly felt surreal, and all she could think about was Starla.

Lula May did a double take at Rose, her posture suddenly stiffening.

"What are you doing here?" Lula May's narrowed eyes darted between the intruders and their matching tops. "What is this all about?"

"Hi, Lula May. Geez." Rose flashed a sarcastic grin. "Is that how you greet someone who helped Starla so she wouldn't be sent to auction?"

Lula May's lips scrunched before spreading into a closed, defensive smile. "I don't know what you're talking about."

"Where's Starla?" Rose sensed time was running out, and she needed to get right to the point. "Don't tell me that Murray already sent her off to some kill buyer."

One of the reporters emitted an audible gasp.

Sheila cringed. "It's in good hands," she said in a half-reassuring, half-indignant tone.

"So, the horse isn't with you anymore?" Ben asked Lula May with genuine inquisitiveness.

Just as Sheila started searching the crowd for the nearest security guard, Rose turned to the two reporters.

"Starla is not safe," Rose said adamantly. "I helped out Starla's trainer under the agreement that she wouldn't be sent to an auction. Lula May wanted to get rid of Starla without anyone knowing, even at an auction with kill buyers. If you want to contact our barn to verify what I'm saying—"

An angry holler from behind interrupted Rose's breathless pitch. They turned to look, all eyes up toward the hotel entryway.

At least twenty feet above the crowd, Mike and Darrell stood near the center of the steel and glass entrance canopy. They were holding dark paper or fabric of some kind.

Walkie-talkies blipped below them.

Without tossing the increasingly tense audience a single glance, the two guys stepped to either side of the canopy, methodically unraveling a large black banner.

A bullhorn suddenly plowed into everyone's eardrums.

"Listen up!"

Under one end of the canopy, almost directly beneath Mike, Tim stood on top of an oversized white planter. "Lula May's rip-off art—she copied us, and she got caught!" he yelled into the mouthpiece with typical protest rhythm.

Tori giggled gleefully and poked Rose's ribs. Mike and Darrell started yelling along.

"Lula May's rip-off art," Rose repeated, chuckling. She never would have guessed Tim's handiness at such harsh poetry, but then again, he did write most of the lyrics for his band's songs. Elliot and Billy, from opposite sides of the crowd below, joined in on the chant while handing out copies of the zine to the dumbfounded crowd.

"Isn't that the big piece you were working on for your show, Lula May?" Ben shook his head slightly, trying to make sense of the two side by side diamond drawings on display.

Lula May didn't say a word. She scoured through the guests standing around the red carpet, flinching when a few of them stared back at her expectantly.

"What are you waiting for? Get them out of here!" Sheila screeched loudly at a passing security guard.

"We're Nothing4U." Tim jumped off the planter as he ran from two uniformed men attempting to grab him. He was able to maintain the megaphone in front of his face. "Lula May stole our album art. Look it up! She's a con artist!"

"Oh, god."

Rose turned away from the disorder to look at Lula May. The artist was leaning into defiant Sheila, as if trying to bury herself inside her big coat. When Mike and Darrell flung more copies of the zine into the crowd, Lula May expelled a sharp breath and closed her eyes, as if in pain. For a brief moment, Rose couldn't help but feel sorry for her.

"Liars!" Sheila exploded with a roar. Nostrils flared, she pointed a shaky index finger at Rose and her friends. "You stupid little punks—how dare you ruin this!"

"She did it to herself," Rose replied sharply, shoving her empathy out of the way.

The crowd *ooooh-ed* at two beefy security guards awkwardly climbing up the columns of the canopy. One of them lost his footing midway and slipped, but he caught himself before splattering on the ground.

"You're nobody," Sheila seethed, her voice shaking. "I'm going to have my people come after all of you."

Rose stared up at the older lanky woman about to combust right before her eyes. She had to suppress a surge of laughter.

"Oh, no," Rose mocked, her hand floating up to clutch an imaginary set of pearls around her neck. "Will we ever have lunch in this town again?"

Tori and Cameron chortled at the same time. Even the two reporters smirked a little.

Cameron stepped forward and lifted his arms, fingers flashing wildly. "Jazz hands?" he teased, even though nobody had a clue of their inside joke about "show biz."

Tori doubled over, laughing aloud.

"Hey, Lula May," another woman's voice called over from several feet away. She waved the zine in her hand. "What is this?"

Sheila's eyes protruded at the growing chaos surrounding

them. She yanked one of Cameron's wrists and shook him hard.

"Hey!" Rose and Tori grabbed Sheila's arm and tried disconnecting her death grip.

"I said, don't touch me," Cameron snarled through a gritted mouth. He was trying his best not to react.

"Whoa, whoa," Ben took hold of whatever arm he could to quell the escalating altercation.

Lula May exploded. "Stop! Sheila, let go!" Her hands went to her head as she burst into sobs. "Sheila, I said *stop!*" Black mascara streaked down a cheek.

"Fine!" Sheila spat, wrenching a step back.

"Give us a minute, please?" Lula May asked forlornly. She and Sheila walked back down the red carpet to the driveway, the two reporters loosely tagging along. They all stopped in front of the limo, immersed in a heated exchange. A man and woman, both with name badges and matching authoritative frowns, quickly joined them. Two security guards followed. Sheila was still clearly fuming as they huddled in discussion, throwing the group hostile huffs every few seconds.

"Where's Tim?" Tori wondered. He seemed to have disappeared.

"Oh my god, he's up there!" Rose pointed at the canopy. Tim had just hoisted himself up to join Mike and Darrell. The other security guards who had tried to climb the columns were now nowhere to be seen. Pacing back and forth with the banner on full display behind him, Tim began reading directly from the zine article.

The audience was starting to piece together the details. While most of them were still gaping at the guys hollering over the grand entryway, plenty were also starting to size up Rose and her friends.

"This is private property!" a man yelled from the crowd up at Tim. "Get down, right now!"

"You know the real story about that horse?" Tim blustered into the megaphone. "Lula May didn't save anyone!"

Sections of the crowd visibly stirred at the allegation. The plagiarism issue was perhaps a step removed from the event and their concerns, but the well-publicized horse was not.

Rose turned to Tori, her mouth open. Tim had never said he was going to bring up Starla.

"Here they come," Cameron muttered, jutting his chin.

Lula May approached with a vacant look, eyes hanging down. Sheila glared at the group from just behind her client.

Lula May swallowed and opened her mouth to speak.

"Get him to shut up," Sheila ordered icily. "Then we'll discuss."

"You think she cares about that horse?" Tim let out an exaggerated scoff. He was only getting more pumped by all of the curious and confused faces staring up at him.

"Look, just tell us what you want," Lula May pleaded through her grimace.

"Oh, no, we're going to tell *you* what to do," Sheila cut off Lula May again. "Now, listen carefully, children—"

Lula May threw her hands in the air. "Shut up! Let me talk!"

Sheila looked at Lula May with parted lips, taken aback by the sudden outburst. "Go ahead," she replied curtly, crossing her arms.

"You guys made your point." Lula May turned to Rose. "How about we split the money with Nothing4U. All the proceeds from my next exhibit, fifty-fifty."

"Seventy-five, twenty-five," Sheila interjected.

"Or whatever they think is fair. Just get those guys up there to stop." Lula May ignored Sheila's sharp sigh. "What do you say?"

Rose licked her lips. The aggressive chanting resumed from atop the canopy. She could almost taste Lula May's utter desperation at salvaging her event. This was probably the best, if not only, chance at getting what they came for.

"We just want Starla," Rose answered coolly. "You make sure she returns to Laguna Lake Riding Club—if she's safe, we'll try to get Tim and the guys to not pursue further action."

"*Try?*" Sheila lowered her chin.

Rose ignored the woman's condescending stare. "What I can guarantee, Lula May, is that we'll all leave this gala. Quickly."

Lula May's face instantly brightened. "Okay, okay! That's easy." Her head bobbed from side to side as she dug inside her pocket. "I'll get Murray on the line right now. He knows exactly where Starla is!"

Rose's pulse sped up with nervous anticipation. Lula May stepped off to the side, covering her other ear with a free hand.

"Murray? It's me. Change of plans."

The group fell quiet for a minute as they listened. Rose could hardly breathe. As Lula May had claimed, it sounded like Murray did indeed know of Starla's whereabouts and was still taking orders from the artist. But they still couldn't completely trust Lula May. Rose got out her own phone and sent a brief message to Gina, who was tentatively expecting her. Only once the barn owner confirmed Starla's status would they even consider leaving the gala in peace.

"Should I have him stop now?" Tori quietly asked through the corner of her mouth. Tim and his friends were still going off.

"Not just yet," Rose said, eyes focused on Lula May. The artist had suddenly paused, listening intently to the other end of the call. What if Murray had already sold her? The cryptic meeting she'd overheard between Murray and Don sounded dangerously close to the mare being discarded for pocket change. Despite her forced sheen of confidence, Rose's insides quivered so intensely that for a moment, she wondered if she was actually getting sick. Just as her mouth watered with nausea, Lula May started walking briskly back to them. Her long coat swung triumphantly with each step.

"Done and done!" Lula May announced, beaming with a mixture of relief and pride. "I told you it'd be easy. Murray's making arrangements as we speak."

"Great," Sheila drawled sarcastically, rubbing the back of her neck. "Now, tell those jerks up there to get out of here."

"When Gina gives me the green light, we'll go," Rose paused. Maybe the guys' vocal cords could take a short break while they waited. She nodded to Tori, who immediately blew a piercing cab whistle between her fingers.

"Be right back. I'm going to tell the staff that we've got this handled," Sheila grumbled to Lula May once all the hollering ceased.

Lula May almost appeared to shrink an inch or two as Sheila whirled around and merged into the crowd.

"I'd really appreciate it if you guys could talk with the band and put some reason into their heads," Lula May said after an awkward minute of silence. "It's really all a big misunderstanding. I mean, sure, I stumbled on their album when I was doing some research. Maybe their album cover just got stuck in my head without my realizing it."

Rose glanced up at the clone image on the banner as the artist continued her self-defense. Lula May could gab for years about how nobody truly owned a concept and how art was, in many ways, a feast of shared expressions within a collective. But no way were those two illustrations some subconscious accident. There was a big difference between a likeness and replica, but Rose wasn't going to dive into the weeds about all that now. A much larger question burned, one that had nothing to do with the art of copying or stealing.

"I have to ask you, Lula May," Rose blurted. "Why did you want to get rid of Starla like that?"

Lula May's mouth instantly shut. She looked away, blinking.

"You could've just left her with us. You knew that. Horses in auctions can end up at the slaughterhouse—or some unthinkable, abusive situations. How could you just hand her off to Murray like that?" Rose's voice climbed a notch with anger.

"Shh!" Lula May hissed, darting her eyes around in case anybody heard. She stepped in closer. "Look, it was stupid. I'm sorry, alright?"

Rose didn't want to lose her temper, but it was becoming increasingly difficult not to. That Lula May thought she had any room for defiance at this point was not acceptable at all.

"You may be sorry," Rose went on in a carelessly sharp voice, "but that still doesn't explain a thing!"

A vein bulged on the right side of Lula May's forehead as she realized a nearby group was eavesdropping. She pressed her eyes shut and stood still for a second. Suddenly she started talking softly in a tumbling, almost stream of consciousness sort of way.

"Starla was supposed to help me. I'm not a horse person, I'm not an equestrian. I'm not even into horses. They scare me." She opened her eyes and sighed. "It was supposed to be for publicity. Good publicity. But we just didn't click, and I didn't want anybody to know. Sheila had already gotten the word out, so I had to hide it all. To be honest, I was angry at how it didn't work out."

"None of this is Starla's fault," Rose retorted with heavy disgust. What a weak explanation.

Lula May's cheeks reddened. "Yeah."

Rose's phone rang. "Hello?" She recognized the number.

"Rose, just got your message."

"Gina!" Rose replied, her heart thumping. "Did you—"

"Just talked to Murray. One of my drivers, AJ, can haul Starla on his way to the area. She'll be loading by the end of day."

Are you serious?" Rose's jaw dropped. "I can't thank you enough! Where is Starla now? Is this for sure?"

"She's in a pasture a couple of hours east," Gina answered. "AJ knows the property. He'll handle it."

"Gina, I'm so grateful for you. And AJ, too," Rose said warmly, flashing Tori and Cameron a relieved nod. "Whatever work you guys need me to do—"

"We'll talk details later," Gina said simply. "You'll be the first to know when Starla gets here."

A wave of light rushed through Rose's body, expanding into every cell of her being. She stood still for a few moments, enjoying the simple bliss of not worrying about Starla.

"Think we should take off now?" Cameron asked. A prolonged

honk, at least five seconds long, blasted through the urban corridor, echoing off the buildings on either side of the busy street. Expletives exchanged, quickly followed by a screech of tires. Typical road rage.

Rose jolted back to reality. Lula May was already sulking away, fur coat and all, mumbling something about finding Sheila. Rose felt simultaneously grounded and floaty, unfazed by all the wary eyes still on her and her friends. It was a state of mind, on another level entirely, that she would never forget.

39

"Think's looking cute tonight, see that?"

Gross. Rose hoped the jerk didn't see her eye roll. She kept facing staunchly forward while winding through the crowded room behind Tori and Cameron. *Don't touch anyone.* Even the slightest nudge could be interpreted as an unwelcome invitation for who knows what.

A crazed guffaw bellowed from the depths of all three hundred pounds of the hefty bearded guy. Rose could feel the Ice Cave's resident prick still watching.

"Just keep swimming, babe." Cameron eyed the small stage. "They're starting soon."

They eventually wedged into a tiny spot along the far side of the room. Rose planted her feet and crossed her arms into a defiant shield. The view would be better from here than by the emergency exit where they'd watched the opener. Dozens of more people had squeezed into the place after the turquoise-suited ska band had finished their thrashing and jokey set. Their fun and upbeat music had relaxed the antagonistic Ice Cave crowd enough that she hadn't detected any other random fascist signals so far.

Making sure she saw every face in there in case someone else decided to mess with her, Rose threw imaginary pies at every skull present, aiming right between the brows. Over and over again. An unlikely giggle suddenly bubbled inside her. Did any of these skulls sense the string of cuss words she was silently and gleefully hurling like piss-filled balloons? That's all they were to her tonight—random skulls, some mean and some nonchalant. Definitely, anyone who had the audacity to step in here was hard as hell. Or were they? Maybe they were just full of their own delusions, all fake and slurpy inside, benign as a baby bunny if it weren't for their ballsy mouths. Her lips formed a tight line, halfway repressing an inward smirk. What was the point of tiptoeing around when she existed just as much as all these other fools?

Clearly, she was bouncing on an emotional seesaw again. She had no idea why, but she'd been on it for days now, unable to hop off. Maybe it had something to do with her birthday earlier this week, though she really didn't feel like an official "adult" yet. Rose gently brushed a fingertip over the new ink on the inside of her left wrist. It was hardly tender at all now. She was glad she had taken Mike's advice on booking with Sal, the best tattoo artist in town.

While Tori and Cameron began talking into each other's ears about something on his phone, Rose tuned into another nearby conversation between two dudes. One of them was enunciating over the loud room in that spitty, inebriated way.

"Man, all those spots…Cuckoo's, Hong Kong Café, Country Club, …things'll never be like those days again…"

Oh great, the punk rock police are on duty tonight, Rose grimaced. Bragging about the old days and mild gatekeeping about the "authentic" punk experience was a common thing to overhear at shows. She glanced at her friends. They always welcomed a chance to covertly make fun of the guys who blasted their invisible legitimacy badges around, but Tori and Cameron were now bickering and laughing at each other in their usual way about something else.

"Check it out—elite artist Lula May tapped to headline stand-up comedy special!" Cameron cackled at Rose as he read from his phone. "Now *that's* gonna be funny!"

"Awesome," Rose snorted. Then she felt someone throwing hard looks at her from across the pit. After a quick scan, she met the burgundy-haired woman's hostile and darkening stare. It was very deliberate, like she really believed she had something to be suspicious about. Then Rose noticed the context. A gaunt mohawked dude, presumably the woman's date, was staring at Rose in a way that no boyfriend should.

What a hassle. Not wanting to deal with an incensed chick and her desperate hookup, Rose turned her gaze away from the conflicted couple. The dude was in the danger zone now. Best to stay far away from those two.

On the stage, a guy with a bass guitar that looked tiny compared to his Goliath-like frame casually bantered with his two bandmates. A ratty sneaker with flailing brown-stained laces propelled over the audience and hit one of the speakers. No one in the band noticed or, if they did, they certainly didn't care to flinch or even look over. *Lucky that wasn't a bottle.* Rose forgot her annoyance at the couple across the room as she checked out the bulletproof group on stage. The shirtless platinum-haired drummer settled into his awaiting rickety stool, quickly followed by the front man with the now-famous boyish face and low-slung guitar. These days, they were accustomed to significantly larger, slicker venues due to massive record sales and a glut of mainstream radio play, but this crowd still treated them as the dudes who used to barely fill the local roller skating rink—hence the flying shoe.

Suddenly, almost every skull in there swiveled toward the stage.

"Look!" Rose pointed her finger, brows raised with surprised delight. The dog barked, strutting around the platform. Medium-sized, long tail, cream-colored with dark brown spots, he casually sniffed random cords and inspected the speakers like a total expert. "How *cute!*" Squirming from the unexpected dose of adorableness, Rose couldn't help but grab both of her friends' arms on either side of her.

"Huh?" The sapphire glow from Tori's phone highlighted the creases of mild frustration on her impeccably made-up face. Realizing what the buzz was about when Rose burst out laughing and cooing at the dog, whose head had disappeared while very earnestly rummaging through a paper bag by the drum set, Tori looked back down and began speed typing. "Oh, yeah. Cute."

Cameron tapped Rose's shoulder and leaned into her ear. "Trouble in la-la land," he explained in a low voice. "They started recording at the Casbah this week, and Tim's pretty much disappeared again." He shrugged. "Or she's just hating on cute doggies, I dunno."

The recording studio? The Casbah was known for hosting a tight roster of local music legends. Rose had been so consumed by her own stuff lately that she barely knew or remembered what was going on with Tori, much less Tim and Nothing4U.

"Heard that, dork," Tori replied flatly as she finished typing. "And I do like dogs. As long as they aren't mine."

Cameron pursed his lips and nodded. "Right."

Rose felt Tori looking her over carefully. She knew that hesitant vibe.

Tori fiddled with her phone. "Do you guys want to get out of here? I know that wasn't the plan, but Tim and the guys are still in Newport Beach…" She gestured at the screen.

"You mean, right now? But…" Rose couldn't believe her ears.

The posh coastal community was a twenty-minute drive, even if they really gassed it. Cameron balked next to her.

"I know, I know," Tori whined, her knees bending up and down with each guilty syllable. "But wouldn't it be fun to get some fresh air? We haven't been down there in months!"

Cameron's gaze flicked to the ceiling and back. "Yeah, ditching this once in a lifetime show to freeze at the beach sounds just *amazing*." He checked his phone. "What are they doing there, anyway? Isn't Island Plaza closed by now?"

Rose giggled, imagining the Nothing4U guys walking past the upscale window displays at the sprawling open-air shopping mall.

"Some impromptu bonfire, according to his last text." Tori cracked a wry grin. She held up her phone to share a photo Tim had just sent.

"Big fire," Rose commented curtly. The blaze looked way crazier than the neatly contained flames she was used to seeing at the beach, but that wasn't what stood out the most. Two older brunettes, one tall and the other petite, laughed in the background. Despite their blurry outlines, both appeared nothing short of absolutely gorgeous.

"Ran out of wood, so we got some trash from the garbage can," Tori recited Tim's latest message, her eyes dancing. "We'll be here for a while."

"And we will be *here* for a while." Cameron made sure to over-emphasize. "Right, Rose?"

Rose fingered the edge of the old bracelet from Moose wrapped around her wrist. "Sorry, girl, but I'm with Cameron." She offered a mildly apologetic shrug even though she was secretly relieved. "I swore I'd be home by curfew, anyway."

Rose fully expected Tori to debate more. But instead of launching a keynote on why they should hunt down Tim at the beach, Tori just stood there, blinking stonily at her phone.

"See, Tori?" Cameron continued in a school-smarmy voice, trying to lighten the mood. "Birthday girl calls the shots tonight, okay?"

"Come on, that's all over now," Rose shooed off his comment with a wave, and she meant it. She had always hated when people made big deals out of birthdays, especially her own.

Booming drums heaved through the room with the weight of an undertow. The lead singer stepped to the microphone, and aggro guitar chords surged into the first song, eliciting the crowd's full attention. A coil of mostly dudes was already igniting the pit with stomps and shoves. That kind of intensity was expected, but Rose sensed that everyone was ready to overindulge in their usual tendencies tonight. Nobody planned to allow the band to play without reminding them of exactly where they came from.

To hell with your platinum record.
Love,
Orange County

On the far end of the stage, the curious dog zeroed in on the pit, brown eyes exuding both playful inquisitiveness with experienced self-restraint. His body was perfectly still except for his wagging tail, which thumped side to side in almost exact rhythm to the drums at certain parts of the song. After a ruffling body shake, one of his ears flipped up, and Rose glimpsed some white puffiness tucked inside. Bemused, she wondered whose idea it was to protect the dog's hearing. Considering the band's heavy touring, it was nice to know the rock star pup had someone looking out for him in that way.

"See those cotton balls in his ears?" Rose yelled to no one in particular. She just couldn't take her eyes off of him.

Cameron was fixated on the pit, tense and getting primed up. "Wanna join me?" He turned to his friends.

"I'll just watch," Rose laughed.

"You gonna be on that all night?" Cameron extended an arm and snapped his fingers in Tori's face.

Tori jerked up from her phone and shook her head.

With a devilish smirk, Cameron shoulder-checked a handful of people in his path before barging into the frothing mob. Their elegant and polished friend had disappeared for the time being, replaced by an imposing, ready-to-wrangle brute.

"Ha!" Rose was always entertained by this side of him. She turned to Tori, expecting her to be just as gassed at the spectacle. "What's wrong?" she asked, taken aback by such a look of drudgery.

"Some hoebags are with them," Tori answered through rigid lips, keeping her focus on the pit. She looked almost too angry to even make eye contact.

"Screw him," Rose hollered through the music. "He's always doing whatever *he* wants." She paused, knowing the next few words might sting. "He's like a dream killer. Remember that trash Marvin?" The last thing she wanted was for Tori to get so prematurely involved with the guy that she, too, dumped her personal plans. Rose did respect Tim a little more after Lula May's fancy gala, but that didn't mean she'd ever stop being blunt about his other antics, especially if her friend was affected.

Tori's entire stance stiffened at the mention of Marvin. In the Park family, Marvin's name was the equivalent of a rare terminal disease, one that got exponentially more contagious with each utterance. Even Claudia's flippant exterior shattered if he, or even his now-defunct band, came up in conversation.

Rose shifted her weight, slightly relieved that Tori couldn't hear her nervously clear her throat over the raucous music. Of course, she didn't want to bring up bad memories or make hurtful comparisons. But Marvin literally *was* a dream killer—blasting Claudia's plans to oblivion by convincing her to forget everything and everyone and move in with him, only to end up cheating on her with some super-desperate groupie-type. What else did that make him? Claudia never did reapply for school, instead winding down a bumpy road of miscellaneous part-time jobs and even shorter relationships. Quite the downgrade, considering she'd originally earned spots at some universities that plenty of students would now kill for.

Tori's expression was blank. Maybe she was picturing that gloomy day when a younger Claudia had returned home, humbled and solo, straddled with two stuffed duffel bags and a pathetic, tear-streaked face. Whatever she was thinking, Rose didn't regret saying a thing. She wouldn't be a real friend otherwise. They needed to look out for themselves, not chase after romance as if their *lives* depended on it. Who did these guys think they were?

"Look, I don't know about you, but—" Rose stopped to correct herself. "Actually, I *do* know. You're not going to get played like some loser who's got nothing going on!"

She wasn't implying that Claudia was that, but she was sure that Tori understood her awkwardly-delivered message. At this point, pretty much every dude they'd met lately had proven to be nothing but total letdowns. That included Ethan.

Rose bristled every time she thought of him, which was hardly ever nowadays. She was more concerned than saddened when he'd announced he was heading back home to deal with some serious family business. But, as a friend, she didn't think a text during the holidays was an outlandish expectation. By then, he had abruptly stopped updating his social media, too.

She'd especially expected a reply after messaging Ethan about Starla returning safely to Laguna Lake Riding Club. If he had bothered to respond at all, Rose would've gladly briefed him on how she now had two part-time jobs: one at the barn to help support Starla's board while Gina searched for a potential new owner, and the other as a store clerk at In Absentia. But if he was cutting her off, she'd be a fool to continue updating him on a horse he no longer cared about, and an even bigger idiot to confide how the new barn manager was awesome to work with unless it involved her rude and overbearing assistant. Rose had even made a new friend recently—Jessie, a boarder her age who was also one of the coolest people she'd ever met at the barn. Like Tanner, Jessie's horse was also a dark Quarter horse who liked to gallop on the trails, not that Ethan would know. Was every guy out there either a selfish jerk or, at best, immature and egotistic? Either way, the turnoff was extreme.

"Ugh!" Tori staggered sideways but quickly regained her balance. Two guys standing a few feet in front of them had veered back into the girls from the pressure of the increasingly out of control pit. More people stumbled and jostled as an invisible quake roiled through the crowd.

Rose took hold of Tori's elbow and led them to one of the floor-to-ceiling columns. Ensuring nobody was standing right behind you, regardless of what was going on in front, was never a bad idea.

Just as Rose wondered if Cameron would be able to find them, she saw his tousled head squeezing through a stampeding curve of limbs and silhouettes. Contrary to the pandemonium, he took steady and composed steps on his way out of the pit. Behind him, shadows mauled and clobbered, framing him like a moving painting. Suddenly his left side lurched in reverse as something reeled him back in.

Startled, Rose stood on her toes, unable to regain a decent view. Standing at five foot two was hardly helpful.

"Where's Cameron?" she yelled. Tori's head was now moving along with the drumbeats, seemingly unaware.

Rose's stomach ground with unease as she scanned the mob. Still nothing except the vicious circle. Was he getting trouble from some loser homophobe or something? No sign of the cute dog researching the stage, either.

"Just landed on my ass so hard, a contact popped out!" Cameron suddenly emerged behind them, disheveled but pumped. He rubbed an eye and shook his head. "Pits are for slamming, not taekwondo, geez!"

Rose and Tori keeled over as their cackling was drowned out by the audience's instant roar for the next song. "Smoked You" was one of the early hits. Everyone in the Ice Cave knew that nowhere else on the planet were people seeing this played live in such an intimate venue. Those days were long gone.

Even the huge resident pile of turd, who'd somehow oozed his way into their section, donned a mildly nostalgic grin as his chapped lips blathered something that actually didn't appear malicious or hateful. But that wasn't the only thing that Rose noticed about him.

"Someone needs to learn how to wash his hands," Rose managed to eke out while laughing hysterically. "Stye-city right over there." Her abs were almost at the point of getting sore, but between the wild crowd, familiar hit song, and Cameron's lost contact lens, she just couldn't hold back—making fun of the bully's sorry derma-predicament was like an automatic reflex.

"What?!" Tori cracked up harder.

"*Stye-city*," Rose delivered the two syllables as clearly as she could and cautiously tilted her head in the general direction of the pus-filled swollen eyelid. Her ball-busting mood was on a roll. Sinking to the jerk's level wasn't exactly the smartest move, but any retaliation for all of his racial and homophobic slurs was just too tempting.

And really stupid.

His auburn eyebrows jumped sky-high, exposing only one large green eye since the infected one barely opened. Besides the common eye zit, he apparently also possessed superhero-level hearing.

Uh-oh. Rose looked up at him. His incensed green eyeball had never looked so cruel. One of his even more gargantuan friends looked over with simmering curiosity, sensing an opening for potential conflict.

Some gazes flicked away from the band and focused on the small group by the column. A scene from a recent nature program on lions and gazelles flashed through Rose's mind. Instantly regretting her cocky comment, she darted a wary glance at her friends.

Tori and Cameron were on alert, heads up high as the chunk of the audience in their midst was now partially ignoring the music and sifting closer around them.

"You say something, *chink*?"

A thousand neutral responses flew through her brain, but Rose was too afraid to pick one. Self-consciously, she rubbed the tip of her nose. An out of place stench was permeating the area. Even a barn in a record-breaking heatwave wouldn't smell like this.

"You speak English, *chink*?" the prick demanded.

"Um, yeah," Rose stammered, blinking back carefully contained fear. Was this the night she was finally going to get jumped in here? Suddenly all she wanted more than anything was to be back home, tucked inside her boring and wonderfully safe bedroom.

"Um, ya," the prick mocked in a high voice.

Cameron covered an abrupt cough with a closed fist. Rose turned to look at him and *bam!* The meat of the foul odor hit her senses like a cement wall.

"Somebody fart?" Cameron asked loudly, attempting to chill out the tough guy. "Can't even breathe..." He pressed his fingers on his nostrils. Next to him, Tori's deer-in-headlights gaze disappeared for a moment as she tried to shake off the smell with a bothered shudder. A couple of nearby onlookers grimaced through the thickening airborne funk.

The prick remained undeterred. "Look at me when I'm talking to you, *chink*." Somehow, he was able to growl yet still be heard over the pounding music.

Next to the lead singer, a guy in a pit-stained shirt with four familiar bars on the front raged into the microphone, raised his arms to jump off the stage but instead tripped off the edge, slamming headfirst into the choppy mess below.

The pandemonium was at an all-time high. Under normal circumstances, it would be quite entertaining. But with the giant bully escalating to attack, combined with the unsympathetic congregation hoping to witness a show of a different kind, Rose was petrified and hopeless. No amount of bragging rights was worth the situation she'd just gotten her friends into. Even the super athletic gazelles in the nature program couldn't all outleap their ferocious predators. What chance did Rose and her friends have of any escape?

As Rose frantically racked her brain, a clumsy arm sideswiped her side. Skittish, she looked with a jolt, assuming it must be a left field assault from some random observer. When she saw the burgundy locks and staggered mohawk, she was certain that the sour couple had joined in to aggravate the situation.

But the woman's sunken eyes didn't even register Rose. She was hunched over and teetering with each pained, shaky step. The boyfriend was holding her up, struggling to keep her standing as they wound through the tight crowd toward the exit. For whatever reason, she was trashed and hurting bad, without any clue of the confrontation they'd just walked right into. The angry prick ignored them as they tried to pass the small space between him and the high schoolers.

Just as they took another step, the woman lurched forward, almost like the guy who'd slipped off the stage face-first. Her boyfriend tried to catch her in time, but she completely ate it. Rose could faintly hear her moaning as she wrestled on all fours. For some reason, even with her guy's help, she kept slipping.

"Ugh!" she wailed. "What the…?" Her hands slipped and arms spread, the bottom of her chin hitting the floor again.

"Get up, get up…" the boyfriend urged impatiently. Stooped over her, he was clearly uncomfortable with their vulnerable position.

This was Rose's chance to track an exit. When the woman slipped again, a conspicuous movement a few feet away on the ground caught Rose's attention.

Nobody else seemed to notice the dog weaving around the shadowy maze of legs—especially when the woman, still on all fours, opened her mouth and expelled a long, gurgling retch. Mustardy liquid gooped over one of the tops of the bully's boots.

"Aargh!" Now the prick was really furious. He propelled the besmirched boot right at the couple, kicking the guy down to the floor.

Pushing his friends' arms, Cameron muttered, "Go, *go!*"

Rose darted through the first barricade of bodies in a concentrated blur to the door, hyper-aware that her friends were right behind and counting on her to pick up speed. Her knees almost buckled with relief as they pounded out of the critical radius of the prick's reach, into more of the general audience still fully engrossed in the music. While sprinting to the exit, she glimpsed the dog again. He was curled into a focused U-shape, his muzzle buried deep under his tail, investigating the most fascinating mess imaginable.

The trio exploded out of the entrance, turning a few of the security guards' heads.

Rose ran with such momentum that it almost felt like her legs were trying to catch up to her torso. Her friends sprinted right behind her, and their maniacal laughter bounced off the pavement into obnoxious echoes. They were soon far enough away to slow down to a pumped walk.

"Did you see her puke all over him?"

"And that pooping dog—he's like our hero tonight!"

They soon got to their cars, giddy and breathless. After a few more jokes about their close call, they hugged each other goodnight.

Cameron opened the door for Rose and bent forward at the waist into an exaggerated bow. "Run along home, my dear," he said with an outstretched arm. "Miss Tori and I are going to get some drive-thru munchies. Text us later."

Rose buckled the seatbelt and waved back to her friends as they bounced a few spaces down to Cameron's car. Some greasy fries with ketchup sounded heavenly. As the one with the early curfew, she'd normally feel a little jealous to miss out.

But who was she kidding? With a contented yawn, Rose started the car. She now had tons of responsibilities with Starla and the barn. Frankly, going home early to prepare for a busy morning with horses felt pretty awesome.

40

𝕿he road was silent. Rose let some cold night air cut in through the top of the window. She was so tempted to make a quick stop at the barn. Her parents knew she was staying out later tonight, but she didn't want to push it by worrying them. Besides, she'd see Starla first thing in the morning. Even though Starla was not technically "her" horse, Rose sure felt like Starla's guardian these days. If only she had the money to buy Starla...but that just wasn't realistic, especially with college coming up. For now, working part-time to help offset Starla's costs while basically spending as much time with her as possible was a pretty good alternative.

At the next empty intersection, Rose stretched out of the window to look up. The obsidian sky was mesmerizingly clear. She could have stayed like that for hours, just shivering and tripping and trying to visualize how the black nothingness surrounding each glimmer went on forever. The moon was nowhere to be seen. Each tiny fleck of starlight seemed to shoot out more energy than even the sun at high noon. White-hot Capella beamed down, ancient and brilliant.

A recognizable scent got her attention. She drew in a long breath, feeling the coldness stream through her nostrils. No, she was a bit far from the barn to actually smell it. Probably from her imagination, or just wanting to visit Starla.

The traffic light switched to green. Her foot lingered on the brake. If she was going to see Starla, she had to turn in the other direction now. *Not this time*, she decided firmly. It was late, and Milo was undoubtedly waiting for her.

The terrier's ecstatic sniffs were easy to hear through the front door when Rose fumbled with the keys on the porch a few minutes later.

"Shhh," she whispered, slowly opening the door so it wouldn't bonk his little nose. "Hi, sweetie!" Milo sprung up and down, his tail wagging out of control as he trailed her to the kitchen. The strange scents from the crowded show on her jeans were irresistible magnets.

Nothing looked more heavenly than the white Roma Angelo's to-go box greeting her from the top shelf in the fridge. Salivating, Rose wolfed down the two bruschetta slices while standing over the kitchen counter. The tomatoes and garlic were so fresh and flavorful that the bread didn't even need to be toasted. Next time, she'd make sure they ordered extra. Still a little hungry, she searched the cabinets for an easy final snack. The box of crackers and package of oatmeal raisin cookies didn't look as appetizing, so she settled for a tall glass of water and carried Milo up the stairs.

The late-night silence of the house was beyond soothing after the intense Ice Cave show, especially with such a close call. Rose shuddered again at her foolishness. She and her friends were lucky to make it out unscathed, and everyone knew it. Rose washed up in the bathroom as quickly as she could. Milo sat upright and watched patiently from the white bath rug before scurrying off.

When Rose joined Milo in her bedroom, he was already stretched against the headboard, right atop her pillow. His ears cocked toward her cooing, but his eyes remained shut tight.

"What a tired baby," Rose giggled, pulling on her soft pink pajama pants. Just as she reached for the duvet, her shoulders dropped with an annoyed sigh. She'd forgotten to turn off the darn kitchen light.

Milo's eyes flew open and bore into her as she stood up.

"I know, I know—Mommy will be right back," Rose assured him through a deep yawn. Milo lowered back into position with zero interest in leaving the bed. Blinking sleepily, Rose silently cursed her mild OCD-like tendencies. Going back downstairs right now sounded just about as fun as getting food poisoning, but trying to sleep with the lingering light in her thoughts all night would be pointless.

A figure stood in the hallway just outside her door.

"Oh!" Rose yelped, jumping with shock.

His head jerked toward her with equal surprise while shuffling awkwardly down the hallway. He was mostly obscured by a large rectangular object in his arms.

"Dad!" Rose blurted accusingly, a hand resting on her heaving lungs.

Milo instantly appeared between them to inspect the bulky item, his nose wiggling with curiosity.

"Oh, thought you were sleeping," Dad replied, carefully lowering the rectangle to the floor.

It was a frame of something—photo, painting, map?—but all she could see was the backside. And it was big. Over four feet wide, larger than any of their family portraits. Judging from the fragile condition of the beige dust cover, it was also much older than anything she had ever posed for.

"What is that?" Rose shook her head at the perplexing sight. "What are you doing?"

Dad glanced back and forth between her and the frame. He wasn't usually so clammed shut—a little quiet, maybe, but never secretive like this. His mouth was drawn tight as if holding back something.

Milo ran his black nose around the nearest corner of the object and promptly dug his little teeth in.

Dad quickly pulled it away.

Rose stared at her father, slightly taken aback by his protective arm work. Was she imagining things, or was he purposely hiding the front of it from her view?

"Okay, what is this, Dad?" She stepped forward. Milo mimicked her. *Don't smile.* It was like she and Milo were teaming up and cornering Dad. If she laughed right now, she didn't want her father somehow using that as an opportunity to wave her off.

Milo took note of Rose's insistent voice and went at the frame once more with his open mouth.

"Hey, hey." Dad lifted the mystery item away from the terrier again. From Milo's playful grunts, it was clear he was beginning to think this was some sort of game.

Rose smirked. "You'd better let us see it." She stifled a yawn. "He's not going to let up, you know."

For several stiff seconds, Dad's eyes locked down onto whatever was on the front side.

"Okay."

He maneuvered the frame in a two-point turn and leaned it against the wall so it faced forward.

Rose's grin faded. A cold shiver swept from her stomach to her arms. Her eyes crawled over the swirls of blazing tangerine, dips of lilac, and crevices of stones and shadows embedded on star-roasted dirt. She tried to breathe out deeper in order to counter her increasingly shallow inhales. The landscape stared back through the human-made filter of the painting, reflecting eclipsed memories and runaway dreams. If her dad wasn't standing right in front of her, she might have sprinted back into bed to hide under the covers—forget the stupid kitchen light.

Dad's lips were moving, but the churning of elsewhere in her head was too strong to tune out, and she could hardly make out a single word. Something about Grandma?

Her gaze kept traveling over the image, creeping toward the center. It wasn't like she was unaware of the figure in the middle of the scene. But how was this anything but completely chilling? Dozing off at the Quonset hut during break on that distant Halloween morning was the last time she thought she'd ever see this again. But here it was, delivered late at night by Dad. It was like seeing an alien, or...

A raspy, high-pitched screech started in her right ear, faint but familiar. Was that her imagination, too? She was almost too afraid to keep looking.

Despite the eeriness of a dream vision appearing in a random painting, her curiosity only grew as she scanned each millimeter of detailed landscape. With bulletproof patience, the figure in the foreground waited in her peripheral vision.

A man leaned close over his horse, reins loose in one hand, as they jumped over a wooden fence. The overwhelming familiarity in his gaze radiated like a solar wind burning right through the canvas. But he was expecting something more than just landing the jump. Even his horse's left ear was flicked back with awareness. Above and behind them, a dark gray raptor bombed through the air, calculating their relative speeds. Small straps dangled from each of the bird's ankles, just above some very noticeable talons. The man's gloved hand hovered out to his side. An invitation for the raptor to return.

"...almost looks like charcoal, even though it's watercolor. Aunt Esther sent it as a surprise for your birthday, it just arrived a little late. I'm sure you already noticed Grandpa's horse. There's another package on the way with some of his belongings that Aunt Esther said you should have. We'll talk about it tomorrow, okay? Goodnight." He gently patted her on the head, a rare display of affection that she used to yearn for as a kid.

Rose watched silently as her father retreated to his room. Never in a million lifetimes would she guess that Aunt Esther would be so thoughtful toward her. Or that Dad would talk of her grandfather having a horse. Why hadn't she, of all people, ever known of this?

Her head still tingled in the spot her dad had just touched. Behind her parents' closed bedroom door, their soft voices were probably going over what had just happened. A small smile played on her mouth. Nobody had ever surprised her in such a meaningful way. She would cherish Grandma's artwork for the rest of her life. And she had so many more questions now.

Rose turned around to admire the painting, eager for one last indulgence in its vivid, dreamlike shades before turning in.

Both of Milo's ears cocked up when he heard Rose gasp.

✦✦✦

Nothing was wrong with her eyes.

Rose stared up at the white ceiling. Shifting in her bed, she tried to come up with a logical cause for the glitch with her 20/10 vision. Milo was strategically curled against her shoulder and randomly fluttering his paws as he finally plunged into a deep snooze. His human was back where she should be.

All of Rose's exhaustion was long gone, replaced by the shock of having just experienced something that she couldn't reconcile. Rose was spooked enough to leave the painting out in the hall. She wasn't sure if she'd be able to sleep at all if it were in her room right now. Not until she figured out what had just happened.

It wasn't the angle it was leaning on the wall, nor was it the generic lighting from the ceiling. While her dad had explained the painting, Rose saw on it, briefly, the wild colors from her dream.

Then, every bright pigment vanished. The painting was black and white all along. It had reset right in front of her.

She flipped onto her side and forced her eyes shut. A tornado of questions thrashed around her head, but she couldn't single out one racing thought. It was like Halloween morning all over again. A cosmic prank. Focusing on anything besides how optics had just completely messed with her was impossible. She peeked through her eyelids again to see if her room looked the same. Even with the lights out, everything appeared normal. There was definitely nothing wrong with her eyes.

Rose grabbed the headphones on the nightstand and plugged them into her phone. She had to get her mind off of that painting. The screen lit up with a text from a few hours ago. It was Mike, asking how her week was going. She felt a little rude for not replying to his text from the other day, a link to a review of some restaurant she'd never heard of, but she was with Starla at the time. It seemed his random and periodic messages never seemed to mesh with whatever she was doing. He wasn't at fault or anything, but still…the clumsy timing was something to note.

Scrolling through for some music, Rose clicked without looking. She needed to get sucked into something else—anything else.

The first sentient cello notes of "Cold" began. She looked at her big Cure poster, the band's pale faces illuminating like dim moons in the dark.

What is the story behind Grandpa and his horse? And that bird? For the first time since sinking into bed, Rose calmed down enough to delve into the possibilities. First of all, from the looks of his youthful face, Grandma had probably created the black and white image from a scene before the Korean War. Early 1940s, maybe? If so, that would've been even before Rose's dad was born. She'd always heard of Grandpa's hobbies of photography and cars, which everyone deemed bizarre and eccentric (to put it nicely) at a time when most people around him were just trying to survive with decent food and shelter. But horses or huge birds? Never came up.

Her family's reaction to her obsessive equine tendencies made some more sense now, especially when it came to her dad and grandma. It was clear they weren't very fond of Grandpa's horse streak. That was what she had to get to the bottom of, among other things. The discord between her and her parents had simmered down lately. Though still unresolved, she could feel, in her bones, the hidden history of her family about to unravel. She didn't want to force anything, though. It would happen soon. This old painting was a huge step down that road.

"Thank you, Grandma," Rose whispered.

The woman sat on a blue embroidered cushion directly in front of the in-progress image, stroking the canvas surface with alternating pressures. Through the window, beams of light gleamed over her petite frame, creating a golden-white aura that seemed obviously reserved for the woman widely known as the most beautiful human around. She was well aware of the designation but thought little of it. Beauty was just as much a curse as an asset, in her experience. She paused to nudge a tendril of satiny raven hair over an ear and back into the firm twist. As she scrutinized the image, deciding where to add on next, a gust of wind and high-pitched bird chirps swirled over the room's sun-drenched wooden floors and full bookshelf. A few strands of wavy hair escaped again, grazing the tops of her dewy cheekbones. Just outside the single long window, in the vast green meadow framed by miles of rounded hills in the distance, stood an enormous spirit tree. Its heavy branches swayed, slow and knowing, rustling in the moving air with broad, oceanic sweeps.

She continued alternating between delicate pulls, gentle dabs, and deliberate wrist flicks. This nook of the Hermit Kingdom's rural silence was interrupted only by the random mutters that escaped her rose petal lips every other minute or so. This was her designated alone time: twenty minutes every early afternoon, carved in stone. It was never long enough, therefore absolutely mandatory. She could read, write, or paint without worrying about meals, children, or her husband's brazen hobbies. They all knew not to even approach the closed door unless a limb or life was at risk.

When the bristles hovered over the small blank space she had reserved for her husband and his horse, a sharp and exasperated-at-one's-spouse sneer formed on the woman's lips. Her hands and eyes continued with unfazed accuracy. So far, nothing on this planet had ever disrupted her when she had a task, not even his outlandish pastimes.

Rose snorted mischievously, abruptly knocking her out of the zone. She knew that sneer well, and it looked so funny in that otherwise idyllic, olden days scene. Why Grandma would continue painting something that annoyed her so much was a real brain-teaser—a ridiculously hilarious one.

Milo's head popped up, and he repositioned a few inches away to avoid Rose's stirring. Settling into the sheets, he let out a little sigh.

"Sorry, baby." Rose shook her head at herself and quieted still. But Grandma's curled, griping pink lip and concentrated brushstrokes reappeared in her mind, and Rose had to smother a new burst of giggles into a pillow. The more she thought about it, the harder she cackled. Was she really making fun of her grandmother across dimensions? The idea of teasing the dead family matriarch cracked her up so hard, her eyes were watering. In a way, it was just a spectacular relief to really laugh about something family-related, even if she did feel kind of like a maniac.

Rose dabbed her face and relaxed into a deep stretch, extending her arms and legs as far as they could reach. It always felt nice to sink into bed and give her body a break these days, especially with all the new work she had at the barn.

In the past couple of months, Rose had brushed up on the basic tasks that she used to do in exchange for riding lessons, plus other aspects of horses that she'd always wanted to experience— lunging, stretching and massages, to name a few. She even observed sessions with their new equine acupuncturist Hana, who seemed to be Starla's second favorite human. Rose was so grateful that Starla was now in safe hands, and learning so many different ways to help the special mare was a dream come true. Even though Rose still felt like she didn't fit in all the time in other parts of her life, she was fully at peace when she was with Starla.

"It's one of their quirks, you know," Gina had told her recently. The barn owner had once again just received major attitude from Starla, only to witness the mare sweetly nuzzle up to Rose a moment later. "Mustangs are sometimes known for choosing a person and not really taking to others, so I'll just let her do her thing."

Milo's eyes were now shut really tight, like he was purposely pressing them extra-closed. Rose sighed and shut her eyes, too.

She and Starla usually practiced something new a few times a week and explored the trails on other days. Once a week, Starla got a full day off and just enjoyed a long turn out, and then a chill hand walk around the property. They were far from polished but had nonetheless made some significant progress, which Rose was both proud of and grateful for. As Starla's fitness improved, so did Rose's skills. Starla's lead changes were now pretty much on point, and she even seemed to enjoy popping over a course of small verticals. Starla still disliked plastic bags but, unlike some of the other horses at the barn, she was pretty unflappable when strong winds hit the area. Rose was also super stoked on recently teaching Starla to follow her without a halter. After a few weeks and a lot of laughing, the intelligent mare learned to move along with Rose's arm as well as voice cues. It was all just for fun, and Rose couldn't wait to try teaching more on-the-ground tricks. But the most gratifying part of their relationship had nothing to do with training. Whether in her stall or turnout, Starla always somehow knew when Rose was approaching. Even from a good distance, Starla would stop whatever she was doing and elevate her head, zeroing in on a specific direction until Rose came into view and their eyes locked.

Gina wanted some exposure for Starla at a couple of schooling shows this upcoming season. While she appreciated Rose's super casual foray into liberty training, it wasn't an extremely interesting topic to her. Most of the potential buyers she had in mind would be looking for a more formally trained horse, ideally one who could pack around a kid or adult amateur as a confidence builder. Rose wasn't so sure about Starla as a show horse, even if just for schooling shows. In her opinion, Starla seemed more of a no pressure, trail and light arena type, but Rose kept telling herself that she was not the professional in the situation. She didn't have much of a choice, anyway. Gina was generously covering the vast majority of Starla's costs, so Rose's job was to simply support the situation as much as she could.

A spark of electric blue flickered in the corner of her eye. Her phone was glowing under a pillow. Probably Cameron or Tori taunting her with their midnight snack. Smirking, Rose began thinking of some obnoxious replies as she reached over.

A completely unfamiliar phone number stared back at her on the screen. The area code wasn't even 714.

Pulled this guy from auction. Knew him as a kid. John's coming to evaluate him first thing tomorrow. Are you around? We're at Laguna Lake Riding Club. Tanner says hi.

Rose froze.

Another message came in. A photo. One look and it was like she got punched in the stomach.

All warmth drained from her body. She gaped at the dark, listless eyes. At first glance, he appeared to be looking out in front of his gaunt face. But his—no, the—empty gaze also somehow went inward. He hardly "looked" at all.

Rose's mind raced with a frenzy of possibilities that had condemned him to this state. She had plenty to shuffle through. Every instance of animal abuse she'd ever heard of was permanently etched in her memory, often resulting in haunted, sleepless nights. The resignation in this horse's eyes was palpable and, as a prey animal, the lowest crevice of rock bottom. She wished she could see more of him to get a better idea of the rest of his physical condition, but a lot of his body was out of the frame. One thing was ominously clear: no matter where this horse had come from, Laguna Lake Riding Club was the safest place he'd been in a very long time.

What should she do? She gripped the phone, recalling all of the times she'd glanced at the dumb thing, expecting a text back from Ethan but seeing nothing.

And now here he was, asking if she was "around."

Bristling, Rose leaned back against the headboard. No. He wasn't going to just insert himself back into her life with some random, one-sided request. She had to stand up for herself.

Sorry, can't help. Rose tried to be polite but nonchalant in her answer. Delete, type, delete. Right above the cursor was that heart-wrenching photo. She tried to ignore it but looking away didn't help. Milo's tail wagged as she scooped him up and drew him close. Snuggling with him always helped her think.

"Stay," Rose whispered a few seconds later, petting Milo from head to tail. She quickly changed her clothes while rehearsing justifications to present to her parents. Just before she left the room, she turned back to her dresser. Carefully, she slipped the wooden mala bracelet over her wrist. Any mountaintop Buddhist energy couldn't hurt right now. In the hallway, the painting greeted her again. Rose lingered for a magnetized moment.

Was that the barn smell again? As soon as she noticed, the scent was gone.

A few minutes later, she was reversing out of the driveway. She waved to Koko, who was watching her from the side of her yard. As the dark houses and angular hedges of Camino Drive passed in a glassy blur, Rose could still feel the stab of ice that had plunged into her when she first saw the photo. All she could see were those eyes. She hadn't even bothered to reply. After convincing her very taken aback parents about a horse emergency at the barn, she had jammed out the door before they could change their minds.

Rose barely noticed the ancient sounding car dealer commercial on the radio that she'd heard since childhood. Everyone who grew up in SoCal, at one point at least, had joked about the three-worded jingle that sounded like "pussy cow."

What am I doing? Once she turned onto the main road, echoes of her confident little speech to Tori at the Ice Cave pecked all over her conscience. Talk about cringe. What would Tori think of Rose just jumping into the car after a couple of sudden texts from a guy who had disappeared for months? Teeth rattling from the cold, she grumbled at herself under her breath. Her stupid jacket was still hanging on the stair banister, too. But there was no going back now.

Rose blinked at the dashboard as the aggressive b-flat chords from her morning alarm song finished off the commercial break, launching into an amped-up, Fullerton-fueled cover of "Ring of Fire." The sounds instantly triggered a cavernous, thunderous chopping in her head. She dialed up the volume, letting the intensely familiar music fill the car just before it got too loud. It felt odd to not be stirring awake in her room, blinking the night away as the song faded the cacophony from that relentless dream. Reliving that panicked ride with Fender was rare lately. Sometimes she even missed it.

Rose peered into the thick ground clouds that draped over the silent street ahead. She opened the window an inch, letting a slice of air frost the left side of her face. Then it went all the way down as she breathed, plunging inside and cooling every smoldering, conflicting thought until she reached the narrow street of Laguna Lake Riding Club. Starla was probably all cozy and sleeping with her cute right hind leg cocked up just a bit. An uninvited return was there, too.

Rose had zero obligation to Ethan. A part of her still wished he would give her a reason to feel otherwise. But dwelling on his decisions was a serious waste of her time—a lesson very much learned after her third message to him went unanswered.

But she absolutely could not turn away from those empty eyes. Whoever that horse was, he was inevitable. And that was all on her.

The music pounded on, dead-on, hitting the frequency that melds the aerial chopping with the terrestrial galloping. A small pocket in the overhanging gloom wisped open, connecting reflections from high above. The thundering burst out of the trees and passed, fading into black. Moonlight glowed for a few seconds before everything masked behind darkness again.

Rose could barely see the parking lot within the thick white vapor. Whenever there was fog, this part of the neighborhood always had an extra dense layer of it. She heard it had something to do with the small lake deep in the nature reserve, but she wasn't clear on how that exactly worked.

She stepped out of the car. Other than the conspicuous white trailer near the entrance, the place had never looked so unoccupied. The fog morphed as her mass cut through, curving and unfurling around her like the first hidden layers of a painting, seen but unnoticed.

A clop emanated from just beyond the fence. It was impossible to see more than ten feet ahead, but only one horse would be out here at this hour.

Veins buzzing, Rose headed to the hitching posts. Despite the overwhelming desire to rush over, she forced herself to slow down with careful and measured steps. This horse was a total stranger. Anything could frighten him.

A cloudy veil floated between horse and human, thinning and drifting. His translucent outline slowly crystallized into a commanding, distinguishable portrait. White warmth softly streamed from his nostrils. His left ear tipped toward her, but not a single other muscle or hair stirred. From the shape of his head and sleek conformation, she guessed he might be a Thoroughbred.

Frail, tall, and dark bay, maybe black.

Rose's heart dropped through the earth.

He was the mysterious image that had invaded her mind when she was with Starla in her stall.

Rose tried to maintain her composure. She had never seen a horse like this in real life.

He needed help. Now.

She fumbled for her phone to call the barn's longtime veterinarian but stopped when she remembered Ethan's text. John was coming early in the morning.

Horror clobbered her as she scanned the horse's body. She couldn't fathom what he must have gone through. The man-made abhorrence was undeniable. How could people be so vicious— and especially to a species that had literally trained, toiled, and warred for humankind for thousands of years? And yet, horses never look back. They don't look down on the egregious even though they are superior to who sucks their blood.

Exploit. Use up. Throw away.

Evil.

Watching the steam flow from his nostrils, Rose tried to align her breathing with him. She didn't know exactly why, but it was what she had to do in that moment.

His dark eyes flickered. His potholed spine, the hairless ridge of an imploding tent of flesh, willfully held up. The visible parts of his coat were just dilapidated, with sores and marks that he would always retain even if he no longer actively felt. A nearby light illuminated his starving patience. And still, he was even more stoic than the pressure of time that heaved him down, closer to the ineludible and awaiting earth.

Was that a little blaze on his face? Rose wanted to make sure but didn't budge. His silence was thoroughly imposing as he breathed in this new place and new human. Despite his punished physical vessel, he still somehow possessed a dignified air. She didn't hear the faint voice greeting her somewhere in the distance.

The air from her lungs spun into the fog, whirling with a soft vibration and weaving into the remnants of his. She thought of Starla, stolen from her home, separated from family and forced to bend to human greed and selfishness. Like many others from her land, people had destroyed so many, so violently, without a second thought. It wasn't only horses and burros. But through her own sheer will, Starla had survived and adapted, eventually calibrating into Rose's far-off existence. Even with some unknowns ahead, Rose was grateful every time she thought of Starla. All she wanted was for Starla to know that she was permanently safe and loved. A simple, quiet justice.

Things weren't perfect, of course. Hard secrets remained, and Rose's family still had plenty of healing ahead. Some days, it clouded almost everything, or it simply hovered as an obscured and muted backdrop. But horses were the ultimate protectors whenever that perennial rootlessness emerged to haunt her. Just a few minutes in their presence easily undid years of human damage.

And right now, deep in the fog, she too was standing tall. No one's guilt, expectations, or mistakes would define or dictate her path. She had chosen every challenge that had led her to this place, at this hour, right in front of this regal, betrayed horse.

His protruding bones and wasted gaze ignited a revolting fury in her, searing Rose inside out. If only she had one wish. And it wouldn't be for her parents to sit her down with a solemn explanation about the past.

Hell no.

Rose's eyes flashed as her two worlds meshed in a moment of sheer fantasy. She was back inside the lawless room where she and her friends had hung out just hours ago. There, the human scum responsible for this horse were surrounded by a hundred menacing, jeering, steel-toed pricks, all ready to destroy. There was no way out. It would be the most cataclysmic night that place had ever seen. Seemed fair to her.

The fog whitened and thickened but Rose had never seen more sharply. Everything was a message. Right here, breathing in the watery air, with the damp soil under her feet and fire blistering her insides, a dormant piece of her had activated. This horse had traversed an incomprehensible, excruciating journey and prevailed to encounter a new road in his life. The outright strength, both physical and emotional, required to achieve such a feat was absolutely mind-demolishing.

Sandy's unsolicited advice suddenly made perfect sense. None of this was personal. It wasn't about Rose or even her innate love for horses. And riding them was just not enough. All equines deserved so much more—*especially* after they stopped carrying human agendas on their backs.

He released a short sigh.

Rose's body rippled with a soaring awareness. The recent years disconnected from horses were a mere blip. Her map was now filling in with the vibrant shades from her dreams. What she once thought was uprooted had actually just been pushed underneath the surface, waiting in silence to rear back up.

The old language of all species didn't need words, only energy. *Maal* had guided her to the other side. The nonhumans had awakened her ability to connect on another level.

But first, this powerhouse of a horse needed to heal and reclaim his energy. If he had made it this far, he at least had a shot. And as long as Rose was alive, no person would ever pontificate what work he should do, or which sport he would excel at. *No.*

He didn't owe a goddamn thing. Not in this universe or anywhere else.

Horses were above revenge. They had always communicated this very clearly.

Rose's nightdream of brutal punk rock vengeance may be a silly imagining, but it was also an imminent glimpse of a parallel track on her grid.

Her mouth watered as she imagined her prey one more time.

Rose had never met a slob who covered their tracks very well. So she would let those scumbags—whoever and wherever they were—think they were in the clear for now, all sliming on the down low. But she knew how to stomp her way around the underground, too.

And she would meet them in that pit.

ABOUT THE AUTHOR

Linda Jisun Lee is a writer, artist-curator and independent researcher based in Los Angeles. She previously worked at the RAND Corporation, directed a contemporary art gallery in Los Angeles, and lobbied at the United Nations Human Rights Council in Geneva, helping to secure the adoption of a human rights resolution. She holds a BA in International Relations and a Master's in Public Art Studies from the University of Southern California.